Hunted: Magics Heir, Book Two

G. L. CRAMB

ISBN: 978-1-7369696-1-8 (paperback)

MAGPIE PUBLISHING

*In Honor of a friend, who's honest opinion
I could always trust in. Thanks Ron.*

1

Predator & the Innocent

A muted orange, fringed in red, still fills half the darkening evening sky under spreading fingers of billowing cumulus. Their underbellies glow in those same fiery hues with the failing sun. In my mind's eye, the glowing clouds can surely be mistaken for rising plumes of smoke. Defended by the fiery clouds, the inky sky above is beginning to push the sunset towards the horizon. Still, the entire far skyline seems ablaze and screaming of a different time altogether. A chill breeze, contrasting the scene, washes over me even as it did on that similar day. The colourful twilight sky is setting the valley's thick forest, behind its huge lake...*afire*. Finding myself taking a moment, I reflect further upon the memory. Why not? It is, after all, quite significant to this very eve. Those of smaller minds in this land called *Aeryth* are of little consequence. And those of any consequence are more the more under the thrall of *my* council, ever as we have schemed.

I am called Mensæ now, a name worthy of my talents.

Leaning into the railing on the third-story balcony of my room at this hunter's lodge, every detail of that night long ago on a distant shore materializes crystal clear within my memory. Ruminating, I find myself peering back over that bay to the city of Esperance. Notwithstanding that it had been quite memorable, my mind can relive it in complete clarity and detail. One of many traits that make me special, as it does all my compatriots here at this otherwise deserted mountain lodge…on this particular mid-winter's eve.

This land called Aeryth, was new to me then, those forty years past, having first set foot upon its shore, that very eve. Though *that* night, the burning sky from north to south was indeed and verily aflame. Looking east, I witnessed raging fires, not a sunset. On the left horizon, fires engulfed the structures within the city of Esperance itself, set afire by our army of orcæn troops even as they were forced to retreat back to the sea and into the few hundreds of giant galleys, they had arrived to Aeryth upon. But more than the city itself was ignited and burning that night.

To my right upon the open sea, all of the ships of our armada lay ablaze as well. For while Prince Aegèas, from the Mid Realm and heir apparent to the throne in Kings Court, had driven our invading forces back to the sea, his fleet of every imaginable type of sea vessel and 1,000 strong swept through our anchored fleet of 300. Having sailed in from the north and the harbour at Kings Court and every harbour betwixt there and Esperance, they rained fury and devastation down upon our elite galleons with torch arrows and flaming spears from ballistae. Small barrels of oil were set afire and catapulted from their ragtag decks and onto our more majestic fleet, as they sailed swiftly through the anchored warships on a stiff breeze. Our invasion from across the Southern Sea was turned back that night, and our armies were utterly vanquished.

I smile to myself. Aegèas became a hero that sun and would soon rise to the throne over all of Aeryth. But the invaders were not entirely vanquished. As a fact, the true and more powerful nemesis had made it successfully to shore unnoticed and we are now meeting at this very lodge, discussing our successes and plans of further conquest. As the advisor and seer to the now seated King of Aeryth, I am also the governor to this council. I have come far and accomplished much since that night. I take my roles seriously–king's advisor, council governor, and seer to the crown. Though a true seer, I am not.

But as close advisor to the king, my chambers in the cæstle at Kings Court are adjacent to the king's, and with such proximity to Aegèas, my mind mægic allows me to intercept the king's *sight* and claim it as my own, denying the king his very own mægic and cementing my place as advisor and seer to the king.

Those convening here, like myself, are wielders of this same ancient mægic. It has become clear to us that our particular form of mægic is mostly unknown and never practiced in Aeryth. Our successes have been easier for this fact. But, though muted to history, 'tis indeed that mæge elders, Source-Sayers, escaping from the Wizærdii of this art, is what had brought the practice of mægic to Aeryth more than three millennia ago. And now, for these past forty years, our stronger, dominant mægic is now taking seed in the courts, keeps, and mountain lairs throughout Aeryth.

Our council, meeting this week at the lodge, is made up of seven mægi. We carry a specific mandate set down by the Three Eye Council, who in turn sit as the extreme rulers over all of Destinæa and, as they see it, the whole of the world.

In theory, my council of seven are under the thumb of the Three. But practically speaking, we are separated by a great sea. A sea that took three months for we and the orcæn invaders to cross, losing a third of our force to watery graves upon the journey. And then we, all seven I dare say, also have individual ambitions. We are loyal to the Three, of course, as to not be means a torture worse than death by many fold. But we will be given leeway if the result will benefit the Three in the end. We are ones of a mind to take full advantage of such a gift.

Our mission originally conceived, to find at the least the Druidæ and even more to our benefit would be to find the Elders, Source-Sayers who wielded the other five ancient mægics to full effect. Few in Destinæa know this story, me being one that does.

Though sure there is more to the tale, I understand the Three feel that the five other ancient mægics were stolen from them and are rightfully theirs. And with these other mægics once again under their sway, the entire vast world, and indeed the heavens above will be under their exclusive dominion. The Three already hold complete reign over all that they survey, and when my council has accomplished our goals, they will rule all Aeryth as well. We have been sent by the Three across the great Northern Sea with a trained army, just as similar groups had been dispatched in centuries past to the other three corners of the compass. south, east, and west out of Destineae. Separate councils, each made up of eight acolytes, had been sent searching after the stolen mægics. Each expanded the empire but without finding and regaining that which the Three seeks most. When these other mægics were not found upon the land in the other corners, it was cyphered that the traitorous Source-Sayers must have travelled north across the sea.

I and the others were tutored long and thorough in our art, gained through strong bloodlines. A vast army of orcæn were bred for the sole purpose of undertaking our charged mission. Though this army was destroyed, we eight acolytes, of course, survived. We are the true mission in any case. We have been mostly successful in our charge over these past four decades, though the Three do not know it yet and will not for some time. But time is a commodity of which the council has plenty and even more so the Three. After all, the Three have been searching for three millennia, a century more will not matter.

Finding any of the Elders holding the true mægic has not happened yet. But the council knows that mægic exists in Aeryth and then so must the trail to the Druidæ and then further to the Elders. I believe that I have even encountered one of the Druidæ and I am eager to pursue it. In the meantime, the council continues expanding its control over Aeryth, each member in a position of power over great numbers and increasing more every year.

The Druidæ are the answer, and I can feel we are on the verge of a breakthrough. The Three have said that the Druidæ are the keepers of the knowledge and mayhaps even on a par in the Arts as myself and my compatriots. But for some reason, the ancient mægics that I was tutored about are only displayed in small ways around Aeryth. Could this land be only a steppingstone to the Elders of the Mægic, or is their mægic only being hidden further or deeper in some spot here in Aeryth not yet discovered by this council? Mayhaps this is an effort to thwart us, the Elders knowing that someday the Three would find them and exert their right.

Some recent happenings are encouraging though. Word from Spæctre in Tullamoor speaks of a boy that controls beasts and holds another mægic in his staff while disrupting his business and killing his agents wholesale. I intend to discuss it further with Spæctre on the morrow when we convene. Further, this boy might be the offspring of the king's daughter. The same daughter that was spirited away by the man that I believe to be one of the Druidæ disguised as the lass' mentor. That effort foiled even more plans that the council had set in motion. These Druidæ may be more aware than I thought, working in ways similar to our own.

The council had schemed to have a king's courtesan from a wealthy royal family murder the king's wife and then be exposed for it, thereby killing two birds with the one stone, as the saying goes. Discrediting a royal family that has the king's ear–oft times opposing my counsel to the king–and opening an avenue by which the king's daughter would be betrothed to a council ally family, thereby solidifying more future control by the council. This mentor stole the girl away before a wedding could be consummated, setting back our plans for a time.

Capturing this lad who clearly displays one of the ancient mægics and mayhaps has a connection to a member of the Druidæ will become an imperative for me and the council. We are here to discuss this as well as other pressing matters.

These further thoughts of the council pull me back to the here and now and why I have convened the others here at the mountain lodge the king has just recently frequented. We are meeting away from any prying eyes at a time the lodge would normally be closed for the season. Each of the original eight acolytes will be present save one who has vanished into the Northern Reaches two decades afore. I cannot help but wonder, due to recent events, if the Druidæ are somehow responsible for that disappearance as well.

Looking out over this unique horizon, I recall the night we boarded the skiff to shore from our command vessel. Compared to the other ships of the orcæn fleet it had truly been a luxury craft that suffered no hardship in the three full moons it took to cross to this land. Each of the eight had our own bodyguards and servants to attend us. And over those last seven suns of battle, while the armies fought ashore, we eight entertained, in our fashion, a like number of well-to-do citizens gathered up in forays by our personal bodyguards. We used our specific mind mægic to learn the language and ways of our 'guests.'

On that last night, our guests were arrayed on deck with the obvious success of their homeland in evidence as they saw many of the invading ships afire behind them, flames licking the horizon. They could not be helped but to be encouraged. I surveyed each of them...seven men in various lordly attire and a woman in the obvious finery of her station at court. It was, even so, the way of life back in Destinæa.

"Eyes forward, if you please." I struck a loud and commanding voice to swing their attention.

A tall, lean, and obviously brave man with a noble bearing stepped forward and addressed me.

"I see your fortunes have turned somewhat, Master Mensæ sir. Mayhaps I can act as an emissary to strike a truce between our armies," he said.

"There will be no truce...sir. All of you, disrobe, now!" My curt return.

Our guests looked about at each and the other, a fear finally setting in at the gravity of their situation. All went quiet for a moment–the only sounds the rigging clanging against the gunwales and the waves lapping against the hull. They had been lulled into a mistaken sense of security as they had dined and drank in luxury as civilized 'guests' of their captors. I knew what they were thinking. Their situation would be remedied with ransom or favor of a sort as their station would typically warrant. It was what civilized enemies did amongst nobles, after all. But now, swords could be heard being drawn, and chuckles heard from the ugly orcæn guards. Our *guests* remained cowardly and compliant. In their time aboard, the noble lady had commented in private that these 'orcs' seemed to be an unfortunate cross in bloodlines betwixt a strong lean stock of man and a toothy, large-eared lesser being, and she could not truly disguise her disgust. What manner of men would even attempt such vile experiments with bloodlines? We would. They were pale with black beady eyes and a curve to their spine. Drawn faces housed large, toothy mouths and overly large and pointed ears tucked flat to the sides of their heads. Yet they were, strong and fearsome looking to be sure, and subservient and knowing their place.

Each of the council stood across from their own individual 'guest' of like build and stature. Mine carrying the look of a well raised academic. Each of the guests were now beginning to undress, resignation and fear in their movement. Mayhaps we would but toss them overboard and leave them to swim to shore, I read my guest's thought. The noble lady, however, refused.

"I will do no such thing!" she screamed in defiance. Anger boiling there with a bit of panic creeping into her voice.

Her host, Maya, the only woman among us eight, nonchalantly addressed her.

"Then my guards will help you, though they are known to get a bit handsy." Maya smiled and her guard attendants chuckled ever louder.

A guard moved forward from behind her and placed a hand on the lady's shoulder. She gasped and stepped away from his grasp, and reluctantly started to disrobe. She had managed to turn all eyes to her.

I eyed Maya closely, as did the other council mægi. It is seldom that a woman advances to such a level in Destinæa's crown city elite. She would need to be tougher than any man and ambitious, extremely talented, and smart as well. I, of course, know that Maya is just such a mæge. She has aligned herself recently with Chalmæn. An inspired move on her part, as Chalmæn is ambitious and of like mind. A powerful ally.

The noble lady, I never bothered to learn her proper name, shook and in near hysterics, finally finished. Maya's guards grabbed up her clothes immediately. All the guards on deck stared brazenly at her nakedness, openly licking their lips. I watched as Maya approached her and put a calming hand to her forearm. Then with a sky bolt fast move, ran a knife across her exposed neck, quickly stepping back to avoid the bloody body collapsing to the deck. Maya's eyes seemed to sparkle as she looked at each of the mægi in turn. The guards shuffled and groaned at their loss.

While the 'guests' stood in shock, Mensæ nodded and each of them found a similar fate at the hands of the guards behind them. Little struggle amongst them as they were still in shock at what had just transpired. I could not help but smile at Maya's guile, sending a message to her compatriots that she was not one to be trifled with...and just maybe with a little mercy with a quick death to the noble lady. *Mayhaps*, that was in my mind only.

We eight quickly donned our new apparel and climbed down into the waiting skiff tethered alongside the ship. The captain had orders to sail immediately back to Destineae to inform the Three of all that had happened. I gazed back with intent from the bow of the skiff as six others rowed, and Maya stood at the rudder. He could see looking over her shoulder in the distance the fate of their ship.

"Mensæ, what is it you see?" Maya queries me across the sound of oars rhythmically rattling in their iron brackets.

"Alas, the captain will not be able to fulfill his last order."

Once on shore, there was little discussion amongst we eight. Pushing the skiff back into the waves, having set it afire, we quickly gathered what little we had brought with us. Our plans had been laid in detail on the journey over, assuming we would find what we were looking for. We would travel out from our landing spot and assimilate into Aeryth society. Once gaining a foothold, we would then start our search and further work according to the direction of the council of Three. We would meet back two years hence to this same location to take our first council. That was near to four decades ago.

I step from the balcony as well as the memory and back into my rooms, pulling the glass-framed balcony doors tight against the cool night air. I am taking my eve-meal alone and the table is already set as one of the lodge's help sets down a steaming bowl of soup. I smile at her and place an extra coin on the table next to her as she finishes placing the meal out on the small table. The lodge has a small working crew, gathered specifically to cater to their unexpected guests and their off-season stay.

She smiles at her luck to be making coin this time of year.

***

(Elsii)

Whilst I sit atop the old oak tree stump outside the barn doors-it is as large and flat as a table-I watch as poppa and Jardon (that's my big brœther) work at their hunt meat and skins. Poppa has two large doe hanging from his trestle and a third carcass on his butcher's table with its hide stretched on a rack. Jardon is doing the quartering of the carcass meats. Poppa is scraping the hide and I look up as I hear and then see a single figure approaching on horseback from the trail that leads out of the woods wearing what I recognize immediately as the livery of the king. Poppa and Jardon haven't heard him yet. But Mum always said I could see and hear a doe afore anyone else would catch sight. I slip off the stump, hurry inside the barn, and climb up into the loft, settling in the hay and gazing down from the lofts loading window. Poppa finally notices and stops his work to meet the man. Poppa is surprised somewhat, as the king and his entourage had left the lodge nigh onto a full moon past after the last hunt, and we are preparing the lodge to shut down for the off season.

"Captain Caän, was something forgotten from the king's party? I don't remember any staff alerting me! I would have sent it on to Kings Court straight away," says Poppa, and I hear a little concern in his voice. It would not be good business to hold anything belonging to the king and his entourage. The king is always generous in any case, Poppa always says.

The guardsman approaches and dismounts. He knows Poppa, o'course. This is the guardsman that was assigned to the king's advisor, and one who Poppa got on with so well.

"Nay, Dùghall," responded Caän. "I come on command of the king's advisor, Mensæ. He, in turn, has been commanded to hold a council of the advisors and regents to the greatest houses from across all Aeryth. You, and your great lodge will host it. I've been sent to Dùghall arrange it with you." He placed a small sack of gold coin into the Poppa's hands.

"Another of those awaits you after Mensæ's departure at the conclusion of his summit," Caän said, leaning in towards Poppa. "The only condition is secrecy, master. As few as possible must know and each sworn to complete confidentials, sir."

"Of course. As you wish, ser," replied Poppa, knowing it will be easy after all. Who has he to tell, but for us family? We will be the only ones working. All others are long gone and will not return afore next season. He will have to make do with us. Mum and my five brœthers and sisters.

"They shall start arriving seven days hence, Dùghall. My master, Mensæ, shall act as governor to the council. He shall require the king's usual chambers as his own. Expect six other council members and their small parties, mayhaps. Seven to stay in the lodge and two score in the barracks. The guardsmen will tend to their own needs but for the accommodations of the barracks. Keep only a small staff to tend the council for three or four suns at most," the Captain finalized, and Poppa nods in instant agreement.

"Now then, sir. Can a weary rider find a hot meal and a bed for the night?" asks the soldier.

"Follow me to the kitchens, ser," replies Poppa with a grand smile. "My wife has a hearty stew simmering on the stoves. Let us stop by the brew shed and I'll bring in a small barrel of hard apple ale as well if it suits you. We've just finished a new batch." Captain Caän gives Poppa a wide smile.

"Jardon, lad," yells back Poppa. "Come take ser's horse and give her some feed and care."

Then Poppa and the captain head towards the lodge kitchens. Watching close, I see Poppa weigh the coin sack in his large hand with a glee. Must be gold coins, sure certain.

The captain left out on the morrow's morn.

Just as the captain said, the council members begin arriving on the seventh day, and I am close by to watch. Real close. Cause I hide under the porch in the shadows. They couldn't see me at all, cause I stayed in the shadows. The first to arrive is Mensæ, Captain Caän, and a few other guardsmen. Master Mensæ is there to meet all the others when they arrive to the front of the lodge. And I am there too, lying flat under the porch, staring through the stairs, but back in the shadows where nobody can see me,

Next to arrive are a man and fancy dressed lady. The coachman called out loud to nobody but master Mensæ, which I thought was peculiar as he should already know their names if they were in his summit. He called Baron Chalmæn and Baroness Maya. I remembered the baron as he was at the king's hunt, not two moons ago.

The baron's wife is clearly a force to be reckoned, my sisters would say. She stands tall with her chin in the air like she smells a fart, and eyes Mensæ close when he's not looking her way. I get chilly bumps looking at her. Mensæ called her Lady Maya and it suited her. They talked a moment about lands the king had given and titles that went with them. I did not understand. But I gathered they lived far to the south and way out west near a place called Coffs Harbour. Their keep stands upon cliffs jutting from the sea. It all so sounds mysterious and adventurous to me and thought I should watch them close during their stay. I knew from my lessons with my sister that a keep meant a cæstle, so I knew they must be royalty 'cause that's who lived in keeps and cæstles. It is on a great island off the west coast of Aeryth, reached only by a wide stone bridge over a chasm of crushing sea that hammers the cliffs below. They made it sound mysterious and grand, like Poppa's tales of such things, Mensæ said they were a lord and lady now, just as they had planned. The Lady Maya is beautiful. But she does not look friendly to me. And I double my thoughts to watch her close.

Next to arrive is a strange man, arriving on a grey speckled mare. Mensæ called him Spæctre, but he reminded Mensæ that he goes now by the moniker of Haledon. I thought it strange that a grown man would change his name. He spoke of a new Lord Tullamoor and a vigilante who had disrupted their plans. I was not sure what that was. Mensæ said that they would discuss it later, as he was intrigued, 'cause he had heard the vigilante had mægic. I caught my breath at that.

Later that same sun, a tall man with a long black mane of hair flowing upon his shoulders arrives. I had slipped back under the porch to watch. He had what Poppa called goatee whiskers 'cause they looked like a goat's I guess, and his eyes were coal black. I knew I'd always remember his face. He and Mensæ talked about the markets in a faraway city called Newcæstle and the black market was doing especially well. This is confusing, but I knew I could ask Jardon about it later. Big brœthers are good for such things. His cloak clasp was polished silver and gold, two snakes winding about each and the other.

Later another man came by carriage and was garbed in what Mum calls royal colours, and he and Mensæ talked of goings on in a city called Esperance.

Last to arrive is a short man with a grizzled look about him. His whiskers on chin and cheek do little to hide his pock marred face. He seemed to be sneering at everything and had an ill attitude. He and Mensæ talked about his training special soldiers in a place called Dæmons Due in the mountains on the far side of the lake. I listened in, o'course.

"Andras, how are things proceeding at your camp?" queries Mensæ.

"We've fewer candidates since the supply from the north has been disrupted with the death of the younger Tullamoor, of course. The new lord there has hindered it even more than the rogue vigilante. I'm sure you are aware. The one people are calling Drægonheart. It seems he has moved on though. A good omen, I am hoping," replies Andras.

"Spæctre, er…Haledon, will have things moving again from over near Cliffside. There is a very "hungry for coin and power" son of a baron on new lands there, recently granted by the king this past year. There are plenty of his type, I'm pleased to say. Haledon has his ear, of course, and will have the supply chain back intact before long," Mensæ assures Andras. "Fewer candidates are coming from the northeast in any case."

"Aye, 'tis true, that. And it gives me more quality time with the older candidates. We have some that are showing encouraging results," grumbles the grizzly man. I've never heard a man speak in such a hoarse voice.

"As for the vigilante you've just spoken of, I've assigned your most recent graduate to a Kingsman's patrol to take him down and bring him to me. The king would be happy with just his head, but I have questions for him. He was foolish enough to tip his hand to his whereabouts, and I have high hopes of bringing him to Kings Court for an interrogation only I can perform. we will speak more of it later."

The way Master Mensæ says some things makes me shiver, whole body shivers.

2

Prey Unaware

Melancholy and wonder. Six full moons have passed since I first met the Druid Eschereon on the bridge just outside this small village and Esper Keep. Both the village and the keep are a wonder. I ponder that nothing...and everything has changed in my life. I am still Arias Côeurdrægon, but I have discovered that my blood lineage is not what I have lived these past seventeen years. Thoughts and feelings of my life with Da have not changed, but my family has grown bigger in ways I could never have imagined. And so, I come into the village, away from the druid's keep, from time a'time to give myself a little perspective.

Sitting against a small fountain wall adjacent the barter square of the towne on the west side of the village and smiling to myself, I wonder that after my long and arduous journey I have ended up in such a place. I take in the sights and sounds of everyday life here, the village waking to a new sun. Further down a byway to the square, youngers are playing, trying to keep a hoop rolling over the cobbled stone street in front of them with just the touch of a stick. On my way to the square, I had passed the laundry strung up behind many a townfolk home, each abode made of simple stack stone and mortar with wood shake roofs. When I reached the square, the smells of bakeries and food vendors added to the experience all the more. This is a place of peace and simple life.

It is barter day on the square, and I enjoy it most of all the days here in the village. The townsfolk and people from afar outside the village walls come once a moon to barter and trade for goods they need with goods they have either crafted themselves or no longer need. Though they have a simple system of coin for smaller necessities and foodstuffs within the town itself, larger transactions are made here in a barter system passed down through many generations of the common folk living on this side of the Barrier Mountains. The many small, scattered villages all have their own barter day bazaars, one sun in a moon cycle. King's coin is virtually unknown here, especially at this farthest point north in all of the Mid Realm. As a fact, people here do not consider themselves a part of the king's realm at all. They pay no taxes to the king and he offers no protection to them. To Kings Court, this land may as well be part of the Northern Reaches, thought to be unreachable and useless lands of mountain, stone, and mostly desolation.

One would think that, with a keep rising above the village and sitting against the mountain and all, this would not be true. This is, as a fact, the most mystifying part of Eschereon's abode. As I look up over the village rooftops, I marvel that I alone can see the keep. Neither the villagers, Sæm nor Alænèa, anyone for the matter, nor even Eschereon himself can see the whole of the keep rising above. I thought my friends were playing a joke at my expense at first. But I learned this to be a true mægic of an era long past. The druid is able to explain the mægic and even show me how it is formed, at least in small part. The keep, it seems, is protected by ancient mægic wards that render it unnoticeable to the naked eye. I have learned that the entire village has a different variety of wards placed upon it. Every stone of it makes it unique in all of Aeryth as well. And somehow, I am immune to some of it. Mayhaps my acute awareness of mægic auras explains some of it. Ever since Alænèa had awakened the sense in me, I have immediately surpassed even the elders of her village on the ability to recognize them.

And so, as I sit against the wall of the fountain with a foot upon its basin's stone ledge and looking out at the square as it comes to life, I take time to reflect on my arrival and the time spent here, trying to rein in anxieties that of late have begun to surface in my mind. I find my thoughts wander to old, dear friends a world away...and to Finnie. She is especially on my mind of late. The pull to her is indescribable to the point of wanting to just leave everything here and head back to Middenvale. Eschereon has explained that it would be unwise now, and this only fuels my anxiety. I push these thoughts aside for the moment and turn to other memories. These, too, are crystal clear to me.

On the day of my arrival, the druid had been expecting me as if it was a prearranged time and place upon which we were taking our first meeting. It harkened, in a manner, to the way that I had met the Elder in Sæm's home village in the Northern Reaches. A blind recluse, the Elder met me as if he'd known me his entire life, calling me by my full name and with knowledge he could not possibly have learned aforehand from my companions. I had felt the druid react to me in much the same manner.

Eschereon named me an enigma after meeting me and my peculiar traveling companions that sun, but I think it just the reverse. Da's final note to me was true in its words to be sure. The druid that he had sent me on this quest to find did have answers for me. But they are answers to questions I have not even brought with me, and they only produce a myriad of further queries that I could not know existed.

And then there is the mægic. These things that I can do, things that I have done not even of my own will or design, have names in the druid's lore. In this learning, I am amazed, and the druid, with *my* stories, is as well. Eschereon is ofttimes aside himself with wonder and glee, he's proclaimed, but one cannot tell it from his almost always stoic expression. Well, there is a slight smile from time a'times, but I have to be quick to catch it. Along with his usually expressionless face, the druid's entire countenance and attire is of a like. From the everysun same binding braids and beads he wears in two places along his long, mostly grey beard to his simple draped robe with a thousand hidden pockets, voluminous sleeves, and two amulets about his neck. A skull cap with colourful runes stitched around it sits upon his head at all times. But, if I am not mistaken, I do notice a change in the jeweled rings the druid wears on both hands some suns. Some of his long fingers even carry two a'times. Aside from the ladies that walk the streets in Seas End, I have never seen such a thing.

I have so queried Eschereon about this and learned that each ring indeed has a purpose, but the druid reveals them not. So, he says, do the amulets about his neck, just as my amulets from my mœther and the tinker I'd met in my travels. Just so, my queries become the druid's, as he is most curious about the amulet from the tinker. He says it is very old and carries a very strong mægic that he cannot discern. The runes amongst the filigree are from a language he is not readily acquainted with. It fascinates him, and he copied the runes to research in his vast library. He thinks it a product of a Source-Sayer, mayhaps, most ancient and powerful of mæges.

One thing became clear early on to me. Sæm, Alænèa, and I felt comfortable, safe, and close to the druid almost immediately. There is an inherent truth in what he speaks, and there is always trust in his wisdom from our first meeting. He is always candid and does not shirk away from any subject of query.

Eschereon is never in a hurry to do or tutor anything, and so it is up to me to draw from the druid the answers I seek. These sessions subsequently lead to other studies and queries that I have not expected. It seems a strange way to tutor an apprentice, which the druid seems to think I am, though no words to that effect have ever been spoken. My first queries were about why my da was put to oath by Mœther to carry me across the whole of Aeryth as a younger just barely having reached his fifth year-end. This took an unexpected turn. I recall the conversation as if it were yestersun. To a fact, I am able to do this with most any memory my mind holds. And so, I recall with total clarity and detail the whole of that first sun in the druid's keep.

Bane and Talon had no desire to enter the village that Eschereon was leading the others to, and they soon disappeared after they had determined, in each their own way, that I was in no present danger. Bane silently vanished into the tall grasses and Talon took to the skies again, heading towards the peak of the lone mountain the druid's keep sat against.

Sæm and Alænèa strode aside to me as we followed the druid, leading our horses across the stone bridge and on towards the village and its mountainside keep. This was when I first expressed my wonder at the impressive keep, its three tall and wide turret spires climbing one above the other up into the mountainside above the walled village. Arched aqueducts (I knew them from the drawings in books I'd studied in the schoolhouse in Middenvale) wound their way behind the keep's spires and up towards a snow-capped peak high above. It reached even still higher into billowing clouds. The stone of the village walls and the keep appeared to have just been stacked in place, showing no age to them. The look of washed granite sits about them.

"Isn't it amazing?" I finished my awed description.

Alænèa and Sæm turned to me with wide eyes and furrowed brows and Eschereon ahead of us even turned to stare at me.

"Of what are you speaking, Arias?" Sæm spoke first. "I see great stone arches reaching up to the mountainside and into a high pass in the distance. Are these the...'aqueducts' you speak of? The walls that circle the town we are approaching do look as if they've just been laid to be sure. But I see no towering turrets and spires or battlements. All that is visible above the town seems to be a winding lane up to a stone abode built into the mountainside. It is curious though. I have never seen a village with walls at all."

"I've never seen such a village either," Alænèa agreed. "Though my experience is limited to the Plain and the tomes of the Elders. But I see no towers. I see it as Sæm does, Arias. My eyes do see an aura about the town though, even in the sunlight! Everything I've seen since passing through the Poppy Sea is a wonder to me."

I noted a small smile creep onto the druid's face as he looked first to me and then, with a quirk of his head, to Alænèa as well.

"You are all correct in what you see," explained Eschereon, shocking us. "It is just that you each have different mægical ability. I am especially taken by Ariastone's sight. Not even I can see the keep without a mægical device. He mentioned them earlier and I thought that the keep's wards had somehow failed. And, dear lass, your recognition of mægic by aura is an ability only a few carry. Remarkable. I believe you can learn the mægic of warding."

Little did we know then that it was Alænèa that would have the true talent with mægical wards. Or at least in recognizing them and cyphering their meaning.

"I believe I will be quite busy with the three of you in suns to come!" he exclaimed. "And to your remark on the fresh look of the stone that makes up the town's structures and streets, you are seeing the work of the protecting wards placed upon them much more than a millennium ago. A couple, mayhaps. The towne has not changed but for its residents in all of that time. There is an exception in one square and alley within the village. Ask anyone how to get to Drægon Alley. Lore holds that there was once a fight with a drægon there. The tale speaks of drægon's breath destroying the mægic of the wards, the only thing known to have done it in over a thousand years." Eschereon smiled as he told this story of his village.

"Do you believe in the myth of drægons then, druid?" I asked him, smiling at the thought.

He called back to me over his shoulder, having started back towards the towne.

"Are you asking if I believe in the myth of drægons or do I believe in drægons, lad? I can say that as a boy, my pæder pointed to a lone beast with great wings flying high over this very mountain and he named it such. I had never seen a drægon before that nor since, so I cannot say for certain. He was known to tell a tale to entertain me. But then, there is the Drægon Alley in this very village."

Going pensive for a moment, I thought in a world with true mægic, could drægons not be possible as well? I determined I would like to see Drægon Alley.

Before we had made the gates to the village, Eschereon addressed us again.

"As I have said, no person, aside from your friend Ariastone here, can see the keep, and they live beneath it unknowing. The abode you see high on the mountainside at the end of the winding path is where they know me to live. There are other mægics to keep this secret from them as well. I will explain those to you another time. It would do no good to tell them otherwise, and it is for their safety that they do not know. Please humor my deception." And with that, he turned and led us into the small towne he said they called Esper which means 'Hope.'

It was a quiet morning that sun when we first entered Esper, and a soupy fog still hung knee-deep above the ground and swirled about our feet as we walked the cobbled stone ways. Lilit and Jilly sat atop Paint's saddle taking in this new scenery, and the clip-clop of the horse's hooves was the loudest sound to be heard. On the inside of the gates, open to all, Eschereon explained, I could see that the towne was much larger than it appeared from beyond the walls. We headed up a main travelway, with a few shops closest to the towne gates and then a number of structures that just offered up the very brightest of colourful doors in red and blue and lavender among others...residences mayhaps. The windows with broad slatted shutters in complementary colours to their doors were held back tight with iron shutter dogs to the clean, smooth stone wall faces. Large bronze or iron lanterns hung over each doorway.

The street had a gentle rise and as we came upon the next corner, the fog had disappeared, and a shop owner was sweeping the dust along the walkway outside her shop. There was little more to sweep along the pristine travelway and walkway above it.

"Ga-morn to ya, Sage!" she said addressing Eschereon, and he smiled a greeting back with a nod and a touch to his cap to her. She stopped her sweeping for a moment and looked up to the furions sitting upon Paint's saddle. They gazed back at her in unison, their heads swiveling on their upright bodies, staying fixed to her as we passed. She just smiled and pulled at her earlobe, and they mimicked her gesture in unison, eliciting a loud chuckle. She paid little attention to Sæm, Alænèa, and myself.

At the intersection of the next byway, a man stooped with a huge canvas sack upon his back. There appeared to be sheared wool showing at the top and bulging from loose seams. He turned to us as he passed in front of us.

"Morn to ya, Sage" he said, giving an abbreviated greeting salute to the druid and taking care to keep his load on balance. "Bilby, catch up, will ya?" he said to his younger, who could not have seen his fifth year-end and had stopped to stare at the strangers. He quickly ran to his da, carrying a few dropped pieces of wool in his small hands.

"Best to you, Cantor," returned Eschereon.

We, at last and a time later, had passed through the whole of the towne and had come up to a stone wall enclosed paddock. The stableman had heard the hoof falls of the horses, and he and a lad met us at the gate. There was a small grassy pasture off to the right and a stable house set tight to the mountainside as it climbed quite steeply on this side of the towne.

Eschereon gripped the man's forearm warmly and greeted him with a smile.

"Pètyr, I trust you can care for my guest's steeds? They'll be here for a term. This is Ariastone, Alænèa, and Sæm." Greetings were made all around.

"They will be well cared for, Sage," replied the stableman.

"I'll be by later to brush them down," I added.

"O'course," replied Pètyr, with a knowing smile. "I'd be doing the same." He gave me a nod of approval.

"Well then, I have not made arrangements for a mornmeal for such a party. Shall we go across to the inn? It's small, but their larder is always well stocked and Maäm Mary is a wonder of a cook." We all heartily agreed, not having a proper cooked meal since leaving the Plain.

Leaving the stables, we proceeded towards the inn. It was a cheerful building to be sure. Like every other structure in towne, it had a character of its own. Welcoming in its very appearance. It stood alone and apart from the adjacent buildings, and the property was surrounded by a painted white picket fence which was covered in flowering vine. A long, deep covered porch ran the length of the building, with a wood shake roof and thick, carved wooden posts holding it up. Planters with flowers of every sort adorned the porch with large wooden chairs and small tables arranged about.

The yard would be shaded most of the sun, as a large tree with canopy stretching wide in every direction protected it. A bench sat under the tree, and I felt a bit of my Middenvale home calling to me as it resembled the tree outside of our cottage there. Birdhouses hung everywhere and two large maggies with shiny black and white plumage sat on the back of the bench, watching a tall goodman going about pruning and weeding activities. The man heard our banter as we exited the stable yard and, seeing that we were headed his way, came to greet us in the middle of the lane.

"Hail, Sage, and welcome." The man grasped the druid's forearm with one hand and lay his other upon his shoulder in a genuine show of fellowship. "Are you and your guests joining us for mornmeal?" I got the feeling this man would give the boots from his own feet for a stranger in need, his warmth was so genuine.

"We would indeed love to partake of your wife's fine fare!" returned Eschereon. "It seems my new friends have not sat at a proper table and a warm meal in quite some time."

"Let us remedy that then." He turned to the three of us. "They call me Giorgie. Please do as well. Mary makes a wonderful porridge, and her eggs, sausage, and peppers will warm your innards to your toes."

"That sounds wonderful, master keep," I said. "I am Arias, and this is Alænèa. The tall one with the biggest appetite is called Sæm. Your words have my stomach growling aloud!"

"Let us find the cook, then. She is most like to be guarding her kitchens from intruders, with pots boiling and pans sizzling as we speak. Come, come. Let me find you a table inside the soup hall. Sage, she'll be so pleased you've come to visit!" And with that, the goodman and innkeep led us inside.

In the coming moons, I would visit Maäm Mary's dining hall often, never attempting to enter her kitchens, but enjoying her fare and company greatly. We became fast friends, with Giorgi discussing all manner of things. Mary, like her husband, is a wonderful person, prone to soft hugs and a kind word. And Giorgie's maggies (he calls them magpies for their taste in Mary's berry pies cooling on the windowsill) are fascinating creatures. He has trained them to travel the whole of Aeryth to the druid's friend somewhere on the coast in the Southern Reaches, with messages to and fro. A message could reach across Aeryth in four suns instead of forty on a fast horse. In suns since, I have wished they knew the way to Middenvale.

That sun and the many that followed were filled with revelations that would change my life in so many ways.

After a filling mornmeal among warm hosts that sun, we were led up a winding path to a stone abode in the stone mountain, as there was no apparent entryway to the druid's keep that only I could spy. The others swore that all that was there was a crumbling cliffside of the mountain itself. Just loose rock and gravel, untraversable. Myself, I felt I could simply climb a small hillock to reach the keep's base, but there were no evident portals nor doors of any kind. If I strayed from the path towards it, I had an overwhelming sense of the futility of such an act. After all, there were no entrances there. I followed the druid to his abode, my mind in conflict with itself over what my eyes insisted they were seeing.

Within the druid's stone home, we found a large, comfortable, if simplistic, living space. The central room we had entered held seating and a long wood table in front of us. A large window on the front wall brought a good amount of light into what, by all appearances, a comfortable lodge-style abode. The ceiling reached high, mayhaps three times my height, with massive wood beams traversing the room from front to back and embedded into the stone walls. A large wagon wheel sized light fixture hung from the center beam directly over the large table with a dozen oil lamps that cast significant light about the room at dusk or in the dark of night.

An impressively thick and colourful rug adorned the stone floor and oil lanterns sat on a few tables or hung as sconces upon the stone walls. A large stone fireplace occupied most of the right wall, with two very comfortable chairs crafted of thick leather and stout wooden arms and legs worn smooth with age and use. A well-stocked wood pile sat upon the hearth, and a thick timbre mantle was inset to the firebox's stone chimney above. Further on, to our right and past the sitting area about the hearth, was a simple kitchen with its own fireplace and iron stove. Four thick, heavy doors stood in the back wall. One to the right of the kitchen suggested it led to a larder. Another lay open and revealed a bath. The others, one on the back wall and the other on the left wall, were open and showed bed chambers.

The left wall drew my attention most. Heavy wooden bookcases rose near to twice my height and ran from the front wall, then six long paces down this sidewall. A step ladder was attached to a bar atop the shelves so that the highest shelf might be reached while standing upon it. The ladder rolled on wheels below and the track above. A depression lies worn into the stone floor below the iron wheels, suggesting it had been used much over long years. Every shelf stuffed tight, one to the other, with leather tomes.

Books that would take years to read. Two large, comfortable chairs with small wooden tables aside them sat in front of the shelves. The three of us were drawn to them, unable to keep ourselves from lightly running our fingers over the bindings in awe. One last chair and table sat in the front corner of the room. A high circular window brought light directly upon the table and chair that sat higher than the rest in the room. It was a scrivener's table where a scribe can sit to copy words from one book into another for distribution. Upon the table sat an open tome, loose papers, an ink well, and writing plume. But there seemed to be a layer of dust upon them.

"Welcome to my home," Eschereon proclaimed, bringing our attention back to him. "Please excuse my housekeeping. I spend little time here. It is mostly for show and the few guests I receive."

"Come. I've more to show you and then we might get properly acquainted."

He strode over to the thick door to the right of the kitchen and opened it into what was clearly a functioning larder, just as I had suspected. But he directed us to follow him, a smile upon his face. Stepping past the food-stuffs and kitchen pots and tools, he faced the blank back wall of the small room, where naught but a mop and pail sat in the corner. I looked over Alænèa's shoulder with Sæm peering over mine in turn. We watched as Eschereon mumbled words in a language unfamiliar and at the same time traced a doorway in the wall with his walking stick. An audible click rang out, and he pushed at the right side of the wall. It gave into the mild pressure and swung inward, revealing a small foyer and a shallow staircase running up and off to the right in the direction I knew the keep to be in. A light shown from that direction.

A short climb up stone steps found us entering a vestibule in the shadows of a great structure held up by massive, fluted columns. We could go left or right, and Eschereon took us to his left. We made our way around what turned out to be the underside of a great double-sided circular stair made of polished granite steps and polished stone balustrade and found ourselves at the back of a huge, three story entrance hall. Our exclamations echoed in its vastness. Granite columns carried low arching beams from the outer perimeter and strategic points within the hall. The hall was circular to match my recollection of the first tower's shape from without. Great arched doors stood closed across the hall from us in a direction that faced the village. I recalled that I had noticed no doors from the outside earlier.

"The keep's great hall has seen few guests over the past two millennia. Let us proceed to my working chambers," the druid explained as he exited through adoorway on the left side of the hall.

Beyond it, we climbed another stair of stone and proceeded across a great battlement that led to a second tower. We were already high enough that looking out over the parapet, we could survey all of the towne. Entering the second tower, we climbed two additional stairs winding along the outside of the tower walls to find ourselves entering a long wide hall. Though the keep's outer walls were made of stone, here we found ourselves walking on deep, plush rugs. The walls were paneled in hardwoods of walnut, I guessed, with tremendously detailed cloth murals hung intermittently betwixt oaken doors that giants would have no need to duck under. Eschereon led us through one such doorway, and as I entered, I found myself dumbstruck.

As my eyes slowly perused a two-storied chamber, my jaw going slack to see endless intricately carved woodwork upon shelving rising from floor to ceiling with books of all sizes, bound in all manner and colour with titles etched in gold upon them. When I had once confessed to Da my love of reading from the schoolhouse library, which carried mayhaps half a hundred books, he told me a tale of a great library he had visited. I had laughed at what I thought was his exaggeration. I realized that this must be that very same chamber he spoke of as his description matched in detail. To one end of the chamber stood an enormous fireplace, burning and giving off the most comfortable glow. Four heavy, stuffed, double-seats of softened leather sat as a framed square around a low oaken table in front of the hearth. Other chairs were scattered about the room and adjacent to windows looking out over Esper and much of the valley below. In one corner on the hearthside of the chamber sat a man on a high seat behind a scrivener desk. He was truly a scribe then. He rose from his seat and joined us.

"Therrien, see who has arrived finally. This is Ariastone Côeurdrægon and two traveling companions, Sæm and Alænèa," Eschereon introduced us.

"Yay, Sage," rejoined the scribe with a wide smile. "You have the look of your mœther's bloodline mostly, Ariastone. And your lovely friend, she is of course from the Plain. Most curious. Sæm, you say your name is? Could you be of Ètœn Bearheart's bloodline?"

It seemed he knew a great deal of me and my friends. More than only a scribe then.

"Yay, sir. Sæm, I've found is indeed my Da's brœther's son, and so family," I blurted out.

Therrien's forehead furrowed and his eyebrows raised as he looked to me and then to Eschereon. "Oh, dear... Eschereon, he does not know that Ètoen is not his true pæder."

My jaw dropped for a second time since I had entered this room.

"Therrien," the druid said. "Might you bring a tray with tea for us all? We can sit afore the hearth and have a chat."

Six full moons have passed across this sky above the druid's keep since that sun, and I find myself both equally enthralled with what I've learned of mægic, and as much, longing for my past and simpler life. I come to the village center on barter day to be amongst the towne folk, and more frequently these suns, I venture out into the surrounding countryside, visiting homesteads asking if I might be of help in the everysun chores. Asking for nothing more than to satisfy the longing.

3

A Tinker and Innocence Stolen

"Mummy, can I have a biscuit, please?" I ask, tugging lightly on me mum's smock as she stands over the ovens. Almost frantic, she is. But I am hungry. Mum's biscuits are the best in the whole territory Poppa always says, and he surely knows the right of it.

"Hush, Elsii, lass. I've no time now. It's a madhouse 'n only yer sisters to help. These men are generous, mayhaps, and the Lady Maya ever more so, but they're wanting things just so. They want what they want, but don't want to see the help at all. We're needing to fill their tables and then disappear afore they arrive. Strange folk, for ministers and royals and such, but a blessing this being the offseason and all. Their coin is plentiful, it is," Mum 'splains while still busy over the stoves.

I shouldn't of asked. But I really am a bit hungry. Mum and Poppa and everybody in the family has been almost loony with the company that just arrived. All the staff has already gone away to their homes on the other side of the mountain, and it is only us left. I have two older brœthers—they have whiskers even—and three big sisters. Kersti is married now too. Her and Thoms live in a cottage over the hill behind the pasture, but they are here early still, helpin'. I have my own cottage too that Poppa built for me past the hedges in the garden beyond the kitchens. The guests don't know it's there, so it's my secret place. You can't even see it 'cause the hedges are so tall at the back of the garden. Mum lets me sleep out there a'times, me 'n Huni.

I back away a bit and am about to leave…really, when Mum sighs real loud, slumps her shoulders, and smiles. Then she turns to me and stoops to look me eye to eye. She'd pulled a hot biscuit outta a basket she was goin' to send off with Stella for the guests. Whenever Mum looks at me like this it is to tell me somethin' portant…or hug me.

"Elsii, my little, dearest lassie," she says with a smile as she wraps the warm biscuit in a cloth and places it in my hands, then grasps 'em in both of hers. "Here's yer biscuit, golden eyes." That was her special name for me, 'cause my eyes are gold and sparkly. "There's some just churned butter in the corner with the buttermilk creams still atop." She always says somethin' real nice afore she gets serious.

"I want you to make an oath to me, can you," she says, dead serious…'cause oaths are weighty stuff (that's what Poppa always says). I just nod.

"Whilst these guests are here…four whole suns more, they are sayin', I'm wanting them to never see ya a'tall, lassie. Not in the hallways, not in the dining hall…nowhere. You gotta be a ghost! You know the game we play when Auntie comes calling a'times?" I nod and smile. Auntie is always sayin' mean things, and uncle too so sometimes I never even visit when they come 'round, just hiding and spying on them. They never know.

"I swear an oath!" I tell Mum and mean it. Even lick my fingers and put them to my heart. Asides, it will be fun. The only thing I will miss is scavenging under the big table in the dining hall. The guests always are losing coin from their pockets, letting it fall under the chairs and table at mealtimes. I have a stash of lots of coin in my cottage from scavenging.

"Mummy, can I have somethin' for Huni too?" I ask. Mum raises her eyebrow but pulls a piece of jerky from the jerky sack on the wall and hands it to me. Huni used to scare Mum. But she realized now we love each other and it's okay, as long as she isn't seeing her all the time. So Huni can't come inside. I think that's why Poppa built me my cottage.

"Remember your oath?" Mum raises a brow again at me. This is serious, I think, repeatin' it twice and the brow thing again.

"Course I do, Mummy. I'm a ghost!" I whisper as I run off smiling, arms wide. But then I stop and go over to the corner. Unwrapping my biscuit then breaking it apart to scoop a big dollop of butter into it, I notice a bowl of honey and add two fingers of honey to it.

I sneak out to the garden, then behind the hedges to my cottage, making sure nobody is watching. Not even from the windows.

Though you can't see it behind the hedges, me and Poppa painted my cottage real pretty. The door is as tall as me and painted mulberry. That's purple but so are mulberries, and Poppa said I should name my cottage and so I call it Mulberry Place 'cause Huni likes 'em. It has a window too with a shutter that comes down over it if I sleep overnight in it. Me and Poppa painted it yellow.

He also crafted me a cot and mattress, and I have a chair and a small table for eatin' on too. Mummy gave me a real warm and pretty quilt for my cot and an old ratty blanket, and I put it in the corner for Huni. She doesn't mind it being ratty. She is there now, all curled up in it. As I come in, Huni comes over to say morn to ya and I give her the jerky. She runs her body and arches her back along my leg as her thank-ya and goes back to her corner to tear the jerky apart with sharp teeth and claws and devour it in a flash.

Huni is a wolf badger. And Poppa says wolf badgers are just about the meanest creatures in all the forest. Bears and mountain cats won't even bother them, nose-a-nose. Huni even eats venom snakes. As a fact, she eats anything, but she loves honey most. She climbs trees and sticks her head right into holes with bees buzzing and comes down smilin'. *She really likes honey*!

She is big too. When she stretches, she can lick my chin and hug me around my waist. When I lie on my cot, she squirms into me an' sticks her nose under my arm. It tickles so, but I let her 'cause it means she loves me...and I love her. I really like all the animals, o'course, and they all really like me. The horses and pigs and chickies and even Mad Red, the craziest rooster. He attacks ever-buddy but me. But Huni and me love each other most of all.

She saved me when I was little, ya know. Once upon a time, just like this morn, Mum gave me a bowl with a biscuit and honey drizzled atop and sent me out to the garden till she could get the mornmeal done for the guests. So I went out and sat down on my rock to eat and watch the flutterflies in the flowers. Sometimes they let me touch them or they come sit on my shoulder. Anyway, I was examining a large flutterfly as big as my hand when a huge, hooded venom snake rose its head up out of the bush and stared and hissed at me. It weren't more than an arm's length from me. Next I knew, a big, ferocious wolf badger was next to me, swaying afore and back, starin' at the snake. Then quick as flash, they were twistin' and turnin' and rollin' in the bushes. Then my Huni came out with the venom snake dead in her mouth.

I screamed for Mummy and Poppa and when they came a-runnin', Huni was curled in my lap with her muzzle in my honey bowl and the venom snake lying dead on the pathway. They gasped to see what was happening. Me scratchin' and pettin' a mean wolf badger and a huge, venom snake laid dead on the path. 'Twas long as Poppa is tall. Huni and me have been together ever since.

When we have guests at the lodge we mostly eat when we can. Early in the morns and eve-meals in the kitchens late after the guests have eaten. Poppa says the whole lot of them are together summitting, whatever that is. Talking 'portant stuff for the king and the other royals, he says. They have lots of guards out in the lodge barracks too. Thom and my brœthers, Sten and Chez, are mostly helping with their horses and grillin' and smokin' meats for 'em. But they mostly keep to themselves and stay out on the grounds.

I keep my promise to Mum, and none of the guests ever see me. But that don't mean I can't see them. I'm a good ghost and a good spy too. Learning when Auntie comes to visit, I know some tricks and hidey holes. Mum lets me stay in my cottage at nights, so she don't know when I sneak out to do my nighttime spying!

Poppa will most like have tanned my hide if he knew what I was doing, but to me it's just having fun being sneaky. In the cold weather, Poppa keeps plenty of firewood in the guest rooms next to the fireplaces. But what the guests don't know is that the fireplaces open from the back as well as being open in the front on the room side. The lodge is built with a large dining hall on one end of the ground level with a couple lounges on t'other end. One is for the goodmen with smokeweed and pipes and it has an ale-bar asides. Thom tends to it most nights. T'other is for maids and maäms awaiting on their menfolk and where they drink and whisper together. With this summitting, there are no other women, so the Lady Maya smokes and drinks with the menfolk. They don't seem to think anything of it.

The kitchens are to the back of the lodge rooms, betwixt the dining hall and the lounges. All the sleepin' chambers are on the second and third floors. The king's man, Mensae, Poppa called him, is using the king's chambers atop on the third floor. The lord and lady are using the chambers that we normally keep for the king's lady.

The secret part is the back stairways from the kitchens. They go direct to the upper floors and into halls betwixt the sleeping rooms where all the backs of the fireboxes can be serviced and the staff can bring up meals and such, direct to the guests. In the middle of the night, when the fires burn low, logs can be added without entering the guest chambers. 'Tis quite a fascinating thing, and Poppa and Sten showed me how it worked one sun. There is a chain that attaches to the back stone of each firebox. It runs over a pulley, Poppa called it, and 'tached up to a great iron ball on the other side of the pulley. A counter-weight, Sten 'splained. Sten can just pull down on the iron ball and with the firestone greased up, it can rise up mostly silent, and a log can be placed into the fire from this hidden service gallery betwixt the chambers. Four bed chambers can be serviced from each hidden way. The other end of the hall, away from the stairs to the kitchens, has a door leading into the guest corridor, but it is hidden behind a great rug that Mum calls a tapestry.

But there is also something the guests might not like if they knew about it. It is a peek hole in the wall just atop the fireplace mantle. Poppa uses it to see that the guests are asleep afore opening the back of the firebox, but it can be used for spying too.

Being a curious sort, I find the peek holes irresistible. So, each night of the summitting, I been sneaking out of my cottage behind the hedges into the kitchens and then up into the secret halls. Poppa and my brœthers will not be up till much later, as they know the guests will tend their own fires while they are awake, and they have been awake to the wee hours each night. My sneaking confirms they were all up and about, well into the nights. I wonder why they can't do all their talking at their sun-time meet-ups together? But I notice that there seems to be a difference in the nights. The king's man doesn't talk to everybody in the night meetings and neither does the Lord Chalmæn and the lady. Ser Mensae talks most nights with Master Haledon, or the ugly and mean man, and sometimes with the one with the pointy chin whiskers. The lord and lady speak to the master from the south, and Master Ugly as well.

So, I wander about to spy on them, just like I do with my auntie. I have to stand a log endwise up and climb upon it to reach the peek holes, and most times I don't really hear or understand what they are saying a'times, but the fun is in the sneaking! It's the last night of the summit, and I am watching in on the lord and lady, and they are talking real serious to a man in a black cloak who says he was sent to them by Master Mean and Ugly. Lady Maya hands him a small rolled-up parchment and her voice rises quite loud and says, "Get it done!" It seems to me her eyes go red as blood, and the man goes stiff for a moment. He takes the parchment and makes to leave straight away. I close the peek hole and climb down from my log stand and am going to sneak across the guest hall to the other hidden hall, but when I peek out from behind the tapestry, I hold back 'cause the man in the cloak is still standing outside the lord and lady's chamber reading the small parchment. He looks dazed, like a startled doe, but finally turns and heads down the hall. He makes to put the rolled-up parchment under his cloak, but he misses his pocket and I see it fall from his cape and onto the floor.

I want to call out to him that he has dropped it, but Mum's voice comes to mind and I stay quiet. When he is gone, I finally sneak out, scoop up the parchment, and disappear behind the tapestry on the other side of the hall. I can give it to Mum on morrow's morn, and she can return it. Nothing more exciting happens so I tippity-toe back down to my cottage and fall to sleep straight away.

The morn's sun is bright already when I wake to much noise and talking in the garden on the other side of the hedge. This seems quite unusual to me as the gardens behind the kitchen are mostly for Mum and the kitchen help. Guests might meet in the more formal gardens but not typically here. I can clearly hear the Lady Maya speaking. So, quiet as a chippie, Huni and I leave our little cottage and crawl beneath the hedges to spy what is happening in the garden. A couple ladybugs climb higher into the bush above my head as I wriggle closer to the garden side of the hedgerow.

Peering from under a prickly holly bush, I am most surprised to see all of my family lined up next to each and the other with big smiles upon their faces. Lady Maya is handing out heavy coin purses to each of them. Master Mensæ is there as well, and the lord and lady's guardsmen are standing behind my family with longswords out and held upright in a sort of salute to Poppa and Mum. The lord is saying that they are most pleased with the hospitality and service provided them during their summit and are leaving momentarily. As almost an afterthought, the lady asks if everybody is present to receive a purse. I watch as Mum pauses a moment and then says, "Well, there is l'il Elsii, my youngest lass, but she is but an eight year and wasn't about to be a bother."

The lady's eyebrow rises, and she makes a purposeful look to the captain of her guard. I see it and wonder as it seems a bit sneaky, like Poppa gives Mum when he's keeping a secret from me. I scratch at my leg, but do it quiet like, so as not to draw attention.

"Well then, please give this final purse to her as well," she says and steps back to stand beside Mensæ and the lord. The lord nods to the captain. I'm thinkin' I'm wrong about the Lady Maya, her giving Mum a coin purse for me.

Mum takes in a great breath and smiles a great smile, and I almost crawl out from beneath the hedge to run to her. But then, of a sudden, I see all the guardsmen step forward most quick and thrust in unison their longswords. Poppa, Sten, Chez, and Thom try to reach back to no avail, and my sisters and Mum just look to the lady with wide eyes. I see the red blood blossom from grievous wounds on their smocks, and it seems a gurgle comes from them as they drop to their knees. Tears are welling in my eyes but I am too much in shock to utter a sound, and I watch as Mum looks in my direction.

I am holding my breath as my family falls unmoving now upon the ground. But from the corner of my eye, I am sure I see a grin spread upon the face of the Lady Maya.

"Captain, send three of your men to find this lass and deal with her. And let us be off immediately," the lord barks in a most evil voice. The captain and the other guards follow the three of them towards the stable yard and three of the guardsmen break off from the others and immediately head towards the lodge and the staff quarters looking for me, I am sure. What am I to do? My chest hurts and I cannot move. Something hard is caught in my throat. Huni is growling deep in her chest. Finally, I find myself taking a great breath and realize I've been holding it all this time. Huni is licking at my cheek.

A chill grips me, and my grief gives way to panic. They are looking for me and will probably not stop until they find me. Where can I go? Of a sudden, the garden is very cold and silent, and I'm gripping the twigs in the dirt below me. Would my auntie take me in? I think not...and I know not where her homestead is. I am just an eight year-ender. I have no coin nor do I know anything beyond the lodge grounds really. But I know the lodge grounds well...and if I can hide, the guardsmen might lose interest or think I have run away, and they might not chase after me. I can then leave and follow the road and cross the mountain and...and...if I had coin, somebody might help. Coin. I have mine in the cottage hidden, and there are all the purses in the garden...with my family.

I climb from under the hedgerow and run back into my cottage. I grab my shoulder bag that I carry my treasures in and put my coin purse in there too. Then I run back to the garden. It is hard to go in there. I force myself to walk in but I cannot tear my eyes away from Mum and Poppa. I stoop and touch Mummy's hair. Their eyes are staring past me though and cannot see me, I know, like Gran's at her wake. I start picking up the coin purses. Why would they give them coin and then do this? Some of the coin purses are sitting in pools of blood, but I collect them anyway, not looking. I keep turning back to Mum. It looks like she is trying to tell me something. A raven caws from somewhere behind me. The hairs prickle the back of my neck and I look up towards the lodge. A guardsman is staring back at me from a window on the second floor. My breath catches in my throat and I turn and run towards the woods. I run and run and try to think. He sees which way I am going. I stop. And then I change directions and head across the deep grasses in the pasture, heading towards Kersti and Thom's cottage. It is on the other side of the pasture and out of sight in the trees. I can hide there. I think I can hear them yelling betwixt themselves in the distance from the woods on the other side of the pasture where I started.

I finally come to Thom and Kersti's cottage and run in, out of breath. I jump onto their bed and just sit in the corner, hugging Huni who has been following at my heels this whole time. I squeeze her tight and start to cry... exhausted and panicked. I can feel my heart pounding like it wants to burst from my chest. The scene in the garden won't leave my head, no matter how hard I squeeze my eyes shut.

After a time, as I sit in the quiet, hugging Huni has calmed me. I tell myself I have to be smarter than them if I am going to escape. And I start thinking more clearly again. My stomach is growling now, and as I peer out the window, I see that the sun is half across the sky already. My shaking has stopped and I get up from the bed, my face sticky from tears and see a bowl of apples. I take one and give another to Huni. Just the simple doing of it calms me. I look about the kitchen and see some smoked sausages hanging on a hook. I have to fetch a chair to stand on to reach them, but I do and bring them all down.

A small bird flies into the window pane and startles me.

Thinking clearer now, I reckon if I were the guards, I would be searching wider and surely they will come upon the path to this cottage. It will not be safe here. I ponder that there are more places to hide in the lodge, and I know them all. They will suppose I will be afraid to return there...and so that's where I need to go. I will be smarter than them. I have to be.

I go the long way around the pasture, keeping behind bushes and trees and being silent as can be. I cannot even hear myself moving. The wind tossing the tall grasses to and fro is making more sound than I am. Coming to the barn first, I take one of Poppa's knives and stick it into my shoulder bag. In the stables, the horses are anxious as it is feeding time and there is no one to feed them. I reckon I can hide in the hayloft, but then think better of it. They are sure to look there. I would, and I'm only an eight year-ender. Almost nine though. Running my hand along the stall doors as I walk through the barn, Willow sticks her head over her gate and snuffles at me. I press my head to hers and reach up to scratch at her jaw, just the way she likes.

Leaving the barn, I can hear them off in the forest, yelling betwixt themselves. But I don't know if I hear two or three voices, so I creep into the shadows and slowly make my way towards the kitchens.

"We gotta be real quiet, Huni," I whisper. "One of those bastards might be here in the lodge still." Talking tough and grown-up helps to settle my nerves. Slipping into the kitchen, I pull the jerky bag from the wall and then fill my bag with apples 'n grapes from the fruit bowl mum keeps on the table. Then backtracking to the stairs, I lift the door to the cellar, which is hidden behind the tater sacks and under the stairs, and me and Huni climb down into it. I don't know how to light an oil lantern so it is dark and chilly but I have my jumper on since this morn, and I pulled a blanket with me that was hanging on the back of a table chair. We curl up into a dark corner betwixt two barrels under the blanket. The chill isn't so bad and Huni next to me warms me as well. Just as we settle in, I hear noise above me in the kitchens. I stiffen, but then sigh as the noise moves away. I close my eyes 'cause I can't see anyways.

Startled awake and out of the nightmare I'd witnessed and was reliving in my sleep, it takes a moment to realize where I am, but it comes back in a rush as I hear all kinds of commotion in the kitchens above me. From the sounds of it, all three of the guardsmen left to find me are right above me. I start shaking fierce and Huni starts nuzzling deep into my armpit. In a reflexive manner, I find myself rubbing her head and deep into her fur as well. In the doing it I catch a little calm.

The three soldiers are in the kitchens for food, I reckon now, as it is most like to be getting on to evemeal time. I know my stomach is grumbling...and I have to pee. Moaning to myself that this is not a good time, just seems to make it worse. I get the nerve to move out of my corner betwixt two barrels of pickled cucs and other garden pickings that Mummy has prepared for the season and feel about the wall to find a place to squat. The cellar seems a bit brighter than earlier though, and I find my way. I cannot help but to think Poppa would have laughed, and Mummy would give me a scolding. I choke as I know neither will be happening. I find a corner and squat.

Just the act of doing what I need to do seems to give me a strength, and even an anger begins to boil up, replacing my fear for a time. The guardsmen are talking as they bang about above me. I cannot understand what they are saying and with my immediate fears subsiding, a courage and a curiosity begins to replace them.

"I'm going to climb the ladder to see if I can hear what they're saying, Huni," I whisper. The act of telling Huni what I am about gives me the daring to do it.

I make my way to the ladder. After being in the dark so long, I find that I can now make out a bit of my surroundings. The lantern light from above seeps around the cracks of the cellar door and floorboards. I creep quiet to the ladder and start to climb, one step a'time, listening to make sure there aren't any loud creaks as I ease my way up. At the top of the ladder, I can hear them louder, but still cannot make out what they are sayin'. They talk a bit funny with 'accents', Mum told me once about some other guests. She said folk talk a little different in faraway places and some talk so as you can't even understand them.

Feeling brave and knowing the cellar door is behind a tall stack of flour sacks, I press my head into the door above me and it lifts a bit, maybe the height of my finger. I blow a breath out as there is no squeak at the hinges. But now, I can hear them and make out what they are saying. They are eating now, clear from the sounds, and sitting at the kitchen's table 'cause I recognize the scruffing of the bench against the floor.

"Captain's gonna be peaved we ain't found her and got back yet," one is sayin'.

"He'll have us run through with a sword if we return without proof we've takin' care of it. He'll want a hand and no less," another says.

"I'll gladly bring back her head for the trouble she's caused," speaks a third voice altogether. I like his voice least of all and catch a breath at what he has said.

"We need a scheme then," says the first. "She's tight in some hidey-hole she knows, hopin' we'll just leave. It was clear she was at that cottage over by the pond, leavin' the door open when she left. Mayhaps, we were close to getting her there before she run off again."

"She'll be gettin' hungry and cold soon, the nights being what they are this time a'year. And it's a long ways to any other village or towne, hereabouts. A wildcat or some other creature'll have her for a meal if she wanders about these forests."

"If she tries to head out, she'll be doing it on the trailway," the second adds.

"She might try to leave, ne'er the lesser. We need to guard the trailway out, sure certain," the third says.

"Settled then," says the first, something thick being chewed in his mouth. "Here, draw straws for the trail. It's gonna be cold there with no fire, mind. Everything has got to be on the hush."

All I hear is chewing and gulps of ale for a time, and then I near fall down the ladder when one pounds the table and the other two guffaw.

"Hucks, you're the lucky one then, dress warm," says the first. "Chutz, you get the pond cottage and I get the barn and the lodge. The animals will let us know if she sneaks into the barn, most like, so I'll be here in the lodge proper. Let's catch the little bitch and be done with it. If she doesn't turn up tonight, one of us will ride up the trail at first light, but my coin is on finding her hereabouts."

I climb back down into the cellar, real quiet. They have the right of it. I have been planning on staying hid till they give up and leave. I shiver and retreat to my spot betwixt the barrels, pulling some jerky from my sack before pulling the heavy wool blanket over my head, making a little tent for me and Huni. Giving Huni the bigger piece of jerky beef, I start chewing on the other, making my own plan, now that I know theirs.

I can't stay here, sure certain. So I make a scheme too. If they are going to guard the trailway up from the lodge, I'll need to get past him some ways. They are right, the forest is full of hungry creatures at night. But I have a wolf badger to help keep me safe, and I know a way around the guard on the trailway. On the other side of the barn, there is a creek, and a good path alongside it. I know it well as I've caught crayfish in the creek oft enough. The creek wends up into the forest, but eventually it comes up alongside the trailway. I will follow it till there, where I'll be past the guard and then I will get back onto the trail where I can move faster and be safe.

The guardsmen are right in all that they'd said, to be sure. Poppa and Thom took me with them into the closest towne last year. It had taken us three suns to get there by wagon. I know the way as it is simple. I will need to follow the trailway out from the lodge and then turn right when I get to the main travelway. But even that is a long way.

It has been a long time since the guardsmen have left the kitchens, and so I gather my sack and blanket and climb the ladder. My stomach is as tight as can be, but I slowly push the cellar door open and crawl out. They are gone.

It takes me a few moments to adjust to the moon's glow, lighting the kitchen through the windows, but it almost seems bright after climbing from the dark cellar. As I reach the back door, I notice my brother's pack hanging on its hook above the bench. Thinking it will serve me better than my shoulder sack, I climb up on the bench to retrieve it. I hear nary a sound from the lodge and I wonder where the guard might be. Banishing the thought, I decide to bring the woolen blanket with me as well. The tall leather boots (they come near to my knees) that Poppa had made me are there too. I change into them also. I roll the blanket up and tie it to the top of the pack. I pull the pack over my shoulders and cinch the straps tight. It hangs down past my waist but is easier to carry than my sack.

Gathering my nerve, I sneak out the door. I tell myself, sneaking, I have always been good at, and this is just like avoiding Auntie. The moon is already high in the sky, and it even throws shadows it is so bright. I run from shadow to shadow till I make it to the creek, and follow the path into the woods. It is darker here but I know the path and it makes the going quiet. Crickets and bullfrogs and hoot owls are louder than I 'member them. Breezes in the leaves seem to hiss at me time a'times too. Once I stumble over a tree root and cuss out loud. But it is a whisper cuss, so I brush off my knees and keep going, Huni on my heels all the way. I have gone a good ways down the path, looking in the direction where I know the trailway to be, worrying I might come across the guardsman, and I surely do. Well, actually, I first see a small glow and cypher it to be smokeweed. I do not realize I am so close to the trailway, but he is on the other side and so I continue down the path, being extra quiet.

'Tis quite a further bit down the path afore I meet the trailway, which is a good thing, but I am glad to reach it. The moon shines bright on the road, and I can move faster.

"Mum would say, 'don't dally,' Huni. So let's get a move on," I whisper, more for me than for Huni. She just looks up at me and keeps pace, sniffing about as we go. The moon is still bright and I see my breath afore me in the nippy night air. A wolf or coyote or something else is howling off in the woods. I tell Huni it's a long ways off.

My pack gets to feeling pretty heavy from time a'times, but then I'll hear another sound behind or off in the woods and I'll speed on my way again. I am chilly to my bones and the sun is peeking through the trees just a bit when I stop dead to my tracks. Sure certain, I hear a banging of metal to metal likened to a camp plate and cup. And then there is a huff and a whinny too. And just past a clump of trees up ahead, I see smoke rising. Being real cautious, I walk real quiet to the end of the trees and look off the trail. There is a tinker's wagon. And the tinker himself is bending over a campfire, cooking meats on a pan by the smell. I recognize him for the regular tinker that came to the lodge last springtime.

Of a sudden, tears just start raining from my eyes and I run right into his camp and hug him tight around the waist. My crying is even loud to my ears and I can't even make myself stop for a while. He pats my back and leaves me to it.

"Well then," says the tinker, with a small warm smile, after I get myself together some. "If I'm not mistaken, you are Maddie's little lass, from the hunter's lodge I'm just now headed to. I'm thinking you have a tale. Why don't you sit a bit with me and mays-be have a bite of mornmeal, and you can tell me all of it."

I let the heavy pack slip off my back and sit close to him, him being someone I know and aren't afeared of.

And so I tell him the all of it, and I see an anger building in him. My thought is to turn about with him and get as far away as possible in case the guardsmen come lookin'. But, he is of a different mind. I tell him I can give him all of my coin if he will just get me to the village and away from the guardsmen. I tell him the guardsmen are young and strong and quite vicious about it all, but this does not sway him. He seems an older man to me, though he stands straight and is very tall. He is grey of hair and whiskered and even carries a long walking stick, though it is much fancier than the one Poppa sometimes used.

"I've a hidey-hole, back of my seat in the wagon. You'll sit there until I deal with these guardsmen, but I will not be turned aside from this task," he states, whilst packing more of his camp supplies back into his wagon, in a studied manner. He looks most determined. I am scared but do as he bids me.

The tinker, he says I can call him Mæster Rõghæn, or just Rõghæn if I prefer. He finishes loading up and hitches the wagon to his two great burden horses. I try to help where I can and he smiles that I do, though a sad smile, it seems to me. He does not even blink to see my wolf badger friend climb into the hidey-hole with me. I hug her tight, a fear rising to my throat.

We remain quite quiet as we head up the trail, back towards the lodge. His eyes are watching the tree line as we go, as I have told him the where-abouts of the one guardsman last night. Sure to it, the man steps out from the woods, mayhaps twenty paces afore us, long sword ahand. He speaks aloud so the tinker can hear.

"Stay your wagon, master tinker. The lodge ahead is closed. You can turnabout, just here, and be on your way," the guardsman says in a most affable manner. Though as I look out from my hidden space behind Mæster Rõghæn, I see he looks more than a bit disheveled, the night being a long one for him, I wager.

Mæster Rõghæn stands up and makes to stretch, as if to pull the kinks out of sore and tight muscles. I even hear a crack from his neck. He gin-gerly climbs down from the wagon with his walking stick ahand as the guard makes to make up the distance betwixt us, walking on the quick.

"Well, that is most unfortunate, as I've come a distance and it's a ways back to the main travelway, don't you know?" he responds to the guard with a wide smile. "So as not to make it a bust, would you not have an inter-est in looking into my wares? I'm sure I'll have a thing or two to suit!" The tinker stands leaning heavy upon his staff and appears much more fragile than earlier this morn and it gives me a fright.

"I've no time nor need for any wares you are peddling, man. Be on your way now," he says, playing at his sword's pommel and lifting it just a bit and in a threatening manner. The two are but a pace and a half and apart and looking intently, one to the other.

"I've never known this lodge man to need a guard upon this trail, especially if he isn't in residence... It cannot but make me wonder..." and just as he is speaking it, Huni crawls up aside me and I give a small yelp. This makes the guard's eyes go wide and Mæster Rõghæn takes full advantage. With a swiftness and strength belying his age, a quick strike direct to the guard's neck and two following to either side of his head, the man collapses to the ground into an unmoving heap. The tinker relieves him of a few things, including his long sword and coin purse, and proceeds to drag his lifeless body to the woods.

"Let us continue on, lass, and see what we shall find at the lodge," Tinker Rõghæn says. "And when we are, please remain a bit quieter. Though it did aide in this encounter, we might not be so fortunate in the next." I nod my assent.

We continue down the trail and pull out from the treelined roadway to hold up some thirty or so paces from the stable yard and barn, very much to the surprise of the other two guardsmen. One is in process of mounting his horse and the other turns to the wagon drawing his sword in the process. Tinker Rõghæn leaps from the wagon and does a remarkable thing. He just plants his staff in front of him and starts whispering to it! The guard on the horse sets out and is approaching fast. Tinker Rõghæn just keeps whispering. I do as he has requested and stay quiet and low, peering out under the wagon's seat. Huni can feel my distress and is tense and ready to spring.

And then, mayhaps four paces afore the tinker, a whirlish appears. Small at first, it swirls and pulls up the sand and gravel in the ground under it, and quickly grows to the height of two men. A wind swept in, all around us and the whirlish of sand and stone head directly towards the horseman. It was a vicious swirling weapon aimed at the fast approaching rider. Unable to stop, the horse and rider buck and scream to the onslaught of sand and stone. The rider is thrown, lands hard, and lies unmoving. The horse, its hide torn in many places, bolts off. I feel sorry for horse but have naught but ill-feeling for the man on the ground. The whirlish is gone and the other guardsmean, shied at first, continues on with sword drawn, renewed anger on his face.

They engage, with sword and staff, and the tinker is very adept against the swordsman. But a piece of wood is a poor weapon against a long sword, I think, and so, I draw Poppa's knife I'd taken from the barn and hold it to me, should the tinker fall. I need not have worried for it though, as Tinker Rõghæn once again takes advantage and in two fierce strikes inside the guardsman's reach, sets him down for good. Alas, while we are fixed on the battle afore us, the rider has risen and has creeped around the wagon and appears just afore us and behind the tinker, unawares.

Thinking only that I cannot let this guardsman kill again, I shriek and burst from my hidey-hole with knife ahand even as the swordsman raises his sword. Huni takes the moment to show why a wolf badger is a fearsome and wild creature. She pushes past me from our hidey-hole in the wagon and leaps with claws and teeth bared upon the tinker's attacker. I follow, in fear for my creature friend. He takes my dirk in the shoulder of his sword arm, even as Huni is growling as she takes bite after bite out of his ear and neck and rakes his back with her claws, both fore and hind, her growl fierce and loud. And then, all goes dark.

When I open my eyes, Huni is licking my face with intent, and Mæster Rõghæn is laying a wet cloth upon my forehead. My head is throbbing. I push Huni away, but giggle a bit in spite of the pain.

"Welcome back, little one. You have given us a scare! The brute threw you headfirst into the wagon in his agony at your very brave attack, to save a tinker you but met this very morn. You and your spirit creature have acquitted yourselves quite well. The danger is now past, and we can see to settling the affairs of your family," he states, a sad smile again painted upon his face. I look about to see he has carried me into the lodge and lay me upon Mum and Poppa's bed. I pull the quilt to my nose and take in their scent. The scent of Mummy and Poppa.

"Rest a bit. I'll come for you soon, and we will make a memorial for them," he continues and I nod as a tear finds its way to my cheek. Huni curls into me and I close my eyes thinking of all of them, finding a deep sleep finally.

It is the morrow's morn when I wake again to smells in the kitchen. Huni and I make our way to the kitchens, where Mæster Rõghæn is busy at pot and skillet, and it smells wonderful. He is just finishing, and we sit on the benches on opposite sides of the family table near the garden windows. Looking out, I do not see what I feared I'd see. The garden is back to its bright and sunny state. Flutterflies jump from flower to flower, and Poppa's birdhouses are busy places to colourful winged creatures in countless variety.

"Eat, little one. We will visit them after."

We do. And I say my fare-thee-wells to all of them. Mæster Rõghæn has made graves for them, each and all together out from the garden and on a nice knoll and under a great tree. But there is an extra grave and I ask him why.

"I fear the captain of those guards will return when he has not heard from them. When he does, I think it wise that he sees an extra grave and does, mayhaps, assume you are gone as well," he explains. "I will dispose of the guards' bodies and let him think what he might."

I sit and cry for a while and gather flowers to the graves of my family. The tinker says some kind words over the graves to try and comfort me. I tell the story to him, the all of it, and explain that it's my fault because I had picked up the small parchment in the hall the night before and had not returned it. I hand it to him and tell him I was going to give it to Mum first thing, but it was too late. He unrolls the parchment and his eyebrows raises as he reads it.

"Nay, little one. It was not you having this that caused it. But rather the reason it was written. Do not concern yourself about it in that regard, you can trust me on it." And that is all that he says. I know there must be more to it though.

He does not ask where I might go and nor do I mention it, but we leave together on the buckboard seat of his tinker wagon with Huni tucked at my feet.

4

Assassin

I am not too happy with the situation, but I am a soldier and Kingsman and so I will burden the slight. Though I command this patrol and each man is hand-picked and honed to my expectation of a Kingsman, I have been sent an 'elite' soldier from the king's advisor's personal guard to join my patrol. The man is clearly adept and indeed masterful at any weapon I've tested him with, which I insisted upon from the onset. They have sent reassurances that I am still the unit commander and the man will follow my every order to the letter. But he remains untested in the field. An unknown quantity in a real fight. Not a seasoned veteran like the others under my command, who I trust with my life, as do each and the other under my command.

Though the other men accept him into their midst and ranks, there is no easy camaraderie among them. Charan keeps mostly to himself but works in concert with the others when commanded. He is a loner, but a good soldier in spite of it. A masterfully elite soldier, but for this one fact. Hence, he can never be truly a part of the unit.

Our orders are explicit. We are to venture beyond the Barrier Mountains and hunt the rogue vigilante. The king and his advisor feel certain it is there that the criminal has escaped. As they are known as seers and are said to have had a vision recently, I feel certain that this will be a chase that will allow the king's justice to be served. It seems, until now, the king's gift has failed him in this one thing. They are to bring the vigilante back alive if it is possible, but his head will suffice if needs be. The affair is somehow related to the king's only daughter and this one issue disturbs me most.

'Tis near two full decades past since Agleasia has vanished and some fault has been placed upon my greatest friend in all my history as a Kingsman, Ètœn Bearheart. Rumor holds that the rogue might even be a bastard son of the two of them. The thought of killing Ètœn's son does not sit well with me. But I am a Kingsman and will carry out any decree from my king, just as Ètœn himself would. I know, also, to the depths of my soul that my friend would never betray his king, and that there is more to this tale, for Ètœn's part, at the least.

We have traversed the Barrier Mountains two full moons past, entering through a known pass, due north of Kings Court. Entering is the easy part. Finding a way completely through the mountains has taken near to a grueling fortnight. Our guide insisted the way is not safe for horses and we have lost two in the effort and nearly the life of one of our own. Charan had been instrumental in saving that soldier's life. No sign nor talk is heard of the vigilante early on, and we have already visited a number of small villages in our quest. Taking cue from the folk we meet, we move onward to each next town as we traverse the countryside, east to west and always northward.

I've come to lament the king's vision has not been more specific. As we come to each consecutive settlement, village or towne, I split the company up into smaller units, canvassing the residents for possible sightings or information. We have little to express to people in way of description, but for the lyrics of the outlawed songs sung about the lad, his sigil and his unique hair. None of which is of much value on this side of the mountains.

Two full moons and a fortnight since leaving the mountain's passes and three full moons into our search, we have come finally upon a larger seaside towne. Again, I command that my unit break into teams and canvas the towne in search of our target. It has become routine now. Four teams of three are sent about the task, leaving Charan and myself as a team.

Charan and I are having an ale and mid-sun meal on the outskirts of a market square when our luck changes. We are just dropping coin for the meal and the server is holding it up with dismay as he calls over the patron of the cafe to discuss it.

"Other than the occasional trade ship that stops on their way to the inner sea and Seas End, we don't see folk from the south. And we see few king's coin. But I guess it'll trade fair enough. What would bring the king's soldiers past the mountains and way up hereabouts? We're quiet and peaceful-like, up here. Don't hardly have work enough for the sheriff," said the cafe's owner in a bit of a rambling fashion.

"I am Alærik, captain and kingsman in the guard. The king is in search of a bad sort that owes a debt," I explain and give a description over to the man. The man's eyes light up for a moment as he looks out and about furtively.

"Would there be a bounty for knowledge of such a man?" whispers the keep, knowing it isn't a proper thing to be asking.

"If you have solid knowledge, I might spare a few coin," the captain responds.

"Well, if the lad travels with two weasel pups and has a similar accent as you, I have seen such a man." This makes Alærik sit up a bit straighter.

"And where would we find this man?" Alærik queries further.

"Man, I would be hesitant to name him. A lad of sixten-seventeen year he appeared to me, though he carried himself with some confidence. He also carried a fair number of weapons, now that my mind wanders to the memory. A beautiful bow for one. And I saw about his pack, dirk and short sword as well. But his interest, while here, was the barter market it seemed. He volunteered his service to the farmers setting out wares or helped to raise vendor market tents. He seemed most happy joining in the preparations for market, but he had brought no thing with him to trade." He tells his tale.

"The market lasts two suns here, and he took his mid-sun-meals here, sat at the table just next to where you are sitting now, both suns, talking with local folk. He seemed an unusual sort in that." The keep continues. "I know not where he was headed next, but he spoke a good deal of Esper, a village far to the north and east."

"And when was this?" queries Alærik.

"Twas but a little more than a fortnight, at the latest barter market."

Alærik places three silver upon the table to a wide smile and a nod from the keep.

Some asking about gives us what we need in way of directions to this Esper village and taking quarter in an inn to the east end of towne, We make a plan to head out on the morrow's morn.

***

As it happens most times when the weight of the past creeps upon me of a sudden, I find myself first in this same square again, and then I leave even this quaint towne of Esper and it's wondrous fine and happy folk, venturing out to the even more peaceful pastures and homesteads about the valley.

'Tis Eshereon's tales and lessons that have led me here this sun. Assure, I find his lessons exceptional…stunning even. Yet and still, some leave me longing for my past.

In these past six moons since we've been here in Esper, I've experienced shock and marvel and wonder, sure certain. The druid's stoic countenance notwithstanding, he delivered shock and awe upon us from that very first sun. To me in particular, more so. His scrivener, Therrien, held the honor of being first to deliver upon me that first shock of many. Da was not my true pæder.

In following suns, Eschereon tells me more of my true origins in that very same library he'd first led us to. As he speaks of my mœther, my mind has, in a miracle opened itself to memories I did not know I held. She was ever-present in my very early years and I know her, of a sudden. My mind has always held memories precise and with such clarity that I can recall exact words spoken from any given sun in my past. So, this is a most confusing revelation.

"Druid…Mæster," I say, as I rise one sun during those early lessons in his library. "How is it just now I carry a limitless tale and memories of my mum, yet just yester's sun they did not exist to me."

"Twas my doing I'm afraid, lad. We thought it prudent and for your very safety that you could not recall her as you left out with Ètœn," the druid explains.

"You can simply delve into a person's mind and do such a thing?" I ask incredulously.

"Nay, though it is written that there is powerful mægic in the world that can allow just such a thing, I cannot. However, I can, under the right circumstances, hypnotize your subconscious mind to forget for a time. What I do can never be permanent. Under the right circumstances, the memories return," he explains.

"You say that Ètœn Bearheart was not my pæder, but then, why do I not recall my real pæder?" I query, as it is just so. As much as I've searched, I hold no memory.

"Mayhaps it is because you have truly met him but once, aside from when you were an infant child. That was the day we sent you off with Ètœn," he says as he tells the further tale. And as I revisit that sun within my mind, I recall not just the old man, who stands before me now, looking the same to me as the man who spoke to me as a five year-ender, but another as well.

His words spring to the surface of my mind in that same instant. He is staring with intent into my eyes. He has spoken to me after my mœther, but before the druid.

"Arias, son," and there it was, proof to myself that the man I call Da, is indeed not my blood pæder. "Though years and leagues separate us, they are but constructs for others to be guided by, we will always be connected in a much more permanent manner. This is but the beginning of your journey, and if the muses warrant, we shall again meet further down life's byways." And he kissed me on my forehead. Even then, I felt no strong connection to this man, and at that age, what he had spoken to me held little meaning.

From those early suns, near to six full moons prior, my life, and sure certain, Sæm's and Alænèa's as well, has changed in remarkable ways.

Eschereon teaches the three of us lessons in the ancient mægics, discovering those that are unique to each of us. This holds a surprise for the druid, as he explains.

"The wizærdi of old were able to pull the mægic from the ether that their countenance, or spirit, was most attuned to. There were those that were strong in their connection to beasts and creatures; others were seers, and able to see in dreams or have immense feelings of what might come to pass in others' lives. These you have witnessed yourselves as you've described to me. Others could pull healing powers from within and without. Still others could harness nature's forces about them...and still others could move objects with only thought," he explains.

"And each of them was nuanced in their ability, of course, some much stronger in their abilities than others," he continues. "The strongest amongst them were called Source-Sayers, as they were able to tap the very deep essence of their mægic, the very source of it, in the ether about them and were able to perform tremendous deeds because of it."

"I've read in the older tomes that there began a great experiment with bloodlines and is the seed of the legends that the Elders in the Plains and in Sæm's village hold to, I believe," he lectures. "And if I am not mistaken, all the three of you are, to some extent, the byproducts of these wizærdi of eons gone by."

"In the case of Ariastone, here, mayhaps the very purpose of their designs," he mutters, with hand upon his chin, in wondering thought it seems to me. And then in a more overt voice to address us all…

"You see, neither I nor any of my compatriots, as far as I know, have met anyone with your unique abilities, Ariastone. Nor even yours, Sæm and Alænèa. It is a wonder that you have found each and the other," he states looking beyond me in thought, and I wonder at his comment about his compatriots. Are there other druids, then?

But the direction of the lessons takes a more studied and tedious turn once again as they are sometimes wont to do, and my thought query is lost in the continuing lessons. The day becomes unbearably long again and my mind drifts and reaches to my past once more.

That all lay upon yester-sun now, and hence, I find myself here at the barter market, with my intent to once again venture out from Esper. I need some time away, my longing for times past heavy upon my shoulders. I finally eye my friend, Chæda, in the marketplace setting out his wares, and I smile. I will aid him with his barrels and troughs and ask if I might travel with him to help about his homestead when he has finished at the market and heads home. He smiles as I approach and welcomes me as he has done in earlier markets.

I've visited Chæda's homestead a few times in the past, helping him with his farm work and farmstock, as it suits me and helps put me at ease, and ate with his family as well. He barters his wares in Esper's market and I help him with his wagon, which he uses to display his troughs and barrels. It seems such a simple thing, but I've learned since, that his craft has a demand. He fashions feed troughs of every size and sort and these are nothing special, mayhaps. But for their sturdy construction, his water troughs and barrels are known far and wide to be superior. They are known to last a lifetime with nary a leak nor split of wood.

He crafts each with a care and of wood harvested from a small forest that lays about his homestead. He fashions their metal-binding straps in his own small forge and constructs each as his pæder and grandsire afore him did.

In suns past as I watched him work, lending a hand and some muscle from time a'time, he gladly explained and showed the family secrets of their making. He said the wood he used was from a certain stand of tree and it was a good part of the secret, but the true miracle in the crafting was the sap extruded from a special vine his family had found within the same forest, and it was a variety he had never seen elsewhere. He showed me how he carefully brushes the sap to both tongue and groove betwixt each slat of fine planed and sanded wood. It acts as both glue and sealant to each of his barrels and water troughs.

His homestead is a small working farm, mostly for family needs, but he also trades with neighboring homesteads for goods they produce as well. He explained that they each farmed some different crop and creatures and trade amongst themselves. In this way, they stay friendly and each committed to the welfare of others. It is a simple and good life, and I envy him a'times. And so, at the end of the morrow, I help him pack up his barter goods and travel back to his home with him. It is a long and relaxing trip as we spend one overnight on the way, allowing us to catch up as friends might.

Totally unlike me, and proof I have found calm and can relax here in the countryside, the sun has risen high enough to shine a few rays through the barns loft door afore I awake next morn. Shuffling and clattering, horse snorts and whinnies awaken me on this first morn here in the loft of his barn. Peering down and over the edge, I spy Chæda, a look of concern upon his face as he gathers supplies below me. Lilit and Jilly poke their heads out of their straw nest and rise, even as I do. Swinging my legs out over the loft's edge, sending straw chafe floating down into the morn suns rays, the furions sit up next to me and look down as well.

"Ho, Chæda, what are you about and can I lend a hand?" I offer, picking straw from my hair and gazing down upon his bustling activities.

"Ma's worried sick over a kid goat that's wandered and hasn't been seen since yester's morn," he calls back to me.

"I've a mind to finding the l'il creature afore Ma drives me to the brink of sanity about it." He smiles. "They're like her own babes, the wee ones, you know."

"Let me go for you, Chæda," I return. "I've some experience in just these kinds of things and would like to be in your wife's good graces for an extra helping of pie that I can smell she's baking!"

"Ha, I'd welcome the help then, and I'm sure she'll offer you a whole pie if you bring her precious kid home to her. I'd have sent Finn looking, but he's headed over to the Makka homestead fetching a new harness and gear we've traded for."

"Fear not, I'll find and bring her kid home," I say, already dressed and climbing down from the loft.

After a quick nip of buttered corn muffin offered up by Mæve, Chæda's wife, I am on my way.

It is a very pleasant morn, with a comfortable breeze swaying the tall grasses and bending the tops of the trees I can see at the edge of the stand of wood to the east of the homestead's pasture. These trees are thicker and taller than any I've seen in my travels about the valley and many are of the variety Chæda crafts into his barrels.

But I head away from that wood, as I know the small herd of sheep Chæda owns pastured to the west of his homestead, and the goats often follow along to play and eat amongst them. I know also that the creek that flows through the homestead falls into a deep ravine a bit downstream in that direction. It is a perfect place for a young kid to get in trouble.

Smoke from the cottage chimney can still be seen in the distance even as the sounds of life there fall away as I reach the side of the ravine I'd recalled from my travels here and about. Sure to my reckoning, the bleating of a young goat can be heard over the baying of the sheep ahead of me. The bleating is echoing about the deep gully. A double helping of berry pie is in my near future, I wager.

As it turns out, I still have a bit of a challenge rescuing the little fellow. He is at the bottom of the creek gorge and it is easily between two and three pole to the creek and bottom below. Lilit and Jilly are peering over the edge of the sheer-sided chasm-like ravine with me and though they might find a way down, I need to find another place to descend.

About two hundred paces further on, I see an opportunity. There are plenty of hand and footholds and even a couple of small trees are growing against the cliffside. Though nearly vertical, I reckon a way to the bottom and back up again.

I cannot make the climb down with any of what I carry, however. And so, I shed my pack, bow, and staff at the top and begin a slow and studied climb down. The furions think it great fun and have little trouble making their way down. It seems they are laughing at my more feeble progress, climbing back to me, off and on, with encouraging giggles.

Dropping the final few feet from a sturdy branch of one of two small cliffside trees I've used as support on my way, I don't need to go back searching for the missing kid. He is waiting for me in the soft ground about the stream and is busy playing with the furions.

"Hey, little one," I speak to the playing kid. "Mæve was sure you were a wolf's dinner guest and here I find you having the time of your life, chasing crawfish in a stream.

"No matter, I'm to deliver you back home, and I'd appreciate a little cooperation if I'm to climb back up this craggy cliffside with you."

I bind his legs to his dismay, but I feel it is necessary to keep him still if I am going to safely ascend the way I came down. Tucking him into my tunic, he quiets down for me. The return climb somehow looks more treacherous than the way down. But there is nothing for it, so I make my way, hold by hold, back up, sending the occasional torrent of stone and loose rubble from errant footholds back down the cliffside.

After a grueling climb, with the kid's head popping out of the neck of my tunic from time a'time, assessing our progress, I finally breach the upper edge of the river gulch. Standing upon the trunk of the small tree growing near the top of the wall of the ravine, I pull myself back up and unto the pasture land with plenty of sheep bleating a greeting to me and the little goat pup.

The little kid is bleating and kicking up a storm as well, sensing he is back up with his barnyard friends. Pulling the kid from under my tunic in an effort to relieve the little guy's stress and myself from a further rib bruising, I concentrate on untying him and setting him down. As it turns out, the sheep bleating is not in greeting for us, but mayhaps in warning that we have uninvited guests.

As I rise up, I am immediately aware of a patrol of Kingsmen not twenty paces from me and approaching in a great arch, ever closing around me. Da's last day springs to the forefront of my mind.

"Stay your hands and remain where you are!" yells the patrol's captain.

In the moment that I have to assess the danger, I note he is a tall, grizzled, and quite competent soldier. There are three crossbows aimed at me and one bow, notched and drawn asides. The captain is still mounted, but the others, save the bowman, are advancing with crossbows and swords drawn. My mind travels back to Da's last encounter with Kingsmen and then I glance towards my weapons, piled a few paces away where I had left them, and have already decided that is my first move.

I have become complacent in my six months at Esper with the druid. Though he has been tutoring more in mægic and further defenses, life has become calm and peaceful and my sense of danger has greatly diminished. At that moment I realize it now to my folly, even as I hear the whistle and then the thud and then before the pain of it has reached my senses, the force of an arrow strikes my right shoulder and pushes me backward towards the cliff's edge. My heel hits upon a rock and I stumble further backward.

With my mind racing, I have no control as I go over the edge flailing backward, an arrow lodged in my shoulder and the faces of Lilit and Jilly in helpless distress. The pain of the arrow finally reaches me, coupled with other searing pains joining in as I fall into the tree I had just stood upon on my climb back up. My right leg catches in the limbs and my body twists, arresting my fall for just a moment as I feel my leg dislocate at the knee in the continuing freefall.

Next are sharp jutting rocks that I had used as foot and handholds, but now are punishing weapons pounding my body. I watch in slow-motion as all of this is happening to me and I have no control. My body cracks once again into the lower tree as pain strikes my hip, and tumbling, I fall now towards the rocky face of the ravine wall…and then, all goes black.

***

(Captain Alærik)

Charan and I stand on the precipice of the gorge and look down to the lad's body. His left arm and right leg lie askew to their rightful place and Charan's arrow is very evident as it protrudes from his right shoulder.

"I meant only to incapacitate him as I saw him glance to his weapons," Charan states in a nonchalant manner.

"Aye, your aim was true to your purpose as I know your skill, and it was a wise decision. 'Twas but a dark luck the further part of it," returns Alærik. He cannot fault Mensae's assassin's decision to do such.

"Our orders were to return him whole to await the king's further purpose if possible, but his head may have to do by the look of it," Alærik elaborates. Knowing it is his friend Ètœn Bearheart's son makes it heavy in his heart.

"Brësson, make your way down to him and string a rope about him and we will haul him up," Alærik orders. After some moments, a yell reaches up to Alærik.

"Cap'n, the lad still lives, but his breath is shallow, and he's lost a fair amount of blood," comes his cry from below as he examines Arias. Brësson is the team's medic and as such is a good judge of it.

"Well, then, remove the arrow and wrap his wound. We're bound to try to get him back to Kings Court alive if the fates will allow."

With a rope secured around his chest, his men pull the lad's torn and mangled body up the gorge's rugged side and finally land him on the ground above. Off to the side, and most queer, two small fitchets watch carefully from a distance in the tall grass, scowling at us, it being my impression.

"We'll not be able to transport him tied up on a horse the whole way in his condition. 'Twas blind luck we stumbled upon him this morn. The king's advice that we might find him near sheep and a ravine proved true. A seer, he surely is," Alærik muses. "There is a homestead there in the distance. We'll requisition a wagon and then return to the port town where we came upon the information that led us to him. There we can board a trading vessel back down the coast to Kings Court."

The Kingsmen remount, with their capture over a packhorse, and head towards the homestead.

5

Seized

(Sæm)

𝕴 cannot understand Arias. Holy Scribes, the druid's library is a wonder! While Arias has disappeared into the countryside yet again, I am sitting at a table under a window in the keep library, deep into tomes of ancient histories. Three more are piled up on the corner of the desk as I am near to finishing the one presently in front of me. My mind whirls as I cannot decide on which book to start next.

Eschereon is off with Alænèa somewhere, practicing wards and spoken spells. She is getting quite good at recognizing ancient runes containing mægic and is learning the art of imbuing a lasting mægical effect into objects with written runes. She delights in pulling pranks on Arias and me with her newfound skills. Locking chamber doors and making tea kettles whistle while sitting cold upon a stove plate. We are forever needing to learn new spells to unlock or dispel her wards. Just yester's morn I had tried to fill my washbowl and the bowl expelled the water as fast as I poured it in! Less humorous is her trick to keep my food stuck to my evemeal plate. Yay, she is quite adept at her pranks and quite whimsical about it too. To my dismay, she finds me her most frequent target. Good fun has its bounds, one would think!

But I find the library my favorite place in all the keep to escape within. A warm breeze accompanying the sunlight swirls in from the window above me, occasionally putting a creak to the shutters aside it. From time a'time a bird alights upon the windowsill and stares down at me curiously, bobbing it's head to and fro. Therrien, Eshereon's scribe and confidant, sits on a high stool across the library from me and under another window. His plume quill softly scratches against parchment offering a comforting background refrain to the birds outside my window and the tales that from the pages as I try to absorb each of them in turn.

Stories from over an eon past, such as Titans in battle amongst themselves or leading troops of smaller men in battle against other armies led by another Titan. These giants were near immortal, living hundreds of years, and stood half again and more against the height of a normal man. They had reflexes of a jungle cat, the strength of a bull and were fabled like gods in these tales recounted in the books upon the druid's shelves.

There are books of man's conquests and knowledge of any subject ever known or dreamed in the minds of men and much of it lost to time but for these very volumes. Remarkable things and amazing creatures and plants and beings lost to time and the people of Aeryth today. Marvelous past civilizations here in Aeryth, and if one can believe it, distant peoples in faraway lands across the four great seas around the points of the compass. There are even tales of drægons. What is most remarkable, if Eshereon can be believed (and somehow I believe), is that a great many of these books were written by druids of past ages themselves, and the tradition continues to this day with Therrien in this very chamber. This gaining of knowledge seems to resonate deep within and I find that once I've read a book, it resides forever in my mind, there fit me to recall at any time. Eschereon has even tested me for this very thing, coming away astounded. My appetite for it is insatiable, and especially for the histories of the lands hereabouts and in the Northern Reaches.

"Therrien, have you read of these fantastic beasts of past ages in the

Northern Reaches?" I query of him, having picked up a bread roll filled with meats and cheese and slathered in a rich oil of some sort, I point it at him, my mouth still half full.

The scribe smiles back at me, seeing a lad with an insatiable appetite for the books, sure certain, as well as anything that is around that I can sink my teeth into. A green oily dollop on my chin evidence to the latter, no doubt. I know it and see it in myself.

"Do you see that I have much time on my hands for such things?" he scoffs. I just smile and take another bite, ruminating over this last bit I've been reading while listening to the scribe's scratching.

"They remind me greatly of the rumors of the creatures roaming the Wending Wood back home. Some with claws as long as your plume, legend says, and the look of lizards, but twice the size of a man. I thought such tales were to scare the youngers from venturing into those woods, but mayhaps there is truth to the stories?"

"Aye, Sæm lad, these are true recountings in the tomes, or so says Eschereon, and he is one who might know. And I've never known him to speak an untruth."

This last gives me pause as I am just now reading of a great drægon that roamed the skies in eons past over the Northern Reaches and especially about the islands just north of the keep, lying across what are called the Dæmon Straits. Alænèa and I spied these very islands looking down from the cliffs just north of Esper Keep. With that thought, my mind shoots off on a tangent, recalling the many pleasant hiking trips Alænèa and I have taken in the lands about the keep. A smile breaks out upon my face as I use a linen to wipe my chin, having finished my mid-sun snack, washing it down with some cider, and pondering what Therrien has said.

***

(Alænèa)

Eschereon and I are touring Drægon Alley in Esper village below the keep. I cherish these little trips with the druid. They are less frequent when Arias is around as the druid's greater interest is with my friend from the west. So, when Arias takes one of his 'brooding' trips out into the countryside, I can corral the druid into my sphere of influence and get some more personal instruction into the mægic abilities that are awakening in me.

We have been visiting upon most every stone building within the towne. At present, he is showing me how every fired clay block that make up the structures of the towne carries a stamp on one corner or another, unseen to ordinary folk, and they are actually runes of ancient mægic. Runes put there by mægii working with masons when the towne and keep were built, two eons ago. Runes that subsequently were imbued with stronger and stronger compounded mægic over ages by those whom Eschereon called Wiccans. Here, within this alley, there are no signs of the runes upon the stones that make up the buildings. In fact, the style of building here is different from the other parts of the towne, as if this one area alone has been rebuilt. Indeed, the druid explains that it had been, many times over the centuries.

"Something happened here quite out of the ordinary, Alænèa, and mayhaps like the legends say, this very spot was visited upon by a drægon. A mighty beast of legend. My pæder hinted to me that such beasts were real and the tomes within the keep's library speak of them as actual and fearsome creatures. I've never known the writings of druid's past to be anything but truthful. It is our one higher oath above all others, that we will speak truth."

"Yea, Eschereon, I will attest to your 'truth at all costs' ways, though I've found, like the Elders back home on the Plain, your truths sometimes come wrapped in intricate riddles and webs of prose aimed at deception!" This brought a rare smile to the druid's face. He explains, indeed, he needs to sometimes mask a greater truth that he thinks is more than one might be able to handle, and it had become habit. But I am becoming more fluent in druid-speak and am able to fathom out Eschereon's true meaning more each sun.

I love how the druid has taught me to call up a mægic from the ether about us, where he has taught us all mægic flows, and direct it into an object and hold it there with a special rune designed to that purpose. Objects can be 'taught' to repel other objects or pull them tight, with only special incantations able to unlock or mute the original spell for a time. Eschereon explains that some even take special cantations or song with specific intonations to alter a mægic spell affixed to an object.

"Alænèa, you have a natural talent for warding. Mayhaps, you have bloodlines leading back to the powerful ancients of Äsguard, an island nation of Wic'cha and Source-Sayers. It is where ancient and powerful mægic was used to craft great weapons and amulets of power. Things forged for specific people and holding power for only those of strong links to their bloodline. Lords and kings have been made and toppled with just such objects."

These are terms foreign to me, Wic'cha and Source-Sayers, though I have no doubt Sæm knows of them, his head always in a tome, these days.

"I've no lofty intentions of such things, Mæster druid. Though if I could use it for protection of men such as Arias, wrongly persecuted by such other men, I would gladly use it so," pausing, I look back to the druid. "But, where is this Äsguard? I would, mayhaps, visit it some future sun to better learn the deeper mægic of warding."

"Your thought to protect young Ariastone, unto itself, is a lofty and virtuous endeavor, Alænèa. His mœther has gifted him even such an object," the druid says, letting go her query of Äsguard altogether. She, of course, sees this and vows to have Sæm research it for her.

"Yea, I know, Sage. Sæm and I have been studying his amulet closely since you'd made it known that was its purpose. Sæm has it even now and is researching the runes attached to it so we might learn more of it."

The druid's eyes widen at her remark, and the significance is not lost on Alænèa.

"But surely, he is safe here of all places, Eschereon. After all, it is where you brought his mœther, the king's daughter, to be safe beyond the king's reach."

"And he was, they were, for a time. But then, we all had to leave and split apart and send Ariastone off to places unknown with Etœn Bearheart. With him, she sent her amulet, gifted to her by Ariastone's true pæder, half a dozen years prior. She had hopes it would shield him as it had her, should there come a time he would need it. The king's men were closing in upon the towne of Esper by pure happenstance just then. The king leaving no stone left unturned back then in his search for Aeglesia. We took no chance those many years ago, and it was our hope that the amulet would be of use should it become known that Aeglæsia had a son."

"We had all gone, those twelve years past, to differing points of the compass, each unknown to the others. In such a manner, should any be found, we could not disclose the whereabouts of the others. Aeglesia was in capable hands and I have friends in all corners of Aeryth, and because the king knew nothing of Ariastone, we thought him safe in a faraway land with Ètœn Bearheart."

"That he now wanders about without the protection of the amulet gives me some pause for concern. I feel there may be greater forces working to find him in these suns."

And the concern shows on his face to my eyes. I determine that when Arias returns to Esper after his latest sojourn, we shall make him wear the amulet at all times.

**

(Finn)

Loud voices reach me even afore I make the pasture's edge, causing me to slow and stay still within the treeline. The sheep are bleating a storm, and the voices are curt, certainly not friendly. Poppa has sent me to the neighbors to fulfill a barter, and I return to find Arias is in desperate trouble.

I recognize what is happening and have the good sense to not interfere. I've heard tales of the king from across the mountains. What could I, Finn, a mere lad of only fifteen year do against a company of soldiers? Though I have never actually seen a soldier from the king's army, I ne'er the lesser know that these men are most likely Kingsmen for they are in garb, alike to each and the other, and even from the treeline, I see like sigils upon their breasts.

My breath holds tight within my chest as I cannot understand the scene unfolding afore me. My new friend from Esper, Arias, being surrounded by these soldiers carrying weapons of war, has just been hit with an arrow to his chest, sending him over the edge of the gulch. I know the ravine at that location to be nearly shear and deep to three pole at the least. I do not think that Arias can possibly survive such a fall, even without a bolt in his chest. My heart sinks.

Exhaling a great sigh in concern, I can naught but watch the further happenings. One of the soldiers climbs over the edge and some little time later I hear shouting to and fro from above and below. I find myself shivering in anticipation when it becomes evident that they are pulling Arias up from below with three soldiers heaving upon a thick rope.

The skies have taken a sudden turn to the dreary, with a chill breeze shoving me from the back, with leaves rustling in the treetops above me. But my whole attention is on the scene not fifty paces afore me as I stay hidden aside the path and in the trees.

They have pulled Arias from the ravine and it looks dire to me. Arias appears limp and beaten and broken. The arrow I do not see, but his shoulder is wrapped tight. This gives me a little hope that he might actually be alive. The soldier that has gone below is pulling himself back up over the edge, even as there is some discussion happening within the group of Kingsmen. One has pointed towards the smoke rising from Mum's cooking stove chimney at the cottage and a chill grips me once more.

I watch as two men callously throw Arias over the back of a horse and the others mount and start towards our homestead. I want to charge ahead and warn Poppa, but it will be impossible without being seen and so I think that unwise.

After the soldiers head out and onwards towards the homestead, I venture out myself and head over to the ravine. The Kingsmen have left Arias' staff and pack where they lay and I think to retrieve them. Looking after the soldiers, I can see they are well on their way now towards the homestead. I hope there will be no trouble there. These Kingsmen seem an evil sort.

6

Coffin

Excessive barking against horses' whinnies and huffs aside the clap-clop of hooves draws me from my hammer and anvil. I peer sidewise out the barn door at a company of soldiers as they slowly ride into the homestead yards. It is a sight I've never in my life seen afore, and my thoughts are that it will not be a welcome thing. I ne'er the lesser try to finish my work whilst the iron is still hot enough. I've stacked a number of fresh made barrels against the barn the scent of newly sawn wood thick in the air. Also lined up in front of the barn are a few feeding troughs, newly crafted as well. The company leader seems to take notice of them. Mæve has noticed their arrival as well. I hear the door behind her bang shut against the spring latch as she steps out onto the back porch.

As the soldier captain dismounts and glances back to her he heads towards the barn. I lay my hammer aside, wipe my hands on the rag tucked over my wide leather belt, and come out to meet him.

"Well met, sir," the soldier smiles, extending his arm in greeting. I take it in return, nodding. "I am Captain Alærik of the King's Guard." I take stock of him and his contingent mounted behind him. My brow immediately raises, as I see the lad, Arias, draped over a horse. "What might I call you?" the soldier continues.

"Chæda." My voice and face grow more solemn as I glance twice more, back to the lad.

71

"We are on the king's business and have need of a wagon. I can compensate you now for its worth and the trouble." A formality for goodwill as they are going to have a wagon in any case, I am sure.

"I've no use for a king's coin as we use it not here north of the mountains. But my only wagon I have need of. 'Tis the only way to get my barrels and troughs to market."

Alærik eyes the feed troughs once again.

"I'll pay three king's gold sovereign. For the wagon and one of your larger troughs…a lid to nail atop of it. 'Tis thrice their worth and gold is good coin on either side of the mountain. That is the last I'll say of it, and I'll need that lid crafted by dawn." Alærik's tone has changed and leaves little doubt I will have no choice more in the matter.

I cannot hold my tongue any longer and finally ask the captain, "What could a lad so young have done to bring the wrath of a king…and a dozen soldiers this far north to bring him back?"

"No concern of yours, farmer, but to say it was high Guines." And even as he speaks it, Mæve, who has been listening to the exchange, realizes that it is the lad Arias that we are discussing and that he lies strapped to the burden horse and is in dire shape. She comes running now to see what has happened to him as he is pulled down from the horse and laid to the ground.

"The fates be dared, what have you done?" As she kneels beside him, her hands shake to see him so broken. She is no healer but feels she must do something anyway.

"We must send for a healer!" she insists.

"Nay, we will not. He will be traveling back to Kings Court in a box nailed shut. You may clean his wound and wrap it again in clean linen, but that is all." Alærik taps the longer of two newly crafted troughs with his toe. "Make me a lid for this one, master woodsmith. And bring round my wagon. Brësson, you stay here with the lad and the woodsmith and help with dressing the wound clean. That's all to be done for him. No one is to touch him past that. I'll send relief a turn past sundown."

"We will take our leave now and set camp out of your way, sir and mäam. Honor our bargain and we shall leave you with your gold on the morrow's morn." With that, the soldiers withdraw a hundred paces from the barn but still in sight of it.

Mæve and the medic tend to Arias after the two soldiers carry him to a bed of straw in the barn. Even if she was allowed through, she does not know how to help the lad. He is but a little more than two or three years older than her very own son after all. She cannot imagine how a king in a faraway realm can want him so bad as to send a whole company of men to hunt him.

For my part, I go about fashioning a lid for the trough that will be Arias' prison for a trip back to Kings Court, if the fates will allow him to even survive the night. But I will do my little part to aid the lad. And so, I in the least will craft the wooden lid to allow air and light to pass betwixt the boards. It is a small thing, but I have hopes it will help. I also line the trough bottom with straw, so as to cushion the lad's broken and misaligned limbs.

Finishing, I gather Mæve to come back to the cottage to get some sleep. She refuses me though.

"I'll just stay to keep a cool rag to his forehead, Chæda. They have allowed me that little thing. He is so broken. Bruised and cut and hardly a breath escapes him. His fever rages, and I'm not sure he will ever awaken. I must do this little thing at the least." She turns back to Arias and trades the rag that has grown warm, for another soaked in cool water, squeezing a few drips between his lips while doing so.

I am worn but with a mind to in some manner do more for Arias. Thoughtful, I retire to the cottage to find Finn sitting at the kitchen table, a great concern on his face. I have forgotten entirely about my son in the wake of all that has happened.

"You've seen the soldiers and what is about outside?" I query Finn.

"Aye, Pa, and I saw what happened to him." Finn tells me all that he's witnessed.

"I gathered his pack and weapons and carried them back." Finn nods to the corner where they lie. "I've been thinking on what to do, Pa. Arias has said he is apprentice to the Sage of Esper. I think I should take his things and seek out the Sage immediately and tell him what has happened."

After pondering a moment, I nod to my son.

"We must use care not to alert these soldiers of your intent, Finn. Arias' horse is still out to pasture. He will not let you sit upon him, but he will bear the burden of Arias' things and will let you lead him. I will secret his rein and bridle out to you. Only one soldier is left in the barn and he watches over the lad. When dusk arrives, make your way out, keeping the barn and cottage between you and the soldiers' camp until you are out of sight. Then make haste to Esper and the Sage!" Finn nods his assent.

"What do they want with him, Pa?" asks Finn, and I tell all that I know.

"They are taking my only wagon to East Port. I intend to follow them and retrieve it after they're done with it. My hope is they will just abandon it on the docks. Poor Arias, he is in terrible condition, and I fear he will not even last the travel time." I shake my head to just the thought of it. "If anything can be done, the Sage will know. Be safe but reach him as soon as you are able."

We go about our scheme, and Finn is gone by dusk, heading to Esper and wishing that Paint will bear him but knowing he will tolerate but one rider.

The morrow's morn brings the company of soldiers back to the barn.

"Peers, unsaddle your mount and hitch her to the wagon. You'll be coachman."

I have brought out my largest trough and filled the bottom with straw. I place the lid I'd fashioned alongside it. The captain orders Arias placed in the trough and the lid nailed to. Before they do, Mæve reaches in and gives his hand a gentle squeeze, and I place a water skin upon his chest. Alærik grabs it up and stares at the two of us. His eyes glaze with a far-away look for a moment, and he tosses the skin back atop Arias' chest. His man, Peers, nails the lid, and three of his compatriots help him lift and secure the trough upon the buckboard wagon amongst his bags and other saddlery.

In the commotion, I see Arias' furions climb unseen, up under the wagon, and find a home atop the spare wheel secured to the underside of the bed. They have no intention of being left behind.

As the Kingsmen leave out, mud kicks up by a dozen horses followed by the buckboard. Mæve and I stare after them, the scene looking every bit like an undertaker leaving out with a coffin box atop his wagon.

***

(Finn)

The sun has finally stretched past the trees on the horizon behind me though not enough to produce enough warmth to make a difference. I've walked all night knowing it is crucial that I reach the Sage in Esper as soon as possible. I am exhausted. I've just crossed the Maírín River, its rock-hewn bridge spanning the hundred paces of the shallow waters that gurgles over and about its boulder-strewn bed. Though not deep, it is swift and ever-flowing and said never to have known a dry spell.

I finally give in to the fatigue. This, a good place to rest a bit. After letting Paint's rein drop, allowing him access to the cool running waters and plentiful grasses, I sit two paces from the water, my back against a large boulder. Relaxing with a sigh for the first time since I've left the home-stead, my calves are sore from my all-night walk. As I rub them my eyes roam over the landscape around me. My mind leaps to the intent of my task…getting word to the Sage of Esper, and it brings to mind something my mum had told me about this place I've chosen to stop at.

My mum had said that the river was named for the Sage's lady long ago. Because of it, weddings are commonplace on the bridge. It is thought to be a good heralding for a long marriage as the love of the Sage for his lady has become legend. The banks are said to be in constant bloom with the flowers that the Lady Maírín loved most, a league in either direction. And to my memory, I cannot recall a time when I have passed over the bridge without seeing flowers blooming on her banks.

I ponder what this means in regards to the Sage of Esper. I have never met the Sage, but all describe him first as old before wise. My mum once told me that even as she and Pa were married on this bridge, her mœther and hers before her and for six generations back have likewise been betrothed here. Each making the long ceremonial trek to be married here for the grace and good omen of it. This, I ponder, measures the Sage to be impossibly old. As I sit, the scent of lavender wafts strongly to my nostrils as I survey lazily the endless purple along the banks. I close my eyes a moment to rest just a bit more before continuing my journey.

***

(Captain Alærik)

A sense of calm envelopes me. It has taken more than three moons to accomplish the king's task, but it is now complete. Or near complete. It still remains to bring him back to Kings Court, the only question left unsettled to my mind is will he arrive alive or dead. Still unconscious and with a broken body after a full day on the travelway with no change, the odds are stacked high against him. I've been warned to take no chances as this vigilante has proven to be very dangerous. He has a reputation that has grown even greater on the tongues of bards.

But I can see that he is just a lad, and now feel a bit of regret that I have not let Brësson set his dislocated leg and broken arm. I've made the decision to keep him incapable of any fight on the journey home. Mayhaps, as the son of Ètœn, he deserves more from me. And his hair seems to mark him as the son of the king's daughter as well. Alas, his future remains dim as the king's purpose will not be for him to live a long and prosperous life. This lad can more like expect a much shorter and tortured life if the king intends to let him live at all. Reasoning it through now, the lad's best fate may have been to have died a quick death from his fall into the ravine.

***

(Lilit & Jilly)

The furions find their way up and into the bed of the wagon next to the trough that holds Arias snug and helpless. There in the wagon-bed, they can hide amongst the saddlery and a few bales of straw packed around the box holding Arias. They have stealthily visited him off and on throughout the sun of travel from the cottage to this eve's camp. He remains unmoving, though sticking their noses betwixt the planks left separated in the lid, they can sense he still lives. Now that dark has settled about them in the dead of night, they lick and paw his nose and cheeks in an effort to arouse him. All in vain.

Though unable to wake their friend, they are determined to help him. And so, while foraging for their evemeal about the sleeping camp, they retrieve and fit through the slated lid dates and jerky they have pilfered from the slumbering soldiers. They stand a hidden vigil over their friend.

With the new sun comes first elation and hope for Lilit and Jilly, then further despair. Well into the morn, the ride has become rough on the travelway with the road especially rutted and filled with potholes for a stretch. The furions hear a pained grunt from the trough when the wagon hits a deep roadway hole. Springing from their hidey-hole aside it and abandoning caution, they scramble atop the box and stare down betwixt the slats of wood. Arias stares wide-eyed back at them, perspiration beading his brow and lip as he looks up at them in pain…unrecognizing. Their usual connection with him lost.

***

"Ugghhh!" My eyes fly open to excruciating pain. My back of its own accord arches up in reflex and reaction to the torment… It is everywhere in my body. My head aches, pushing reason from me, and spikes of agony pierce me from my left side and then a burning, gnawing hurt crawls up to my now barely conscious mind from my right shoulder. I become instantly aware that I cannot move my arms or legs. *Panic.* My chest aches deep within as I gasp and gulp for more air.

I try to focus on anything to wrap my mind around what is happening to me. My eyes flit about in increasing despair. In the moments that follow, my brain seems to grasp that I must be in a coffin, and it is moving. But somehow, light is streaming in through the lid of my coffin. Of a sudden, two rodents…rats?...are sticking their noses betwixt the wood and snuffling just over his face. *Panic…and darkness…the dream ends.* And with it, my scream stays trapped, still within my throat.

7

Sage

(Finn)

I awake with a start, the heat of the sun bearing down on me. *Panic*. The sun nearing mid-sky, I've slept the entire morn away! Looking about, Paint has retreated to the shade of a tree. A sigh of relief escapes me that the horse has stayed close about. Easing down to the bank of the river, I splashe cool water to my face. Quickly retrieving my pack, I rummage out some jerky and a few travel biscuits and then set about gathering Paint's rein. There is no help for it now, I'll just have to try and double my pace for a bit. I must reach Esper and the Sage as soon as possible.

I have made the Maírín bridge, and that is my halfway mark. I know as I'd accompanied Pa to the barter market more than a few times now. Mayhaps, if I keep a pace, I'll reach Esper by nightfall.

***

(Alænèa)

I cannot help but laugh at Sæm. As I walk into the library, he stands over a stack of books on his usual reading table, the top one open and the tome seems half-finished. He has to stand as the stack of books is as if fused together and likewise glued to the tabletop. Eshereon's lessons in ward use has been invaluable to this Plain's lass for pranks upon my friends.

Alænèa the prankster. How my life has changed. And Sæm is my favorite target. I'd used a ward similar to the one I'd etched to keep his evemeal stuck to his plate a few suns past. That one proved quite amusing as well. He literally had to cut his food away from his dish, truly working for his meal.

He knows who has done it, of course, and probably even knows the exact ward I'd crafted to set the prank, hidden as it was. But, taking time to cypher the counteracting mægic apparently hampers his time reading, so he simply has decided to stand while reading. He will eventually need to act on the problem when he is ready to read the second book in the stack. I walk over and release the ward with a concentration needed to summon the mægic Eschereon has taught me.

Standing back, hands to my hips, and as much as I try I cannot stifle my smile.

"Læne, that is a good one. The hidden rune was artful!" I like how Sæm has given me a personal nickname, one that only he uses to date.

"And you let me catch you stumped for a time, Sæm, how sweet of you. Or were you just that engrossed in your tome? The ward was plain to see on the last pages of the top book, so as you'll know." His eyebrows raise, as he slowly nods his head side-a-side, smiling.

"I have another planned for Arias, but it seems he remains absent and brooding about the countryside. Oh, and by the by, Sæm, Eschereon had concern that he had not been wearing his mœther's amulet these past few moons. Mayhaps you should return it to him."

"Oh…I'd completely forgotten I had it! I found reference to all but a few of the runes embedded within it, but there are a few still I've not been able to cypher. I'll just copy them and continue my research and he can have the amulet itself back."

Sæm's become the absent-minded academic of late. A weighty title as he's not reached his seventeen year-end yet.

I do not mind Arias' lone trips out to the countryside, even if I don't quite understand his need. Eschereon has more time to spend with me, helping me to realize my abilities as regards the ancient mægics. The Elder Shèlah oft times hinted the ancient mægics were about more than the special auras that I can see, but she really taught me little of them or what her special ability was. Eschereon's lessons change all of that.

Arias has helped as well. His abilities are remarkable to all of us, most especially Eschereon. His lessons in what he originally called his *Calming* but has recently renamed the *Knowing,* because it, to his mind, becomes a deep *Knowing* of both oneself as well as one's surroundings and environment. After learning the technique himself, Eschereon agreed and certainly thrilled himself to have learned something so astonishing and new, even at his age.

Our warding lessons have advanced greatly over these past two moons, and Eschereon has postulated that if I (we) can recognize a difference in auras (and hence, different types of mægic), mayhaps we can likewise perform more than one type. He is right. With much experimentation, we have learned that I can move objects with only the thought of it. Actually, it proves more complicated than that, as I have to learn to recognize, then learn to gather, the appropriate mægic from the ether and push it to do my bidding. Learning that mægic exists in the very ether about us has all the three of us in wide-eyed awe throughout our time with Eschereon. Knowing that our bloodlines must have mixed significantly with wizærds of ancient times gives us some sense of wonder as well. For that is what Eschereon has taught us. The ability to use mægic is literally in our blood.

After leaving Sæm to his reading, I meet up with Eschereon in the kitchens. Though he himself can claim but one of the ancient mægics, he is well versed in the others. He has promised to help me visualize the mægic I've just discovered but cannot replicate. A fortnight past, I had awakened from a vivid dream where I'd been climbing a great tree in the Old Wood that Arias, Sæm, and I had traveled through after leaving my home on the Plain. In the dream, I was grasping for a piece of fruit hanging just out of my reach. I really wanted that fruit. I found myself willing it to me even as I stretched past safety to grab it to me in the dream. It seemed to bend on its stem, pulling the attached limb with it and towards my hand. The dream faded in mid-reach, and I woke with arm outstretched towards an apple on my bed table. A moment later, I lie dazed and grasping at my injured nose as the apple had flown unerring into my face.

Arias and Sæm laughed aloud at my story the next morn, claiming fate's reward for the pranks I'd visited upon them. Eschereon's eyebrows raised and had me trying to reproduce the mægic he felt certain was involved. To some success. It has remained a feat of hit and miss and chance, but I've been able to 'push' a feather plume into the air from where it lies upon Therrien's writing desk and scatter his papers in the doing.

Eschereon meets me in the keep's kitchens. He's brought with him the same plume I'd had the previous 'success' with. He also has an idea. Studying more on this ancient mægic least seldom practiced, he said, even in the era where mægic is most common, he has found writings by druids tutoring its use.

In the center of the table, he has formed a pile of flour in the shape of an inverted cone. Atop and at its very peak, he has placed, ever so lightly, the plume. As he has me sit on the bench next to his experiment, he is lighting four candles on each corner of the table. Finally, he drapes a thick cloth over the curtain rod above the only window in the room. We are now in a quite darkened room with his pile of flour and its plume crown the center of attention.

"My reference tome suggests that the apprentice learning this mægic should start light and small with as few distractions as possible. I'll stand behind you and whisper instructions." His voice seems to just hang untethered in the air above and behind me.

"Now, Alænèa, this mægic's aura is blue. Push all but the candles and the pile of flour and its feather plume out of your mind."

"Give me a moment, Sage." At this point, Arias' lesson of finding my *Knowing* comes to mind, and so I let my mind and body reach for it even as he has taught me. Finding the calm of it, I take in the flour and feather with the candle's glow staying in my peripheral vision only.

"The flour grains are lightest, Alænèa. Only dust with no weight." His soft words float to me from above and behind. "The mægic's blue is here with us too. It's always there, all about you for your gathering of it. If you let your mind see it, it hangs near the candlelight just now. See it from the corners of your sight."

"I see it."

And I do! It is there, like a swirling haze at the perimeter of my sight.

"You'll need just a little for this. Coax a swirl or two over to the pile. Push it around the pile. Let it just touch the surface of the flour, bringing a few dust grains up into the air under the feather, around and around, under the feather."

My concentration does not diverge. I simply do as the voice instructs. My eyes and thought intent to the task. The blue mægic comes at my call, a blush against the flour, lifting a dozen grains into a swirl under the feather. I can see the tiny bits of dust like little brilliantly shining stars, circling round and round the pile under the feather. The blue mægic haze does my bidding.

"The flour is substance, and the blue mægic can lift it. The feather has little more weight than the flour dust, but the blue mægic is real, and it lifts the dust. And the flour dust is real. Coax the blue mægic to bring the dust up to the underside of the feather now, still swirling. As they make contact, they will grab and spin the feather." And I know I am making this happen as well.

Before me, the large, white feather plume lifts off the flour pile just a bit, and the brilliantly shining stars of dust grains start spinning it. I watch in wonder.

"Now, Alænèa, push the blue mægic up…and over and set the feather down upon the table next to the flour."

I do one better. I push the feather up to the ceiling, have it spin there for a moment, then pull it down and have it circle the pile of flour before bringing it to rest aside it. My heart pounds and my hands shake. I have done it. I swing round on the bench, rise, and fling my arms around the neck of the druid, hugging him tight. A real smile graces his face this time, and I have caught him at it.

We are about the evemeal table, Eschereon, Therrien, Sæm, and myself. A huge roast prepared by Therrien as reward for my success earlier. I am regaling Sæm with my tale and too full of myself for words when bells roll all about us. In all our moons here, I have not heard such a thing.

"Therrien, will you meet our guest, please?" He nods and leaves us.

"I've set a ward to notify us when somebody approaches on the trail to my mountainside abode. Shall we go and see who has come?" I smile. How clever. A simple ward, but how did he manage the sound of bells? A query for later.

When we arrive out of the pantry and into Eschereon's mountainside home, which for us has been simply the foyer to the keep in the mountain, we spy Therrien heading down the trail to meet somebody. Arriving at the window and looking past Therrien as he has stopped now, I gaze upon a lad, no more than fourteen year, if I am to guess. But what matters most is that he is leading Arias' horse, Paint.

We hurry out the front door and to the lad. He pulls Arias' pack, staff, and bow from the horse's back even as we approach.

"Therrien, can you see to the animal? Lad, come with us. You look exhausted."

I am aside myself with worry, not knowing what this portends.

"Sæm and Alænèa, might you gather a bit for him to eat and mayhaps some tea? We'll be by the fire."

Eschereon leads the lad into his home. In less than a turn of a sand glass, he has eaten and explained all that he saw two suns prior.

"Pa said he'd be following them. He said it was to retrieve his wagon, but I know he meant to know what would happen to Arias. He overheard that the Kingsmen planned to travel to East Port where they would charter a vessel to Kings Court. Pa feared Arias would not make it. Sage, he was so broken, and they would do nothing to give aid beyond wrapping his shoulder to stop the bleeding.

Pa crafted the lid to give him air and planned to sneak a water skin into the trough with him. But he remained unconscious by the time I had left the homestead."

Eschereon queries the lad a bit more about the Kingsmen that have taken Arias, and then, "Therrien, escort our friend down to the inn and ask Giorgi and Mary to take care of him for me. Make arrangements for a horse when he is ready to return home. Sæm, Alænèa, we have schemes to think through.

Thank you, Finn, for your efforts and quick report. Please excuse us, as we must act swiftly."

Eschereon sees the lad out, thanking him yet again and expressing his sincere gratitude. He then immediately turns to us.

"We will leave in the morn afore sunrise, I think. It will do us no further good to leave tonight. We will plan to reach East Port early morn five days hence. It will be hard riding at that. Alænèa, you are not familiar yet on horseback. It will be especially hard on you. Are you up for it?"

"This is Arias, Eschereon. I will not slow you, I promise."

It has been near now to nine moons that I have known Arias. He is a brother to me. I feel more determined now, than when I had decided to sneak out from my home on the Plain to follow Arias and Sæm. My feelings are strong about him and since our time in the life ponds together, I know our destinies are to be entwined. We must find a way to secure his freedom before further harm can come to him.

8

Bowels

"HUuuuhH...HUuuuhH!"

Sparks afore my eyes, thunder pounding inside my head. I am here again, but where is here? Pain racks my body as I arch my back and my mind tries to catch up. It's different this time. But familiar, so I settle a bit. I'm alive, if still in my coffin. I find if I lie perfectly still, the pain is bearable. As my eyes adjust to the darkness, there is a source of light so images take form. Looking in front of me, soft rays of light are moving back and forth along a further wall… outside of my coffin. I stare through an open crack in its lid. It is a big crack about two fingers wide, and it seems incongruent with what I know about coffins. The lid is a good hand's width above my nose.

I open my mouth to say something…anything…if only to hear my own voice. But my mouth is sticky and dry, and I cough and gag and pain explodes throughout my lungs and the whole of my body again. I reach for my throat but only my right arm obeys, and with it comes shooting, searing pain from my shoulder. But as I'm pulling my shaking hand to my throat, it collides with a soft, wobbling skin that I recognize immediately as a water skin. Fumbling, my fingers mostly numb, I'm able to dislodge the skin's cork stopper and somehow push and pull the skin to my mouth. My fingers will not listen to my brain and will not squeeze the skin, so I wrestle the stem of the skin into my mouth with tongue and teeth and press it with a numb lifeless hand to my chest.

The pain in my shoulder as I do this is near unendurable, but the water flows. The first gulp I nearly choke on and spit it all out. But the next I take slower, and I'm able to swallow. Smaller sips now, but I don't stop until I can no longer suck anymore from the water skin. My arm falls to my side as I take in a deep breath, and I feel tears rolling down my face from the sides of my eyes. I learn that if I pull my breath in slowly, my chest does not ache as much.

Lying still to ease the torment in my body, my senses take over. I feel my body is swaying in sync with the moving rays of light against the wall outside my coffin. I'm in the hull of a ship! Searching my memory, I look for the source of this knowledge, but though I know it to be truth, I can find no memory of ever being on a ship. This gets me thinking…about why I am here at all. And a dawning sets a panic aflame in my mind. I don't know! I don't know my own name. I don't have any recollection of anything outside of the here and now. But I recall vividly the other time I woke in the coffin. Pushing the panic down, I decide that these thoughts are doing nothing to aid my situation, and so I let them go. Pondering this, I find I am amazed that I can do that very thing. I close my eyes for a moment. When I re-open them, I take stock again of my here and now. Reasoning that if I know things such as the feel of being on a ship, I must have memories that have been stripped from me, hence some brain trauma. I know this but know not how.

After I settle again, I become aware that I am being watched. The rats… but no, not rats. They are staring from each side of the coffin lid. Inquisitive eyes and light snuffling. Not like I am food. How do I know that? They are furions…the word instantly comes to mind. Also called ferrets or fidgits. I know this. And they have no business on a ship at sea. This is not their native habitat. Again, I *know* this. One of the furions is pushing something through the opening betwixt the slats. It lands on my neck. Reaching up, ignoring the shoulder pain with feeling slowly returning to my fingers, I find the object deposited on my neck and pull it up to my nose. A date. In this moment, my stomach comes to life and groans loud enough to startle the furions. I eat the date and look desperately at them for more.

It is like they understand. They leap off my coffin lid and disappear, only to return moments later to push something else down and to me. Some sort of meat jerky and another date. I am just swallowing again when a great lethargy envelopes me... *Darkness.*

***

(Sæm)

She does not complain, but I can see that she is quite uncomfortable. Alænèa has ridden a horse a number of times over the past six moons. Well, smaller ponies mostly, alongside Arias or myself or the both of us from time a'times. She gets along fine with the animals and has become quite comfortable on horseback, but for short periods of time only. We have been riding fairly hard for three straight suns on fully grown horses raised and trained for this type of travel. She has not trained for it. Reaching back to a time I had experienced the same, I understand what I see in her this eve.

She stretches her legs, then pulls them in, squeezes them together, then gets up and walks a short while.

"Alænèa, come sit. I think I can help." Her eyes go to me, hope and a bit of desperation on her face. Eschereon looks up at us with a raised brow. Intuiting the situation, he goes back to the business of preparing an eve-meal for us. I begin a massage of Alænèa's calves, squeezing deep into her muscles as she sighs and leans back against a tree.

"We will arrive into East Port on the morrow's eve. My first hope is that the Kingsmen have not already left on a ship to Kings Court. Traders do not sail regularly from the port heading south. If we are too late, and they have managed passage already, I will secure us passage on the first vessel headed south. My hope is that there will be one such soon. If they have departed, it will make our task much harder."

Eschereon has our attention, even as I've moved my massage up to Læne's sore thighs, and she moans under my hands, her expression a desperate thanks. I try to hide my smile.

"We may be taking a boat out onto the sea?"

I see the longing in her eyes for such an adventure, pitted against the greater fear for Arias' well-being.

"We have a much better chance of freeing him if they remain in East Port still. One company of Kingsmen is a more manageable situation than the cells below the king's castle."

The gravity of the circumstances, spoken aloud, hits Alænèa harder now and me as well. My experience in Tullamoor where the rightful heir remained secreted away in a hidden vault below the keep for five years comes unbidden to mind. Sleep comes in uneasy fits throughout the night, with dreams of Arias in such a place.

Our questions regarding Arias and the Kingsmen are answered in part half a sun's ride yet out from towne. Eschereon is hailed by a farmer on a buckboard who knows him even at a distance. His identity becomes clear as we approach.

"Hail, Sage. I am Chæda, and I see that my son must have made good time in reaching you. I am grateful to the fates."

My first thoughts are that he has retrieved his wagon, even as his son said it being his intention. What happened to its cargo remains the unknown. We surround his wagon, the three of us anxious to hear his tale. I settle our horses, Alænèa's and my own, and listen as Chæda speaks from his buckboard.

"I fear you are too late though as the Kingsmen's captain and one other have left on a trader yester mid-sun, headed south to Kings Court. The others left out to the south on horseback still, there being no room for their steeds and themselves aboard."

Eschereon nods and places a hand on the farmer's shoulder.

"Thank you, Chæda, for sending Finn to us. Critical time has been saved for the effort. What might you be able to tell us of Arias' state, if anything?"

"That mayhaps I can speak to, Sage. You see, I did follow the Kingsmen the entire way to East Port. And I did camp each eve a ways from them, but not so far as I could not hear a scream of agony coming from their camp the last eve afore they arrived. The fates know I was glad to hear it, as when they left, he still lay unconscious and terrible with a fever. 'Twas to the least a sign he still lived."

I cringe to hear this as does Alænèa. And to hear him say it appears a good sign, my stomach tightens to a knot. We have arrived too late.

After we part ways with Chæda, Eschereon looks to us, and I am sure he recognizes our fear and the feeling of helplessness in our demeanor.

"Hope is not lost. Do not fret overmuch, the two of you. I am not without resources and friends that will aid us, even in Kings Court. I did not solely believe we would still find them in East Port. I have lived many years, even within the very walls of the king's cæstle, and know a thing or two about what we are up against…and what we might do." He has about him still an air and a confidence.

Eschereon's resourcefulness shows itself when we finally reach East Port. Though it takes a precious additional sun to make the arrangements, Eschereon secures us berth and passage on a swift vessel that will take us direct to Kings Court. The boat might very well gain some time on the large trader that carries the Kingsmen and Arias. We find lodging and await with little patience. We will need to stable our horses here till we return.

***

(Arias)

I awaken to light streaming directly into my coffin. But it is not my coffin I have discovered. Awake, off and on now for near to a whole sun, I reason, I have learned more of my circumstances. I cannot recall, no matter the effort spent trying, what has put me into a feeding trough, though I know with surety that it indeed has that better purpose. I lie in a bed of straw and happy for it, as my left leg and left arm are…one dislocated and the other broken. The pain reinforces the notion and remains a constant to my predicament. I appear to have sustained a wound of some sort, as my right shoulder is bandaged under my tunic. It is nice that somebody has taken the time to give aid in that regard, if not towards the other ailments. Mayhaps they have no experience in healing methods to address the others. This surprises me, as I somehow know exactly what should be done.

The furions are a wonder to me, and most certain have saved my life. They are ever-present and are often dropping pieces of fruit, cheese, and scraps of bread into my box. While I've been awake, I've seen no other come even within shouting distance, though my throat remains too dry to try such a thing. Though the fruit helps a bit, I wish somebody would refill my water skin. I think on this a great deal. My chest warms at the thought. I feel a swoon coming on and take the time to smile up at my unlikely rodent-like friends as darkness consumes me once again.

***

(Alænèa)

I think it a wonder, and though my mind cannot help but fret over Arias being on a vessel out to sea with no land in sight, it captures my attention in most every other way. At this very moment, I stand as far forward as I am able, leaning into and staring over the bow rail and into the surf as four great sea animals breach the sea's surface in great leaps and bounds. Awestruck, I have no words. We have been at sea four suns now.

By contrast, Sæm seems quite familiar with sea vessels. He recites to me all the many terms that sailors use for the parts and pieces of the boat, explaining that he and Arias have indeed sailed near the width of the inner sea in their journey to find the druid. He proves quite adept at working the sails as the captain orders his small crew about, having quickly become one of them when the skipper finds he has the knowledge and abilities of the best on his crew.

Eschereon has 'sea legs', as well, and more. We have berths–hammocks actually–in the forward hull, but I find myself from the first night, up on deck wanting to sleep under the stars. I settle myself on the deck foremost as possible and where it feels most exhilarating with the bow cutting through the water below me. Eschereon is not found in our berths either, but rather he spends time well into the night, standing aside the first mate at the ship's helm and talking to the wind. I discover later that it is precisely what he means to be doing. He explains that even though he helped us to discover our abilities, his is mægic over the elements. As he stands at the stern, face hardened and intent, wind fills the sails to greater extent as we no doubt are gaining little upon little on the trader carrying Arias.

***

(Arias)

I hear a loud groan escaping my lips, and a jolt that jars my entire body, as the lower end of my box hits something more solid than the swaying deck that has been my home for a time I cannot have measured. My over-worked nerves constantly remind me of my damaged limbs as they scream at me. My conscious mind once again taking over, I spy through the spread slats of the lid, two men staring back at me, brows raised. Mayhaps they are thinking the box carries dead weight, but it is not yet so. I hold memories of waking a few more times while on my seafaring trip. Once I found a replenished waterskin. It did not remain so for long.

I've become accustomed somewhat to the enduring pain I feel while conscious. What bothers me more and occupies my mind most every moment remains my inability to recall who I am and how I came to be where I now find myself. Taking stock during my waking moments and feeling about my person, I find naught save, my waterskin, now empty, and an amulet as it hangs around my neck under my tunic. It warms to my touch, and I feel it important that I keep it on my person.

My sea voyage has apparently come to an end, and I now remain awake and quite aware. Hearing first the surf lapping against the piers which seems a hauntingly familiar sound, and then shortly after, the cacophony of noise and voices all about me as my box recedes from the boat I've called home, I know somehow that this is a very large port towne. My escort loads my box upon a buckboard wagon I spy as we reach the front of the pier. A new part of my journey, and not so comfortable as the last.

Cobbled stone roads jar me relentlessly, the straw below me doing nothing to soften the continuous bombardment against the raw nerves about my broken limbs. Excruciating agony coursing up then down the left side of my body holds me at the brink of unconsciousness. I am in no mood to enjoy the sun and fresh air that comes with being removed from the dark hull of the ship.

Then we stop.

"He's s'poused tur meet us up here, ain't he?" I hear one of the coachmen say as I stare up at their backs. After loading my box upon the wagon, my many escorts have become but the two. I have learned more of who they are but not entirely so. Each wears a sigil upon their leather breastplate. It is a black raven over a golden häalberd. It seems familiar to my mind, but I cannot recall from where.

"He'll be here, sure. It's Cässin on duty this sun. Ah! I hear 'im even now." And I hear even as they do, an annoying squeak along with a shuffling of feet over gravel.

Off-loaded onto a wheeled cart now, again quite roughly in my opinion. The squelch and grind of wheels on an axle that has not felt the love of any grease for some time. Rolling down a gravel ramp now, switching back then forth but ever downwards and after quite some time brought to a halt against a tall iron gate. Taking time to observe my caretaker now, calm restores to my worn body at the pause as he fumbles through a ring of large keys, searching for that special one. He stands tall with whiskers grown long for this time of sun if he'd shaved this morn at all. A dark shadow hugs his jaw in any case. He carries a heavy load upon his person…most settled about his waist. His uniform struggles to contain it. His arms are massive and he stands on the legs of an ox. I reflect he could lift my box on his own in spite of his belly.

Finally finding the key to match this lock, the iron gate swings open with another high-pitched squeal. My box on the cart maneuvers through and the process at the gate reverses in a slow deliberate manner. Lantern light from iron hooks upon the stone walls to either side shines the way as we progress further into the gloom. A massive arched wooden door with huge black iron hinges appears to be our target. The squelch of the cart wheels now annoying beyond reason for one in my position.

We arrive into a greater hall having past a dozen or so openings with iron bars stretching across them. A dungeon, I cypher, though I've never been that I can recall. The eyes of the giant gaze down through the slats and settle to mine.

"Welcome to the Bowels." A sad smile visits my new gaoler's shadowy face.

9

King's Advisor & Friends

(Sæm)

Dimly lit but bustling, the pub we find ourselves in again this eve has immediately become my favorite. 'Tis our third eve in this particular public house. The scents and sounds and obvious atmosphere of fellowship and joy within the place nearly drives our real purpose here from my mind. Eschereon sits opposite and Alænèa to my right. We hold council and eve-meal at a table in the front corner near the windows. The dining hall, not overly large, carries the scent of the house ales as well as seared beef that arrives to neighboring tables on buttered iron platters, still sizzling from time spent on the kitchen's grill plate. Laughter ever-present, it clearly is a local favorite and why we are here. I watch as the portly server with splattered tunic and buttons near to popping approaches with our own sizzling plates.

We've been in Kings Court near to a fortnight now. Eschereon has made discreet inquiries around the docks and with others. The others have contacts within the cæstle itself, hence the druid's claim fulfilled that he is not without friends in the king's court. His queries have led us here. Whilst Alænèa and my temperaments are ramping up in anxiety over Arias, the druid has remained ever calm.

First, he's learned that Arias has arrived still alive and still nailed within the feeding trough he'd left Chæda's homestead in. Dock hands as well as king's soldiers on patrol about the docks have transported him from the trader's vessel to a wagon at the pier's mouth. This information comes easily. Where they carried him is now the greater mystery.

Eschereon's contacts within court turn out to be the youngers, now grown, from families that he knew during his time as Arias' mother's tutor and confidant. We have learned he had been such those first weeks in Esper with him. I recall the shock upon Arias' face as he learned his mœther was the king's daughter and watched back then as he had put pieces together in his mind.

It seems that even as royals age, and their staff with them, the staff's youngers are brought naturally into the family business of tending to them. And so, Eschereon has learned that Arias currently abides in the roughest and darkest of places, referred to simply as the 'Bowels,' and again, it is why we dine and council at the 'Bottoms Up' beer parlor and inn.

As it happens, the Bowels are the dungeons beneath the gaols serving the south gate garrison. The guardsmen, unlike the conscripted soldiers assigned for a time here, live within this community as they work their whole lives in their specific line of work. It takes a special breed of man and soldier to do the work of the king's gaolers and executioners. They oft eat here. Eschereon hopes to gain some insight from these very men on a scheme to rescue Arias.

The druid spent time at the bar afore we sat to evemeal, as he'd done on the two previous nights we'd eaten here. Listening mostly, as the guards drink and jaw-bone about their sun. He does not need to nudge them much to learn even more of Arias' fate. He explains just now, it ofttimes being the topic of most interest, owing to tales that he has been visited most every sun by Mensæ, the king's advisor. I recognize on Eschereon's face that this gives him much concern.

"What worries you so about this Mensæ, Eschereon?" His look getting the best of my curiosity.

Pausing to look across the table to me, he spends a further moment sopping up some gravy with a piece of crusty bread before replying. Even as he continues pondering his reply and absentmindedly taps his fingertips in rhythm against the tabletop, I catch an old local at the next table of a sudden turn back to his own evemeal plate. He's been listening to us. Eschereon draws my attention back with his words.

"I can't say for certain, Sæm, other than to say that even in the first weeks after I arrived here, three decades past, having come to join Arias' grandmœther at court, I've felt as much. His counsel held great sway over the king, and it seemed even then an unnatural thing. I took care in being… unobtrusive in his presence."

I contemplate the druid's words and then my plate, as I cut into my thick beefsteak. When I look up again, the old man from the adjacent table stands over us, his finger–the only one left on his right hand–lies upon the back of the fourth chair at our table. In hindsight, I become aware that I've noticed him both the previous nights we'd taken evemeal here.

"Pardon." A gravelly voice from a mouth collapsing upon itself to very few teeth, it seems. "'Twas rude of me listening in, but I did even still, and I might be of help as I think you're needin'. You're the king's daughter's tutor from the south, aren't chya?" He stares at the druid. "You haven't changed a bit in all these years."

"I don't recall…having met you, stranger," says Eschereon, studying the man with intent now.

"You wouldn't have noticed. Mind if I have a seat?" Eschereon nods, but the man has already pulled the empty chair out and is shuffling into it.

"My nephew back then, he worked the stables up at the keep. I'd visit him after my shift down here as I had a love for the great beasts, ya see, and it was a great place to come after being in the Bowels all night." Eschereon's brow raises a smidgen at this.

G. L. CRAMB

"'Twas there at the stables I'd see ya, escorting Aeglèsia down for a ride most days. I'd swear you look the same even as I've a foot in the grave." The druid nods.

"Anyways…I've been seein' the three of yas here the past three eves and overhearing ya jes now, I'm thinkin' to myself, I know a bit about what yur talkin' at. Mays be I kin help. I know the Bowels better 'en most here. Lived 'em nigh on ta forty years. Woulda been a few more if tweren't fer that Mensæ." Turning, he spits at the ground then turns back, drawing his sleeve across his mouth, spitting without teeth being a sloppy affair. Then he boldly slaps his hand, missing four fingers, on the table afore us. We understand without having to ask.

Placing a large hand to his shoulder, the druid welcomes him, understanding more than we do, sure certain. Our new friend, Vidarr he calls himself, raises his disfigured hand, showing no shame, and gives a short wave to the barkeep who sends a server over with an ale quite swiftly.

"He's my brœther's grandson, that one. His papi owns this place. He's a good lad," he says, turning his scrunched mouth into an odd-looking smile. He raises his stein in a toast to us, I assume as he says naught but nods, and we return the gesture.

"Fen there's brœther, he's a gaoler in the Bowels, even as I was." His eyes drift off a moment. "And we talk, ya know, as two with the same 'speriences."

"Farrell says he heard…wasn't 'sposed to, but he did, that the lad they is holdin' is Aeglèsia's son. Is it true?" Eschereon nods slightly once more. "Well, he's in rough shape 'n Mensæ and the king won't let a healer near. Nobody but the gaolers and that Mansæ, but I'm proud ta say Farrell's done a bit."

At this, I note Alænèa's hand on the table tighten into a fist. Mine as well. He is alive, and Arias, being a healer himself, is no doubt working his body to health no matter his condition. He'd told me the tale of how he'd

98

taken a crossbow bolt through his side. I feel Alænèa's same anxiety but hope as well.

***

(Arias)

I do not respond to Cässin as I do not feel any welcome in his words. The Bowels, he'd said. It does not conjure attractive thoughts in my damaged mind. Coming to grips over these past suns with my health situation, and I somehow know that I have knowledge of such things even though I cannot fathom from where or who. I know my mind is presently broken even as my body. But I also know the body can be repaired. I hope as much for my damaged mind. I feel my gaoler a hypocrite as Cässin does nothing to make me feel more welcome. On the contrary, the transition to life in the Bowels is excruciating.

Well, actually, the final resting place for my battered body may be marginally better than my box, but the getting there is hell. The fates seem less than kind.

Cässin, my new gaoler, unceremoniously and without forewarning, tips the cart my box lies upon forward, and every nerve in my body responds as the foot end of the trough slams forward into the stone floor, jarring me from foot to head. I slide forward inside the box as gravity pulls me and my knees buckle, both the dislocated one and the battered but one not yet broken, till they hit the lid of the coffin that is not and I think in the moment still might be.

My only thoughts now are the blinding raw pain of it. When the cart falls out from under the trough, I sense a weightlessness alongside the pain for a moment before the head end of the box plummet to the floor. My head whiplashes forward then back and a flash—a memory—surfaces for less than a moment and then vanishes. But the resulting pain slides away as my mind grasps for the memory. A wolf with remarkable eyes.

Left to deal with my pain, I settle back into the comforting straw under me as the squelch and squeal of the retreating cart lessens. Alone with my new memory, my first memory, I struggle to make some sense of it. A wolf. It is a strong memory with a sense of emotion accompanying it. Shaking off my pain as if it were just a discomfort, I attempt to study the memory… It fascinates me. Alas, my attention returns to the present as Cässin has returned.

Jolted back, a more apt description. An iron crowbar has been hammered betwixt the lid of my box and the top of the trough. With a grunt and squeals, the lid and accompanying nails are being pried apart. But my gaoler, being quite strong and determined, makes short work of it.

He glares down at me. I stare wide-eyed back up at him.

"Yu'll be more trouble than yur worth, be my wager. 'Spose ya woun' be gettin' yurself outta that pig's trough on yur own, willya?"

Shaking his head, he turns and walks over, and fumbling with his huge leather key loop, finds the match to the large iron box lock in the gate of a much more spacious accommodation than I'd become accustomed.

Whilst his back is to me, I do my best to test his wager. With forehead glistening, I quickly learn he'd collect on his bet. I can do nothing but pull my right arm and hand to my face. My body numb to any other attempt to move. I know I lie utterly helpless when he turns back to me.

Not wanting to lift me, Cässin has a better scheme. Incapable of doing naught but watch, my eyes go to his large, worn boot as it makes contact with the top edge of the trough and he pushes it, spilling me with an excruciating roll onto the stone floor. Groaning heavily, I think to not give him the pleasure of hearing me scream. I now lie on my belly seeing stars, head against the stone pavers, unable even to lift or turn it.

But what I spy somehow gives me a little hope. There, hiding in the shadows behind a couple of stick brooms leaning against the wall, are the two furions that have made the sea passage with me. Who are they? They become my last memory afore my gaoler rolls me over, and with two great arms under my own, darkness gratefully takes me as I succumb to the pain with another pitiful groan.

I sense it has not been long when I awake once more. Cässin finishes the dragging of my traveling trough to the other side of the large chamber, then tosses the lid inside. As he finishes and dusts his hands as if in an 'atta-boy, well done' his attention shoots to the other direction from which I'd first arrived. On his face…alarm. I hear it, too, now,. More keys and the jiggling of a lock. Cässin attempts to straighten up his unkempt person.

The sound of a rush of boot falls greets us now, followed by a small company of soldiers in full battle regalia. The reason for their pomp apparent immediately. A tall regal figure with a gold circlet about his head and dressed in fine attire, though with a military feel about it, strides into the dungeon. Another man of only a little less stature follows, his raiment much less bold, but with piercing eyes, the equal to the first. The lord of the keep? Somehow, I feel he is even more.

The lord paces fore and back, along the outside of my cell, staring must intently at me and taking in my whole person.

"This is truly him, Mensæ? This is what bards are singing about?" He stops his pacing to leer. This man does not care for me for some reason, and I feel it might mean I'll be leaving out in the same box I came in. I just stare back.

"It is he, sire."

The king? For some unknown cause, a dark mood envelopes me.

"You have till the next full moon to query him and give me cause to not have his head on a stake. He'll have naught but water until then."

My mood darkens all the more.

The man called Mensæ bows his head a bit, and the king and company leave as quickly as they had arrived, Mensæ pausing a moment to give me a small smile. Cässin stands stiff in the far corner saying nothing. The bang of a far off door leaves me and my gaoler alone again. He lets out a breath I think he had held the whole time of the visit.

Time passes as I lie on my bed of straw in a cell made of stone with iron bars along two sides and iron chains with wrist clasps dangling at their ends bolted into the stone walls. Apparently spared that form of detention by virtue of my present condition. Cässin has filled my waterskin, but it lies where he has tossed it and out of reach.

Over the next few turns, I witness the big gaoler delivering food, I imagine, though it holds no discernable scent, in large pewter bowls to other cells down the hall I'd been wheeled through upon my arrival. So I am not alone in my circumstances. Cässin has retired to another room off the greater chamber where I reside. I can see him seated and enjoying a meal delivered by a rotund, but pleasant-looking lass that has presented also with a young lad in assistance, a large pot for my compatriots. She lingers after sending the lad off, to chat with my gaoler. She leaves shortly after with a smile upon her face after a quick peck and a squeeze of her bosom by the big man. When he lifts the lid on his large evemeal bowl, I spy a bewitching steam arise, and with it a scent that finds its way to me as well.

While Cässin dines, I become acquainted with my friends from our voyage over to visit the king. Two…furions, the word comes immediately to mind. They are quite agreeable company, climbing about me and sniffing and licking the underside of my chin. They wear what resembles black masks about their eyes as the only white upon their otherwise dark-furred bodies trails from their snouts around their ears and halfway down, to their bellies. Twins, but for a slight shade difference in the furry hides. I find it most diverting to just scratch at their proffered heads and long furry bodies and tails. Remarkably, when I glance longingly at the waterskin out past my reach, they go over, and the two of them drag it to within my grasp. I later note that they are the only thing bearable during my stay.

Always aware, the furions disappear to the back of my cell when a bell chimes and Cässin's lady friend returns to collect her pot and plate and mayhaps more as she and the big man retreat to a further chamber, giggling.

10

Interrogation

I have fallen into a fitful sleep while watching my gaoler looking in on his charges, banging on bars here and there, and checking to see if they haven't expired since his last round, not wanting to deal with a corpse before bed, one might guess. Before I retired, I had a chuckle though. The big man had just hung up his keys to a hook on the wall behind him and searched now about his table, confusion and furrowed brow upon his face. Next to me the furions presented me with a nice chunk of crusty bread with a weighty brick of cheese.

Awakening from my fitful slumber by the clanging shut of the thick door I'd first entered the dungeon through, I realize there's been a changing of the guard. The new gaoler comes 'round, unlocks my cell, and enters, holding his lantern high to better examine me. He takes his time about it and notes my eyes returning his look.

"They say you are the rogue the bards have written so many ballads about. Ser Drægonheart. Is it so?"

I study him for a wondering moment, my breath caught in my throat. I play the name over and over in my mind, saying it to myself. His words mean naught to me. With a scratchy, dry, and totally new sound to myself, I listen as I respond to his query. I hold no recollection of this voice that is speaking aloud from my very lips.

"If it is, I'd like to hear them, as I know not even my name, and yours that you've given me sounds strange to my ears."

His eyebrows lift and I struggle to clear my throat. He picks up my water skin and leaves me lying just as I was, not bothering to lock the cell gate as he walks over to a hand pump against the far wall and over a stone basin. He unstoppers my skin, fills it, and returns it to me. With a nod, I take it from him in my only able hand, pull the stopper with my teeth, and take a deep swig.

"Thank you. Your comrade at arms has not been so generous." A knowing half-smile graces his face. "To be truthful, I recall nothing afore waking a few times on my long trip here in that box over yonder." His eyes follow mine.

"Well, I can tell you, the king thinks you are him, sure certain. As such, you are destined for the gallows or the broad axe, though if tales speak truth, your deeds warrant just the opposite to my way of thinking."

"And what deeds are those?" I query, highly curious to hear his reply.

"They mark you a vigilante, rescuing all manner of person. Mostly youngers from traders…slavers. But there is more in the king's reasoning. More, I think for who you actually are, not told in the ballads."

"And who might that be?"

But even as I make the query, the sounds of the backdoor slide bolt being pulled and the lock being rattled, has my new gaoler turning to leave, slamming and locking my cell bars again.

It turns out that our late-night callers are from the cæstle, but not the king and with considerably less pomp…or guards, if you will. It is Mensæ, at least, that is what the king called him, and with him but two guardsmen, though each, quite lethal in appearance. They wear black leather mixed with black cloth and black wool cloaks. Two small, dull silver curved blade replicas, one the opposite to the other and half the size of my smallest finger, adorn each of their collars. A personal sigil of the king's advisor, I wager, and meant to evoke fear. Each carries a real blade to match the sigil at his waist and a thin bladed short sword as well. My mind, to my shock, appraises such things at the first.

Mensæ himself stands garbed in a robe of deep grey and though mayhaps meant to convey a solemn and conservative countenance that might be expected of a sage. The lining of his raiment boasts soft silks dyed in royal reds. A reflection of his ego, I think. These immediate, studied reflections, are a curiosity to myself.

"I'll speak to the prisoner alone for a bit, gaoler." And with a nod, one of the guardsmen escorts my gaoler out. A gesture to the other and he retreats out the door they've arrived through.

The man the king calls Mensæ casually wanders to my gaoler's side room and returns with a stool. Placing it just in front of the bars, he takes his seat and studies me for a few moments. I return the favor.

"We were not formally introduced earlier. I am the king's counselor. Mensæ, I am called. You?"

I'd been propped up against a stiff pile of hay when I'd been dragged into my cell earlier. A blank look returns his query.

"The king does not like you, lad, but a'times I've been able to sway him. Mayhaps with a bit of cooperation, your fate could be less dire." His smirk quite irksome to me, I ne'er-the-less make to reply.

"Mæster, I fear my mishap has left me unable...to give any aid, though I would certainly like to avoid the ire of your king." My inquisitor's left eyebrow raises upon his forehead in what I cannot mistake for good cheer.

"MY king is your king, young Arias...Bard?...Bearheart? Which is your bastard name anyway? And my ire alone should trouble you, lest that of the king should so befall you."

He seems quite serious, and I, sure certain, know that my predicament and further health depends on the whims of my gaolers. And so, I mean to be frank with him.

"Ser, I assure I mean no disrespect. I will unerringly try to satisfy your queries. But, your naming me, though if slight difference from what others have recently called me, and even your statement that I am indeed a citizen of this realm, is new knowledge to me." His eyelids seem now to lower in a deeper aggravation.

"No more games. You are the bastard son of Aeglèsia and have sought refuge to the north under the protection of one who is called Eschereon, mentor to her in years past, though under another name himself. I will know of both of them, if you have any hope of leaving this place alive."

Though outwardly calm, his tone of voice strikes me as exceptionally intense. I believe his statement to the depth of my soul, but know no matter his words, he will not let me leave alive in any case. It being of special interest that his specific desire concerns knowledge of my alleged mœther and a mentor of hers. I, of course, know nothing of either.

The drip of water hitting the water basin across the chamber and light shuffling about of my prison compatriots in the other faraway cells drift to my ears in the vacuum his statement left as I say ne'er a further word and but study him with intent.

Seeing no outward sign I will be giving him the information he desired, he speaks again.

"Let us try this another way, Arias Côeurdrægon…" And a sneer and a smirk comes now to his lips. It does not bode well for me, I think.

Of a sudden, two things happen to me. I feel flush, with a warmth and tingling sense visiting within my head, and at the same time an equal sensation strike my chest so that I reach up and place my hand over my tunic, under which lies the amulet upon my breast. There comes a heaviness that seems to press me into my straw bed, and in my mind I feel an…intrusion. I know of no other way to describe it. My body's pains and very essence fall away from my consciousness and all that remains, an 'outside' force trying to press thoughts into my brain. But my mind is not having it and denies the pressure.

When I can finally concentrate on anything else again, I look to the king's counselor and witness a confusion about his face and a bead of sweat lying on the side of his forehead at his hairline. He stands from his stool, grabs hold of the bars of my cell, and stares at me hard, his person as close to me as possible without being in the cell itself. My chest still tingles about where my gemstone talisman lie against it, but I let my hand fall away from it.

With a pensive look about him, Mensæ calls to his two guards and leaves without further word to either my gaoler or myself. For my further part, a lethargy envelopes me and I fall into a sound sleep.

In the coming suns, things are not pleasant. Though my sun-time gaoler will replenish my waterskin from time a'times, no food nor even gruel comes my way scented or unscented. But small items of foodstuff in Cässin's personal chamber go missing and appear afore me as gifts from my furion friends. A piece of bread, a date, or meat jerky. I hold conversations with them in quiet whispers now.

My nighttime gaoler is called Farrell, I've learned. Though seldom and far betwixt, I speak to him a bit most every eve. I had shocked him on my second night in my cell when I gathered the courage to help myself to fix my broken body. Dragging myself to the bars of my cell, I lie against them and wedged my twisted leg betwixt two of them tight. This was an excruciating process in and of itself. When I pulled and twisted my body against the present nature of my leg, I screamed and fainted away with the pain of it. But when I awoke, I found Farrell staring down at me, and when I looked to my leg, my foot and lower leg were once again aligned as they should be. I begged Farrell for some cloth and sticks, telling him my purpose that same night, and he returned to me with a long rag and two pieces of the lid to my old box-home. With an almost equal pain as when I re-set my leg, I managed with teeth, one hand, and the bars for support to squeeze my broken forearm back into its proper place. Wrapping strips from the rag about it and twist-tying it into a knot, I had done all that I knew to do with it as well.

Farrell tells me he remains under orders not to aid in my healing, but he will not stop me from my self ministrations. Likewise, he will not give me food. But he does speak to me of Mensæ. I wish, each night afore I lie back to sleep, that my body will heal and relieve me of my pain and further, that some way to escape my predicament will present itself. My chest warms to both of those ideas.

Two things, nay three, occupies my time as the suns creep by and near to a fortnight since I arrived. First, I find I am healing but become more anxious to my situation. My splint is slowly helping my body to heal my broken arm and I can put a limited amount of my weight to my realigned leg. The furions continue to supply me with scraps of fruit and food that my gaolers deprive me and this keeps Cässin, my day gaoler, wondering where his treats disappeared. Farrell, my night gaoler and a good sort, spends some time conversing with me after Mensæ leaves me each night. We speak of his family and life in King's Court. It helps to calm me after the king's counselor's increasingly severe probing interrogations each night.

Second are these unceasing sessions of query. Mensæ has visited me most every night and the time spent the same as that first, his temper slowly growing with each episode. When he does not occupy my time in what has become meaningless attempts to solicit information I had no memory of, he proceeds to a more sinister approach. This unnerves me most, but especially this past night.

Ultimately, and not just by the by now, these immediate events turn my thoughts to escape. For a dozen suns I lie in no condition for such thoughts, as my body's excruciating pain and the slow healing process occupies my time. But these last two suns and eves find my mind more and more cy-phering strategies to this end. Mensæ's attitude towards me has of a sudden changed, and so must mine as some memories have surfaced now with his efforts.

Farrell, upon his return and the counselor with his guards having just departed, leaves me in a full sweat, eyes wide, pressed against the stone wall of my cell. I dare say, Mensæ left in a similar state. I sit trying to make a sense of it all. With hands shaking, I reach for my waterskin. Farrell leaves me to my thoughts and returns to his alcove, seeing I am in no mood for our usual chat. Looking to him, I take note that he does even the same as Cässin each time he retires to his space. He hangs his heavy set of keys upon a hook behind his chair.

This night likens not at all to my others with Mensæ. I knew it would not from the beginning. He posed none of his usual queries. We are past that now.

"We will dispense with our usual prattle this eve. I know you carry ancient mægic within you, and I'll have knowledge of it as well as of your mentor, a druid. It is clear he has trained you well enough to resist my lesser probes into your mind. That all changes now." A smirk and a slight rise in one side of his upper lip exposed a yellowed couple of teeth.

He's mentioned this druid before, and though I have no memory of him, I hope he had indeed given me some training to fortify me against the coming onslaught to my mind. He had not.

In prior interrogations, I had felt…perceived…endured… None of these words can actually describe the experience, his probe into my psyche… my very mind. Each time I know it to be an intrusion and I resist. Farrell let slip that prior criminals that had been "interrogated" by Mensæ have come away profoundly changed in mental faculty. I cypher that my amulet has somehow been an aid to me in my resistance. I know not how, but its warm-ing reaches into my body and mind clearly coincides with his probes. My hand slides unconsciously up and over where my tunic covers it even as he speaks.

Something is different for me this time. In spite of his threat, a confidence has built up within me over these past dozen days when he's had no success. It is a false sense of security and nearly costs me my mind mayhaps but releases in me memories of a sort as well. They are near the death of me.

Mensæ starts this session as the others before. He focuses his attention to my eyes and as before, I find myself helpless to look away. It happens immediately this night, and the amulet heats my body beyond its normal function. I 'feel' Mensæ's 'spirit presence,' I've come to call it, pressing me to open up to it. This time, however, I decide to press mine to his as well. I feel him flinch at this but then disregard it as though it did not happen. I feel, nay know, that he is familiar with this, but not in a comfortable sense. I press even as he presses in anger now, I know. A discovery. If I let my guard down just the slightest, memories…my memories…appear to me. But even as they appear and I know them as such, I see equally real, his memories as well. He does not seem to realize this, and I back off, my mental blocks up once more.

"You are not invincible, I see." A glee in his eye. "This night will reveal all before I am finished with you!"

I fear, but then hope he has the right of it. Though his memories are presented to me and I have no real desire to weigh them, mine are also and this drives a keen curiosity within me. He seems to ponder what he's seen in my memories. It is then that I realize that I've retained those memories he's accessed in my mind. I can recall them at will now and they are mine again. He begins again, and this time I become curious about his memories. Mayhaps they will be an aide to my escape attempt that I am determined will be in my near future.

This time I see memories of a council at a mountain retreat with a group of compatriots, for I know it as such even as I see it…experience it… Then

a fleet of burning ships at sea and a disturbing scene aboard one of them…
Then a skiff landing ashore with the very distinct and same faces from the
later council members. The memories roll back an inordinate number of
years now…hundreds… and a meet with a man Mensæ recognizes as his
superior and a mage of incredible power of mind and mægic.

Of a sudden, the connection breaks with a raging, searing stroke of
intense pain in my head as Mensæ rises and steps back away from me with
a scream, loathing and shock upon his face.

His guards come running as he steps forward again, banging his staff
with jeweled head against my cell's bars. I find myself in a sweat, my tunic
soaked through and staring up at him as if seeing him for the first time. He
falls silent as he is approached by Farrell and his personal guards.

"The full moon first rises on morrow's eve, gaoler. Per the king's decree, this prisoner's head is forfeit the morning after. Alert the axeman!"

And as I said, Farrell retires leaving me with my thoughts and new
memories to sort and study with but one sun remaining before my execution.

11

Vanished

ware that my time is spare, I spend the night making a plan of escape. It is not totally a hastily conceived notion, as I've been pondering its finer points for a few suns now. It relies on a great many things to happen in my favor and no little bit upon my furion friends. But one of my recovered memories has involved these very same creature friends doing similar things at my bidding.

Farrell's late night gabbling with me after Mensæ's visits lay the groundwork for my hopes. He one night spoke of how the dungeons came to be known as the Bowels. It seems that all the bath and toilet chambers in the king's cæstle up the hill, along with all the slop pot shoots and kitchens drains empty below the keep into sluiceways filled with flowing waters from aqueducts feeding them even further up the mountainside. These smaller sewers feed a larger one that in turn lies below these very dungeon chambers and cells. The smell, as I'd encountered my first day here, does indeed waft up from the two large iron grates on the stone floor that my gaolers' apprentices routinely wash the floor's grunge, grime, and occasional blood into. Oh, and our cell's slop pots also. The Bowels, it is an apt name. I intend it to be my escape route as well.

I know the grates can be lifted, as the lads do just that as need arises time a'times. They are not large, but I cypher that the larger of the two I can fit through. In the dead quiet of the night, I can make out the sound of flowing water below.

Two other things will need to happen, and on the morrow, or my fate will be sealed. Cässin's lady friend must be randy…a good wager, and the furions–I know them by their names now, Lilit and Jilly, as they were part of my recovered memory–will need to play the biggest part.

Cässin sniggers upon hearing my fate for the coming morn as Farrell informs him with the changing of the guard. Once alone with his charges for the sun, and me his featured guest, he cannot help but twist the proverbial blade to my gut.

"I'd take your order for a last evemeal, Drægonheart, but king's orders remain. No food for ya still. Mayhaps it's best. No shit leakin' out one end whilst yur lifeblood is gushin' from your neck. Easier on the cleanup sods in any event!" That seems to tickle his humor, allowing a guffaw to tumble from betwixt his rotting teeth.

"I was more hoping for a word with the lady that brings it back in the stores." I put on my most jovial air. He kicks the bars on my cage but smiles an evil smile.

"Oh, she'll have a word, this eve… I'll leave the door ajar, mayhaps, so's ya can hear a little."

I pace about the cell a bit, off then on throughout the sun, trying to limber sore and aching joints and willing a strength back into them. My leg remains pitifully weak and my left arm has little strength. Fortunately, my shoulder is near to healed and I have a strength about it. Swelling about my head and face has diminished greatly and my ribs, though sore, hold a pain that seems manageable.

While Cässin attends to other duties, I work with Lilit and Jilly but I need not have bothered as they respond to my specific retrieval requests as if they understand my every word. Cässin leaves the Bowels entirely from time a'time, but when he does, he takes his keys with him. These times will not work. I patiently endure the gaoler's smirks throughout the sun.

Some inborn function tells me time nears my window of opportunity and as it does, a bell chimes down the long hallway from which Cässin's lady friend, with my compatriot's gruel, will arrive. Cässin rises and gathers his keys to open the thick door and let her in. As her assistant delivers the eve's dinner fare into tin bowls and plates aside their gated cells, Cässin escorts his lady back to his corner, carrying his evemeal. She stays a bit, and I can see he ladles his peculiar charm on thick this eve. Though my lips might not show, my eyes surely have a sparkle to them in hopes he will be a successful suitor this eve. I need to wait till she returns later to find out my fate. For sure certain, this buxom lady holds it in her bosom and betwixt her thighs.

Cässin has finished his evemeal and has three ales in washing it down. He's done his eve chores about the Bowels and has returned to his corner. He sits whittling on a chunk of wood to no great avail when the doorbell chimes. He looks towards my cell and winks. I wish him well.

Returning with his lady friend, they sit about his table and chat. I can see naught of her as she sits across his table and behind a wall. I hear as he laughs heartily and she giggles coquettishly, and when he gestures in invite to his lap, she comes round and does just that. He makes a point of looking my way from time a'times, a smirk as my reward as he fondles her breast and squeezes her knee.

As many a time afore, he eventually takes her hand and draws her back to the store's chamber. As he promised, he leaves the door ajar as his secret pleasure, mocking me.

I set to work. Expressing my need for the keyring that my gaoler left conveniently hanging on its assigned hook, Jilly and Lilit work as a team, and climbing the back of Cässin's chair, soon have the keys dropping to the floor. The noise not enough for them to hear over their passion in the far chamber. My wonderful furion friends expeditiously drag them to me. Quietly returning the keys to their hook and closing my cell gate, I make my way over to the iron grate in the floor. It lies just aside my traveling trough which sits in the same spot Cässin had left it at the far side of the room.

Using my right hand to lift it my left being useless, I prop it against my box. Hearing a flow of water within, it remains black as pitch with no light from the wall lanterns able to penetrate the dark. The water does not sound too far away, but with a leg still far from healed I will do serious damage if the fall is too great. There being nothing left for it, I shimmy my way to where I remain half in and half out of the hole in the floor. The fidgets climb atop my shoulders, more confident than I. I drop.

My knee gives way and I fall back and onto my arse into a swift running water. To my amazement, aside from the striking pain in my knee, it is not much more than the height of me. Lilit and Jilly have bounced to safety on either side of the rock sluiceway that I find myself sitting in. They are chattering to either side of me. The water or the sewer I am in carries a nauseating odor and bits and pieces within it, and it is fortunate my stomach has remained mostly empty for quite some time since I sit gagging for more than a moment. Pulling myself up to my feet, I discover the iron grate still within my reach. I pull it into place as the grey water drips from my hand to my face. To my ears, its tumble to the floor proves deafening and I pause to hear if my gaoler comes running, but it does not happen. I've freed myself into the sewers and smile inwardly at my success.

I cannot help but wonder what they will think of my disappearance. Cell locked, keys hung where they were left. I have vanished and Cässin's dalliance will cost him dear. I think there is not a more deserving fellow.

My direction takes no thought. Follow the streaming flow about my ankles. Farrell had said the Bowels empty into the sea eventually. I can at this point reach to either side and feel stone walls, and extending my arm above, I easily touch the ceiling. My concern, therefore, keeps my hand above should the ceiling become lower and force me to crouch.

An elation fills me as I step forward into the blackness, not being able to help the quickening in my pace in hope of setting foot all the sooner into open air and true freedom. My haste becomes my downfall and quite literally, not fifty paces forward. But the chittering of Lilit and Jilly cheer me on as they scurry in the dark aside me.

Of a sudden, my hand falls away from the ceiling, or rather the ceiling rises to greater height. As I take in this surprise, thinking prior it might actually fall and constrict my progress, I catch my breath as the floor falls away as well. I instantly sink into a deep pool of chill waters, and a relentless pull drags me down as a panic grabs hold of me.

Struggling with but one good arm and one good leg, it becomes futile and I give up the struggle with a burning chest filled with but half a breath. I let the riptide have its way as it pummels me against the tight sides of an underwater shoot. Seeing stars, I gasp for a breath even as I become weightless and airborne, falling what feels a great distance before landing in another pool. This one much more shallow as I hit bottom against my wounded shoulder. The water from the falls above pounds me, and as I drag myself from under it gasping for air in total darkness, I immediately find solid ground. Rolling over, half in the pool but head out, I find relief as an even deeper darkness envelopes me.

***

(Alænèa)

Vidarr has come directly to the inn where we are staying. His eyes search as he bursts through the front door. The squeak of its hinges draw our eyes to him. Both Sæm and I notice and gesture him to us. His body's mean and manner a quiet anxiety, but it surely shows on his face.

"What is it, Vidarr? What has happened? Is our friend alright?" whispers Sæm as he pulls the old man into a seat.

"Aye, for this last day only." He growls in his usual manner. "Where is the Sage? You must act afore morn. Best yet afore Farrell comes to duty if there is to be a chance now."

My breath catches in my throat as Sæm's eyes squint in concern.

"Eschereon is out making further arrangements and is to meet us back here for mid-sun meal. Have an ale and a bite as we wait then. We can hear you out and all that you know as soon as he arrives. We can do naught till then in any case." But he cannot keep it in.

"This night is the first of the next full moon and Farrell says the king's counselor has no further use for the lad and has named the morrow's morn his meet with the axeman." I wish he'd waited with this specific news. Nerves throughout spark within me as my mind races.

We have made a scheme since two suns passed and Vidarr has told us his story and that of the Bowels. He explained the nature of the underground sewers of Kings Court and the eventual flow out onto the sea. He'd even been to one of the portals on the rocky slopes of the southern river where they empty. This is the key to Arias' escape, he had argued. The 'Bowels' are the last of the king's keep to sit over these sewer ways. And access through floor gates are possible entries to the gaol chambers themselves.

Eschereon is out even now securing passage away from Kings Court and back to Esper. Sæm has just returned from a smithy, purchasing some tools Eschereon thought we might need. A great hammer sits at his feet.

Even as Vidarr's ale arrives to the table, the druid pushes through the front door of the inn. The clatter of plates, cups, and laughter about us belies our mood as Eschereon approaches. Our mid-sun meal becomes a brief affair in the noisy dining hall as we discuss further what the old man can tell us about Arias' situation. Even still, Sæm devours his share and then some from my plate, I bid him welcome as I cannot eat.

"This is dire news, sure certain. But we are ready to move even now. If you can meet us at the south gate in two turns time, Vidarr, your help in directing us to a starting point to our search would be greatly appreciated." Eschereon ends our conversation, and we part ways.

Our preparation means settling our account at the inn, procuring a skiff at the riverfront, and transferring our supplies to it. We row the small boat to a mooring as close as possible to the south gate into King's Court. We wait there for Vidarr.

For our part, we've arrived early and sit quietly and stare up the trail to the gate, listening to the river lap against our skiff and hearing youngers at play. We watch as fishermen, single and some in pairs, dip rods into the waters. Eschereon especially pensive, myself running my fairly brief history with Arias in my mind. Even so, I count us close friends.

Our time with the druid has brought us to understand and care for each and the other. Arias continually amazes me with an innate ability to channel his mægic, even as he'd just learned a new thing. Even as I constructed a ward, he knew how or could see through it to dismantle the effect. He could move things with his mind at great distance. I've seen twenty paces. He had episodes likened to a seer, Eschereon said, when a vision of a near future came upon him. His gift with any creature became more than evident and recently he'd been able to even control the winds to his whim. His aura always strong to my sight and different from any other.

And now his fate hangs on this very sun. It is left to us to save him from an errant act of king's justice. His fate is tied to a bloodline he has no control over. Our charge does not even seem possible. To squirrel our way up into what will most like be a myriad of sewers beneath Kings Court, to find the 'Bowels,' the dungeon cells where he is being held awaiting an executioner's axe fall on the morrow's morn. There, we must overcome his gaolers and secret away the way we came. I glance to Eschereon. Somehow I think this man can make it possible.

"Yea, Eschereon, I see the old man just now coming through the gate!" I say, noting Vidarr hurrying to us as I stand on wobbling feet to wave at him.

He gains our mooring after maneuvering down a hill strewn with more rubble than grasses. Sæm extends an arm to help him step across and into our skiff. He finds seat on the bench next to me, and then Sæm pushes us off and into the river proper with an oar. The druid sits at the stern over a rudder, and Sæm settles upon the center bench and takes up the oars, looking to Eschereon.

Vidarr had explained our goal lies a good bit downstream, but I find myself already peering closely at the bank for tunnels or caves, anxious to find the way into the sewers.

With the sun crawling all too quickly across the sky and grey rain clouds giving chase with thunder barking their imminent arrival, the old man gives notice to watch close.

"It has been many a year since I explored this side of the sewer tunnels. The landscape has changed a great deal." He squints up and down the shoreline, holding firm to the boat's side as the choppy water makes it all the more difficult a task.

At long last, with sunlight failing and heavy raindrops smacking us hard from above, Vidarr points and shouts.

"There! Do you see the rusted grate? It's near to covered with the rat-bush. There…just next to the gravel beachhead. Look to the water thereabouts and the debris is thick around the outflow." I can clearly see an iron grate now, and Eschereon turns the rudder, steering us to the stone beach. Sæm and I leap out and pull the skiff into the small beachhead.

We waste little time here, leaving Vidarr with the boat. Eschereon, and what I can only explain as a gathering of mægic from the very air about us, makes the end of his staff glow. We approach the grate with heavy and more frequent rain drops pelting our faces, and notice the constant flow from the cave entrance. The grate itself lies askew, and one swing of Sæm's hammer sends it collapsing inward. Slipping into the channel that carries the outflow from the cave, we pass into the dank, dark, and quite smelly tunnel.

The three of us enter, one following the other, but as soon as we cross the threshold of the portal the way widens with the tunnel having a running trough down the middle and dry ground to either side. Eschereon's staff lights the way to mayhaps five paces ahead of us. The radiance about his staff shines its light in a limited manner, and so he varies in an alternating manner to light the way first from our waist upward and into the ceiling and then back down so that we can maintain a solid footing as we advance. The light from the cave's portal dissipates completely as we round the second bend. There are many such. There are no byways that we come upon and that is good fortune as we would have no way of knowing which direction we should take as the meandering and twisting tunnel has quickly confused any sense of direction any of us hold.

Going remains slow and the stench accosting our senses soon becomes severe. I wrap a scarf about my face but it does little good. The trek seems endless as it takes us on a serpentine route deep into the stone mount that Kings Court sits upon.

It has been two turns of a sand glass before anything changes. It is alarming when it does. Fissures appear, some level to the eye and some rising in an ascending manner from floor to ceiling with leaking water in some cases flowing quite hard. The way becomes wider, and Eschereon's light does not reach across the breadth of the cave tunnel. But still no byways present themselves, and we feel hearted for it. We do, however, now see from time a'time large and nasty rats, their eyes aglow against the light from the druid's staff and immediately scurry away from it.

Well into what must surely be dusk in the outside world, we come upon a problem that needs some exploring and cyphering. Before us lies a large cavern with a high ceiling and a shallow pool covering most of it. A pounding stream of water pours from a trough high up the far wall. It is as if the tunnel has come to an end. We all stand and study the cavern, willing there to be a way forward. Sæm sees it first across the pond. There winds a passageway tight to the wall opposite us, rising up and around the pounding falls. But as the druid makes his light follow the way up the wall, a scene appears that makes my skin crawl.

Sæm and Eschereon are already making their way directly across the pond to address the situation. There seems to be a pitted battle amongst a group of rodents… Large rats it seems, and as Eschereon turns the light to them, their ghostly eyes glow and the majority retreat up the passageway. I follow along the dry walkway against the wall, heading towards them from the opposite side of the pond.

Sæm appears about to skewer the remaining rodents when I scream and fall. Something lies across my path and I have tripped.

"Some light, Eschereon, if you would."

Even as he directs his light to me, the something I had tripped over groans, and my two companions rush to me. To us. To Arias and I. My heart fills with joy even as it aches to see his condition, made more a dire scene as he is hidden mostly in shadow and soaked through and through.

Of a sudden, the two rodents Sæm had just been intent on slicing through, jump upon Arias and me. I know them instantly, of course. Lilit and Jilly! They have been fighting off a contingent that clearly wants a piece of Arias.

"Ho, Lilit and Jilly. I had not recognized you and nearly poked you deep. My apologies!"

They seem to take no offense as they lean against Sæm's legs in warm greeting. They, sure certain, are remarkable, empathetic creatures and quite loyal it seems to their friends. It is a wonder that they are somehow still with Arias through his capture, transport, and gaoling within the Bowels.

As I kneel over Arias, Eschereon arrives and studies him from over my shoulder. All three of us will him to be okay. He stirs and with another groan gazes up at us with a look of confusion. The furions are under his chin, sniffing and licking him towards full consciousness.

***

Opening my eyes to three strangers gazing down upon me, the whole of my body fights over which symptoms to recognize first. The chill of the water half my body lies in or the ache of the head, ribs, and strained limbs interrupts in their healing by having been pummeled in the rock funnel I'd nearly drowned in before being spit out to where I presently lie. The strangers seem to recognize me and show sympathetic faces which leaves me some little relief. They pull me out of the water, and the elder in the group lowers his staff and it lights the four of us to a greater extent. Mægic, I know somehow, and I think back immediately to Mensæ's insistence that I disclose all I know of persons that can wield it. Even as he said he knew that I could. I thought at the time his queries but strange talk of myths.

"Oh Arias, you have the look of a half-drowned, malnourished dog. But I'm so happy to see you that I'll not even complain that you've tripped me into this cesspool." The girl with large eyes leaning closest whispers in a chastising, yet grateful voice.

"I feel a fellowship with you, all three, though I recognize none of you. I'd be grateful for a little fresh water." My voice sounds a bit gravelly as I watch the three of them gaze from one to the other in concern, and the lad reaches for his water skin right away.

"You are ever most resourceful and proven so yet again, Arias. We will be anxious to hear your tale. And we will need to see about your memories. I've seen where a blow to the head can cause such a thing." The elder states while examining me closer. "Will the king's guard be close behind?"

I drink deep from the tall lad's skin.

"Nay, I think not this way that I've come. Cässin, my sun-time gaoler sure certain cannot fit through the escape hole. And I left no evidence as to how I left, I believe, in any case. Farrell, my nighttime gaoler, gave me a clue to the how of it, though I doubt he knew it."

"Well then, mayhaps introductions are in order once again. Though you've known us for a lengthy term, all the three of us. I was even at your mœther's bedside for your birthing." A smile that somehow looks rare crosses his face.

"This is Alænèa and Eshæm, that you call Sæm, and I am called Eschereon the sage, though your da named me druid when first he spoke to you of me."

My brow furrows.

"Hmmm, Mensæ, my inquisitor and the king's counselor, queried me about you much this fortnight past. He showed a keen interest in you and my mœther. He found a way of looking into my mind just last night though I think I frustrated him, and his effort released a few memories within my mind with the attempt. I saw my da and heard his dying words to find a druid. And my friends here, Lilit and Jilly, I know again."

I feel a guilt for some reason that I've let Mensæ gain some important knowledge he should not have. In the balance, I but gained a few old memories. Eschereon's face goes blank for a moment at my news.

"Even if they know not how you made your escape, they will be searching with utmost urgency to find you. Mayhaps it is time we retreat out of these sewers and make a further escape."

"I'll not argue against leaving these bowels below the Bowels, but I may need your staff as aide as my dislocated leg though back in place is not yet healed. Will it lose its glow in another's hand?"

"Let us see." And he hands me the staff.

With both hands firm about it, I make to pull myself upright with Sæm and Alænèa's help about each arm. The staff's glow grows two-fold and all looked to me.

"I once named you an enigma, Arias. I find that description holds all the more." And in the greater light, a wide smile can be seen clear upon his face.

12

Hunted

(Mensæ)

It will not be in my favor to have this lad speak to the king again. He holds a mægic much more powerful than I could ever have expected. Not since Běelzel, and he is one of the Three, has anyone dared to violate my mind so. I thought it not possible but for the Three. I'd killed the last who tried in a thrice…always in control. But this whelp, not yet a full man, maneuvered his way in. What did he learn? *Too much!* I should have ordered the axe man then and there, but he riled me so.

The depth of his discovery remains unknown to me, but he has seen our arrival. He knows Běelzel. *It will be over on morrow's morn. No need for worry.* I'll inform the king his justice will be done then. But there is the matter of the druid. He was called such by Ètœn Bearheart in his death throes. I watched it happen in the lad's memory. But even as I broke through into his mind, he found mine…too easily.

Did I break through? Or did he let me in*? It was a ploy.* His mægic is strong.

"Captain, we will return to the Bowels now. Call for the axeman. The lad dies this night and not on the morrow. We leave immediately."

"Shall I send word to the king?"

"Nay, I will handle the king. Bring four of your trusted."

Chatter and shouts from ahead carry to us as we near the door to the dungeons proper. All goes quiet as the door's bolt is pulled open by the captain of my guard. Not unusual in and of itself, but the shouting has been.

It must be the changing of guard that I'd interrupted. The two guards I've come to know are nose-a-nose, the sun-time guard Cässin sweating profusely. Looking to the cell holding the king's bastard grandson, I notice now he is no longer there.

"Where have you taken him? The axeman has been sent for. The king has moved his justice up to this eve."

Farrell, I note, pauses a glance in Cässin's direction.

"He's gone, Master Mensæ. I arrived just at the hour to find his cell locked but empty."

"Where is he, Cässin? What is the meaning of this? There are no last meals for this prisoner. Where have you taken him?"

"Nowhere, sir! He's…he's just vanished. I've just now returned from the store's chamber about to do last rounds when Farrell here arrived to the outer door. I let him in and we have just now found him vanished with no way for it."

My ire outweighs concern at this point and I push forward, my hand about the thick neck of huge body of the guard. Ne'er the lesser he falls back against the wall, the captain and his guards with hands at the pommels of their blades and short swords. I pry his mind open like a heavy baked potato, not caring the damage. It appears he does not lie, but for the wench he'd taken to the store's chamber to have his way.

There are but two ways into the Bowels. I and my guards came one way and met nobody. And with lock on the keep side, it seems unlikely he escaped in that direction. The sun guard unlocked the other door which takes a key from Cässin's belt to unlock, so he could not have left unseen in that direction unless added by him. His mind shows that did not happen. He has either vanished or is hiding still within the Bowels.

"Captain, tear this place apart. Leave nothing unturned nor unopened."

It takes far less than a turn of a sand glass to accomplish my order, and he remains vanished.

"Unless he lies to the bottom of a floor drain and we've looked there as well, he no longer resides here, Mensæ."

"No mægic can let a man pass through stone walls, captain. I know not the how of it, but he will not escape Kings Court. No vessel nor wagon leaves the city without being searched from this eve till he is found, captain. Make it so. And he dies on the spot. I'll see every house and business alike searched if I must."

In his condition, he must have had help. Again a druid comes to mind and mayhaps the same man. Just as the king's daughter vanished. But he had two moons to arrange that. This happened of a sudden with no clue in the guard's mind. They are dangerous, these druidae, and more clever than I have thought. They must be found and forced to reveal their secrets. The way to that end, if not through the druid himself, just may be this lad.

"On second thought, captain, the rogue must remain alive." I will not fail in my interrogation next go round. I will be prepared.

***

We travel a serpentine route through the sewers and come finally to the tunnel's entrance and a rocky beach. The others politely ignore the smell of me, I think, having spent over a moon in garb, now mostly rags, with my own crusted excrement chafing me. The waters of the sewers make my odors all the more fresh again.

The elder's staff gives what light we have, as the darkest of storm clouds engulfs the sky and with it the moon as well. The lap of the waves and especially the brisk breeze are a wonder to me though.

An old man sits aside a skiff here, pulled up and unto the stone beach and clearly waiting on us. He beams at me as we approach.

"You've escaped the Bowels… Mayhaps the only prisoner to ever do so, lad. They were not built for anything but cruelty and a final solution for it. Any that enter expect nothing less than the king's ultimate justice after a pitiless wait. But you have come out whole. My grand nephew would be thrilled, though I will not tell him the how of it till he works there no more… And he'll enjoy it all the more for it then!" Giving a faint smile, I think that mayhaps I have escaped but feel in no way whole for the experience.

"This is Vidarr, Ariastone. His nephew, Farrell, is the nighttime gaoler," explains Eschereon. I nod.

"I'll say your nephew is a fair man, Vidarr. And he made my stay less harsh than it need be. He is also the unwitting source for the knowledge and hope I had for my breakout." The old man just gives me a knowing smile and says no more.

Half a turn later, the moon breaks from the thick clouds for a bit and lights our way up the river. We are in the roiling waves to the center of the waterway where the deep current moves swift.

"There!" Eschereon's voice enthusiastic as he points straight across the bow.

The moon's light has overtaken that of his staff that I have been holding out over the bow. Against the horizon, a sleek cutter's silhouette appears. We are headed directly for it, and a collective sigh arouses among us. Just as quickly, the clouds overtake the moon once more and it disappears into the darkness. But it gives Sæm and Alænèa fresh vigor on the oars, and an impression for Eschereon to steer towards.

Hands aboard are waiting to throw us a line a while later as they too had seen Eschereon's light slowly making its way to them. With rope secured about my chest in a makeshift sling, the crew pulls me aboard as I am in no shape to climb aboard of my own accord. A mate is assigned to the skiff and safe return to shore for Vidarr. The sailor will be left behind. In near silence, sails are hoisted and quickly catching the winds. We are headed out to sea. Though no moon or stars to navigate by, the ship's captain clearly knows these waters and has us advancing at a remarkable clip.

"We travel direct to open sea for the first of the trip, as I have no doubt the king's counselor will have ordered all vessels detained and searched. We most like would never had made the docks if we were afoot. The moonless night in this impending storm favors us. Let us hope our luck holds." Eschereon settles deeper into his seat.

Sitting now in the captain's cabin around a small table, we are discussing a further plan. I am grateful to these three of which I hold no memory. Sæm speaks next.

"Arias, I apologize as this whole affair is likely my fault. Here then, take back your mœther's amulet and replace it about your neck."

Sæm passes an intricate piece with a unique stone at its center. A glowing white with the sparkle of many other colours seems to flow within it. I quirk my head not understanding. Eschereon recognizes my confusion and explains.

"Arias, your mœther sent that amulet with you a dozen years past. The runes woven into its setting form a ward about its wearer, making him invisible to mægical sight. Seers cannot penetrate its veil and thus it offers protection should a seer turn his or her sight towards you."

It does not clear things up for me as I do not understand why I am sought after. I say as much.

"We must find a way to heal your mind and regain your memories. Though it no doubt saved you in the presence of Mensæ, it will be a danger to you now." Eschereon wears a mask of worry.

"I think I might have a solution, Eschereon." Alænèa glances first to the druid then back to me. "Arias, delve into your *Knowing* and see if it helps"

I return her insightful plan with a blank look upon my face, sure certain. Sæm comes to my rescue.

"Arias, you taught all of us a technique to calm one's body, mind, and spirit and once achieved, you reached a state in which all things become clear and the way forward is evident. A mentor taught it to you as the *Calming* but since, you have come to call it the *Knowing*."

"Well, if it will be of help, you'll need to teach me as I have no memory of such a thing."

"Aye. I can do that. Let us find a place topside and get comfortable, Arias."

We've outrun the storm, and the night is now temperate and breezy with the full moon dominating the sky amongst a myriad of stars. The sails are full, and Sæm and I make our way and find a spot on deck. He against the fore mast and I under and betwixt the gunwales at the bow. We are close enough to each and the other to hear anything above a whisper but far enough away to feel a personal space to take in the beauty of the night. After the three fortnight I spent in a box and then in the Bowels beneath Kings Court, I feel an exhilaration and freedom tenfold. The furions sneak up into my lap and curl there.

"Take in a few deep breaths, Arias, and relax as much as you might."

Sæm speaks to me now in a broken cadence as I listen to the rhythmic clang of metal hooks and leather bindings upon the sails. They bang a beat against the backdrop of the sea lapping against the bow, and I watch as the moon creeps lazily across the sky. Sam takes me to the *Calming*…the *Knowing* they had said I named it now, and I know it now…and again.

There I take in the world about me and as I do, Sæm comes into my line of sight again. And I know him now. Then I am swamped in a sea of memories sharp and clear. Sights and sounds and smells of my life past. Sam and Alænèa and Eschereon. And then the rest as well… and the death of Da and my entire quest to find the druid. Then there is Finnie and my eyes fill with moisture and a tear leaps to my cheek from overflowing lid. My heart swells then aches then settles again. My life returns to me.

A cool wind hits me then, or it is the thought and more recent memory that does the chilling. They are not my memories either but Mensæ's. They play before me as if my own. His recent summit with six compatriots from a far away land. Glimpses and bites of sounds and spoken word in parts and pieces that do not all make sense. But a slaughter there of a family on his command. A rolling back to some forty years passed and his arrival upon the shores of Aeryth with the same group and one more asides. A little further back the memories spread, an ugly scene of murder invades my mind of his command ship during the raid my grandsire, the king, did repel. Finally, a fear instilled within his very bones by an elder he named Běelzel, an evil master of mind mægic.

My forehead furrows and I come awake from my *Knowing* and stare at Sæm.

"I must speak with Eschereon, Sæm. Your trick worked and in the *Knowing* of it, a terror has taken hold, so I do not know if I should thank you." My hand reaches to his shoulder.

He but nods, and we make our way under boom and around mast, high stepping rigging to the stair leading back below decks in search of the druid. With a last look at the wide night sky, a sigh escapes me as we go below. We find the druid in our shared cabin, his nose in a tome reading from some ancient scribe's hand. He looks up and swings about from his bed hammock and meets me at the cabin's small table. Alænèa hears us approach from above and joins us now.

There is little room for the four of us, and we are bent of neck to stand upright save Alænèa, so she finds a spot to lean against the bulkhead as Sæm slumps into a hammock. Eschereon and I sit on small stools on either side of the small table nailed to the deck.

"Eschereon, Sæm had the right of it and my mind has recaptured my memories, including some from my inquisitor, Mensæ."

His eyebrows raise.

"And how is that possible?"

I had never disclosed my time with Finnie. And this is my first chance to discuss my experiences in the Bowels.

"His verbal queries went nowhere, of course, as I had no memories that he could force from me and he believed it so, I think. But he has other methods. He tried several times to... I know no other way to describe it, but to say he tried to force his mind onto my own. To probe mine with his."

Eschereon sits up straight to the hearing of this.

"You recognized that he was attempting this?"

"I've had some experience with my connections with Bane, the furions, and Talon. Joining with their spirit selves is not un-similar. But this was different. And he could not accomplish the task and became quite frustrated as if he'd not encountered such denial before. I believe my amulet the cause of his failure as it warmed upon my chest with each of his attempts." And I reach for the amulet picked up from the tinker several moons ago.

Eschereon pulls at his beard, stroking it in contemplation of this news. "There is more."

"You purposely let him in." A statement not a question on his part.

"Yea... In his previous attempt, I glimpsed a few memories of my own. He had in some manner broken through the barrier that had kept me from my own memories...and I wanted more."

"So, even as he was now seeing your memories, you were seeing his?" I nod.

"And when he realized it, both he and his mind revolted in disgust... and fear."

I then tell Eschereon of the memories of Mensæ's that I had experienced. He listens attentively, concern growing across his face though he attempts to disguise it. I've become more adept at reading such things. My friends have as well.

"This man that hails from distant lands that attacked at the very heart of Aeryth is now advisor to the king? How is this possible, and what does it mean, Eschereon?" Sæm speaks up, no longer swinging in his hammock but hanging on my every word.

"I have some idea as to the 'how' of it, and the consequences could be most dire, I fear. We should get some rest now, especially you, Ariastone. If you indeed have regained your memories, then other talents are there for the awakening as well. You are an excellent healer and should turn your efforts to healing yourself. You will need your utmost strength in the suns to come, I fear. I must take some time to cypher and ponder what you have told me."

He rises and make his way out of the small cabin, searching for more air and room to think proper. We have just been left in typical Eschereon fashion. Told a bit but left wanting. The three of us stare about at each and the other, all thinking just that, sure certain. Alænèa is the first to speak now.

"The druid has the right of that last part, Arias. You need rest and healing." I nod, and they remove themselves from the cabin, ducking through the narrow cabin portal, pulling the door to behind them, and leaving me to settle into a hammock. My furion friends join me, curling together aside me.

In a thrice, my further knowledge and memories restore and allow me now the insight to do it. I sink into the *Knowing*, willing my subconscious to take up the task of accelerating the healing of my body and to ponder on Mensæ.

Three suns hence, I again sit naked astride a stool with sudsy water about my feet, a large bucket of sea water afore me and soap and wash linen in either hand even as I had done the three suns prior. The chill of the morn invigorates on my mostly healed body, the clang of the rigging, the flap of the sails, and the lap of the waves ever-present about me. Once again I attempt to scrub the stench of my captivity from myself. I hear Eschereon approach from behind, knowing him by his scent and sound or lack thereof, he being always quite stealthy. I turn to his approach.

"I will still be hunted, won't I?"

"Not just you, Ariastone. Not now. We must make immediate plans upon our return to Esper."

13

A Way Uncertain

We make our way to Esper and the druid's keep before the end of a
fortnight near mid-moon cycle. It is now not more than a crescent
and gives less light than the surrounding myriad of stars. Bane meets us at
the gates, pacing to and fro as we approach, and Talon circles above in the
night sky, letting me know he is there, screaming out his remarkable echoing fight cry. I had reached out to each of them the morn after regaining my
memories and found each unsettled as they had lost the spiritual connection
we shared while my mind and memories had been aimlessly lost and thus
cutting in two our ever-present link.

I dismount and Bane comes to me, jumping up to place his front legs
about my shoulders in an almost human hug, his weight substantial. He
lets out a contented growl deep in his throat. He is taller than me now in
the effort. I bury my head into his fur. I feel the same. My gang of creature
friends are whole again and I feel, at the least and in some measure, safe for
a time. He does not leave my side as we enter Esper.

The common tasks of caring for Paint soothe me at the stables that
night. Bane lies in the straw of the stables watching me, Lilit and Jilly
curled beside him. His copper and gold eyes are intent on my every action,
satisfying himself I am fine. When I return to the keep, he follows. I sleep
a deep, sound, and worryless sleep that night with Bane at the foot of my
bed, the first in two moons.

Eschereon brings us together in his library seven suns after our arrival back to Esper. After mornmeal, Sæm, Alænèa, Therrien, and myself are gathered to hear him. He has sequestered himself away these passed suns in a flurry of activity and reading histories.

"I must put off for a time your training, Ariastone, and Eshæm and Alænèa as well. Your capture and the tale of it recited by you has made a great difference. I have sent a magpie off to a friend, and he will organize a meet to discuss how we must proceed." Eschereon looks studied and intent. A seriousness about him I've never seen before. He paces slowly across then back about the chamber.

The druid and Giorgi have trained his birds, even as the king used ravens, to carry messages across Aeryth to close friends. They are maggies, though Giorgi renamed them magpies for their love of his wife's pies.

"It is my intention to leave before three days hence, and I would greatly suggest you all do the same. It will not be safe here for the foreseeable future."

Though his demeanor remains grave, my spirits are lifted, as I think it finally time to return home and to Finnie. My thoughts drift there, but Eschereon looks to me and I know he is about to dash my hopes.

"Ariastone, though you wear your mœther's amulet and it protects you from the king's *sight,* he will be guarding your old homestead awaiting you and will double his efforts. Any attempt to return there at this time would be folly and put your friends at risk."

A tightness grips my chest at the thought of putting Finnie and the youngers and my dear friends back in Middenvale to danger. I sigh.

"Where would you have me go, Eschereon, and why not with you?"

He leans back against the firebox mantle and crosses his arms. A great raven alights upon the sill in an open window across from us and looks in upon our group. All eyes turn to it in the moment and it flies away once again. The druid's brow furrows as he turns back to us.

"Your memories stolen by Mensæ, Ariastone. They are the reason we must remain separate."

"I don't understand, Eschereon."

Sæm, ever quick to these things, has already cyphered the answer.

"You said your memories were of Eschereon at the time, Arias, so the king, when he cannot find you, will turn to who you know. Did you also lose memories of us to him? If so, we will be of danger to you as well." Sæm explains, and panic falls upon my shoulders to think I have endangered all of my friends. I think back to my encounter with Mensæ.

"Nay, he had put the idea of a druid deep to thought with all his queries of them. When he prised open my memories it was furions and Eschereon that occupied my thoughts and hence memories of them sprang upon me. The meeting on the bridge, and then his one on one teachings to me. It is chilling to think he holds these same memories, even as I hold his."

"And he will use them to solicit a *seeing* of you and I from the king. From those, he will cypher our whereabouts. You have an amulet from your mœther to guard against this, I do not." I find his comment disturbing, but it also niggles at my brain for some reason. Alænèa catches and expresses it first.

"But Eschereon," she says. "It was Mensæ that stole Arias' memories. He is a seer like the king. Why would he need to involve the king?"

Eschereon leaves the mantle, crosses the few paces back to the table and presses his long fingers to the tabletop, leaning towards us.

"Because *he* is not a seer, but much worse."

His statement hangs before us, puzzled looks all around.

"He is a mæge of some power, I believe. But if he is who I think, he is not a seer. Rather, one who can steal the *sight* dreams from the king and pass them off as his own with the king none the wiser. He is a dangerous man. To you, Ariastone, to me, and more importantly, the whole of Aeryth, if I have the truth of it."

"If I'm not to go with you and cannot return home. Where is it you would have me go?"

"To a place you three can remain safe, and more importantly, where you can learn more of this threat and therefore how we might battle it. I am suggesting you return to the Plain within the Poppy Sea. And there, take further lesson from the Elder."

Shèlah, the Elder, and the Elder and great seer in Sæm's small village within the Northern Reaches, had tried to tutor me of some monstrous evil mægic that existed across the great Southern Sea. Wielded by mæges set on holding cruel dominion over all that exist in the world. But their stories were from two millennia past and myths of the ancient mægics that no longer existed in Aeryth these suns. Well, strictly speaking, they did exist. I'd seen the proof of it with my own eyes. And these past six moons, I had even practiced them here with the druid. Could these old legends hold any truth today? Eschereon seems convinced they are truth and even now a dire danger to us.

I just then notice that the others have turned to me.

"You would have me hide away, Eschereon. And what will you do?"

"Not just hide away but learn more and grow your abilities with practice with the others. I've gathered some reference tomes for the each of you to take with you." He points to a stack of books piled upon the table.

"The elders will have other knowledge that will be of use. I mean to travel and consult with others like myself. I carry wards that will protect me to some extent from a seer's mægic, and I will be ever on the move, which will be the greatest protection, I believe."

"I will travel with you, Arias. I found the Effleæn a fascinating people and can learn much more from them." Sæm states and studies what Eschereon has found for us, but Alænèa is hesitant.

"I've just escaped from the Plains. Must we go back?" she asks.

"Think of it not as a prison, Alænèa, as you know the way out now. Think of it rather as home and a place you can seek solace from time a'times." After a moment, she nods. A sigh escapes me as I acquiesce as well. My heart aches that I cannot travel to *my* home even as Alænèa wishes she could stay away from hers.

Three suns hence find us in the stables preparing for our departure, packing our camp gear, Eschereon's loaned books, and travel food enough for a few suns. I need another trip up to the keep to fetch my pack and weapons.

Having met the druid there at the stables, we are shocked at who we find. He has cut his long beard near to nothing and trimmed his hair back as well. He looks a great deal the younger for it and most assuredly different. Trading out his simple cap of runes, he now wears a wide brimmed hat with a conical crown and an old weatherworn cape with a hood to it. He has a great leather satchel and a wide strap to drape over his shoulder and across his chest. He carries his staff. His other garb simple, he reminds me of someone from my past. The stableman had left to a large old shed aside the barn, and is returning now upon a wagon. A tinker's wagon! And that is what Eschereon reminds me of, a tinker!

He will travel in disguise it is clear. And one that he has apparently employed in the past.

"A wonderful deception, Eschereon. You look the part most authentic."

"Ha, and rightly so. I have plied my craft in this trade for countless years, traveling the whole of Aeryth as a respected tinker, mind."

We all just shake our heads in wonderment. All but Therrien. The druid's scribe knows, of course.

"A last word before I leave, Ariastone. Heed and take care. Mensæ will most assuredly come hunting you now that he has some knowledge of your abilities and you are a dire threat to him in what you know. Though you have some protection from his mind mægic with your tinker's amulet, and a true Wic'cha's crafted work, I believe. Your companions do not have the same, and Mensæ could and will attack them with his mind mægic."

"Wic'cha?" My eyes narrow to him even as I reach for the amulet under my tunic and sitting next to my mœther's trinket.

"Study the tomes, the three of you. They hold some answers. Old knowledge that may be of some aide to you."

The stableman's help opens the gates, and Eschereon climbs atop his wagon. A snap of his rein and a clip of his tongue gets two stout grey mares moving forward and we watch as he starts his way down the main travelway through Esper and towards its only gate.

Myself, I head back up to the druid's keep to gather what remains there. My pack and weapons are in Eschereon's private study at the top of the far tower, as he met me earlier to show me again his great map of Aeryth, carved into a huge wooden table, pointing out where he is first headed.

"Arias," he had said and this drew my attention immediately to him, as he had addressed me casual which is unusual for him. He always calls me Ariastone, and Sæm buy his given name as well, so when he'd used Arias, it caught my attention of a sudden.

"One other thing before we part. I know you have given some thought to your mœther since you have arrived here. I do not know for certain if she even lives, but her and your pæder had once discussed traveling to his home for her safety." He pointed to an island in the mouth of the great inner sea.

"They call it Asgährd, and it is near impossible to reach on seas always roiling without the aide of a seafaring captain from the very island." I slipped the information away to the back of my mind. With the further preparations for our departure, I had left my things there.

Having arrived back to his study, picking up my pack and staff, and all that was left for me to gather, I turn to leave and notice Eschereon's great spy glass sitting on a tripod stand at the window where he would a'times look up to the moon or out across the valley. Drawn to it, I meander over and turn it in a direction across Esper's front gate. I put my eye to it, hoping to see the druid's wagon. I do and then stiffen.

I have to swirl the knob as he had shown me, but when I do, what I first see gives me further pause. The travelway out from Esper meets a crossway, mayhaps a half league out. There sits the tinker wagon and a dozen coal black horses about it. Another rider sits aways from the others grouped about the wagon. All the riders wear black and Mensæ's personal guards come immediately to mind. Worry for the druid crowds my thoughts, and I watch further. After about a quarter turn of a sand glass, the riders break away, leaving the wagon to go on its way. But then they turn directly towards me, or rather, the road to Esper.

Pulling back from the spy glass, I begin to run. As quick as I am able, I make my way through the keep and then out onto the druid's stone abode in the mountainside. As I exit, Bane rises to meet me on the track down to Esper. I redouble my pace now. Even as I turn towards the stable entrance, I glance back in the direction of the towne gates. I can make out riders.

Running into the stable barn, the others are gathered, their horses saddled and ready. I push the barn doors closed and gesture them to me, and we gather at the back of the stable barn in the tack room.

"They are here. I saw them through Eschereon's spy glass as they met his wagon on the travelway. They did not recognize him and left after a parley. And then they turned and headed this way. They most likely are entering the stable yard as we speak." Therrien goes off to the doors and peers out betwixt them. He turns and nods to us.

"We will need to hide in here. There is no back exit to the stables," he says upon returning.

We search about and quickly satisfied that he spoke the truth of it.

"They are a dozen, and I believe Mensæ is with them. Pætyr will send them up the hill and then we will slip out."

This would have been a reasonable scheme, but two of the dozen stay behind at the stable gates. I feel certain we can handle these two, but it will not solve the problem as the others are sure to overtake us as we try a further escape. As I mull our choices, Alænèa calls to me. Returning to the tack room, she points to the back wall where she has pulled down reins and some miscellaneous saddlery. She sees something I cannot. Sæm steps up behind me.

Back at the barn doors, Bane paces in front of the doors with a low growl in his throat. The furions stand on the tack table, their heads swiveling from Bane to me.

"Your *Knowing,* Arias." And I recognize her meaning. Alænèa can most times see the aura of mægical items that I cannot see without immersing into my *Knowing* state. I go there now. Behind me, I sense Sæm doing the same.

Of a sudden, looking back to the stone wall at the back at the stables, clear as day, ancient rune lettering appears on the wall. Sæm approaches, running his fingers over the phrasing etched in mægic up the wall.

"The first says, 'Speak the words open me to descend… Then on the second line a word I do not recognize but can sound it out…and finally, 'take care not to tary,' it says."

After a couple of attempts, Sæm sees nothing happening.

"Arias, you try."

I study the phrasing. Like Sam, I can read the runes in the ancient language Eschereon has been tutoring us these past six moons. Like him, I do not recognize the one word, but feel Sæm has been pronouncing it correctly. I try twice with no further luck.

Then, I read it slowly to myself once more and try something different.

"Osha tà da vessèlas" I speak. Of a sudden the wall sighs and blows a fine dust in a great arch back at us.

"Ha! Arias, you spoke the full phrase and not only the word. Brilliant."

We all the three of us approach the wall and push. It does not take much. The wall swings inward, opening to a large cavern with a soft sand floor. There are two passageways to the back of chamber.

"Let us gather the horses swiftly, hide within, and close the door. It appears this is an exit through the mountain, but we will need to decide which path."

When I turn, the others are already busy, and Therrien stands before me with a saddled horse, reins in hand and Paint, with Lilit and Jilly sitting atop aside to them.

"I will not be safe here, Arias, and can be of much help. I've read the histories as much as scribed them. I would for once live them, rather than just scribe the tales from the druid. Take me with you." I nod.

We enter and I draw light mægic to my Bo staff, as Eschereon had taught me. The cavern brightens to it as the others push the wall closed again. We look about and take stock. We have everybody and all of our supplies.

"Well done, Alænèa. You likely saved us all with your discovery."

"A team effort, Arias. As Sæm said, your speaking the phrase and not just the word was key."

"The last line said not to tary, Arias. I believe we are meant to continue with haste." I nod.

"We have two paths to choose from. Which shall it be?" Therrien paces from one to the other and finally speaks.

"To the right, I smell naught but mildew and staleness. But to the left, I hear the sea though very faint, but also smell a salt air."

We each do the same and are in agreement. Bane leads and we follow. The way begins to fall fairly steep from the start and is serpentine, with a switchback every hundred paces or so. It becomes evident immediately that this will not be a simple tunnel leading out to the side of the mountain. We are headed to the sea. This concerns me as I had visited the cliffs overlooking the sea with Eschereon. He mentioned that the keep stood safe from the seaside as none could climb the shear cliffs for a hundred leagues in either direction. And that is where we are headed.

As we descend, I ponder what the stableman will think when he enters the stables and not find us, only saddlery supplies scattered about the floor of the tack room having been removed from the wall. We have been traveling for over a turn when I start to notice a disturbance. A rumbling. The last line on the wall comes back... Do not tary.

"Quickly now! Run!" I yell. I watch as Jilly and Lilit climb Bane's back and hang like possum cubs to their mum. Bane bounds down the tunnel. The ground starts to shake, and I send Paint ahead at a gallop. The other horses follow. Alænèa runs in graceful leaps and bounds in spite of the quacking ground, but Therrien cannot find his feet. We hear great cracking sounds as if the walls themselves are wailing. Sæm and I approach Therrien from either side and lift him as we run. We run with him until he gains his feet.

Only moments later but feeling like an eternity, we bound out of the tunnel and into a huge cavern so that I cannot light it all. The animals and Alænèa have found their way to a side wall well away from the tunnel. We head their way even as an avalanche of boulders, rock, and rubble rumble into the cavern. Great splashes are heard, and I point my staff to the sound of it and will more mægic to the drægons tooth end of it. Ten paces forward, the rock tumbles into a deep pool.

The others make their way to me to gather in the light. All have survived with only minor scrapes and scratches. Looking back, the entire tunnel looks to be filled with the stone. Panning the staff around we see no way out of the cavern, but the far end remains dark as I cannot make the light reach it. After the horses are completely settled, we decide to explore further. We have not traveled fifty paces when we come upon three oaken barrels. Atop them sit four lanterns of a design I've never seen. I could not make out any reservoir for oil, nor wicks to set alight.

Examining them more closely reveals reflecting glass laid within the body, forming four quadrants set to reflect outward. Crystals are mounted both in the top and bottom of the casing, and the whole of the lantern is encased in the most perfect glass work I've ever seen. It takes the shape of an elongated bubble with a lid and bottom made of some very light metal and a handle afixed to the top. A simple knob with for spokes adorn the bottom. I twist it a half turn to see if it opens to allow oil to be poured into the lamp. A hidden reservoir mayhaps.

I near drop it as the crystals come to life and a most brilliant light emanates from the lamp. The three others each pick up a lantern for themselves and do as I had. The light seems as bright as a small sun! Shining them around, we notice others hanging from hooks anchored into the walls. Therrien walks back and turns one on in the corner where the horses are gathered. I look forward.

There before me, floating majestic and still, is a galleon. A smaller one, mayhaps, but it looms large before us. It carries three masts and will easily carry a crew of a dozen with plenty of room in a cargo hold from the look of it. My mind grapples with such a vessel sealed in a cavern with no way out. Approaching along its starboard side, Alænèa, behind me, is drawn to a line of a dozen thirty-gallon barrels stacked against the wall while the furions bound up a gangplank.

14

Escape to Sea

æm and I raise our lanterns high to shed more light to the sizeable ship. There are two gangways actually. A smaller one for foot traffic up to the deck, and another larger, that leads into the ship's hold. Two great hold doors are swung open from top of bulwark to mayhaps two paces above the waterline. The deck above likewise raises open for a few paces back from the gunwales like the hinged tops to a covered basket. Like nothing I've ever seen on the docks of Seas End or Cliffside, it looks a most efficient way to load cargo.

Alænèa calls to us as we are headed up the gangway leading to the deck.

"Everything here is labeled with ancient runes, Sæm. Come help me cypher their meaning. These two on the wall I know… *Torhè Lässa…*"

As she speaks the ancient words represented by the runes, crystals embedded in the ceiling of the cavern come to life and the massive chamber becomes sunlit it seems. Colours come to life about us. The water a deep azure, and the ship mahogany and teak. The walls of the cavern shine grey but marbled here and there with emerald or amber. All of it a wonder. I continue up the gangway to explore the ship.

"Did Eschereon ever speak of this, Therrien?"

"Nay, not a word. And there is nothing in the histories of the keep either. I am gobsmacked to think this sat below the keep unknowing. How old is it?" His eyes dart unceasingly here and there. He proposes an interesting query.

I head to the stern and the hatch to the captain's cabin below. The deck holds no dust, no grime, no wear. It appears just built and recently cleaned. I am relieved to hear a squeak as I turn the hatch dog-levers, a more normal sound in this otherwise perfect ship. Everything about the vessel seems to me sleeker and more efficient than the common ships I've seen and been upon.

Descending the stairway and into the companionway, I step forward to a doublet of doors adorned with thick coloured glass in a nautical scene, clearly leading into the captain's quarters. The door itself a work of art. Entering, I become only further amazed. A small desk sits to one side under starboard port holes, the light from the crystals outside streaming in like rays of the sun. Two chairs and a small settee of fine wood and leather arrange around a low table sat against the port sidewall. In the center of the room, a map table holds great parchments with detailed navigation maps. Barely a dusty mote floats in the light beams streaming in.

At the map, my finger trails to the legend and a date there. 626 A.A. This means nothing to me, but Therrien had followed me into the cabin and sees where my finger lay, contented.

"Mæge dating," he says, and I turn to him questioning.

"Eschereon explained to me that those that first crossed the sea brought the first written records as well. They are even the ones to name this land what we call it today, Aeryth. The A.A. signifies the year they arrived as the first year. Aeryth Arrivatè. Hence, 626 A.A. The king's dating is different, however, and begins with the royal family's first ascension to the throne, or K.A. King's Ascension."

"Eschereon further explained that '1 K.A.' coincides with 1807 A.A. So, that would make these charts…1,181 years old." I feel my left eyebrow raise incredulously, but it soon settles as I've learned prior the unlikeliness of the ancient mægics are but prejudices within my mind.

"1,181 years. Their mægic must have been a powerful force in this world. Their lanterns still work. Their wards and mægic guised runes still hold out the centuries. I am in awe."

Sæm and Alænèa have joined us along with the furions. They have hopped unto the captain's desk, and Lilit is examining a brooch. She sits upon a captain's journal. While the others study the maps, I walk to the desk and slide the journal from under Lilit. The two are captivated by the brooch. It appears to be a folding of rope crafted in gold with a twist of elven vine laced about it, and the plant's blossom at its center is represented by small cut emeralds.

Pulling the captain's chair away from the desk, I settle into it. Opening the journal, I realize immediately that it will take some time to translate. The flowing script is written in the ancient tongue of the mæges. As I look up, I spy Alænèa studying the captain's brooch with the furions. Apparently, the women are all about the jewelry.

Sæm lifts the journal from my hands.

"Therrien and I will work on cyphering this, Arias. It's likely to hold clues we will need. Oh! And Alænèa pointed out that runes on the far wall are key to our further escape." Alænèa looks up at the mention of her name and addresss me as well.

"Arias, the barrels outside are sealed with rune wards. I opened one and found corn grain. When I offered it to the horses, they accepted it heartily!"

More wonder. But my mind has not left our ultimate purpose. To escape Mensæ and his guard. I've known their hospitality once and am not of a mind to repeat the experience.

"Let us look to the runes upon the cavern wall. It would be nice to know we can make further our escape." All in agreement, we retreat from the captain's cabin and return topside to study Alænèa's discovery.

I, Alænèa and Sæm have begun to call the ancient language associated with the runes mægish, as Eschereon began to teach it to us. It seems most appropriate and we cannot find otherwise what they called themselves. Alænèa points the writing out to us, and as I unconsciously slip into the *Knowing*. The runes appear instantly before me.

Therrien, the most practiced in the language, cannot see what the three of us can, so it falls to Sæm, being the most practiced of us three, to translate.

"Captain, prepare your…vessel, know your desire…and you shall be free to pursue it."

"Are you sure that is what it says, Sæm? Is this some sort of riddle?"

Sæm discusses what he sees with Therrien, and the scribe agrees with the translation. It puzzles me though.

"We, of course, want to be free from this cavern. That seems simple enough." Everyone nods in agreement.

"Well, let us get started then. What is next?" My growing anxious mood shows, sure certain.

Alænèa leans back against the boom of the mainmast, a studied look upon her face. The furions are less serious and run back then forth across the boom, enjoying their new playground. Bane has found a spot to sprawl atop the captain's cabin. Alænèa seems to be studying the wolf.

"Arias, Eschereon has tutored us that most often these wards are very specific and indeed literal in their meaning. Though sometimes riddled, one must consider all of the specific parts. I believe first we must have a captain, and so I nominate you to that post."

She looks to Sæm and Therrien, and they say in unison, "Agreed."

I nod and immediately feel an added weight. Even though I have led them in most things these many moons, to have such an official title sets a deeper responsibility to my part in their lives. It had been easier being just their friend. I smile regardless.

"Then my first official order to my crew is to fulfill the second part. Let us prepare our vessel. And first to that end, I name her…but wait, Therrien, Sam, is there a name on her bow or stern?"

They scramble to check and returned to state the negative.

"Then as captain, I name this finest of ships *Odyssey*." The three of my crew give out a cheer, and I feel it done. "Next, let us examine these many barrels and load them now. Let us tend to the horses and get them aboard and settled as well."

The remainder of the morn we keep busy with these tasks. With the gangways raised and the hull doors closed and secured, the four of us, Bane, and the furions once more aboard, we sit for a mid-sun meal from the travel stores brought with us.

When ready, Therrien helps me with the phrasing of my 'desire.' Standing at the helm of the galleon, I turn to the vast cavern wall across from the bow. The ward runes glow with their mægic and I read them again to myself…

'Captain, prepare your vessel, know your desire, and be free to pursue it.'

I speak the words as Therrien has prepared for me. Nothing happens. I speak them again, louder…to the same result. I glance to Sæm as he shrugs. I frown for a moment and look to Sæm as he stands next to me at the helm. He has grown this past year and now stands a half hand taller than I. He has a strong air and confidence about him and looks more the more like my da, broad of shoulder and thick of arm. And intelligent.

"A moment, I have a thought."

And then I leave the helm and return to the captain's cabin. There I find the brooch that had laid over a thousand years on the captain's journal. Making my way back to the helm, I address Sæm.

"Sæm. My thought is that I am not the right man for this role. I've led and taught you near to a year now. I've seen you grow, and I am a good judge of your abilities. I've worked with you aboard another sailing vessel.

You were a natural and that captain would have made you his first mate after a handful of suns and claimed you could judge wind and sail better than even he. Call me admiral to our new found fleet if you like, but you are best suited as captain aboard the *Odyssey*."

I pin the brooch to his cloak's collar. The jeweled elven vine and its blossom glow bright, and I can see a warmth overcome him. I know now I have the right of it. And for all to hear…

"Eshæm Bearheart, I do hereby commission the *Odyssey* into your hands." A wide smile spreads across his face, and he takes me into a hug worthy of his name. Then in a low voice, "Sæm, it says to know your desire. You have no need to speak it."

The brooch still glows. Sæm turns to the cavern wall, and I wonder his desire. Still nothing. No change. The cavern remains still, the waters calm. Sæm contemplates then speaks.

"Arias, Therrien, cast off the bow and stern lines. We can be no more ready than that." As we do, the boat slowly drifts from its 1,181 year mooring. I stare back at the glowing runes and wait.

He breathes in deep and settles, calming himself and falling into his *Knowing*. I see the signs. I know it has become only thoughts and perceptions to him now, taking all things in about him, processing. Then it happens.

A humming fills my body. No, it comes from without. The ship itself is vibrating and the waters about it ripple. The humming grows and is a rumbling now, and I feel the others stiffen to the thought of how we'd arrived into the cavern. The cavern wall afore us of a sudden slumps in great pieces into the water. We are staring out into blue skies and azure water for a moment before the sea level outside of the cavern plummets and the waters about us rise up so that I fear the masts will crash into the cavern ceiling. They don't. Instead, the waters swell behind the galleon and propell it forward with an indomitable force.

The rumbling becomes thunder now and as we look back to the sound, we watch as the cliffs reclaim the cavern. Filling it. The opening no longer exists, a sheer cliffside all that can be seen. We are already well out into the sea and riding a wave even still. Cheers burst from us all around and Sæm's face is alight with pride. With a slap on his back, I say,

"Well done, Captain. Now it's for us to discover just how to sail this ship! It appears more advanced than Poon's trader we apprenticed on. Just look at this helm. Aside the rudder wheel there are three others. And what are these squeeze levers that disappear into the deck?"

"If I were to guess, Arias, I believe the three smaller wheels may somehow control the boom sails. We will need to play with the squeeze rods to see their purpose." I nod. He has already begun cyphering how to captain his new charge.

I happen to look back to shore and the cliffs. A niggling in my mind pulls my eyes there, and then higher. What I notice sends a chill crawling about my spine. There, fifty poles high upon the ridge overlooking the sea, sits a dozen riders in black, each astride a coal black warhorse. Two riders sit apart from the others. One I feel sure certain to be my new nemesis in life, Mensæ. There before me in a cylinder made for it, a spy glass sits behind the rudder wheel.

Sæm has not noticed them yet, but with my grasping for the spy glass, he turns to see. Putting it to my eye, I peer up to the cliffs. Staring back at me through his own spy glass, Mensæ looks pensive.

"Now might be a good time to learn how this ship works, Arias. Each mast has two wheels at the base used to raise the sails. Mayhaps you and Therrien could find out? The foremast would be the place to start." I smile. Sæm has fallen into his role as captain quite easily. As Therrien and I weave our way forward to the foremast, I look back to our hunters. Alænèa does the same from the bow of the boat.

15

A Change in Course

Sæm has captured the wind on our aching backs and arms in short order. And though the exercise proves strenuous, I find it easier than our
time aboard Poon's trader. Even with just the three of us to do the heavy
lifting. Both Alænèa and Therrien take to sailing life as if they were born
to it.

After we have a steady wind filling sails and have left Mensæ and
his guard well behind us, Therrien takes the helm with a little instruction
from Sæm and we three go below decks to tend the horses. Lilit and Jilly
do not bother to join us as the fun of climbing the masts and sliding down
the sails suits them more. Bane claims the bow, putting muzzle into the
breeze and every once in a while treats us to a great howl. I also feel a
sense of security as Talon has made an appearance with his mighty battle
cry. He circles thrice about the ship before winging on to other destina-
tions unknown to us.

All of us find our time on the sea exhilarating and for a time we let go of
the anxiety of the past three fortnight. The very night about us is in agreement as the winds die to less than a whispered breath and we are stilled on
the waveless water. No land can be spied in any direction and after a calm
after mid-sun resting upon the gently rocking deck, we take the time to
gather in our captain's cabin and sit to an evemeal of travel food and fish
caught from the sea. Then we make council.

"I would like to have a purpose other than a life of running from this false counselor to the king." I speak after swishing and swallowing a mouthful of aged mæge ale. We had earlier first opened and then resealed with their appropriate wards each of the casks and barrels we brought onboard before we departed Espers' secret cavern. A few hold ale of a taste none of us have ever encountered and have been aged for over a thousand years. With just the smallest cup, one would swear they can fly and sounds seem to have colour.

"Arias," Sam speaks up then. "I'd like to tell you what I held as my desire afore the cliffside spat us out to little fanfare."

The mæge ale has stolen away the last of my anxieties, and I find myself deep in the soft leathers and cushions of the captain's settee. We sense only the gentle rock of the boat on mostly still waters in this deep sea. Sæm and Therrien have, over the past three days, cyphered meaning to the sea charts and a device to read the stars above. They reckon we are floating near to the center of the north sea, equal betwixt the shores off the Mid Realm and the cliffs guarding the Northern Reaches. Going nowhere without a breeze.

Turning to Sæm, I raise my left eyebrow to his statement.

"And what would that be, Sam?" He gives me a dæmon's grin.

"Your mother, Arias. Let us not dwell on soldiers upon a clifftop. You confided that Eschereon once told you your Da, your blood Da as I'm meaning, more like than not took her to his home for protection from the king's sight. The isle of Asgährd, he told you. Well now, we have a ship, Arias. While this Mensæ searches the west for you, let us circle back to the isles. They are on the charts right here," he says, pointing at the charts afore him.

"Aye, Sæm, they are mayhaps. But the druid also said that only a seaman from those very isles could navigate the waters to their shores."

"Ahh, but we have a ship built by the mæges of olde. It carries devices and mægics of its own. With a fortnight's practice using them, I can get you there, Arias." His confidence in his ability and the ship's as well clear in his eyes.

"Eshereon also said that after connecting with the mind mæge mind to mind, he will always be able to find me."

"But he is headed west, Arias. Heading in the same direction well allow him to find you that much sooner. Let us make it more difficult for him, not less."

"The point is, he will find me in the end. If this is true, and my mother truly is alive and on the isles, I will be bringing the danger she fled near to two decades passed, direct to her."

"Mayhaps, but it will also be friendly ground with potential allies, and we can be waiting on him. Expecting him, not living in fear that he will appear in the night unexpected."

His arguments are sound and I am swayed. I hope he has the the right of it.

"Well then, I cannot deny my heart draws me there. Let us give it a try then. That is if, the sea winds ever return."

I feel a chill dread of my decision though.

The winds do return. Sæm captains us and learns the secrets of the vessel to the extent that he may just have been the most able of captains in this sea and on the finest ship, sure certain. He senses the winds no matter how fickle and rides the waves in any direction he desires. We but do his bidding as captain of the vessel. On the sixteenth sun out of the cliff's cavern, we turn east once more and then north.

The charts in the olde mæge captain's cabin clearly show our destination and with a reference rune placed within the isle upon the chart-map, Sæm and Therrien recognize there are special instructions for the approach to a bay on the north side of the island. The approach is to be precise and unerring to meet the only currents that will feed us safely into the mouth of the bay. Ever roiling seas and shipwrecking rocky spears lying in wait just below the water's surface everywhere but upon the charted path and for any that approach unaware.

We have ventured, upon Sam's learning the ship, well into the great inner sea, and now we are headed back. The charts instruct an approach following parallel to the cliff's lining the coast of the Northern Reaches, not a quarter league out and still well in sight of the sheer cliffs. We are two suns out from the most dangerous part of the trip depicted on the charts. As if to signal that same notion, the skies grow grey and seem a foreshadowing of the sea's expected action as they roil themselves, folding and swirling and liken to savage waves onto themselves. But the seas remain relatively calm this night despite the sky.

I awaken betwixt the gunwales at the bow on the morrow's morn. Bane holds vigil even then with muzzle to the wind sweeping over the bow. Lilit and Jilly are curled next to me on the deck, snuggled tight within the center of a coil of hemp rope. Standing to stretch out the tightness Sæm's captaining has inevitably forced upon my body, I join Bane and welcome the morning breeze with deep breaths and sighs back into the breeze, even as it lifts the hair from my shoulders. Alænèa joins me, handing me a large cornmeal muffin filled with centuries-old dates preserved by the mægic of those times. They bake up fresh, and the mornmeal treat is a wonder. Alænèa leans with back against the foremast and gazes out over azure waters and towards the cliffs as we pass silently by. As I study her, of a sudden she leans forward with a squint to her eye. Pointing now,

"Look, Arias. There upon the cliffside ahead. A wondrous carving in the stone. It must be as tall as the highest of our masts!"

Hand over my eyes guarding against the sun's rise against the horizon, I gaze to where she points now.

"A lion as near as I can make, and all of it carries an aura in blue even as deep as these waters. Quick, go alert Sæm and mayhaps we can study it closer up." She does not hesitate and she leaps and bounds with a surprising ease about her, over rigging and under booms, headed towards the helm and Sæm.

Moments later, he's released the brake to the mainsail and it drops. Then he starts barking orders to the three of us as he swings his vessel towards the cliff's magnificent sculpture in stone. As we near, the lion's relief becomes more apparent. With a moment's capture of a sightline that disappears almost instantly, I am sure I see a hooded figure carved deeper in and in lesser relief peering from behind and over the lion's back.

Sæm's control over his new toy seems complete as we slow and near the stone wonder. The sails are collapsed and sorted, and he yells to me to loose the anchor. We gather then, the four of us against the bulwark and stare in awe.

"Who could have carved such a sculpture in such realistic detail? It has the look of wanting to come alive even now." I examine the deeper shadows above the lion's back but cannot distinguish the hooded figure I'd seen earlier.

"And Arias, look to the runes that lay on the shield that the great cat guards with its paw. Therrien, we'll need your help in cyphering their meaning." Sæm's brow furrows in concentration as he studies that same thing.

"Aye, well you'll need to be drawing them as I see them not. Eschereon had the right of it. You three carry the deepest of the ancient mægics within you!"

"Arias, look there above the stone niche. Five ancient words, each letter glowing a deep indigo. They seem important above the rest somehow."

I notice them now. I can read their meaning as well, as their sounds resonate within my mind as if I am hearing them in Effleæn. The language of Alænèa's people has survived above all others from the time of the mæges.

Grasp Truth and Power Within

My thoughts immediately turn to Eschereon's lessons. "The mæges of olde were a crafty bunch," he had put it. "Ofttimes their messages were straight forward but then a'times they were riddles. And other times riddles within riddles. The game is afoot to cypher which. If you knew the history of the author, clues are available." I query Therrien.

"Have you seen writings of such sculptures, Therrien? Works that rise to the height of this very ship?"

"Art for the sake of artful expression alone would be rare in my experience of the writings by the olde mæges themselves except for works and commemoration of significant leaders among themselves. The olde ones were all about truth at all costs. Hence the fashion and life lived by the druids of today. I'm sure you've noted that Eschereon has never lied to you, though he has fashioned a guise to his words from time a'time."

We, the three of us, have noted this seeming fact. It certainly factored into our almost immediate trust of him. We have discussed it amongst ourselves. Even fashioning queries designed to test it. Eschereon never, as we could cypher, told an untruth to any of us. And though he either answered in a most circuitous manner or he changed the subject, oft leaving one unawares he had done it. He never lied.

So, riddles within riddles are not new to us. But then a'times what might seem a riddle, as it appears impossible to believe, in truth is not guile but a direct answer. Alænèa seems always best in cyphering Eschereon's truths. She said the clues lay in his expressions and manner. Both Sæm and I are adept at such things, but Alænèa the better. Eschereon the best. Therrien has more to say.

"I mentioned the olde mæges specifically as it would seem this is one of their works."

"How could you know such a thing, Therrien? Hundreds upon hundreds of years have passed with great craftsmen and artists living between then and now. The great carved obolisks guarding the river approach to Kings Court and just east of Bladestone. Sæm and I witnessed ourselves.

Themselves a wonder twice this size and they were crafted in this king's lifetime."

"The clue is in the work itself, Arias. Do you see a twisting image of a rainbow just under the rear hip of the beast? The image is one that dates to the earliest writing of and from the ancients."

The image is clear as it rests there just behind the rear paw of the lion, its aura even many coloured. So this great sculpture sure certain a memorial to some great mæge of olde.

"If this is a memorial to some great ancient, then Eschereon, I believe, would judge that there would be in the least something literal in the meaning of the runes."

Grasp Truth and Power Within

"Could there be more to this than just a sculpture in memorial? The runes reference a 'within.' Mayhaps likened to our frost cellar back home, there is an entrance into a cavern behind the sculpture? After all of it, we escaped little more than a fortnight ago from just such a place."

With my speaking it, our eyes make deep scrutiny of the carving before us. A magnificent crafting, the lion's body lies in an alcove, its great forepaw hangs out over the lip and rests against the cliffside wall. Further runes we do not readily understand are chiseled along a spearhead and upon a shield under its other great paw. We decide to give Therrien and Sæm time enough to research the great shield's runes. In the meanwhile, we attend the deck chores of any ship hands at Sæm's direction and then tend our horses below. Later, resting upon the raised topside doors to the forward hold, my eyes leave the huge carving and become entertained by the furions' antics about the masts and booms and rope rigging. None of us have visually seen any indication of a portal to any inner chamber of the cliff.

Alænèa is spending her time swimming at the moment, as Sæm has taught her more than she had learned on the Plains with her Effleæn tribe. To watch her makes for entertainment. Sea creatures approach from the deep to play. Great sea tortoises visit, and she rides upon their backs. And dolpheens, Poon had called them, leap from the depths just to play with her, nuzzling and swimming alongside her as well.

It has been an eventful sun, though as much as we stare upon the tremendous lion in his great niche abode, we discover no more til the sun has made half its journey to sunset. I sit with my back against the mainmast and in my *Knowing*. Bane lies belly against the deck, a constant pant with tongue lulled but for an occasional swipe about his muzzle. Lilit and Jilly are doing the same but splayed around the fore-boom, each of their noses pointed towards the great cat.

The hidden sun creeps from behind a cloud and a beam of light rolls slowly eastward down the cliff face finally crawling across the sculpted lion. As it does, it catches my attention as it shines upon the lion's tail from the west. The tail now appears jagged down its length. No longer smooth but falling in a stepped fashion... *Fates*! I rise and call to everyone.

"Look to the lion's hip! There are steps there climbing to its back. Sæm, can we sidle up to the wall?"

Sæm studies the sea about us.

"The depth does not appear to change from here to there, and if so, mayhaps it will be possible. We'll need all the dock buoys to protect the ship from the cliffside and then lean a ladder there up to the niche behind the lion. Oh, and by the by, we believe we have translated the runes upon the shield. They may be of some aide."

In less than a turn, we've accomplished the task and are following the furions up the ladder. Bane appears not happy to be left behind. Looking over my shoulder, I am not surprised that he paces the deck at the bottom of the ladder. We make our way up and into the space carved out of the stone cliff. It boggles me to think that men had carved such a space into the granite and while they were at it sculpted a great cat twenty times life-size replete with true to scale shield and spear to complement the beast.

Once in the open-air cave and next to the lion's tail, the stair becomes much more evident, though weatherworn over centuries. Each step to itself measures a pace in height, as if designed for men of a greater height than the tallest I've encountered in Sæm's village back home in the Northern Reaches. After ascending up and across the tremendous rump of the enormous cat, we find ourselves in a space that easily accommodates the four of us and would hold thrice our number again with room to spare. The sculpture an awesome feat of craft. The sculpture is not just face carved either. The sculpted detailing found on the cliff face continues back into the cave all the way to the inner wall-face. The great cat itself as long as our vessel.

The furions bound about the head of the lion as I sit back into its mane. Alænèa continues climbing about the sculpture, admiring the details and finding unexpected parts and pieces not able to be seen from its front.

"Well then, Sæm, what is it Therrien and you have cyphered from the runes on the lion's shield?"

"'Twas Therrien done most of the work, of course, but they clearly instructions of a sort. Therrien, mayhaps it would be best if you were to explain?"

"They are the words of the ancients as well, on the spear and shield, as those above the cave, but in the language of the Wic'cha of Asgährd, Arias. The isle of your pæder. It is as if the first a motto, the other instructions to those who might know to visit this as a memorial."

"And what do they say, Therrien?"

"The runes translate specifically... 'Speak that the king might hear. Say with will your desire to meet Ōdæn."

"And who is this Ōdæn?" I query the two of them, but Alænèa speaks. She has returned from her explorations to join our conversation.

"The Elder Shèlah always said Ōdæn gave birth to the idea of the Accadian Plain, my home, in the earliest days when he split the Effleæn of the Deep Wood and the Effleæn of the Plains. She's always referred to him as one of the original Source-Sayers, Arias."

Ancient mægii from distant lands across an unfathomable sea that I so readily discounted in my conversations with the elder in Sæm's home village and Shèlah of the Plains seem to come to play roles in my present destiny, and my companions' fates alike. I've learned that mægic is a true and definable and usable thing from the druid. And histories such as these are an ever-important part.

I think now on these words and their meaning and also Eschereon's lessons as regards the ancients. Ōdæn the king that we should shout at? And how can he possibly hear? Or am I to shout out across the sea to the present king, my grandsire? I have no desire to meet him or his emissaries in the near future. Pensive, I sit back into the carved stone mane of the great cat to cypher the further meaning. The furions are stirring up dust from who knows what past age, and Talon picks this very time to swoop past and share his piercing hunting cry as he did for stone watery prey. His shriek echoes forceful into the cavern such that I think the mighty lion beneath me would raise his paw to cover his ear just beside me and strike me down in the process. I glimpse the three others surely covering theirs in response. Then it strikes me, all that in the moment, what has just happened.

Rising, I look to the great beast's ear just aside me, the king of the beasts he is, and in mourning amongst his friend's battle implements just now. I would like to know this Ōdæn, and even mayhaps, learn more of his plan for me, if there is such a thing as so many claimed. I stand and speak my desire in the Effleæn tongue. It echoes loud.

In response, there comes a rumbling. Lilit and Jilly scramble to my ankles and the others approach, wondering what I have put in motion this time. It turns out to be a wise thing I have risen, for just where I had been sitting, the great cat's mane peels away and inward of a sudden, and a stair down into his head appears.

16

Ōdæn's Gifts

The furions for once are hesitant to be the first to advance into the unknown. I speak a spell at my ever-present Bo staff that I had learned from Eschereon. The same chant that he had used in my rescue from the Bowels. A light clung and grew about the drægons tooth end. We descend. I need not have bothered as when I just stepped off the stair, a glow spread from crystals embedded in the ceiling of the chamber we have entered, just as in the ship's cavern below Esper.

We have clearly entered the tomb of a respected leader. After centuries, the only dust in the chamber is what we ourselves bring in, and it hangs like a mist at sunset or tiny whisperflies floating in and out of our peripheral vision and catches of a sudden within the crystals' light. There are painted images and golden chalices and two huge chairs on either end of the chamber. One of gold with silver filigree with gems in every shape, size, and cut. The seat cushioned in a royal red velvet. The other a deep-seated lounge-style not unlike Eschereon's favorite library chair, of wood and leather and speaking of comfort. They both would leave my feet hanging well above the floor.

The room itself is oval in shape. Along one side are shelves of leather-bound tomes, and on the other sits a long stone shelf holding Ōdæn's forever bed, a stone and bronze coffin with iron feet resembling the paws and furred arms of a lion with claws extended. Runes run the length of its side facing the open room. A rich wood adorns the lower walls beneath the shelf and all around the chamber. It has a warm and comfortable feel, not unlike the library in Esper Keep. A luxuriously thick rug lies near the entire length of the room in its same shape. The only other thing in the room is a square marble cube, a pace to each side and black as the night with a glittering surface that emulates the night stars above. It appears to be a solid cube of the same material and cannot be budged a finger's width if all of us tried together. Nothing sits upon it.

Sounds of awe escape the lips of all of us as we examine the centuries-old chamber. Therrien and Sæm are drawn to the books, Alænèa to the runes upon the stone coffin. I am fascinated by the leather chair. Ofttimes over the past several moons I would retreat to the druid's abode in the mountain and sit upon his leather chair there in front of the large firebox and read or just ponder my travels since leaving Middenvale. Climbing into the chair, I sink deep into it and deeper into thought, falling naturally into my *Knowing*.

In the *Knowing*, I feel a connection to this place. As if I've sat in this very chair before, and my spirit self feels linked in some manner to another spirit being. I've known the feeling, having experienced it with Finnie. It feels very real and just now I experience the chamber through another's eyes... Or rather, he through mine. He studies my three companions, curious to their doings, reaching out to them with our mind. All three turn to me of a sudden, and stare wide-eyed. We have touched each of their minds but for a moment, and still I know the stranger within my mind knows each of my friends intimately now. I feel that this mind mægic is new to him, but he has sensed of in me and died not hesitate to is it. I experience the same with each of them. As with Mensæ, I touch on the stranger now as well, but he is able to keep his mind hidden from me for the most part, and I do not pry. I know him though, that cannot be hidden. He is called Ōdæn, and this is his home now. There are bits and pieces, but they remain unconnected thoughts and feelings and for some reason, will not coalesce in definitive thought.

He is happy to be with us. I feel this as well. He has not touched another's spirit sense or mind in a long time. I know it to be centuries, but his spirit being does not count time in such a manner. One of the pieces of Ōdæn's psyche allows me to feel/see gives me the ability to understand the runes upon his coffin.

As the others gather about me, I speak the words aloud. They are in neither Effleæn nor any language I've seen, heard, or been shown before, yet I know the words and the language now. A gift from Ōdæn, sure certain.

A new rumbling, a softer one than when we had entered but from a similar mechanism ne'er the lesser. With it, the shelf carrying the coffin slides out from its wall and comes to rest precisely over the marble cube with not a hair's width betwixt them in the end. A table of stone lies before us now. On it sits two long stone boxes and a shorter less deep one betwixt them. Each with a cover of thick, hardened glass, and each warded with strong mægic, sure certain. In one the skeleton of a giant Ōdæn lies wrapped in a simple robe. A man at peace with his body's final mortality, but his mægic lingers as an aura about the remains. A dark blue hue.

The other holds the skeleton of a great beast. A cat twice the size of Bane, with tremendous teeth in both jaws, upper and lower and each as long as my oversized hands. A golden aura surrounds the king of worldly beasts.

In the center, a third case covered in a thick, light amber glass encases four objects. A great sword of a size to be judged a standard length to a scale made for the giant of a man that was Ōdæn. A magnificently crafted bow and full quiver. And finally a simple pack, but of an exemplary quality and made of some creature skin.

Here, I place my hand upon the glass, speak a simple rune, and stand amazed as the glass shimmers before disappearing completely.

"Ōdæn would have me share these gifts from him. Therrien, he grants you the pack he came to Aeryth with and begs you choose three tomes from his shelves to carry with you. You will know the right ones when you find them."

He stares at me for a moment, and a shiver runs the length of his body before he dares to step forward to lift the pack from the table. Sæm looks crestfallen to Therrien's luck.

"Alænèa, Ōdæn gifts to you the fine bow of still living Æntwood, with quiver and arrows in complement. They were his daughters and crafted by himself. His spirit has touched you, and they will serve only you now." Her eyes widen. A similar shiver trails through her body as she rises to accept the gifting.

"Sæm, Ōdæn would place his personal sword in your hands. It is unbreakable and crafted with the purest source mægic in the land of Destinæa. You will know its worth when you most need it."

"But Arias, surely not! You are the most deserving of this honor and can wield it in a more proper manner. Sure certain it should be yours." With a smile and a shake of my head, I easily decline his argument.

"Ōdæn, surely knows best, Sæm. He has seen your heart and touched your mind. He is certain of his gift. Accept with grace. You will wield it rightfully." A third time and a shiver covers his body now as he steps forward and lifts the unbelievably powerful sword.

"Arias, surely he would gift you something. Your mægic is clearly the most powerful among us. If he is still with you, ask something of him."

"Nay, Alænèa, one does not ask for a gifting. My gifts come each day it seems in any case. But to set your mind at ease, he has gifted me a thing, though it is unclear to me what exactly the gift is beyond that it involves drægons, so I suspect I'll have little need of it."

"Can we stay a bit longer, Arias? I crave owning a tome from his library. Any book, it matters not if I can even cypher the words. They must be the oldest books in all of Aeryth. I am eternally grateful and still jealous of Therrien." I can see it in Sæm's eyes and know as well he will leave without a single tome. A genuine respect of the mæge that lies afore us.

We stay the rest of the sun and then throughout the night in Ōdæn's chamber. Each of us reads what we can. For my part, I read the books as they are and after simply reading mayhaps two score pages of the ancient tongue, Sæm has picked it up in like manner. Therrien stares, astounded.

They are histories mostly, and when we read first the bindings and then a few pages of most every book upon the shelves, Therrien makes his choices. It will take more time for him to master the ancient script, but he will get there.

We leave out of Ōdæn's chamber on the morrow's morn, and as we do the hidden door raises after us, sealing the stair's portal tight and imperceptible to any of us. The furions sniff about its lost seams, finally deciding it gone forever.

17

Preparing for a Tinker's Bazaar

𝕴've traveled over Esper hill leaving all but Esper's mountain top visible behind me and have nearly made the fork leading either east to the coast or onto one of two southern travelways. The first heads due south to the smaller villages in the interior, and the last leads south and west. I am already settling into my role as tinker to the Barrier lands. In the distance, I spy a company of a dozen riders approaching from the coastal way. They appear to be a well-trained contingent, and I know them for who they are immediately. Though garbed in only black, they are from Kings Court, sure certain.

They will reach the fork afore me.

As they reach the intersection of ways, they await my arrival. Two are separate from the others and hold counsel whilst eyeing my wagon's approach. As I near the group, one of the two approaches and hails me.

"Hail, tinker! Well met! Have you a moment?"

"Assure, ser. I'll just set my brakes and open my wagon for you. It's been a mostly quiet fortnight and I'd welcome some business." The company's men casually split into two groups and make their way to either side of my wagon, still astride their horses.

As I begin setting the wagon's brake, I glance back to the man who sits aside and alone now, who'd been speaking to the company's captain before I'd arrived. I feel fortunate he thinks it beneath him to query a simple tinker, for it is Mensæ. I've shorn nearly all of my beard, wear garment common a tinker, and have a wide brimmed hat that leaves half my visage in shadow, but still he might recognize me as the tutor to Arias' mœther in Kings Court a score and five years ago.

My attention falls back to the captain as he addresses me once more.

"Tinker, you misunderstand. I need but a moment of your time for a few queries if you can spare it."

I sit back with a frown and a squeak to the wagon's seat, letting him know he's been less than polite to this businessman.

"Well then, stranger. What is it I can be of help with? Words bring but a pittance these days." He shows little notice to my snip.

"We seek a druid. Others say he goes by the name Eschereon. Do you know of him?" This man is direct with no banter for parlay.

"Druid? Like the druids of myth and legend that lived among drægons and other mægic beings? Casting spells and the like?" I guffaw in an appropriate manner to the subject.

"There is a hermit named Sage, or in the least, the village folk calk him sage, I think, who lives in the lonely mountain if he will do. He isn't really a hermit, but he lives in an abode cut into the mountainside, so they call him such. And he is old and that may have a bit to do with it. They call him Sage, is all…all the townsfolk and people hereabouts. There is a winding road up the side of the mountain to the west… No, it is the east…one of the two. Mayhaps he is who you seek?"

Actually, there are two mountain abodes. A lesser used one to the east, much like my usual entrance to the keep to the west. My thoughts are that it will be good to send them round the back door, giving Therrien time to make sure the three are off. I keep the captain busy with a bit of useless babble for a bit and for the most part, he sits polite against my lengthy monologue. I can see the ennui creeping into his eyes now.

"….They are a good folk. Not much for a tinker there, but I make time once or twice in a year to visit. The inn is nice, though I doubt they have beds for such a large company. They have good fare in the dining hall though."

The captain seems a bit antsy now at my banter. Anxious to be on his way. The others have pulled away already, shrugging their shoulders and shaking their heads at the over-talkative tinker.

"Well then, tinker. Many thanks for your time."

He flips me a silver from his coin purse and rides away to his lonely and stoic compatriot, awaiting his return with my news. I tip my hat to his back upon his departure. He and Mensæ speak a bit as I set my grey mares headed down the east coast road towards the sea. I will double back after they leave and are out of sight over the hill. My journey will take me south and west.

A quick clipped command to his company and they are off in the direction of Esper. I hope Arias and the others have already left. I have confidence that Therrien has gotten them on their way, and my thoughts by necessity turn to my further purpose.

I had sent maggies to Ferryn and one other as soon as we returned to Esper. Giorgi, my bird keeper, calls them magpies for their love of his wife's cooling pies upon windowsill. No matter their name, they are remarkable birds and Fates sent. They can travel the width and breadth of Aeryth in but a few suns time and make communication an easier task, such as I need now. The birds do not fly to a certain place as the king's ravens do, but rather to a specific person no matter their present location. Each of us Druidæ have two contacts only, and different at that, and send messages via the birds. We've found it a most efficient system. A level of separation and protection for each of us.

Ferryn will get word to his contacts and on and on, till all are notified of a place for our council meet. *A Tinker's Bazaar.* Word will spread, of course, to most every tinker in Aeryth, and it will become an event of grand proportion, which in turn will be an excellent cover for our council of Druidæ. There are nine of us that meet now. Precious few, down from the eighteen that we were five centuries ago. Though we typically meet mayhaps thrice in two decades, the information Arias has passed on to me warrants an immediate council. We are already more than as many decades late in a needed response to the danger upon us.

A few of my compatriots have apprentices, and our hopes are to grow our ranks again. It has been a near impossible task in centuries past, but the founding Source-Sayers work has begun to bear fruit over these past ten decades or so.

Unknown to folk of Aeryth, the vocation of tinker originated with the druids themselves for the simple purpose of an excuse to travel the country-side to mingle and take account of happenings around the whole of Aeryth. And so it continues even to this very sun. Under the guise of traveling merchant and barter-men, the tinkers are welcomed into any community for their mercantile and other services. The disguised druids are ofttimes honored as objective arbiters to minor disputes being unattached and without local bias. Now, tinkers number in the hundreds, and a bazaar such as the Druidæ plan will bring many. It is a solid career for an independent sort with no desire to put down roots.

***

(Rõghæn)

Leaning against the door jamb off her small chosen chamber, I study the lass as she sleeps. She sleeps sound with her wolf badger snuggled close. A wonder that. After taking her from the lodge, the scene of the brutal murder of her family, she acclimated well to a new life on the road with me. Her creature friend a good part of the reason, I am sure. For a full moon and some after, I've continued my trek about the countryside in my role as tinker. I do not mention the events at the hunting lodge, and though I encourage Elsii to speak to me whenever she feels the need, I counsel her against saying anything to anyone else. And so she speaks of her family to me, always pride in her voice, and to her creature friend as well, with whom she can share a tear. I've witnessed such a bond before and know it for what they have together.

More than animal whispering, mægic plays a deeper part I can see. The two carry a spirit bond, sure certain. They can experience each and the other's feelings. The other that I've known with the ability can actually see through the eyes of his creature friends. A deep empathetic connection exists betwixt the two. The creature acts on just the thoughts of the little lass, I am sure. A wonder considering the whole nature of this particular beast. But because she calls me friend, the fierce wolf badger calls me friend as well.

We've traveled all the way to Esperance with the many stops a tinker makes and are finally back to my cottage. My homestead for these past sixty and some years. I'd inherited it from a dear friend I'd shared it with for forty of those years. Like so many friends and folk throughout my life, they pass as only fine memories. He, less than a year prior. 'Tis a curse sometimes, living such a long life, but then I will meet a fresh spirit such as little Elsii and life becomes a marvel once more. I know again the blessing mægic bestows.

Thinking on my true calling and purpose of my life oath, I find it a perverse notion. I have compatriots, some I'd call friends, sure certain, and we all are blessed with the long life mægic can offer. Yet we meet each and the other for the shortest of time only, mayhaps weeks over decades. Our other lives are spent with and among friends if we dare for decades only to lose them after a few tens of years as each passes to dust.

Dust. I snicker at the thought. Pulling myself away from the doorway, my skillet and pots await my attention in the kitchen. I've finished sealing up the cottage against the onslaught we are about to experience. Warding all the windows and exterior doors, the lass will wake soon enough to the howling of winds and sand and desert's dust bombarding my humble abode. Elsii's wolf badger leaps down from the bed and follows me to the kitchen, not too proud to take advantage of every opportunity for a snack.

As I busy about the skillets, the wind picks up and rattles the shutters, and the very floorboards squeak in response. Whilst I listen, intent on the coming storm, another sound intrudes. A bell toll. I know its meaning and so pull the pan from my stove fire and grab a bag I keep tethered to the wall for such occasions. I head immediately upstairs again.

My cottage has been built to three stories. On the first level sit my kitchens and a small table to seat four. Across from it, my firebox and two leather-bound and quite comfortable chairs, one with a footstool stuffed to a perfect height. Upon every available space of wall, shelves are built high and every space within, holds the books of my life and much more. A druid's library holds knowledge back centuries and still more before my time. My times add to the knowledge, and my compatriots as well. My partner of late has also been my scribe, and I'd be wise to find another.

The outside walls are of tightly stacked stone formed on the desert's floor over hundreds of years, and the roof tiles are shells from the long dried away sea. The second and third levels are both under that roof. Three bed chambers and a bath populate the second. Mine is there and the smallest claimed by Elsii. A narrow stair to one end of the second level leads to the third with a steep and slanted ceiling and half-height walls. In its very center lies my destination. And there sits a large maggie, pecking at a small, rolled scroll tied to its leg.

"So good to see you again, Nicolo! What have you for me?"

Reaching for the bird with familiarity, I pluck the tiny scroll from its leg as I offer a treat from my bag. He crows his thanks and shivers and flaps to free himself of gathered sand and desert dust.

"It's quite a storm brewing. Would you rather be off afore it finally arrives, or stay and visit for a time?"

He's always been a fidgety bird and it seems he'd prefer to be on his way again. So, I quickly read his message brought and see no need to send a missive in return. Laying open the bag next to his perch, I let him eat his fill and decide when to be on his way. He glances over my shoulder before tucking in to his bag of treats. I turn.

"You're awake, Elsii. Has the brewing storm awakened you?"

"Nay, the bell is what I heard. Then I smelled the bacon frying and had to decide which way to come first."

A smile spreads as I turn to see her standing at the top of the stair, Huni at her feet.

"He's a handsome bird, Mæster Rõghæn. What is he?"

"He's a maggie, or magpie, if his original keeper were to have his way. He's a messenger bird, quite intelligent."

"Did he bring you a message?"

"He did indeed. How would you like to visit a tinker's bazaar? A hundred or more tinkers bartering their wares all at once in a camp the size of a small village,"

"Oh, I'd love that. Are we going to go?"

"I think it would be a wise thing to do. But after this storm, and by the looks it may be with us awhile."

A warm draft tickles the back of my neck, and when I turn, Nicolo is gone out the window. I seal and ward it against the coming storm.

I cannot send a forwarding maggie to Gantric as my birds are presently being cared for elsewhere. I'd not long ago sent a missive to Gant with the maggie I travel with on my tinker's wagon. She will not return till after the coming storm. However, our system works in such a way that he will be notified by another on the council anyway.

"Come, Elsii. Rashers of bacon and heaps of cheese on taters await us in the kitchen." I do not need to ask twice.

Later, with winds howling and sand beating against the windows, I sit pensive in my chair in front of a fire, a tome open on my lap. Pulling the scrap of parchment Elsii had given me the night we first met out of a pocket hidden in my sleeve, I reread the list. Something of importance to be discussing at the meet.

***

(Ferryn- Druid Council)

The chain of maggies has been started and the council meet set to time and place. We will arrive most like, within a ha'fortnight of each and the other, and when all are judged to have arrived, matters Eschereon has presented can be discussed. Deep matters of concern, and we are desperately behind in gathering this news. We all can expect to be busy and meeting more often in the years to come. It would seem dire times are finally upon us.

For hundreds of years, no threat has presented itself, and our only responsibility lies in the chronicling of the happenings across Aeryth. There have been some changes appearing over the last century across the whole of the lands, however. Most especially, we have noted that there are a number of youngers born with unusual abilities to the time. These youngers seem to be born in the smaller villages or on outlying homesteads. It is a reemergence of the ancient mægics, but in a different manner than the mægics of olde. Often the youngers exhibit more than one mægic and that in itself an anomaly.

The founding Source-Sayers knew this was possible as their writings say some mæges have exhibited the simple 'crossover mægic' with the ability to perform warding for instance. The Source-Sayers efforts, therefore, were concentrated to that outcome. They find that 'pureblood' mæges are hindered in these multiple abilities, but in subsequent generations of 'mixed blood' mæges, and local offspring, more are capable of duo mægics, though of lesser ability and strength of the mægic. There are exceptions though, and these are the basis for the future workings of mægic mixing of bloodlines.

As the designated governor of council and, mayhaps, one of the most learned in such things amongst the Druidæ, save JabberJack, it falls to me to chronicle these very issues. Eschereon, however, has experienced the results of the Source-Sayers efforts firsthand. It will be good to query him about his experiences with the trio of apprentices he's stumbled upon. I have hopes he'll bring them with him to our meet and council. That will be for the bazaar, two moons hence, however. Till then, it is business as usual.

I've made my way, this trip, to the south 'n west of Aeryth. It has been some years since my last travels to these parts. Stumbling upon a large camp of soldiers, I've parked my wagon outside their training grounds. I cannot recall such a large camp of soldiers aside from the king's guard training camps to the north and south of Kings Court. It is most curious, as their sigil is not that of the king's, but rather two spears crossed behind a lion's head of gold. By the looks of the camp, every lad of an age has been conscripted from a thirty and three league radius or more. There are a thousand here and no less.

My first night's campfire made me known to the camp and on the following handful of eves, I do a fair bit of business with the soldiers. They are a disciplined lot on the training field in the heat of the sun, but loose of tongue when visiting a tinker in the cool eves and about a friendly fire. Such is the way of youth, full of pride and virility. Talk of happenstance and love conquests abound.

"Hail, tinker! Have you trinkets for a lass?"

"Call me Ferryn, lad. Have a seat about my fire and an ale, if you have a mind. Cups are just there on the table and the cask has been uncorked. I'll bring what I have for you to peruse. You have a lass you are trying to impress, do you?"

"Aye, and the competition is somethun' fierce with all the horndogs about camp. She's a lass from the village down the road apiece, and I'll have leave in a few suns time." He settles and helps himself to the ale, of course.

When I've returned, his posture belies a stiff training regimen as he sits tall and straight, legs together, though his face has relaxed and his cup rests easy on a knee. He smiles for me as I bring a tray of wristlet and neck charms for him to see. But though he glances at them, his thoughts and eye have drifted to my spit across the fire and the meat wrapped around it.

"I've a few extra coppers if you have enough on your spit to share, Ferryn?"

"Aye, lad, let me cut you a piece then." His eyes light up.

"They dun' give up so much meat to us newts at the mess hall. Always having to prove yurself just for a scrap now'n again." He takes my offering with a glazed look about his eyes and a bit of drool leaking from the corner of his mouth.

"Newts?"

"Aye, newly conscripted, they call us. Lower than the lowest, but we got a purpose with it though, right? Better 'n the docks that way I'd have to say, ya know?"

"Ah, I thought I noted an accent about you, lad. What docks would you be referring to?" I've been waiting on an answer for a moment as he chews on a large piece of hard-crusted bread I'd offered, heavy with a rich butter I make and keep as extravagance for myself.

"Seas End. Tullamoor's goons round up us waifs that ain't got no pa's alive 'n sent us south to the new lord and lady of this keep. Them needing an army, you know. I've a handful of friends from the docks here, almost like home that way…'cept I worry on my mum."

I note his face drop a little before he takes another large bite of the skewered meat offered and more bread to follow it down. He gulps the last of his ale, his old manners showing through a bit, when a horn sounds.

"Sheist! Cap'n'll cancel my leave if I don't get back afore second blow. How much for the wristlet? A silver, then, no time to haggle…and thank ye for the ale tinker! Gotta go…" Grabbing his prize, he disappears at a run.

The next five suns I've learned a bit more. Enough that it will be a topic at our council. How did we not see the signs afore now?

18

Isles of the Dæmon Straits

Sæm put aside his study of Ōdæn's books as he and Therrien have discovered that the end of the new moon's cycle will be our best chance to reach the first of the isles and my destination, the isle of Azgârd and my true pæder's place of birth. They have also discovered something strange about the ship's charts. The lines across the charts reference back to stars in the night skies, but the chart's lines move with charts dating in hundred-year increments. The mæges of old had drawn new charts based on the expected movement of certain star groups in the night sky. The latest chart dates thirty some years past, or a millennium forward from when it had been drawn.

Sæm proclaims this an essential discovery. If we had followed the charts on top of the pile that were dated centuries past, we would have sailed into shoals hidden just beneath the sea's surface and perished in our attempts to reach the isles. This galleon has visited the isles frequently in times past. The captain's journal, once cyphered, chronicles the visits in detail. We will test their accuracy in just a few suns time in the middle of the night and at the end of the coming full moon cycle when the tides will next be right for the trip.

Anxious, we near the island as the seas about it roil in contempt of any who try to approach, showing jagged rocks jutting high above the waves like teeth of a giant kraken in the rough seas. These we can see and sail round, but the teeth hidden just below the surface are the greater danger. We must put our faith in the long-dead sea mæges of olde for our very survival.

We slice through the waves with mainsail and foresail only as the captain's journal advised. Sam keeps us in the deep and narrow current of the only approach to Asgährd, climbing and riding great waves one after the other, riding one's back into each next valley and its sibling towers towards us once again. After a night of a thousand such, the sun finally peeks above the horizon afore us, and the waves settle mægically to calmer seas. We are to the north of the isle now, its emerald coastline to our starboard. Sam turns us in that direction, aiming for what appears to be an inlet betwixt two great granite mountains. As we approach, mayhaps a sandglass turn into the new morn, the inlet becomes quite clear, and the mountainside cliffs resolve into two great sculptures of ancient warriors, saluting arriving vessels or warning the unworthy to stay away.

We are still a far cry out when a great horn sounds against the cliffs in echoing thunder, and farther still, a bell tolls three or four knell in greeting or warning, no way to tell. But Talon answers the sound with his own echoing cry of arrival. Bane makes his way up to his favorite spy spot at the bow, muzzle to the breeze, and the furions scamper along the foresail's boom.

Sæm guides us through the granite warriors and into a great bay. Crystal clear waters await as well as a horseshoe-shaped beach of white sands, a league from end to end. Small craft ply the waters with fisherman's nets hanging about most of them. As we pass through the open gateway into the bay, the cliffs about the heads of the stone soldiers are lined with a dozen archers each, staring and pointing at us as we pass. They do not receive many strange ships, we guess. The small fleet of fishing boats follow us to the docks, observing in detail as we move directly aside them. It is not us they are pointing to, but rather the distinctive flag that flies atop the mainmast. The six coloured rainbow attracts their close attention.

We had not raised this flag. However, it has adorned the center mast since our escape from the cliffs at Esper. It had remained aloft over a thousand years and a product, like the ship, of the mæge captain and crew of old. It is the same design we had seen in the tail of the stone lion guarding Ōdæn's tomb and displayed upon the legends of each of the captain's nautical charts.

Many more bells are ringing now, and even at a distance from the docks, we can see a gathering of people in expectation of our arrival. Fishermen sail close aside us, staring in wonder. Bane paces the length of the ship, peering down at the many small vessels, and Lilit and Jilly run along the gunwales chittering at them. Sæm stays astern, manning the rudder as he shouts orders to the rest of us. We glide in smoothly, as if we've done it a hundred times before. Therrien and I throw our tether lines to dockhands.

Once coupled to the pier, Sæm pushes and pulls a few of his levers, and Therrien and I secure the hold doors as they swing open and down. I smile and descend quickly into the hull to four excited beasts that know we have finally docked. Paint leads them up and out and then down onto the pier. He rises onto his hindquarters and gives a mighty bray so happy is he to be on land once again or close enough to see it, in the least. A dockhand forgetting where he is, falls off the far side of the dock in his rush to give Paint some room. Laughter bursts out from the others about.

A tall goodman with flowing hair and a bit of a regal look about him, starts down the pier and towards us. Two others in less formal attire follow behind him and try to keep pace. We are just finishing bringing our saddlebags, packs, and other weapons and gear ashore when they finally reach us.

"Hail, captain. Welcome to Asgärhd," he says looking back and forth to Sæm and I, not sure which of the two of us he should be addressing. Nonplussed in any event, as we, either one, sure certain appear quite young to be captaining a vessel such as we are. Sæm breaks the awkward silence.

"Call me Eshæm of Falkir, master, and we are quite happy for your welcome after an eventful trip about your island waters. Though the beauty of the destination has made the trip worthwhile," Sæm says as he reaches for the man's forearm and pulls him in tight and strong in greeting, throwing the man off his game it appears.

"You've made the passage without a local captain to guide you, and on a most impressive vessel that bears a sigil from times long ago. All of these things are intriguing to say the least, Captain. I am Lèændár, marshall here in our small port town we call Frejra for its founder and matron. I act as its head of council, if you will. That council invites you as honored guests to eve-feast this sun, if you've a mind to join us." He offers the slightest of bows...well, more a nod, and finds a more proper pose, following his most formal discourse. His accompanying goodmen stand tall and straight of shoulder with hands clasped behind their backs.

We, of course, present as a more casual lot, our life's belongings scattered around us on the dock. Lilit and Jilly stand tall aside me on a barrel, observing the goings-on. Their heads sway this way and that and draw stares among those gathered. Sæm returns the marshal's minimal nod.

"Many thanks for your offer, Marshal. But I am master of this group only upon the seas. Arias here leads us while on land, and so I guess he'll need to address your offer of feasting, though I'll certainly counsel him to accept."

Bane chooses this moment to meander down the ship's gangway, deliberate in his approach and scattering the gathered dockhands as he slips alongside me with an almost casual ease and takes a moment to study the three men. They step back a pace, almost in unison as Bane gives a slow blink and a soft huff. His ears stand as tall as my chest now, and if his size does not impress, the orange hue of his coat speckled in onyx near glows, and his copper and gold eyes draw all attention to him. I retrieve my staff, with its ends of drægon tooth and drægon firestone, and that draws an audible breath from all those about. Standing next to Bane, all eyes turn to me now.

I glance over to Alænèa, who has been kneeling and sorting her pack, and catch a smile spreading across her face. Therrien stands by confused. It dawns on me why. All of this time, they've been conversing in Effleæn. The marshal has addressed us so, and Sæm, in a most natural and comfortable ease, has rejoined him in the same. Though the three of us are quite comfortable in the tongue, it is a foreign language to Therrien.

"Lèændár. We would like nothing more than to join you at your eve-feast and hold council. But if it pleases, we've spent three fortnight aboard Eshæm's esteemed vessel, and though it is a most brilliant ship, we would like to start the sun with a simple mornmeal after a bath, if it is possible? And possibly find a pasture for our most wobbly-legged steeds?" A cautious smile appears on the face of our host.

"Eir, can you see to our guests' needs, would you? Till later then, Arias and Captain Eshæm, sirs. I look forward to dining with you this eve." Turning, he leaves in the same long strided manner in which he'd arrived, leaving one of his goodmen to tend to our needs. As my eyes follow and he exits the pier and back onto the travelway from which he'd first appeared, I notice a woman, nay, a lass more like, of rather unique appearance sitting upon a stack of canvas sacks as she studies us closely. She seems to be following all that happened from her far perch and her eyes sparkle as mine meet hers.

We gather our belongings, saddle the horses, and lead them down the pier following Eir and towards the small towne of Frejra. I feel a warmth and comfort here as if returning home.

***

(Mensæ)

Sitting across from the ship's captain in the dimly lit room of an inn owned by an associate of Haledon's, I note that Haledon has established himself quickly in Cliffside and its environs. Male youngers are being sent off to

Dæmons Due for training and further assignment in the south and west. Haledon has become the counselor to the local baron, and the trade he's established under a similar guise with the recently departed Lord Tullamoor continues unabated. Where the crown's conscription efforts have slacked off considerably as its original purpose has been served, my compatriot's efforts are only growing in this regard here.

This, however, concerns other business.

It has been two full moon cycles since I'd watched Arias Côeurdrægon sail west and out to sea beyond my grasp. I do not know how he has managed it. Sure certain he had aid once he'd reached the village of Esper. Mayhaps they are involved in his escape from the Bowels. The vessel they ride had a different look about it, and it was as swift a ship as I've ever seen. They were headed west, and we will follow, but our trail needs to be overland and much slower. Cliffside will most like be their next port, and we will catch their trail up there. But they have been deceptive in their flight, I know now, heading first west and then returning to the east. Why they choose the isles, I do not know. Following the druid, mayhaps?

What I know, sure certain, is that the king's grandson has somehow escaped and now poses an immediate threat to the secrecy of our efforts in Aeryth, and especially to myself if it is ever revealed to the Three that it was I that compromised the situation. Curse this lad. He has found a way into my memories revealing my comrades and from where we have come. He must be found and eliminated before the Druidæ are informed. I've dodged a bolt it seems, as the man I suspect, nay, know now, after memories revealed by the lad, to be a true druid, was not home to receive the lad's message.

I have a connection now to the lad since I touched upon his mind. It works more precisely in close proximity to him, but my mægic is strong enough that I can never totally lose his general location, especially if he is having thoughts of me. I will find him. And dispense with the threat. Hence my session with this captain this sun.

It is unfortunate that I must leave the king unattended for a time with there being a chance he could experience a *'Sight'* that I cannot intercept. They come few and far between to the man in any manner, and if he has one, he'd not likely recognize it for what it is, having not experienced one in the score and ten years I've been there to steal them from him. He's become dependent on me for such things and will likely await my return to discuss it. We have discussed and decided that it is my responsibility alone to bring the king's justice to the lad. I smile to think that no decision such as this ever remains the king's choice.

"Captain, I'm told you can reach the bays of the isles in the Dæmon Straits? I'd like to charter your galleon."

He has been told who I am and who I represent. He drums his fingers upon the table betwixt us.

"The king has never showed an interest in the isles. Might I ask the intent of your trip there? There is little trade to be established within the isles, we have little to offer, and indeed we must trade here in Cliffside for those things we cannot produce ourselves."

"Rest assured, the crown has interest there just now, and it is of little concern to a sea captain."

This man must be put to his place quickly, or he will be trouble. I send that very thought along with my words. I sense a small amount of resistance. These common folk of Aeryth continue to amaze me.

"It's just that the waters are especially treacherous this time of the year, and all things must be considered. What is it that you will be bringing? And I must say that only Asgährd and Ölympæa are even reachable at all, if this matters."

"I bring my company of a dozen and our steeds."

Beads of sweat almost immediately collects on his forehead.

"Ser, I am the only captain that can steer a vessel clear of the deadly currents and rocks that lie just below the surface on the trip to and fro and about the isles. I would advise against a trip with such a load. The crossing with a stationary load in the hold is challenging. Live horses would double the risk."

"Ne'er the lesser, Captain, we will do just that. When will you expect it be ready?"

"The next possible crossing to the isles cannot be till highest tide, and that won't be till the first sun of the next moon cycle. We must leave a fortnight from this eve to have our best chance."

"We will be ready, Captain. Be sure you are as well." I drop a heavy bag of coin on the table. "Half now, and the other on our arrival."

He will not admit it, but I notice a lifting of the man's spirit at the heft of the purse when he picks it up on his way out.

19

Our Asgährd Reception

It does not dawn on me immediately, but there is reason for me to feel at home in Asgährd. Only later do I learn the why of it. What catches my attention is the lass who sits at the front of the pier, following our movements and progress down the wharf. Her foot rests upon the sacks as she sits and observes, patiently studying, her hands clasped about her raised knee casually and yet intent. She wears an amulet with a large amber gemstone embedded within it. I can see it even from here. I reach for my neck. But for the colour of the stone it resembles my tinker's amulet so close.

Though she sits, from the length of her legs it is clear that her height matches my own. Her eyes shine blue as the water, and she wears a band of soft leather about her deep, auburn-haired head with a single steak of golden blond reaching from her forehead and tucked behind one ear. Three clear runes of gold lie embedded in the leather head band at her forehead, and they shine brightly against the sun. They appear as if they would shine just as bright without the sun. She wears trousers of a sort, though the legs are of a style to make them appear a long skirt when standing. The waist of them rides high and over her hips, and a wide belt cinches them in place. The top and bottom of the belt a woven leather, and at its center a bronze verdant buckle with a single large rune embossed in the same manner as her headband. I know this rune's meaning. *Heart.* A cloak of wool and dyed a burgundy drapes her shoulders, its clasp coin-shaped and also aged bronze and carries another rune. *Truth.*

We have reached the front of the pier now, and looking further about, others like her are walking around towne. Two others I spy along the wharf, doing some shopping it appears. Each is garbed in like manner and with soft headband about their heads as well, though the two others carry but one rune each on the band and in silver-tone, not gold. Their garb practical and mayhaps not as finely tailored as this lass.

Alænèa takes notice also, and the two stare each to the other for a time, studying close and with wondering thoughts, it is clear to see. As we near, she stands and approaches, speaking direct to Alænèa.

"You are Effleæn from the Plain, by the hue of your skin. The Mœther would like a word with you when you find the time. She can be found in the temple upon the hill just there, next to the Æggrazil tree." She points to a hilltop in the distance past the towne and into the rolling hills rising up from the coast. A white stone edifice stands solitary there, next to a massive manna.

"Bring your friends, if you like." Her eyebrow raise as she observes us up close. She takes a deep breath as she watches Bane step up behind us. He seems to sniff the air about her, curious in his own right.

"The wolf wears mægic. I've never seen such." I nod in return.

"Mœther will be anxious to hear such a beast walks upon our shores." She appears quite curious of Bane and shows no fear of the dread wolf. She glances up into my eyes. "And you wear a Wic'cha stone sentient." She glances to my tunic where my hidden amulet grows warm against my chest. Ne'er the lesser, she knows it resides there. Remarkable.

"Wic'cha? What is Wic'cha?" I query.

"Not what. Who. We are Wic'cha. We are the crafters of such amulets. How could you not know this, if you wear one? No, two. I sense two! Who are you? Where did you come by them? And how is it they allow you to wear them? Are you Druidæ? Mœther will want to know these things and will be anxious to meet you as well. You appear to be Asgährdian, but you wear Wic'cha crafting. It is very strange, this." Her brow furrows in thought. "Come see Mœther when you are able!"

"I must head back to report that we have met, if you will be so kind as to give me your names."

"I am Alænèa, and yes, I am Effleæn. This is Eshæm and Arias and Therrien. Arias will need speak to whether we will visit your temple. And what name shall we call you, one who begs names before offering her own?"

I wager she has not yet seen her fifteen year-end, though she has the bearing of one much older. The lass steps back confused and affronted, brow furrowed now.

"Pardon. I am Guin. Guinefere Roux is my full and proper name. I do not understand. You have a man that speaks for you? Your group?" Alænèa's eyebrow raises to this.

"I speak for myself, but Arias speaks for our group, and as I've chosen to follow him, he speaks for me in this."

"Mœther will have more wisdom in this. Please come when you can." She nods to each of the four of us, still confused before turning away.

She seems in a hurry now and disappears in the direction of the temple. Bane senses the woods and also disappears soon after.

"Well, that was peculiar."

"Nay, not really. Though their seated rulers have always been men through the ages, Asgährd has always been a matriarchal society, Arias. The rulers do nothing without consulting the Wyccan, or Wic'cha, their advisors and true leaders in this society. You might say the men are the administrators with the heavy decisions falling to the women." Therrien tutors me.

"Well then, a trip to the temple will be in order during our stay, but first, mayhaps we should find an inn that serves something other than fish. I've a taste for more land-based fare. What say you, all?

From the smiles about, I can see we are of like mind.

We find the perfect place in an inn of sorts, not too far from the quays on the outskirts of towne and in the direction of the temple on the hill. There is a pastured stables nearby, and we take the time to brush and wash our steeds ourselves. Though neither Therrien nor Alænèa are accustomed to such a thing, they join Sæm and I in the task, liking it as much as the horses, I think. Before leaving them, I make sure that the stableman lets them have the run of the pasture for a good bit. The others chase and follow Paint as he enjoys being on solid ground once again.

Eyes follow us, but aside from the interest shown us as we entered the bay and on the docks we are not approached. A stiff breeze meets us as we exit the stables, and I cypher mayhaps, why we have not been bothered.

Smelling of horse and a few suns without bathing, we make our way across the rue to an inn with a bull on its shingle. They kindly show us to their baths, and we hand off our garments for washing as the innkeep says they can do us the service. After retiring to rooms and changing to our only other though less scented clothes, we meet up in the dining hall. I carry my staff and pack as Sæm does. He has with him his gifted sword as well. The others feel no need to carry weapons other than a blade Alænèa always has on her belt

The hall brings with it a cacophony of sounds and smells, very welcome to the four of us. A couple of old locals sit at the bar, drinking their mid-sun meal, but most are gathered in the dining hall. Nothing loud, just the overall din of folk having their meal with friendly banter. The serving lads and lasses keep busy at the peak mid-sun rush. An inn like any other in Aeryth. We savor a meal of roast fowl, beef, pork, and fruits and fresh vegetables, not centuries-old fare kept edible with mægic, paired with some fish. Steaks still run with blood and pork flesh is burned crispy and sopped in sauce. We've not seen its like in three fortnight. And homebrew ale in deep cups. In the end, we sit back and pat our bellies, truly at ease after too long a while in flight on the open sea. Even so, we are aware that the local clientele are studying us…and the furions who have made appearances to enjoy the nuts and cheese I'd ordered mostly for them.

Word from the docks catches up with us and more than a few of the locals stare openly now, it not helping that we speak in Aeryth common tongue and not at all like what we hear from everyone else about us. But they stay polite and when we are addressed in the native tongue, Sæm and I and even Alænèa understand it and return in kind. Therrien sits in wonderment at it all. He's read stories in Eschereon's library most of his life, now he finds himself living such adventures. He studies everything about him in awe.

After our meal and more ale, Sæm finally brings forth the sword he's carried in with him. I can see in his eyes the need to study it more as we have not yet taken much time since receiving it. Slipping it from its scabbard, he lies it on the center of the table afore us. As it slips from its home for many hundreds of years, I see, hear, and even feel it. A silver aura surrounds it and the lightest hum comes to my ears, and the very hairs on my neck raise as my skin tingles in its presence. I notice Sam feels the same. Though the aura may not have presented to others in the dining hall aside from Alænèa, Sæm, and myself, I feel sure others must be experiencing the energy of the wondrous blade. In a corner across the room, a figure sitting with a wide brimmed hat hiding his face in shadow indeed seems to catch his breath and turn to stare at what we are doing. My attention turns to him as the others lean in to study the runes and figures etched along the length of the blade.

His curiosity overtaking him, the man pushes his chair back and rises, his intent to visit us clear in his eyes. As he does, he notices my eyes to him and his eyebrow climbs his forehead as he makes no attempt to divert his interest. As he draws near, he pulls a chair aside to me and leaning into my ear says, "Where did you come by this weapon, stranger? Have a care. If others discover its truth, there will be a call of blasphemy and all the fates fury will break loose in here."

I pause before responding.

"Sæm, here, was gifted it by its previous owner," I say, choosing my words carefully.

"And how would that be possible?" he returns. Though we keep our conversation to whispers, my three friends hear, and whilst Sæm quietly resheathes the sword in a nonchalant manner, they turn to listen in on our discussion.

"If you are aware of its past keeper, you would understand it could indeed be possible." He stares back at me and then turns his attention to Sæm, his face a mask of ever-changing expression as he contemplates what I said.

"What would make him so special as to lay claim to such a blade?" His eyes scrutinize Sæm.

"As I said, he laid no claim to it. It was gifted to him. And mayhaps, it is not about what he has done and rather more about what he is destined to do."

Sæm looks to me with widened eyes, and I think in that moment he realizes he had taken an unspoken oath when he accepted the sword in Ōdæn's crypt cavern. The stranger sits back upon his chair and studies Sæm a bit more. Finally, he swings back around to stare at me before rising and clasping Sæm about his wrist.

"Welcome, stranger. I hope your meal suited. I am Týr. What might I call you?" He's switched to Aeryth common tongue now, which few in the hall understand I gather, as they are more interested in their meals once again.

"Many thanks...friend. As said, I am Sæm. Eshæm Bearheart more precise, but Sæm will do. This is Therrien of Esper and Alænèa of the

Plain. And you've been speaking to Ariastone Côeurdrægon, the leader of this band of misfits." A small smile escapes him as he names our group such. We are, sure certain, different each to the other, but I would not call us misfits in any manner.

Týr steps back to appraise us all after hearing our names. He stiffens just the tiniest bit when he hears my name, I think. But he keeps a calm air about him still and grasping arms with each of us, he pulls up his chair again and sits.

"I've met a Bearheart once. Ètœn, he calls himself I recall. A storied Kingsman he is, I was told. Could he be kin? I've heard the name but once." Sæm glances to me.

"My pæder-brœther carried that name. He was a great Kingsman, I'm told." Týr's brow raises, I think, to Sæm's use of the word 'was.' He turns to Therrien.

"And Esper is the home of a friend of Asgährd and the isles… a *Sage* we call Chèron. It has been near to ten and eight years since I last saw him, but you must know of him?" Therrien's jaw loosens in wonder.

"We call him Eschereon in Esper. I am his scribe." Týr sits up straight.

"Another, quite older goodman, held that post when I visited. Come to think, he had a similar name to yours."

"Therôn is my pæder. I apprenticed and took his place ten years passed."

"I trust he is well. He seemed a very knowledgeable scribe." Therrien accepts the compliment with the slightest of nods. The corner of his mouth turns up, and he offers a perplexed look at this stranger that knows of Esper and his father.

Looking over his shoulder, Týr calls out to a nearby serving lass, she having just cleared an adjacent table. I note she wears a leather band about her upper arm. It has a single copper rune embedded upon it.

"Lôfn, can you fetch another round for my new friends and me?" She nods with a shy smile. Turning to Alænèa, he continues his assessment.

"The Accadian Plain, a most interesting place. I've read histories of it but have never been. Quite impossible to reach the heart of the Plain, I am told. But here you are. Mayhaps it is easier to leave than to enter? Did you know your people—*Effleæn*, do you call yourselves? You are near descendants to us here on Asgährd. Well, mayhaps not so near. Eons ago there was a falling out, if you will, betwixt the two leaders of the founding clans of Asgährd, Ætzir and Væ-nzir. Væ-nzir clan left to settle in the ancient wood across the strait. Some other time I would love to show you the chamber of tomes in Vaihälla, our oldest edifice and a wonder to visit. One can lose oneself in the histories of heroes written in the volumes there.

Alænèa's eyes brighten to the prospect, I can clearly see. Sæm's as well, I notice.

"And the runes we see, the ones that draw mægic to them, do the books in your Vaihälla hold the key to them?"

Lôfn returns with a pitcher of ale to fill our cups and raises her brow to Alænèa's query, sloshing a bit of ale over my hand and wrist as her attention slips a bit. Týr looks to her.

"The oldest of books there are all written in elder rune, but the most ancient of founder runes—the ones said to be used by the Source-Sayers of old—they are in the purview of the Wic'cha, of course. They say they can hold ancient mægic, and I'll not be one to dispute it. The blade you carry is etched deep with many of them, and there is certainly a greater power to it. At least in the hands of the worthy."

I can see Alænèa has a distant, determined look about her. One that speaks to a need to learn more, sure certain. The last remark is not lost on Sæm.

Týr turns his attention to me. "When I visited Esper those many years ago with a friend I hold quite dear, there was another guest of the *Sage*. Our reason for the visit, actually. She had escaped with the druid years before, an unwilling fate and an unfortunate consequence of her bloodline. And you see, well, my friend Illèron Côeurdrægon was in love with her and she, him."

I stare intent upon him now.

"You know my true pæder, the one who knew me but a few suns over my first five years?"

The jab not lost on Týr, he looks at me more appraisingly. He takes a long draught on his cup, his eyes ne'er leaving mine.

"As I have said, his love for her and their youngers is deep. The Wic'cha had *seen* a threat to her and his son and daughter, too. We left immediately for Esper, a dozen years past, as soon as he heard this. To rescue her."

I jump to my feet as I grasp what he is saying, startling the others. Memories flood my mind once again. *Babe in a cradle. Crying, waking me at night. An infant lying across my young lap with the bluest of eyes and a tuft of deep red hair...* Damn, Eschereon! More memories just reveal themselves to me. I have a sister! I fall back into my chair and stare blankly at Týr, a stranger who apparently knows things about me that I don't even know. The others realize the reason for my sudden behavior now.

"You know where my Mœther and sister are? My pæder?"

"No to the latter, and it has been too long. But, yea. Your mœther and sister are here on the isles. Though your mother is not here on Asgährd."

My hands grip the arms of my chair so that my knuckles turn white. My breath catches in my throat and my heart pounds against my chest wall. Granted, Sæm had suggested that we head to the Dæmon Isles for just this purpose; to find my mœther. But I had thought it fantasy. Yet here sits a man that knows my pæder and says my mœther and sister—*I have a sister*—are actually here.

"I am not sure where your sister is stationed these days, as she is a ward of the Wic'cha Mœther and as such, might be on any of the isles or indeed even on the mainland..."

I have not been listening closely, but now his words catch up to my thoughts once again. I interrupt him.

"How do I find my mœther? You say she is not here on Asgährd?" Týr finally notices my state of mind.

"She is currently living on Onæ Parâdeis, isle of the Amâzæ."

"Can you guide us there? Our ship is ready as we speak." He smiles at this.

"You cannot easily reach Onæ Parâdeis by ship, even upon a mæge vessel as rumor says you sail. It lies shrouded in a thick fog from all sides, and the waters treacherous about it, even as you found Asgährd, but with the fog even more so. You must be escorted by the Wic'cha. The isle does not welcome many male visitors. It is home to only women, in fact. Very tall and strong, and a'times well-armored warrior women. They are a brilliant, but solitary sort. They do not…suffer…male visitors well most suns."

We all look at Týr with unbelieving eyes. His tale so…well, unbelievable. He laughs at the looks we give him.

"'Tis truth," he says.

"So whether I want to find my mœther or my sister, I must visit with these Wic'cha?" It more a statement than a question. "And if the sailing is so treacherous, how do the Wic'cha handle it?"

"They don't. Let us just say ancient mægic is involved, and I am not at liberty to discuss it further."

"The lass on the pier will have her way then, though I had intended it anyway. We will visit the temple tomorrow." I notice the same serving lass has been trying to nonchalantly eavesdrop on our conversation. Little birds, alight and listening.

"One last thing, Týr, if you've a mind. My pæder, you've spoke of knowing him well, but say you know not where to find him."

"He is a Strider. A guardian of folk of Aeryth, though they do not realize it. He travels the whole of the Northern Reaches and a'times into the

Mid Realm as well. It being on such a trip that he met your mœther. But he has been gone into the Mid Realm for some time on a search commissioned by the Wic'cha. We've not heard from him and have not even seen a messenger raven in over two years now."

"A guardian? I've not ever heard tell of such a thing."

"You would not. Their mission is done with no fanfare. It is their charge and oath to bring aide and the ancient knowledge to the peoples of Aeryth and to report back to the Wic'cha on what they observe in the keeping of their oath's work. It is a duty akin to the druids, but they play a more active role. Your pæder is a powerful and respected man here on Asgährd. Striders are elite soldiers as well as scholars. Your pæder is one of the best."

Týr departs and leaves me with more to ponder on my bloodlines. I've gone from an orphan from the smallest of villages in the mountains of Western Aeryth to an unwanted heir to the throne, grandson to the king. I have now a sister and mœther I have not seen in over a dozen years and a pæder I have only the slightest of memories of having met but once in my life. And further, there is Finnie and the youngers we rescued from slave traders. I feel my heart skip a beat as thoughts of them surface. They now seem further away from me than ever. Turmoil and chaos roils about me with each new family member's discovery. I dare not venture a guess to what my stay here in the isles might hold for me.

20

Wic'cha

While I brood, the others are busy in their own conversations and leave me my space for thought. Their voices are distant to me as they talk amongst themselves, laughing just now at Therrien's continued wonder at being part of our adventures. The dining hall has near emptied, the local folk returning to their every sun affairs. Lilit and Jilly have ventured out of their home in my pack and are exploring the empty hall, stopping to enjoy the leavings under the tables about us. They are just now sniffing about a puddle of ale or cider and capturing the heart of Lôfn the server who tosses a few bits their way.

"Well then, shall we be off? Mayhaps a tour of town and a trip to see how our horses fare." All are in agreement and with a slapping of knees, Therrien gleefully rises to join me and the others follow suit. The furions seem a little less enthusiastic to be leaving as they have just gotten started on their jaunt of discovery and meal.

Our tour of the small port towne is for the most part uneventful but still great to be among friendly folk, ne'er the lesser for it. Later that eve, we return to the inn for another great meal, and when we retire to our rooms, find our fresh laundered garb folded upon the beds, smelling a good bit less like the sea and sweat and horse. The windows are open, and though the air chill, the welcome scents of the town below my window lead me to leave it be and curl up deeper into the thick bed linens and blankets for the night.

The morrow's morn finds the tip of my nose red and near frozen for my decision concerning the window last night. The washbowl water and cold wood floors reinforce my lack of good judgment. As my roommate last eve Alænèa has been up to her old self with a prank that leaves the laces on my boots as slippery as greased worms. Unable to find the offending rune so I can negate her ward spell, I trudge down into the dining hall with my boots flapping about and making me look the clown. The others laugh at my plight but offer no cure. Fewer guests grace the hall this morn which helps.

"Serves you, for insisting we keep the window open last night!" laughs Alænèa.

A large mug of hot tea and warm taters smothered in melted cheese, aside soppy eggs at mornmeal remedies the inner cold. My buckskins and a roaring fire in the dining hall handle the chilly-bumps up and down my arms and legs. Alænèa finally relents and tells me where she's etched the offending rune. I remedy my boot situation and cannot help but smile at her for her genius.

"I'm for trekking up to the temple on the hillside this morn if any would care to join," I mumble around a muffin running with egg yolk, some in my mouth, some on my chin. All agree with smiles as I catch the drippings and usher them into my mouth. I am playing catch up as the others had arrived earlier than me and had finished up as I just began eating. The furions help finish cleaning my plate as I dust off the muffin crumbs from about my person.

We all carry our packs... Well, Therrien a shoulder bag as he has not yet acquired a pack suitable for adventuring. I have with me my Bo staff as well. Sæm carries his new sword on his back as it is too long to hang from his waist, and Alænèa wears her gifted bow and quiver. We stop in and tend to our horses but opt to leave them to pasture as they are happy to be free of the confines aboard the galleon. And so we decide to walk.

The towne seems no different from the many I'd experienced now in the Mid Realm. Stone abodes line the way in a somewhat haphazard manner, but lines hanging with drying clothes and linen are everywhere and shops cater to every sun life are open and doing business as usual. The smells and sounds are no different here. Life goes on for others even as mine seems to change in remarkable ways daily.

We come to the edge of towne and a well-worn travelway presents itself to us, clearly leading up to the temple that Guin has pointed out to us. Short trees with broad leaves and tall trees with no branches and large fronds bunched on top line the hillside as we go. These are unusual to me but I recall Da speaking of a type similar he found on some coasts in the Southern Reaches. He said hard-shelled fruit hung at the top of such trees, and I can see such a thing on these trees. Ferns cover the ground about us. Other trees I know by name grow in thick groves here and there. Small huts and stone abodes alike pepper the hillside with short fences about them and many goats are tethered, at the least one to a yard it seems.

Large boulders jut out from the hillside and pebble paths intersect with the travelway often. As we trudge our way up the track, I spy a large lynx cat pacing us up among the boulders. I reach out my spirit self and find the cat quite welcoming to it. I feel Bane close as well. We have been walking well into the second turn of a sand glass when we finally come upon a clearing. At its center on a small rise stands our destination. All about the clearing, I notice dozens of piles of painted rocks. The rocks are mostly oval in shape and smooth and stacked one upon another. Some piles stand as high as my shoulders, seeming to defy gravity as the small towers are precarious at best. As the others wander about looking at them, the lynx bounding out of the trees and heading straight for me. I sense no harm and watch in wonder as she bounds about perilously close to the stone stacks, but leaving all intact even as she brushes in and out and weaves betwixt them.

I sense a movement on the deep colonnade surrounding the entirety of the temple and see a figure emerge from behind one of the many pillars even as the lynx slides to a halt a pace from me, lowering its head with large pointy ears. She stares up at me and stretches her front legs out on the ground and towards me, expanding her giant paws and exposing her impressive claws outward towards me also. After a moment, the large cat rises up and approaches me, running her lithe body along my legs as she takes a moment to weave between them and then returns to face me. I sense Bane approaching from behind me now as well. This doesn't seem to disturb the cat at all, and Bane pays no particular attention to her. He is watching Guin as she bounds down the stair towards me, only to stop and reach down to hold the cat in its place.

"You are a strange man indeed, Arias. Fæna has never approached anyone in such a manner."

And even as she says this, the lynx pulls away from her and crosses to Bane, going nose to nose with him and then licks his muzzle and teeth. Bane accepts the act willingly and licks the cat about its ears in return. Guin's hand goes to her mouth as she draws in a breath. Fæna slides down through Bane's front legs and under his belly, only to turn about again and to sit side-aside with him, staring up at the both of us. The others have returned to us now.

Guin quirks her head at the cat.

"The Mœther is expecting you and has sent me to accompany you."

The furions take this moment to emerge from my pack and climb down to join Bane and Fæna, sniffing about the cat as she freely allows their curiosity.

"Who *are* you, Arias? I've never in my life seen animals act in such a manner, and it would seem you have something to do with it."

"I think it is more likely to be *their* nature," I say, that in no way is an adequate explanation, it seems to her.

"We should not keep the Mœther waiting. Please, follow me." Guin turns and starts back up the steps of the temple.

At the top of the stairs, we pass through massive, fluted pillars built of a glittering white stone. They appear to encircle the entire structure, which itself extends a long way back from this front face and easily three stories tall as I can now count very large windows set deep into the interior stone façade, three high. An arched doorway stands tall in the center of the building's face. Matching cascading stone arches step back further into the face until finally a huge wooden double door with arched top above and tremendous iron hinges, buckles, and twisted iron handles shaped as great long tree leaves adorn it. A towering tree with six trunks intertwined have been carved deep into the wooden portal, giving some idea to the thickness of the doors.

Deep runes are engraved into each door in like manner to the tree. They run across the top of both doors, and six individual runes are fashioned into each of the trunks of the tree depicted on the great entryway. The four of us stare at the magnificently crafted entry. Therrien sees the Runes of Elder and is fascinated by them. To Alænèa, Sæm, and myself the door glows in a golden aura, and to me the runes on the tree trunk stand out in different coloured glowing auras.

"Guin, why do the runes on the tree glow in different hues?" My friends look to me, and Guin, already at the door and about to push it open, turns back to us, her curiosity piqued once more.

"And how many colours do you see?"

Alænèa speaks first and says she sees three colours on the tree runes and the others glow a silver hue like the runes along the edge of the doors. Therrien stands squinting at the door, and Sæm indicates that he sees four colours, but two are more faint.

"I see six distinct colours, each bright and strong." I offer my opinion.

She nods in a knowing manner, reappraising each of us now.

"You've deceived me, the three of you. You have studied under a Wic'cha then? For it takes much study and concentration to distinguish each of the wards by their woven colours of ancient mægic. I still do not see the colour of the mind mægic. Do not tell me its colour, I must discover it myself!" The three of us shake our heads to her accusation.

"I see the different colour but know not the meaning of any of these runes. They are not druid elder ruins, I do not think," says Sæm, and Alænèa nods her head in agreement.

"I have not read these runes before, but I feel their meaning in a manner, just as I could in Ōdæn's crypt. I see the one you call mind. '*Thought*' is my impression of it though. It is there, just to the right of center on the tree." Guin nods and looks to me, and I read a bit of awe on her face.

"Come, Mœther will be very happy to meet all of you." Guin pushes one of the two doors inward, and it swings smoothly and silently on the great iron hinges. As I walk into the temple, I glance in wonder at the thickness of the great doors. Bane, Fæna, and the furions follow us in. Another lass in similar garb to Guin pushes the door closed, but only after having given wide berth to Bane. She apparently knows Fæna.

As we enter, the temple's enormous space swallows up any sound we make. One would expect an echo in such volume, but the apparent design of the stone walls eats up any sound. It has an eerie effect on me.

Two winding white marble stairways circle up from the center of the expansive space and on to the second level. But we are guided between the two stairs and into what turns out to be a great reception hall beyond. Groups of lasses of varying age stand around tables or stone monoliths or great bowls of water or mayhaps a different liquid. Some stand about geometric designs and enlarged runes made on the floor with sand or pebbles. Some of the designs glow.

A slim, but shapely elder woman with hair of silvered grey seems to flow throughout the space, whispering to this lass or that lass. She has a warm skin tone and her eyes shine an intense sea green surrounded by amber. All of the girls wear headbands or armbands embossed with any number of elder runes, a symbol of status within their group, I guess. Though she is clearly not the eldest, Guin has more runes incorporated in her garments than any other that I can see in the temple hall. Additionally, they all glow in gold.

"Guine*f*ere, bring your new friends over, please. Everyone else, continue working your wards."

We follow Guin over to a space defined by four standing pillars, half again my height. Then follow the Mœther within. As we step into the area, all sounds from without cease. The animals and Guin remain outside these pillars, unable to enter as if not invited or at the least unwilling for some other reason. And then I see Guin walk about the hall like the Mother had been, giving advice to others. It is a sharp contrast, she being so much younger. Younger than many of the other lasses, too.

I am drawn back to the present as 'Mœther' speaks to us.

"Let us see who has come to visit our island. Seldom do we have guests. Even more rare that they should come without a guide and further, in a vessel displaying the flag of ancient mæges. A little bird tells me you have a weapon that Týr thinks is significant as well. Your names are Therrien, Eshæm, Alænèa." Nodding to each of my friends in turn. "And you are Ariastone *Côeurdrægon*. That is a special name to us here. It is one of our own, and not one found in greater Aeryth."

She nods to me, but also takes time to examine me from head to toe. I give her the same courtesy. She carries a distinct aura, likened to the Elder Shèlah, but it a slightly different hue. She carries herself with an undeniable confidence, bordering on regal but somehow more casual than that.

"You may call me Vicchi. My whole name is long and boring and so Vicchi is fine. The lasses in training address me as Mœther, but outside of my duties here, I would prefer the simpler name, if you will." She smiles, and just as with Eschereon, we feel immediately at ease.

"Vicchi, it is then, and Arias for me if you would not mind." I reach out, offering my arm in greeting. She pulls me into a hug instead.

"Sæm, if you please then."

"Still Alænèa, though my companions seem often to try and shorten it as they have theirs… You remind me so much of my grandmere back on the Plain." Vicchi winks at this.

"Call me Ryen," Therrien speaks up and we all turn to him with raised brows. "What? Aside from you and Eschereon, all my friends and family call me by my familiar. And I thought it appropriate while in Eschereon's company. But out adventuring, I think I prefer the familiar." A wide smile graces his face. We all laugh to learn something new about our friend.

Vicchi ushers us to seats, stone benches, four placed about and defining the sides of the pillared space.

"You have not invited Guin?"

"You are quite perceptive, Arias, for one so young. Please, do not take my comment about your age to heart. In fact, you remind me of Guin in that manner, and I respect her all the more for it. But you will see later my intentions there." Again, with Elders and their mysteries. I decide not to pursue it further at this time.

"Your auras are well defined. You've had some training in the mægics then. I would surely have assumed such with the vessel you arrived upon, though I must admit I had hoped you'd arrive with at least one of my brethren aboard."

We speak then of our time with Eschereon and our escape from Mensæ, and then the tale of my earlier capture and escape from the same man. Her eyes narrow and her hand involuntarily forms a fist in her lap as I tell the tale. After the telling I find myself amazed that I have confided all this to a woman I've just met only moments before. Vicchi puts a hand to my forearm to quiet me.

"You have had a quite remarkable life in your few years, Arias, and I would like to continue our conversation later. You would like to tour the temple? It is quite a remarkable place, and mayhaps a mid-sun meal before we begin again. You've given me a great deal of information to digest in the meanwhile."

And just like that, she ushers us out to Guin, who has been patiently waiting outside the pillared space, seated on another stone bench. Lilit and Jilly are curled in her lap receiving much-appreciated scratching and petting. I assume Fæna and Bane have returned to the outside. All the other students have gone, and I realize that we have been talking to Vicchi for a very long while, sure certain. Our mid-sun meal will be happening well after mid-sun. Sæm's stomach can be heard in protest.

What our Wic'cha friends lack in punctuality, they make up for in quantity and quality, to Sæm's delight...all of us actually.

While eating, it becomes my turn to query Guin.

"Your mœther has a way of extracting the most personal of information from people, Guin. I actually felt the need to tell her everything about myself!"

"I also," adds Sæm. Alænèa and Therrien declare the same. Guin smiles and I can tell there is more to this story.

"When the Mœther is in a hurry to discover a person's true intentions, she has me deliver them to the Sanctum of Forsæti. It is where she interviewed you."

I cannot help but smile. I think Guin is easy to give away the Wic'cha secrets. I tell her so.

"Nay, Arias of the outside world. There are no secrets here. This is knowledge even a first year learns. And it works on all that sit within. The Mœther would have been likewise compelled to answer any of your queries in full truth. Further, I am in my year of truth oath. I wear the veritas rune. I am compelled to answer at all times truth as I know it to be."

"More enlightenment then, if you might, Guin. Your face tells me there is more." She does just that.

"Forsæti and Brågi, were the founders of the Wic'cha and Wærlo'cha here on Asgährd. And they were the sons of Freyja, the Source-Sayer of the Isles. She left them to grow the two sects when she departed."

"We've heard Eschereon speak of these…Source-Sayers on occasion. They were the first mæges to arrive in Aeryth, are they not?" Sæm queries the young girl.

"Yea, that is truth. Though the Source-Sayers were much more than just mæges. Early on, in the times of Forsæti and Brågi, mæges were still quite strong, though they were the first generation born of the Source-Sayers and local peoples, and thus the mægic even then was muted in them somewhat. These are the teachings for Wic'cha novices, but mayhaps these tales are no longer known on the mainland." Therrien—*Ryen*—speaks up.

"The druids, such as Eschereon, keep this knowledge, but you speak the truth. Such tales are at best legends seldom spoken in the Mid Realm these suns."

"They certainly may be tales for another time. I only mention them because the Sanctum of Forsæti harkens back to those times. Founder Forsæti strove for peace, justice, and above all things, truth. The pillars are warded most strongly to that end. Any that sit within are compelled to nothing but truth."

Smiling to myself, I can now see why the Wic'cha guide the Asgährdians. I cannot fault Mœther Vicchi her little deception. She has learned swiftly who the strangers are that arrived sailing the ancients mæges galleon.

"Guin, mayhaps we, amongst ourselves, might discuss a few further truths. Tell us something of the runes you wear. I've noticed all that study here carry some upon their person. There are some that wear many and some with few. There are some newly painted and some embossed in gold. We have studied warding with runes under the Druid Eschereon, and to our folly, our friend Alænèa is becoming quite adept in their use." Both Alænèa and Sæm chuckle aloud, and it brings a raised eyebrow from Guin. "What do they mean to you?"

"These runes are what we Wic'cha are most about. They are the building blocks of our mægic. They are used in helping to protect people, or anything for that matter. With proper use, they can ward against everything from disease to discovery. They heighten protection or strengthen mægic. Likened to the olde Mæges' staffs and stones, they concentrate mægic to a spot. More to the runes' purpose, they are tools to enhance any mægic. We wear the runes to proclaim our proficiency in ward lore. But you would know some of this, as you wear two amulets of Wic'cha crafting. I am most anxious to examine them should you allow me."

I feel suddenly conscious I carry my Bo staff. Eschereon had tutored me some in regards to mægic and my staff. When we had first met, he had raised my staff purposely to the sky and summoned what had appeared to be a flash akin to a sky bolt. And in an intense encounter with a group of mercenaries trading in youngers, I had once experienced such a result myself, though I'd not summoned any mægic a-purpose. I did not believe such a thing possible, at the time. Da had crafted my Bo staff with two stones that I had found as a younger at Moon Lake, at either end, unknowing that they would have this further purpose. I had practiced recreating the mægic effect, but other than producing a light to one end, I remained mostly unsuccessful. He had also advised that I cover the ends of it to hide the stones and runes. I had come to do just that, wrapping the ends tightly with leather. Even as I did to disguise it when I had visited Bladestone, a city filled with soldiers with an eye to finding me. Even now, Guin made no mention of it, as it appears a simple walking staff that a traveler might carry. Mayhaps the Wic'cha can help me draw mægic to it as they draw mægic to runes. I think it an effort worth pursuing.

In the eve, we return to the Forsæti sanctum and the Elder Vicchi, this time armed with the knowledge that our queries will be answered in truth even as hers are. We become the ever-curious ones, and she patiently answers our questions. Finally, I present my most pressing query, though I have waited till the last.

"Vicchi, Eschereon spoke in a time past, even as we stood on the cliffs overlooking the Dæmon Straights, of my true bloodlines. He said that they originated in half here on this very isle. I spoke earlier that it was my search for my mœther that led us here, as Eschereon indicated that he thought my pæder would bring her here for her further safety. Would you have knowledge of this?"

"Mayhaps. I would need to know more to be certain, but I've learned much about you, Arias, and I surmise more. You, by your very appearance, have the traits of an Asgährdian. And how you and your friends speak of your abilities gives me further clues. We, of course, get few visitors here on the isles, and I know of one such person that arrived many years ago. She carried two names. One she kept close as was wise. I know both."

"My mœther's name is Aeglèsia, and my pæder's name is Illèron, so I've been told. I have but one memory of him." Vicchi nods. "I was told by a man called Týr that she resides on a sister isle that is unapproachable by sea and that the Wic'cha have another way of getting there." Vicchi smiles.

"Týr never ceases to amaze me. He and your pæder were as brothers growing up. Illèron, the more clever and talented mayhaps, but Týr has always been the more persistent of the pair. It does not surprise me that he found you afore me and has cyphered who you are. And he is correct. To a point."

The others have quieted and sit staring at the two of us. Knowing that this is a consuming desire of mine.

"To a point?"

"I know the way to Onæ Parâdeis, but it is not a simple trip. And the inhabitants of the isle do not suffer well certain visitors."

"What type of visitors do they not suffer well? And what does that mean?" Vicchi stands and lifts a pitcher that had been set up on a small table in the corner. She fills our cups with a light juice. I sip from my cup, showing patience. Returning to her seat, she lowers herself with a soft sigh.

"Men."

"Men?"

"Lads, men, man-child, any male. No man spends more than a sun upon the isle. It is not tolerated." So then, Týr's earlier fantastical comments to us were borne out in the compelled truth of Vicchi. Alænèa speaks up.

"How can a society grow... even maintain without men. It is not possible. There are functions even the most dense of skull men must perform for a village to survive, and it is not hunting. I've learned such things from the elders back home, even if I have not experienced such. Is there some ancient mægic that lets it not be so?" She smiles and a flush crosses her cheeks.

"Nay, the workings and needs of the body have not changed for the Amæzonaens. And they have their ways that keep their numbers growing, or at the least static and very strong. Let me explain." And she tells us of the Titæns and the Amæz on the neighboring Isles of Onæ Parâdeis and Olympæa. These tales do indeed pass the borders of the incredulous.

She regales us with tales of civilizations much older than the history of the Source-Sayers on Aeryth. The Titans and Amæzonaens were two such. That they still exist upon the isles in the Straits, a wonder in and of itself. Once thought of as gods of Aeyth in ancient times, they have retreated to their ancestral homes on the Dæmon Straits Isles, the coming of mæges to Aeryth being a significant reason for it. Having bloodlines reaching back to mæges, Asgährdians are never allowed ashore on Olympæa. Or not without severe consequence in any manner. Somehow, the three isles found a mutual harmony. For the Amæz need the Titæns and vice versa for the survival of both their races. A mating ritual unique and involving all three islands and all three races.

Alænèa persists in her line of query and Vicchi is obliged to explain.

"The Titæns are true giants among men. A race apart from men such as your friends and descendants of a race extending to the earliest history of Aeryth and eons past. The smallest among them would stand more than half again your friend Sam's height, and he is the tallest among you. They are a society of only men, even as the Amæzonaens live with no men among themselves. Once, in millennia past, they co-mingled, but they were both proud and brutal and each could not bear the other's domineering ways. And so they separated to neighboring isles. But the Titæns are, all to a one, alpha males, and they continued to press any advantage over the Amæz as they are their only equals in which they could procreate. The women of Aeryth are literally too small to mate with even the smallest of the Titæns, though it was once tried." Sam sits up straight, listening intently, his thoughts wondering about this proclamation.

"This is where Asgährdians and our mægic enter into their history. It was our ancestors that brought a truce and balance to each of their societies. We Asgährdians use mægic to protect the Isle of Onæ from the Titæns and supervise certain rituals that allow each to grow…or at the lesser maintain the numbers in their tribes."

I cannot help but wonder about all that this would entail. But it does not change my intent.

"If I cannot visit my mœther on their isle, mayhaps a message could be sent so that she might visit me here?" A small smile, really just a turn of the corner her lips heralds disappointment in this suggestion, I fear…and am proven right.

"The Amæz, or their head mistress precisely, has taken an oath to your father, as he is a friend and they owe him dearly, that they would keep and protect Aeglèsia upon their isle until he should arrive back. They will not allow her to travel here, I'm afraid."

"They may at my request, however, allow you to visit one sun at a time. But this in itself poses problems. You see, the way is open but three to four consecutive suns in a moon cycle, and the path there and fro is complicated and will not be open for another fortnight and seven, even as it's just closed a few suns past."

Vicchi vows to help me though, and plans are to be made to have me guided there. But her aid is promised upon a condition. I am not to tell anyone of the purpose to my visit. She swears each of us to secrecy in this and silences us before we can ask her the why of it.

21

Family on Onæ Paradeis

I cannot say the wait till I can visit the isle of Onæ has passed slowly. We are given free rein over the temple's grounds and libraries and this keeps Alænèa and Sæm busy well into the eves. Vicchi acolytes are there to answer any queries, of which there are many from all of us. But I especially enjoy time alone with Guin, as she gives me guided tours of not only the temple grounds and facilities, but also the whole of the isle. We travel about on horseback, and Paint seems glad to be out and about with me.

We visit two other townes on the isle and each has histories and wonders of their own. The isle itself holds mægical wonders, and Guin has become a prime source of Asgährdian histories. She is well studied in them for one so young. Bane, the furions, and Fæna have become inseparable as well. One day, Guin remarked upon an incredible falcon of unusual plumage she had noticed two suns in a row and I smiled, calling out to Talon to join us. Her eyes widened when he first approached and alighted upon my shoulder.

We have moved to the temple's dormitories and one morn when we four met for mornmeal, Guin joined us in the dining hall. We were seated in a brightly lit courtyard enjoying a meal of thick flatcakes, honey, and fruit, the sunlight reflecting off sparkling white stone walls that were three stories tall and somehow filtering to us below. The younger acolytes populated the tables about us and did not have the look of serious students but rather young friends enjoying fellowship whilst eating runny eggs, smashed taters, and fruits. We noticed her approaching with an wider smile upon her face than she usually carried.

"Arias, gather your pack. Mœther has said the way to Onæ is opening this morn. I've been chosen to guide you there." We all rose as one, anxious to get started, having been forced to wait this past fortnight and seven.

"Oh, no… only Arias," she said as my friends rose with me. "Only Arias will be allowed to accompany me, and even then, Mœther is not sure if we will be granted entry on the other end." The others slowly sat again, looking to me with disappointment upon their faces.

"But I am not a male," protested Alænèa, hoping for special permission it seemed, but saw immediately that Guin could not. "Will you be okay, Arias?"

"Aye, of course. What could go wrong with Vicchi's top acolyte by my side!" We all laughed, the joke betwixt us being that Guin had taken up Alænèa's penchant for rune mægic pranks and delighted in using me to practice on.

I gathered up my full pack, quiver, bow, and with my Bo staff, was ready to go. After pulling Paint from the stables, I met Guin and two other acolytes out in the rear yards of the temple. Alænèa seemed near to pouting as she stood with Sæm and Ryen awaiting me.

"If Guin can bring two temple friends with her, why can't I accompany you, Arias?"

"Adara and Wynn will not be accompanying us to Onæ. They follow us only a far as the portal and will return to the temple with our horses. The way will be too perilous for them," explained Guin. My eyebrow rose to this.

"I'll be gone but a few suns with the restrictions the Amæz put on a man's travel to their isle, and I'll regale you with my adventures as soon as I return, I swear."

"'Tis the missing out on the adventures that bothers me most, and though you are an acceptable bard, 'tis just not the same as living them with you."

With fare-thee-well hugs and slaps we were on our way. Though my human friends were left behind, my creature friends were still in attendance. As I climbed to Paint's back, the furions found their favorite space ahead of me on my saddle, spoiling for a new adventure. Bane, never meaning that I should befall another misadventure as my trip to Kings Court, was within sight with Fæna following close on his haunches. As I looked to the sky, I could make out Talon there, circling above, not much more than a spec amongst the clouds, but I knew it to be him ne'er the less. We were off.

Our travel has been long but not weary-some, as the landscape is all new to me, and Guin's stories of her life on the isle and its history are fascinating. We are headed south and east and after half a sun's ride we seem to leave civilization behind. The terrain has become rocky and more sparse of vegetation. Where other parts of the isle are lush and perfect for growing crops and trees and thus more suited for easy habitation, this part of the island by its very nature is not welcoming. Even still, from time a'time, we see to the distance a stone abode with smoke streaming from a chimney. Some folk prefer the quiet of the landscape, one can imagine.

There seems no visible path to our travels, but Guin turns our party from time a'time at some not so apparent landmark and turns us in another direction. I strain to make out her points of reference, and finally, slipping into my *Knowing,* I see what she sees. Runes that glow to those who know how to look. They are well disguised but for their glow, and thus hidden to all except those knowing to look for them. Simple runes, noticing one to the west of our current path, with its meaning *east,* we turned east. The rune has been crafted/chiseled with care into an otherwise nondescript boulder in the shadow of another. The runes for the compass points are simple and easy to pass as natural features to the stone, but with their glow from being formed of mægic, they are evident to those who are in search of them. Clever.

Showing off, I forge ahead of our party and make the next two turns without Guin's guide. Adara and Wynn looks to Guin with mouths agape, but she just gives me a knowing smile.

"Let this be a lesson, my friends. Our secrets will not always be as well hidden as we think. And do discuss it with Mœther upon your return. Though, I think our friend Arias here has knowledge and abilities that surpass most any other." They stare back to me with expression of wonderment.

We travel the whole of the sun, and we finally stop and make camp in a spot I recognize as being used for this purpose before.

"We will reach our destination mid-morn on the morrow, Arias. That is where we will leave Wynn and Adara behind. We would normally blindfold a guest, such as yourself, but I fear it would be a waste of effort." I nod.

Sitting around the fire, I explain to the two other lasses that I know the secret of the trails signs and that I can see the glow of the runes, which Wynn herself cannot yet see and that I recognize their meaning. They relax a bit more about me as they see Guin show no worry. After all, she is an acolyte in the confidence of the temple Mœther. Conversation becomes easy then, and we have a good time telling each to the other the stories of our lives.

The morrow's morn breaks with a chill wind and the far away sound of the surf crashing against the rocky coast. We have a small mornmeal of cakes and cheese and set off again, not even bothering with a fire. The lands about us are hilly and dotted with boulders the size of small cottages, and we are headed downhill mostly.

Finally we come upon a great monolith of stone which stands as high as me twice over, and with a sheared flat surface facing inland and that sits at the edge of a cliff, overlooking the sea. The drop at this point is most severe. After some words apart with our traveling companions, Guin dismounts, explaining that we must go afoot from this point. I nod, dismount myself, and gather my pack, staff, bow, and quiver.

After I have *spoken* to Paint and the others have left with our horses, we are joined by Bane and Fæna as Lilit and Jilly stand on a boulder welcoming their approach. Guin scratches Fæna about her ears and when the lasses are well out of sight, she turns to the monolith afore us.

"The trip from this point holds many hazards and you'll need to follow my instructions most diligently. It will take us the rest of this sun to reach the Zonæ."

I think that we will somehow make our way down to the rocky beach and board a vessel for the rest of our journey, though no isle to the south or east can be seen, nor any boat below on the beach. I have it but half right. There will be no vessel used in our crossing.

Guin stands afore the monolith now, running her hands across it at chest height, whilst whispering an incantation. She speaks it in a sing-song fashion, using a distinct cadence. Her hands pass over the stone once, then twice, then thrice. She works patiently, as it seems whatever she is doing holds no result. But finally after mayhaps her sixth pass across the stone, runes begin to appear. Faintly at first, but then an aura seems to pull them to more relief against the stone. She steps back now and studies the runes that have mægically appeared. But her brow furrows in confusion. She looks behind us and places her hands to her hips.

"I am perplexed, Arias. This has never happened to me afore."

"I see the runes. You cannot read them, Guin? I will be of little help as I do not recognize them."

"Nay, Arias. I can read them just fine. They are runes of the Amæz, known to few outside of their society. But this is the first time they have made no sense to me. You see, to gain entrance to the gate, all and each one who desire to pass must answer the question presented. There are two queries. One for me and one for you, but mine makes no sense!"

"What are the questions, Guin?"

"They are worded so it is clear to me which is yours and which is mine. Yours asks you to speak the full name of your sister, and I assume you can do just that. But mine asks me to speak the full name of my brœther... but I have no brœther, so it is impossible to do as is asked."

"Aye, I see. And I am at similar loss. I know I have a sister as I was reminded of it by Eschereon shortly after we met for the first time. My memories of her were awakened by him, but they were of a babe in swaddling in a crib or held tight to my mum's breast. I know not her full and true name."

We sit together upon a waist high boulder, staring back at the monolith with its glowing runes and patiently awaiting our response.

"I am baffled it would even present such queries, as they usually relate to the business one has on the isle or the person you wish to see. You've never spoken of it, Arias, and I'd never asked as Vicchi had told me it would not be appropriate to query further. But if we are to solve this riddle, mayhaps I must know more."

As I sit and think on Guin's question of me for just a long moment, my heart swells as a new thought warms me. Something Týr had said to me.

"The memories of my sister I hold clear in my mind, as I said, were of my mœther with a babe to breast. She would smile down upon her as she suckled and whisper, 'my sweet roux one.' Mutti said 'twas cause of her hair being red."

Guin's head quirks and her chin turns to me.

"Who is it you are traveling to see on Zonæ Paradeis, Arias?"

"My mœther."

"But surely your mœther is not Amæzonaen. They mate only with Titæns, and a babe your size would be thrown into the sea. And my full name is Guine*f*ere Roux Côeurdrægon. My pæder's name given me is Guine*f*ere. It means 'white shadow.' My mœther's given name for me is Roux, for the colour of my hair she says." We know now and smile.

"And I am Ariastone Olóryn Côeurdrægon. Eschereon said that my mid-name was given me by my pæder and that it should only be spoken to those I most trust. I did not even know it afore meeting him. She nods, astonishment and wonder in her eyes.

We hug each other tight then and shed a tear…both of us. I can feel hers on my cheek even if she cannot see mine.

"Well, then, long lost sister mine, shall we?"

And standing afore the monolith, we each in turn speak our sibling's name as we stand side a'side, holding one and the other's hand. I start staring at the runes as they blaze in a brighter glow, but Guin turns and faces the other way, looking behind us. As I swing around following her lead, I see the ground ten paces out from us give way and fall in upon itself, revealing a large elongated hole in front of another great boulder, a match to the monolith we had faced, as if they were one cleaved in two. Guin smiles and heads that way. Fæna follows her, and as I follow them both, my creature companions are afoot with me.

As we draw near to the hole, I peer in to see a staircase of stone descending into the ground. Guin pulls her bag across her shoulder and doesn't hesitate to descend. Bane and the furions make their requisite sniffing about the hole but decide quickly to join me as I follow my newly found sister down into the ground. My guard stays up however as I recall our descent into the depths under Esper to escape Mensæ.

At two dozen steps and a deeper darkness as we are leaving sunlight behind, we come upon a large landing where we can all gather together. Having reached it first, Guin pulls a large crystal from her bag. From another small purse, she dips her finger in and when she removes it, she traces a rune of Crimson dye onto the crystal. Guin mutters an ancient word, and the crystal gathers all surrounding light to itself and grows to a brightness to match any lantern and more. After dropping the bright stone in a purse of fine leather netting, she holds it aloft to illuminate the space about us.

"Our long journey begins here, Arias. There is little but dizzying steps downward for quite some time, but have a care. After a while the winding and turning tends to make a misstep more likely, and a fall can do damage. When the steps end, we will take a respite and I'll explain the greater dangers we will face on our trip." I nod as there is little to say, and we continue our decent.

We'd entered the stair a little afore mid-morn, and when we reach the bottom of it, I wager we have spent a turn and a half descending. Any reckoning puts us well below sea level. The stone walls have become moist, and the air, as one takes each breath, heavy and wet. We reach a grand cavern with a stream bisecting it. In an effort to examine it better, I unwind one end of my staff and bring light to the drægon tooth gem as Eschereon had taught me. I will it brighter to a point where we can see from wall to wall the entire space. Guin looks to me and my staff in a new light.

"Well, we will have little need for my meager light now that you've decided to show a bit more of your talent… brœther! The Sage of Esper has taught you a bit more than you've let on." But then she hurries to the wall on our side of the steam, marveling at ancient runes that climb the wall.

"I have never seen these runes on my previous trips under the sea. And look, there is a stone skiff as if it could be used in the stream. But it is like to be far too heavy to float in such a shallow stream and too heavy to even move it to the current's edge. The stream gets wider and deeper further on but does not change for half a league. Surely a stone vessel would not float. What could be its purpose then?"

As Guin makes conjecture, I determine her to be right in that we two would not likely muscle it even a few paces, let it be the fifteen or twenty to the stream. But it is not stone but Ænt-wood I see under more direct light. Heavy, ne'er the lesser for it as I remember Da's mighty warhorse using his strength to drag a log of the very same material from Moon Lake all the way back to our homestead cottage.

"What do the runes tell you, Guin?"

"They say travelers can indeed ride the stream to its very end on Onæ. Though as slow as this flow is, we could walk the way as we usually do in less time. The way is treacherous in footing but I do not see how we can even move the boat into the steam that is not much more than calf deep here. It is shallow for quite some while.

Wait…the runes indicate there is a rune on the bow of the vessel."

I look, and it is one that I know. Alænèa has used it on me in many of her pranks. It commands a surface to become slicker than wet ice.

"Sheerash,"I speak, and with the slightest of experimental tugs, the heavy boat glides across the stone floor with ease.

"Guin, I see another line of runes on the wall where the stream enters the cavern." She walks over to study them.

"They seem to be what we call initiation runes. I can speak the sounds, but I know not what the result would be."

"Mayhaps you all, the creature and you I'm meaning, could try gathering into the vessel, and the rune on the prow may keep the bottom side slick even through the water under the boat. I could push us until we reach deeper waters."

We gather my pack and weapons and Guin's bag, and Bane, Fæna, and the furions board with Guin as the boat sits heavy and still on the stream bed. The waters simply move around the skiff as it remains anchored. My pushing, even as I again chant the rune's name, makes no matter. Guin turns back to the wall where the stream originated and speaks the phrase carved into the wall there.

"Foamæ Flurr Hæste Untàlèe."

This, apparently, happens to be the triggering event. The water in moments has risen halfway to my knees as I stand behind the Ænt-wood boat, and the steam tugging it forward.

"Get in, Arias. I believe we will need no further aide of your brute strength." Guin giggles, and she proves correct in the assumption. Even as I climb into the skiff, the current lifts and pulls us forward.

While Fæna looks behind, sidled tight to my side, Bane crouches tight to Guin, his snout just forward of the bow staring into the darkness ahead. I rekindle the mæge light on the head of my staff, willing it brighter so that we can see afore us. The furions are dancing along the boat's low gunwales as the stream picks up speed and us along with it. There are no oars aboard, and it appears we do not need any. The tunnel below the sea that we find ourselves in, at times narrows to near the boat's beam, and roils in rapids as it shoots us through at ever increasing speed to the next widening cavern. It is all that we can do to hold tight a'times to keep safe within the small vessel.

A few turns of a sand glass, with whiter knuckles and tight stomachs, finds us deposited finally into a large cavern as the stream immediately settles back to a trickle and we glide on a now nearly calm surface and then onto a glittering black sand beach. My light shines up a pathway into a tunnel leading away from the shore.

22

A Tinker's Magic

"Fates allow, will you look at that! Mæster Rōghæn, come see!"

I sit back, mesmerized by Huni. She'd disappeared yestermorn and did not come to bed with me last eve, and I've spent my morn hunting where she'd secreted off to. I now see the why of it. And as I do, I ponder what I've just yelled out. 'Tis just what Mum woulda said. A tear comes rushing down my cheek. For my thoughts of Mum and to see Huni has become one. A mum, I mean.

She has two tiny cubs a'burrowing into her side, and she looks up to me and I can see the pride in her eyes! I know it for what it is. Mæster Rōghæn finds us and proclaims it a wonder that she has been with cubs and he had not noticed, saying they carry the babes for six whole moons afore birthing them. He explains that it is further remarkable that there are two, as most times only a single cub gets birthed by wolf badgers and that Huni being as old as she is, would normally be well past birthing age. But they are cute little things, and I scratch Huni's ears to tell her so.

Huni has found an old trunk in a room Mæster Rōghæn used for naught but storing the strange trinkets and odds that he collects when he is out tinkering. She'd worked the latch open, as Mæster Rōghæn assured me it had been secured tight and made a nesting of the old clothes inside. He proclaims it well that they are being put to use as he should have tossed them years ago otherwise. I can see he has a faraway look in his eyes as he discusses it, like he as thinking of somebody.

Mæster Rõghæn seems to know about everything. I've never met anyone who knows so much. When I ask him how he knows Huni's age, he has me open her mouth and teaches me how to tell an animal's age by their teeth. He tells me a lot about wolf badgers as he can tell me and Huni are "tight as peas in a pod," as Mum would say. He explains that wolf badgers have few enemies in the forest as they are so fierce, and even bears and mountain cats do not usually bother them since they are not easy prey. He continues, telling me how a wolf badger's hide is thicker and tougher than any other animal's, 'cept mayhap a drægons. I, of course, chirp and chuckle to this as I'd learned after much teasing by my older brœthers that drægons are just tales for scaring youngers.

He expounds all the more, seeming to want to tutor me in all aspects of wolf badgers as he sees I've taken interest. They are immune to most any venom, so vipers and sling-tails cannot harm them and become just another meal for them. I can attest to the viper part, as that is how I'd first met Huni. I know sling-tails as Thom had brought one as long as his hand home on a pike one day. Its stinger tail curled up over its back. I can even imagine Huni pinning one with her claw just like Thom's pike and crunching with her sharp teeth into it as a treat and a bit of fun.

He says their favorite food, though most think it honey, is actually the bee larvae, the bees' birthing pod. The honey is an added treat. Mæster Rõghæn does not need to tell me about Huni's claws. I already know what they can do. But learning from him is a wonder. What he doesn't already know, he has hundreds and hundreds of books to tell him.

I could sit and listen to his tales for countless turns of a sand glass and do just that, as we remain trapped in his cottage by the sand storm for over a fortnight. Ten and seven suns actually. I know cause I've carved a small notch to my bedpost each eve of the storming with the small blade I always keep on me since my brœther gifted it to me on my seventh year-ender. Mum was not happy at the time.

We are able to venture to the barn most suns for a turn or two before the sand comes raging back. Mæster Rõghæn teaches me to fill the feed buckets and how to pump water into the trough for the horses whilst he mucks in the stalls. Then we hurry back to the cottage and he seals it up by talking to the walls and we're safe from the storms when they come again. Mæster Rõghæn proclaims me a fitting apprentice and ward. He explains what that means, and I am most happy to hear it. He answers all my queries and names me *In-kwist-a-tiv* cause I have so many. I just say back, "If you please, just call me Elsii." It always brings a laugh.

But most of all I like that he reads each eve from the histories he keeps in all of his books. And in the morns, he tutors me on how to read them myself. He says it is a part of being his ward and that any ward of his needs to know reading and cyphering and mayhaps even schrivening.

Just as I've explored the whole of the cottage thrice over, Mæster Rõghæn announces the storm will abate in a couple of suns. I know not how he knows such a thing as the winds seem to me to be howling as loud as they ever were, but I've learned to trust that he knows. He especially can forecast the weather, calling it ancient mægic that he knows well.

"We must gather our needs for a long trip, Elsii, as we shall be traveling far to the north and through the Furor Mountains and past the edge of the dead marshes."

I, o'course, know nothing of these places, but understand it will be a long journey and love the idea of Tinkering with Rõghæn along the way. I've come to love that life as he carries me with him after rescuing me from the lord and lady's soldiers. I've become adept at reading the faces and manners of customers while they barter, and Rõghæn favors me as a natural to the business. I cheer and clap that we are to head out and take a few trips to Rõghæn's storage room to gather some trinkets and the like to place on his wagon.

As Rõghæn said it would, the storm breaks on the third day, and after gathering the wagon and horses and tidying up the cottage, we set off on another adventure. We will be traveling near to two moons and mayhaps more, he reckons. Huni's new cubs I place in the hidey-hole behind the wagon seat and Huni spends most of her suns in the early part of our trip feeding and loving on them. When she isn't caring for them, I have one or the other in my lap doing the same.

For three suns we traveled over the desert. Betwixt towering cliffs early on, then a flat, sandy plain with no trail but Rõghæn's sense as to which direction to travel in. He points out his landmarks and I put them to memory as he asks, but I feel there is no great need as Rõghæn clearly knows his way. On the third eve, the dry and dusty ground comes to an end, and we come upon the great travelway to Esperance. We've been there and back prior and it feels like familiar ground.

I recall our earlier trip to the great capital city of the Southern Reaches and sigh as we turned north and away from that remarkable experience.

"Aye, Elsii, the southern capital is a great experience, but I assure you there will be many more wonderful experiences on our way north. No cities the size and grandeur of Esperance, but interesting places ne'er the lesser in their own way. A keen eye on your part will make them so."

I take his meaning as he has already taught me a great deal in observing my surroundings with care. From hidden creatures in the landscape to the ways and manners of the folk we meet. Traveling with Rõghæn always holds adventure and learning.

One of the most amazing things I am learning about harkens back to the sun we met upon. He tutors me on mægics. Rõghæn explains that I already possess some of my own, sure certain. I scrounge my brow trying to recall any mægic I have shown, even inadvertent. I have seen Rõghæn's as he has explained that his conjuring the whirling dervish is just such a thing. He later explains that his abilities lie in controlling, in small part, elements of weather and air. It is how he learned also to read the patterns and signs of weather to come.

He tutors me that a mæge taps into mægic that is always around us and indeed everything in nature, and that one's affinity to certain types can draw upon that mægic at will. Rõghæn explains that my mægic is my empathy with creatures, and that all creatures exude their feelings and intent. He says that some who carry this mægic can actually see through the eyes of a true spirit animal. My ability to 'read' a person's manners and expressions and take meaning from them is an extension of my mægic. He explains that I should always trust in that ability as mægic does not deceive, it is always pure.

I think this a trifling thing and not really a mægic until, as I take hold of memories past, I recall times when I can see intent that others seem confused over. 'Tis a fact I'd seen intent in Lady Mæve in the garden that day that I had not recognized afore. I know it now as evil and will recognize it anywhere if I should see it again. It was a distinct aura about her, and I know I would know it again the instant I see it.

Our suns are long betwixt the occasional traveler or small village squares where we proffer our wares, and so I become obsessed with Rõghæn's mægic and pepper him with queries about it. He obliges me and explains how he works his mægic and how he had been taught to recognize and use it. He says he can actually sense what he calls the *elements* mægic about him in nature. He describes how his tutor, long ago, would have him sit alone for several turns empty-minded until he first sensed it. Rõghæn explains he now sees it in shades of colour and can maneuver it with just a pushing thought.

Many times as we ride on, silence becomes the norm, and I use these times to try and will his described mægic into being. I concentrate intensely on a passing breeze, following it through the branches of the trees above. Alas, no colours, no matter the thought I put to it. But then, one morn, as I sit in front of Rõghæn's mornmeal campfire on a dreary cloud-covered sun, I note something about the cubs. I have been staring at them, determined to find appropriate names for the little guys, and notice a distinct hue about them. Though one has the look of a piece of tree bark fallen to the ground, and the other wears a black coat salted in white, both seem toned in a light golden hue. Just the softest of glow that clings to the ends of their fur, it recently begins to grow out enough to stand out from their tiny bodies.

I look over to Huni and note it about her as well, but in a more pronounced manner and know I have never seen it about her before. She is busy about something at the edge of the trees, and as I concentrate on her glow, the fur on her back bristles and she turns immediately to stare at me. I smile at her and she stands on her hind legs and studies me in return. Pressing my feeling of love for her out and towards her as if I were pulling her into a hug, I suddenly perceive…or rather see through her eyes myself staring down at her. I shake my head and fall back onto my bum, wondering what just happened. Looking again to the cubs, it is no longer a slight glow about them but an intense aura of gold. And I feel for them even as much as I felt for Huni. Glancing back to her across the camp, she lies stooped, head betwixt her outstretched forelegs, exuding what I know instantly to be her love for me. Mægic does not deceive.

Even as this happens, I draw my finger back from the sharp teeth of one of the cubs, their names popping into my head. One lies half curled into a ball with his belly pointing out as his brœther nips at his short tail…Bark and Bite.

In the suns following as we travel, I cannot help but explore the connection betwixt Huni and me. I realize after searching with my mind and pressing towards my thoughts of her, I've become aware of her presence even when she is out of my sight. It is a warmth, much like I feel as I physically hug her. I know she has gone out in search of food this morn, and I sit back against a tree on the soft mossy side and think only of her. I push or stretch my mind out to her and immediately sense her presence, even as I know she senses mine. Closing my eyes, as her cubs cuddle into my lap, I let myself lightly fall against the presence of her that I continue feeling and become...absorbed into it. The mægic of it leaves me seeing through her eyes now as she forages about the forest floor, her keen sight and smell becoming my own.

I become more and more aware of folks' expressions and manner as well. I find myself tugging on Rõghæn's jacket when I note a customer's deceit written clearly to me on their face or in small actions. Rõghæn also always seems to pick up on it then, and takes it into account in his bartering. Rõghæn thanks me after, reinforcing that I should at all times listen to my intuition, he called it.

We travel to and through amazing places, whether they be small villages, larger townes, or wondrous landscapes. We, from time a'times, cross paths with other tinkers and the tinker's bazaar is front and center in the conversation. Tinkers are spreading the word. Our travels, though never direct to a point on the compass Rõghæn had gifted me along with the knowledge of its use, keeps us always on a northern track. As we travel, I become more aware of our surroundings. Some because Rõghæn points them out, but others come to me more as a feeling than a perceptive eye as Rõghæn oft comments I should learn and he begins teaching me.

I find by being still, sitting next to Rõghæn on the cushioned wagon seat, and letting my mind settle away from any real thought, a glow might appear in my side vision, and investigating, I'd find a doe off in the distance standing still but watching us. Or a viper curled tight in a dark hole in a log, suddenly bright in my vision. The forests we travel through are now teeming with creatures I've never noticed before. Most small and harmless going about their business, or a deadly cat or full tusked wild boar quietly stalking about us, are evident as well. Most remarkably I am able to sense their intent, dangerous or just curious.

I begin to notice other things in my quiet times also. And they come as colours too. The breeze has a hue, and with it, I can follow its wendings through the leaves and branches. The sun's heat has more than a bright-ness…a glow that interacts with the breeze, causing it to react in return. Rõghæn watches as I become more and more preoccupied during these times, noticing my keen interest in what appears to be nothing at all. He recognizes my behavior and thoughts.

"Just as the sun, though still, can push and pull a breeze, you can as well, Elsii." I would not have thought to try without his nudge.

Thinking on his comment, I gaze down upon myself, not looking directly but with my 'side' sight, as I do when studying the forest creatures around us. I catch my breath, and my skin tingles as I notice that I carry a glow about me also. It becomes more distinct as I examine it, so that in time, when looking directly to a part of myself–say an arm or leg–I can see it! Once I can look directly upon it, I inspect and scrutinize it.

My glow is different from the forest animals. Colour-wise it favors a blue hue and seems more substantial…thicker maybe. As I pull my hand across my arm, it seems I can gather and push it, though there is no sub-stance to it. Spending turns of a glass mesmerized by this new part of me, I experiment endlessly. Hearing Rõghæn's words again, I try all sorts of things with Rõghæn sitting aside me, a knowing smile upon his face. Finally, he comments.

"Push it, no…*will* it out from yourself. Interact with the things you see about you."

"What is it, Mæster Rõghæn?"

"Mægic. It intertwines itself with all things. Some can see it. Some can only feel it. And only a very precious few can bend it to their will. It appears to me that your talent extends beyond any other that I've seen in all my years. You can see it, can you not?"

"I see colours and glowing about creatures…and myself! The wind has a hue, and the sun's light as well. As I smelled the tree moss we just passed under, even the scent seemed to have a soft colour! It is amazing, Rõghæn. You see it too?"

He looks at me.

"I see glimpses only from time a'times. I can feel it mostly. I know it is there and can guide and influence it as my mentor taught me many years past. You are remarkable, Elsii. You know two mægics, and I wonder if mayhaps, more. It has been passed down from our ancestors many generations ago that there would come an age when mæges would command more than just one ancient mægic. Most thought it beyond the possible, but I'm seeing, just before my eyes, those ancient Source-Sayers had it right."

His words make little sense to me, but I pick up on the one clear thing he says. I might be a mæge? Like the tales Poppa would recite to me some nights. Myths only, he'd say, but with valuable lessons. Could he have been wrong? Rõghæn has shown me mægic is real, and now I can *see* it with my own eyes.

"I am no mæge, Rõghæn. They are only in tales and are old and have beards. And are, well, men!"

"No, not yet, Elsii, but one day."

"I will grow a beard and turn into a man!?"

His glee becomes uncontrollable at my words and he laughs aloud.

"Mæges were and are both men and women, Elsii." I look to Huni and sigh. I do not want to grow a scraggly beard. But I will if I must, for mægic's sake.

As we travel now, Rõghæn tutors me in the mægic he knows, and our tinkering becomes an even greater adventure. My dreams of my home in the mountain lodge calls to me less, and the though my hate for the lady survives and remains strong, it comes less to me as night terrors.

23

Reunion

Our troupe of odd traveling companions have made our way up into the crystal tunnel leading to the surface of Onæ Paradeis, the crystals holding a luminescence that light our way. We've progressed to a small cavern that Guin claims to be the halfway point to our destination. She lays a hand to my shoulder.

"Brœther," she says smiling, happy to have a blood sibling, and so acknowledges every chance she gets. I, knowing it to be so, feel the same. "I must tell you what to expect, as from this point on, we are in great danger."

"What danger could there be? Vicchi has said they are expecting our arrival?"

"Aye, and that is the reason for our peril. Arias, we will arrive to the surface of Onæ, and you will be seen as an enemy, no lesser than an unwanted intruder for no other reason than that you are male. And as you travel armed, that too will mark you as an interloper and a danger. You... we will be challenged. You will need your weapons. Do not be hesitant to use them. The first words you will hear will most like be those of a healer. They will not kill us, but we will not be left unharmed. I know this from personal experience. All strangers are challenged, myself included, but as a male, they will despise you all the more."

This seems crazy to me, but I know my sister to be under an oath of truth. So I prepare as best I can. Though a good way from our destination yet, I delve into my *Knowing* and push my senses outward. I join with Bane and the furions and as I feel the Amæzons are not a true enemy, I tell my creature friends not to engage, no matter what happens. I remove my bow and quiver from my pack and carry them instead, thinking to discard them so they will not hamper my movements if attacked. My Bo staff will serve me to greater purpose, I wager. As we make our way forward, I query Guin further.

"Tell me more, Guin, so I might better prepare myself to this strange welcome. You say they challenge and attack every male that sets foot upon the isle?"

"To my knowledge, there has been but a handful of men that they trust beyond reproach. And though one is our father, his favor will not extend to us. For my part, I believe they mean only to take a part in training me as I come of age, though it seems their lessons hold back nothing. I train back on Asgährd most every day in hopes of making it past their challenge without a trip to a healer."

I've seen Guin spar with sword and blade and other weapons back at the temple and know her to be quite proficient for one her size.

"Tell me more on what I should expect."

"The women of Onæ are all warriors. Few are shorter than half and again your height, and they have the strength of a horse–everyone. Speed is your best advantage, as reach and muscle will serve you less. They are all archers of tremendous skill and it is their love, but short swords are their weapon of second choice and they like close contact fighting when not sending an arrow your way. Do your best to stay out of their reach."

"They will attack us as a group?"

"Nay, it will be a one-to-one fight. Their pride will not allow it any other way. Their tradition is rooted in their mating ritual with the Titæns of Olympæ, who must win the right to bed with an Amæz, perhaps dying or taking mortal wounds in the effort. Any lust in their mating is rooted in battle lust."

"But I have no desire to 'mate' with them."

The corners of my sister's mouth turns up.

"And they would laugh at that prospect, assure. They lust for the battle, and sure certain, not your puny body!"

"Hey!"

Guin chuckles. "You will see, Arias."

At these last words of hers, I see ahead a natural light illuminating the unsettled dust in the air. Our travel path has become a stone stairway, and a scent of fresh air beckons. A flicker of light shadow passes before us in the distance. Mayhaps a bird flying by. Guin presses a finger to her lips, and we advance in near silence. I signal Bane and the furions to hold back. Fæna crouches, is ever alert, and remains with the other creatures.

With utmost care, Guin approaches the entrance out onto the surface of the isle.

"It appears they're not waiting for us here. But we must remain ever vigilant, as they will challenge us, sure certain, before we can reach Themis."

Stepping away from the cave that we've just exited, I can't help but breathe deep the fresh air and take in our surroundings. Lush countryside of green grasses strewn with boulders, some the size of our shed back on the homestead. I've not thought on my old home in quite a while, and the thought distracts me. A whine from Bane focuses my attention just in time to push Guin out of the way of an incoming arrow that I sense in my peripheral vision. In the time it takes to pull her back to her feet, two giant warriors in full battle garb are running full speed towards us.

From behind boulders thirty paces forward and left and right of us they are already near upon us. Their strides each are double the length of mine, and they approach at incredible speed. The one to my left, from which the arrow had arrived, is sprinting crosswise to my path and clearly headed towards Guin. A pace ahead of her, an even taller and heavily muscled warrioress is already leaping towards me, short sword in her right arm cocked back for a vicious thrust into my chest.

Slipping seamlessly into my *Knowing,* time slows for me as does the attack afore me. A precious moment to evaluate and react. My body relaxes and my mind is once again in the homestead barn with Da and Moor pushing great logs hanging from ropes tied to beams high above and fashioned like soldiers with wooden arms and legs. I focuse on the incoming targets, Amæzon warriors now, identifying the areas that would be most vulnerable to strikes from my Bo staff.

Twisting to my attacker's left and away from the sword thrust, I swing my Bo hard around and into the lower back of the black-haired warrior as she passes, her momentum pushing her forward, hoping to hit a kidney and at the same time pushing her along in an attempt unbalancing her. Immediately after, I pull the staff back and into ground in the path of the other's legs, just in time to trip her and send her in an uncontrolled fall in front of Guin. She is on her own now.

Glancing up and away from the immediate action, four other Amæzons approach with a small woman betwixt them.

My moment's glance away costs me. A rock the size of my foolish head hits me square in my left shoulder with a force that nearly bowls me over and makes my arm instantly numb and near useless. If my strike has done her any harm, my opponent hides it well. It does, however, cause a hesitation in her attack as she appraises me. I do not wait, however, and twist and roll forward towards her, starting low whilst swinging my staff left to right, side level to her knees. My strike hits her sword, suddenly planted in the ground in the path of my Bo, effectively stopping my strike dead and sending a reverberating recoil of energy back up to my already numb shoulder.

Two things noted in my effort. One: her sword, though it appears a short sword in her hands and next to her tremendous body, is indeed the length of any grown man's long sword… and two: this lady warrior is unbelievably quick and lithe.

Using her sword as a pivot point and with a remarkable twist of her body, a powerful leg catches me on my rise from my squat, hitting me square in my chest and sending me flying back easily five paces. I land hard without a breath to be had. I hear grunts and sighs and personal sounds of battle behind me. Guin and her adversary. Bane stands a few paces away, poised to attack. A glance to the four accompanying warriors shows two with nocked arrows pointed at him. I send a thought to him to hold still and relent and his body relaxes for the moment. I rise to re-engage.

Struggling for breath, I push past the pain and charge hard towards the woman made of rock and sinew, as she in turn bounds towards me. Knowing now I cannot win a battle against her if I fight like the trained soldier that Da and Moor had taught me to be, I take lesson from Sæm instead.

In our travels, as I trained Sæm in the battle techniques I had been trained in, he learned he could not best me in the same manner of battle. He learned the moves but did not use them entirely in like manner. His empathic mægic ability let him anticipate my trained moves. His answer was to strike with no rhyme nor reason of efficient movement, turning my training against myself. Most times his strikes were ineffective, but the unexpected manner would help him land sufficient hits so that the cumulative took a toll on me. I resolve to use the same technique on this warrior queen. These thoughts last but a moment in *Knowing* time, which is well, as we are upon each and the other.

In her charge, she swings her greatsword even as I drop and slide forward on my knees, my body bent back and below her sweep. As I make contact at thigh level, I push up with all my might through my Bo in both my hands and strike hard against her legs. As it once did for me in a long-ago battle, a greater force expels through the staff and she falls head under heals over herself and lands hard three paces behind me, limbs akimbo.

Rising swiftly, I turn and press my attack. I need to try and end this contest sooner than later as I am sure her stamina will outlast mine. As expected, she is back on her feet with just a shake of her head, facing me as I arrive to do further battle. Engaging immediately in hopes to put her on the defensive, I attack hard but erratic. Feigning without need, dodging to no perceptible end, I ne'er the lesser hit her hard from time a'time. Her trained strikes are also finding purchase on my body. Countless stabs from her sword find their way past my best defenses and pierce me time and again on mostly my extremities. I push past with the mental toughness that Moor's lessons had taught.

I am exhausted. And finally, a moment arises that I've hoped for. A mix of determination and desperation shines on her face as she backs a step and sees an opening I've given her…but it likewise leaves an opening to me if she uses it. She does, and I swing my Bo staff with all my strength in anticipation of her attempt. All goes black.

I awake to the words of a healer. Across from where I lie, Bane is sprawled in a corner, alert, with the furions snug against him but standing. All eyes turn to me as they are aware the instant of my awakening.

"You're unlike any person I've ever treated, the fates be praised."

I chuckle, and she stares back, mystified at my reaction. From the corner of my eye, I notice movement immediately to my left.

"Guin had said that the first words I'd likely hear would be those of a healer. She was right, it appears." I watch as a very tall woman, garbed in a simple white gown, examines my exposed body. I see now it is my mœther that has risen to come to my side, a bent smile upon her face.

"She prevailed against me after all, I see. I thought I might have had her there for a moment."

The healer stares down at me.

"Nay, it is you who prevailed, and but for the swift action of Feyre, Rieka might not be with us." She nods over her shoulder where my opponent lies, her naked body exposed in pained glory. She is all muscle and graced with wondrous curves in spite of it. But her body lies heavily bruised and an arm and leg wrapped as if broken and in repair. A large bruise under a great welt and bump rise along the left side of her face. Her eye swollen, black and blue and shut tight within the swell.

"Rieka is second in command of the queen's brigade and undefeated in battle until now. She is fighting for her life."

I, without thought and grave concern etched across my face, roll from my bed to make my way shakily over to her side. Shrugging off a dizziness, I touch her hand and delve immediately into my *Knowing*. Searching, I find her spirit sense and press lightly against it, sending feelings of warmth and respect. As if awakening, she embraces the empathy that I am sending, mayhaps mistaking it for something else. But I am in, and I will make the most of it. My *Knowing* searches her body for the greatest damage and rally her own body's abilities, coupled with my own to effect repairs and healing…until all goes dark.

I awaken to smiles from three very tall women, and my mœther and sister.

"Arias, Eschereon once said he sensed a great mægic lying within your small body before we sent you away and promised we would see you again in your lifetime. Both have proven true this day."

Lilit and Jilly now sit upon my ankles at the foot of my bed, chittering as if in a conversation betwixt themselves. They most likely are.

"Aye, son of Aeglèsia and Illéron, you have proven yourself worthy of Amæzon respect and friendship. You are welcome from this day forward on Onæ Paradeis." Guin squeezes my hand.

"You are certainly an enigma as well, young Arias. The skill to best one of our most elite, one whose wounds heal themselves, and one who can reach within another to give deep healing. Rieka awoke shortly after your touch, saying a great healing force had coursed through her body and she had known it for what it was. She lies in a peaceful sleep now."

I fall back deep into my pillows. Content as I look to my mœther, reaching for her.

"Mūtti."

She smiles, moisture coming to her lower lids, even as mine again grow heavy. I find a warmth and comfort in the ensuing darkness.

24

Relentless Pursuit

(Mensæ)

A whistling breeze and a faint echo calls as we approach the tunnel's exit with caution, Charan and I. Our remaining company remains aboard the Asgährdian vessel with her captain and crew just off the isle's southern coast. He is a devious one, and I respect that. A second *conversation* with him a few suns past and prior to our departure from Cliffside port, revealed his planned deception. He had hoped to carry us to our demise, approaching the isle against seas at their most dangerous, hence dooming our arrival to Asgährd in search of the king's bastard grandson, Arias. A lad who knows too much of me and the others now. A lad who clearly holds mægic as well. For this, he must die, but not before an in-depth probe of his mind. I'd shied away during our last encounter when I realized he could see my memories as I saw his. This will not happen a second time…a last time for him.

Our 'retrained' captain has brought us to Asgährd safely. We have ascertained the boy's whereabouts on the isle as he and his friends are near to celebrities who have arrived upon a mæge vessel. This news alone intrigues me greatly, but the boy remains my ultimate target. Once we found that he spent his time at the Wic'cha temple, we bided our time and waited for when he moved alone and became vulnerable to our purpose. I observed the temple and its acolytes. They seem but young lasses with no mægic present, so I think his interest there something other.

Finally, this very morn, after a fortnight of watching, Arias and the lass he spends most of his time with and only one other lass, headed out from the temple. We follow. After a meandering journey across the isle, ever towards the south and east coast, they finally make camp and send their escort back with their steeds in tow. It was a most curious thing to do, so I had the men intercept her and bring her to me.

My interest in the temple rises when probing the mind of the lass. I find her to be able to rebuff my early attempts at delving there. Interesting, in and of itself. But pressing useful. It seems Arias and his friend are to visit the adjacent isle populated by warrior women by some secret means, and hence their trip out to the wilds here. The lass lies crumpled at my feet now. She's served my purpose well, but I have no further need of her. I have the men discard the lass as I raise my spyglass to study the pair once more. Curiosity stays my hand for the moment, my mind turning the possibilities as we stand watch over their camp.

On the morrow's morn, from a distance and before we can approach them, we watch as they stand afore a monolith and speak, revealing runes that are indistinguishable to me at this distance. I have been mistaken though. It appears mægic of a sort was practiced in the temple. Pondering yet again, I have much to bring to our next meet of the Seven. My further thoughts with the mægic delays my move on the lad, however, and we watch as an opening in the ground behind them appears. We are too late to take advantage of our numbers. I decide to follow him instead. Any lethal encounter will need to wait a bit longer. With his wolf and the lass' cat, in the confines of a tunnel or cavern, it leaves too much to chance to try and capture and press him. Quickly adjusting to this circumstance, I send the rest of the company back to our camp near the ship hidden on the southern coast with instructions for the captain to sail and meet us. He will be able to find us through my mind connection to him now. Accompanied by Charan and one other, I follow the boy and lass into the tunnel. My scheme will need to be developed as we go.

They descend the ravine and enter the newly-opened hole in the ground as we watch. Tis a small test of patience as their small motley group of creatures and themselves descend out of our reach, momentarily. After a justified period, we follow. Not too soon, and apparently just in time, as a mægical shifting of the ground causes the entryway above us to close. The only way forward is down after the boy and his entourage. Though to our purpose, it remains ne'er-the-lesser disquieting to see such mægic in play upon the very ground about us.

Their troupe's descent upon a wending stone stair shows in a receding lantern light so that we can judge a safe distance to follow. Remarkably, crystals embedded high in the circular stone walls above the stair hold their lantern light for a time in another display of mægic. We have no need to light a lantern ourselves. And to greater purpose, I am finding Aeryth, indeed, carries the stolen Mægics of Destinæa. The temple and these isles have become of much greater interest now.

In trained silence, Charan has gone ahead of us in closer surveillance of the boy. Just now returning, he makes his report.

"Another remarkable feat, Mensæ. I've just witnessed them being carried off in a boat upon a rising wave and into a great cavern tunnel. They are gone, well ahead now."

My curiosity piques to a maximum. Were we close to discovering the heart of the Druidæ hidden realm of mægic on Aeryth? We must proceed with utmost caution. It will not do to be discovered now. Clearly, these Druidæ hold tremendous mægics and it will take guile and cunning to advance our purpose.

As we finally descend to the cavern that Charan says holds the charging river, a look of confusion crosses his face.

"Mensæ, the deep flowing river is gone. This stream is but a trickle to what I saw them leaving in."

We've arrived to a great cavern with crystals embedded about and still holding light. Upon the walls above and about a cave on the far end where it appears the stream originated, runes likened to those we saw appear on the monolith in the glade above hold still a faint glow as if they've been recently summoned by the lass who accompanies the king's grandson. They linger now in a dying ghostly flicker. I cannot cypher them, but I become determined to learn this rune lore mægic. Only the sound of the trickling stream and echoing drips accompanies my thoughts, the crystals' light fading as well.

We have no boat or swift river to carry us in pursuit, so we leave out on foot, down and into the tunnel leaving out from the cavern. Footing proves treacherous with slick moss lining the stone floor on either side of the steam. The stream bed itself remains the safest route, and though the ankle-deep water proves icy cold, we take that way. It gives me time to ponder what might await us.

Having traveled easily a turn and half again of a sandglass, we alast come to the end cavern of the tunnel steam. We find it empty but for a small skiff. But it appears clear where our prey has headed, as a single rising pathway leads out from the cave. No glow from crystals remain here, if ever they did. We are far behind them now, I cypher. I do not linger to rest, and the two trained warriors with me do not seem to expect it, and we immediately start our ascent.

The climb is not as hard as the drudge through the lower tunnel's stream, but grueling in its further length. We've finally arrived to a distant light showing down into the tunnel. The exit. Charan goes ahead once more and upon returning says,

"Haste, Mensæ. I believe you will wish to see what is happening outside."

He proves right, and it takes my breath for more reasons than Charan could know.

A light breeze sets a wave through tall grasses about huge boulders, and the sun shines bright betwixt billowing clouds. There has been a pitched battle, I reckon, betwixt Arias and his temple lass friend. Weapons lie about. They are both down, and a great warrioress aside... She is prone next to the lad. Standing above and about them are three other women warriors, their height and size astounding me. They are making final arrangements to carry the fallen away. I cannot tell if any of the fallen three have perished, but I think not as the true surprise at this sight literally takes my breath. Any doubts I might have had about pursuing the king's grandson are doubly banished as I watch Aeglèsia, the king's daughter, help tend to the lad.

She has aged o'course, but I hold no doubt of whom I see. Twenty plus years and the search ends here, on a hidden isle in the Dæmon Straights, draped in druid's mægic to hide her from the king's *sight*. This trip has become more fortuitous with the passing suns. But more dangerous, as well. If Aeglèsia is here, might not the Druid Eschereon be here also or other of his ilk? Have I found the home of the Druidæ that we seek? We will proceed and watch with utmost caution.

The lad is carried to a stone city. High walls, near in height to those around Kings Court surround it, and bright coloured roofs of clay over whitewashed walls and pastel-coloured shuttered windows shine brightly all about and within it. We arrive from the east, the rougher side of the isle. Looking past the city, I see great farms and orchards abound in low flowing verdant hills beyond. Below and to the north, a harbour with small fishing vessels sprinkles in a large bay or moored to a dozen long piers.

The following half fortnight passes mostly uneventful as we remain hidden in the hills above the stone city. We watch the lad being carried into the main keep and do not see neither him nor Aeglèsia nor any sign of the druid in all this time we wait. In fact, as much as we study it, there remains no sign of man nor boy anywhere in sight. As the temple lass had indicated, it is truly an isle of women only, unbelievable as it sounds. Remarkable women ne'er the lesser. Young lasses the height of a tall man and the grown women warriors half again as tall as any man I know.

Foot traffic all seems to enter and leave via the gates on the far eastern side of the city, and only warrior patrols of four come back our way. We remain cautiously hidden.

Nearing a fortnight now, our luck changes. At dusk on a misty and quite gloomy eve, a single warrior exits the city in our direction. As fates would have it, she is the same one that had been carried in by gurney with the king's grandson. She has a limp and her arm lies in a shoulder sling. Still, she looks an impressive warrior. Taking no chance, Charan and Dùghall lie in wait well hidden behind a boulder as she approaches. Ne'er the lesser for it, Dùghall, a brilliantly trained warrior himself, lies mortally wounded aside the woman, now subdued and unconscious from Charan's counter strike.

Bending over this magnificent warrior, I immediately begin to delve into her mind. Her being unconscious will make it an easier affair. But no! Even as her body is tuned muscle and exceptional, her mind resists my intrusion. In twenty-some years, I've found little opposition to my mind mægic, and now over the course of these past few moons, a few have challenged my attempts. First the lad, Arias. Then the Asgährdian ship's captain, and now this warrior woman. The Druidæ are here in Aeryth and active. There remains no further doubt within my mind. The lad will lead me to them, I am sure of it. But first, this mind before me must be breached without damaging it to serve my purpose.

I spend near to the entire night in the effort while Charan disposes of Dùghall's body properly. Finally, with mild coaxing, her mind opens to me. She is both humiliated that the lad has bested her in battle and awed by his power. It seems he has, with the use of healing mægic, aided in her recovery from the mortal wounds he had inflicted. She cannot be persuaded to render him onto us, her respect and awe for him too great. So I play to her humiliation by implanting another thought into her mind and set it to mature. It will serve my purpose just as well.

Erasing any knowledge of myself and her present circumstance, I leave her to recover alone next to this boulder where she will awaken. Charan and I make towards the coast to meet up with the captain of our 'chartered vessel.' My scheme has been pressed into motion. We will wait and watch now.

25

A Need to Flee

It has been a remarkable fortnight here with my rediscovered family. A stronger feeling still, than my experience in the northern mountains with Da's kin; pæder, brœther and cousins, though then I thought them my own biological family. For this truly is family. A sister just found that I remember not and a mœther refound, lost to me since just still an infant. I do what I can to regain some of the time lost.

The Amæzonaens are hosts like no others and though I am a man, they now accept me openly and sincerely, studying me like a new, queer wonder. But I spend near all of my time with my mœther and sister, trying to quench my thirst with a wellspring of queries, and those grow more numerous as they try to answer the ones just presented.

I am learning a great deal and grow ever closer to them, trekking rooms to speak to them of my life with Da as well. We are inseparable for a solid fortnight. And when not with my mœther, Guin and I become closer as well. I teach her to find her *Knowing*, and then we connect even as Finnie and I had. And though it gives us a powerful and tight connection, it sets my longing for Finnie into overdrive.

During our connection in the *Knowing*, my spirit sense no longer wants to call her Guin, but instead her name Roux calls to me.

During my time here, we wander about the city. Other than the fact that there is no man in sight, it is no different than any other I've visited.

The same air, carrying the same scents. Bakeries and stables and inns each contribute to the blend on the breeze. Cobbled stone lanes and stone abodes with coloured clay roofs. Laundry dried on lines behind homes, and every-sun activities happening with everysun folks. The one difference there is, is stark. All of the women are giants, and even the young lasses are as tall or taller than I. Even Sæm's home village seems to be dwarfed in comparison.

When not exploring, Guin and I are invited to spar with the local lasses learning the ever-present warrior trade. Giggles abound whenever I do. Guin suggests the young girls have crushes on her brœther, which mayhaps is the case, but it does nothing to lessen their aggressive attacks against my person. They have heard I'd bested their best, and each in turn becomes determined to land a damaging strike to my person. We are all learning from the training sessions.

My thoughts also turn to my biological father, Illéron. My mœther speaks of him as if it is urgent for me to know of him, and I must confess it is becoming more a need within myself to physically do so. Mœther explains to me that he travels the breadth of Aeryth, vigilant of an age-old threat that the Asgährdians have been charged with guarding against. An evil that, centuries past, the Wic'cha have taken a solemn oath to protect against.

These are echoes of tales I'd heard from the blind elder in Sæm's village and again on the Plains. Why, in such a short span of time, have I now heard these stories thrice, though they are two thousand years old? And niggling at my mind, to what purpose does my grandsire's–it still remains near impossible for me to grasp that my true grandsire is king over all of Aeryth–court advisor, Mensæ, travel all the way to Esper with a company of kingsmen in pursuit of me? His memories, those revealed to me even as he attempted to steal mine, now seem to portend more dire consequences to more than just myself.

But I'd passed this knowledge on to Eschereon. Surely it is all that I can do to fulfill my part. We've put that chapter of my life behind us, and I cannot be more glad of it. There can be no possible way for Mensæ to have followed me. Even as I proclaim this to myself, the amulet around my neck sets aglow so that its heart gem heat distracts me. Of a sudden, the broad sword of a warrior in training slaps me on the shoulder.

"Outlander, another round? You look bored. Your thoughts bounce about behind those remarkable eyes of yours! And mayhaps evemeal with my mœther and I?"

"Aye, another round then, Aschèr. I could use the distraction from my thoughts, as you say! And evemeal, aye. Guin and I would be honored to join you and your mœther. We are thankful for your invite."

My side-eye catches an upturn to the corner of Guin's mouth, and Aschèr sends a flurry of strokes and vicious jabs towards me of a sudden. I keep my grin in check as I defend valiantly, and Ascher's eyes narrow.

And so the suns pass, on into the latter part of our second fortnight here. Seated to evemeal two suns later, Guin suggests we return to the highlands, as the Amæz call that area we first arrived in. It is the forested and wild country that Bane and Fæna have called home since our arrival. I think a hunt a brilliant idea and second her idea.

On the morrow's morn, we meet Bane on the tall grasses just outside the city's west gates, having sent him a thought that we are coming. A sea breeze sends grasses flowing and whispering about us, and the furions leap from my pack at the sight of Bane. They nip and dodge about in play as I take in the fresh air. Though the scents of this city are pleasant enough, this air reinvigorates me. My quiver at my side, my pack and bow on my back, and Bo in hand, I am ready to explore this side of the island. I expect to return to the keep with plenty of game for the cooks in three or four sun's time.

The forests are further west, and we anticipate a leisurely trek along the coastline getting there, just to take in the beauty of the isle. Striding high along a ridge strewn with the boulders ever-present in this side of the island, the bays and inlets are open to our view. Some lined in steep cliffs we must maneuver around and some with golden sandy beaches. One has a lone skiff pulled ashore, but we do not notice anyone to tend it.

Near to eve on the first sun, we are greeted by Fæna. The mountain cat seems especially anxious to see Jilly and Lilit, and they chase about in play as we make our way along the meandering paths of the coast and shoreline. We make camp to a brilliant multi-colour sunset. We've not bothered to hunt during our travels as our conversation kept us occupied during the whole of the sun.

With a small fire burning, we sit about on the few large stone we've made camp around. Bane and the others are out on an eve hunt, we reckon.

"'Tis a beautiful isle the Amæz live on. I can understand why they have no need of the outside world here."

"There is more to it than that, Arias, and as you might guess the outside world would not be welcoming to them in any event, I'd wager." I can sure certain see her point in that. "At the least, not until there is a need."

"What is it you mean by such a statement, Guin? What need would they have?"

"Not them, Arias. I speak of the outside world's need. Have you not wondered why they are all warriors and train all the more each and everysun?"

"I thought you said they must protect against the Titāns of the isle called Olympæa to the east. The isle of naught but men who would pillage and rape them."

"Aye, that o'course is a part of it, but the Wic'cha have taught us that there is more, though lesser in their minds for centuries now. Their purpose of legend is to keep as strong as possible and as well versed in war so that they may come to the outside world's defense when the need arises. There is prophesy that guides them even to this very sun."

I can't help but see the humor and irony of this.

"They train to protect an outside world that would fear and show only disdain for them, and they have done this for a thousand years? It seems a foolish task to build a society around, Guin."

"More years than that, if the writings in the temple are true, and I believe they are, sure certain. They are not the only ones with the same purpose. You have heard Mum tell that our pæder roams Aeryth to the same higher purpose. He is one of the clan of knights templar that the Wic'cha direct abroad. The Source-Sayers of eons past have so directed it, pronouncing that even though it might be generations upon generation and mayhaps centuries away, a threat will arise and we are to remain ever vigilant to it. Though most believe it as just legend or myth now, it has become tradition and purpose for the people of the isles."

With these thoughts settling in amongst my many others, our creature friends slip back into camp even as we are tucking in around the fire for the night. It feels right as they curl about my legs and side. I will remain warm even as the night cools. Fæna's golden eyes glow as she sits and watches over Guin.

The sun rises and we make mornmeal of trail biscuits and warm wine. We vow to do some hunting this sun, and I carry my bow in hand as we continue on our way more inland and towards the forests. Large hares make their home in the tall grasses, and I have no trouble shooting our lunch, which we add some onions to after having found some along the trails. Guin notices what she calls sweet rhubarb growing next to a tree as well. I wonder at the taste, a sweet sugar cane combined with the tang I only know rhubarb to have.

In the after-highsun, my senses become alert to something strange. It hasn't alarmed Bane, but I sense it to our left and upwind to our general path. I do not see anything, but the hairs on my neck rise so that I immediately go into my *Knowing* and extend my senses outward. It is something I've learned to do when I've been 'riding' in Bane's consciousness. And when I do, the wolf's senses go on alert immediately also. Something or someone is tracking alongside our path.

"Be aware, Guin. We have company off to our left."

"I see nothing, Arias. Did you see something?"

"Nay, but I sense something, and I am sure." She nods and furrows her brow in an effort to see or hear what I do. Even as she does, my sense of the presence dissipates.

"It has gone now. It may be but a creature headed in the same direction as us and gone ahead of us now, but it would be wise to be watchful." Again she nods, this time in agreement as she relaxes somewhat.

Tracking towards a tree line we see up ahead, my side-eye catches a figure atop a huge boulder paces distant and in our left to the forest.

"Guin, down now!" And we both dive to the ground. Bane yelps as an arrow grazes his back and he jumps just in time.

"Are they continuing their lessons for you, Guin? That is an Amæz arrow. And the warrior looks to be my old opponent, totally healed. Rieka. We need to move, now." And we do just that, retreating the way we came, and just in time to avoid a second arrow.

Entering my *Knowing*, I search for Guin's spirit presence as we run and find it immediately. To her credit, she slows but a step and smiles as she lets us meld in mind.

"Wow," she thinks at me. *"This is amazing! My senses have multiplied tenfold, Arias. Watch! Another arrow is tracking to our right."*

I've noticed as well and have turned more left to avoid it. It strikes the ground where one of us would have been. Reaching out with my mind now, I bring Bane and Jilly and Lilit into the fold. I feel Guin shiver but smile all the wider.

"Arias, I'm thinking she is meaning to drive us to some point, some purpose...and wow!" Her thoughts of greeting reach my creature friends, and Bane howls and the furions chitter in delight.

"Yes, and she is serious about it too. I sense she is gaining. Let us redouble our efforts till we can find a safe place to stand our ground for a bit."

With a whistle and a twang, her arrow strikes only a pace from us, and we make our way further west now. I reckon the trail we have arrived on is more east of us. She is keeping us away from it and running in the tall grasses. She leaps high upon a boulder and shoots down on us. Though she remains sixty or more paces behind, her aim is superb and deadly. She keeps us away from anything that could serve as defense against her arrows. I reckon we will continue her game until we find such a place… But we don't.

It seems clear that there is purpose to Rieka's behavior. Guin explains that she is known as the best archer on the island and if she had wanted, her arrow could find any of us. I think to separate and send Bane off to her flank but take a Guin's comment to heart and have him stay with us. Fæna has left us but I feel her presence off to our left and tracking along with us. I reach out to Talon and he instantly knows the situation. He is not near, in truth near to the other side of the isle, but he takes flight immediately and starts toward us, leaving his meal on a rock.

As we continue our run, fleeing who is supposed to be friend not foe, we still feel this must be a test or training exercise. One that if we are honest, we are losing. Guin has been with me as I reached out to Talon and knew my intent. She can see I am serious in intent to stop and fight Rieka in some manner. I perceive the fear of that in her eyes and feel it with our connection. She speaks aloud.

"No, Arias, there is something not right here. We must not turn on her. There will be another option soon, I just know it."

I nod while we are, of a sudden, heading downhill towards the coast. Then we see it. The abandoned skiff in a small cove we noticed earlier. I feel sure Rieka means to drive us here. She wants us on that skiff. *Why?* The arrows have stopped, and we pause to catch our breath.

"She wants us to take the skiff, Arias, but why?"

"Let us see first if that is true." We can see her behind us now, standing on a ridge above us. I know we are easy game to her now. I change our course to the east and immediately an arrow slices directly in front of me, burying into a scrub tree to my left. I look back to her. She has not moved and stares openly at me. I nod.

"To the skiff then. I feel a need to leave the isle at this moment." Guin looks back and forth betwixt us, the warrior and myself. Her thought clearly one of not understanding. Rieka's stiff unyielding posture unreadable to her.

We turn and head down the steep hill towards the cove. Somehow I know no more arrows will follow us. But this warrior has angered me, and Talon soars ever nearer to us. I dissolve the connection betwixt Guin and I just as we reach the beached boat, a small two sail skiff that looks very worthy. This startles Guin, and she looks to me then quickly up to Rieka.

"No, Arias!"

Even as she shouts it, the echoing war cry from Talon reverberates around the hills of the cove and directly out of the sun above the Amæzon. I watch as Talon sinks his claws into her in a sweeping motion and sends her tumbling over the edge of the ridge. The fall will not kill her, but she will need to seek out the healer and explain the fall. Hopefully, it will be an enlightening conversation. I have every intention in being there for it. We will sail the skiff back to the city and demand an answer of her, in front of her queen and peers.

"We must go see that she is not seriously hurt, Arias."

"Nay, I can see through Talon's eyes that she is well enough to make her way back, but it will most likely be a painful trip. It will give us the time we need to be there and meet her with the council there to query her intent. Help me pull the skiff from the beach. Do you know how to sail?" She looks to me, astonished to my attitude and intent, but she is in agreement, I believe.

"Nay, do you?"

I give her a warm smile.

"Aye, and I'll teach you."

In but a few moments we are all aboard, even a reluctant Fæna, and Talon sits preening himself upon the prow. We set off with the receding tide. Guin looks back, hoping to see the Amæzon.

26

From Spit to Fire

If not for our harrowing flight and escape from Onæ Paradeis' most dangerous warrior, I admit that being at the tiller of a sleek sailing skiff with sails aloft feels exhilarating. Misty, salted air streams by and wets my face with each slap of the boat's hull across a wave, forcing a smile across my face. Each time I've put to sea…well, those times I'm not nailed in a box…and even then, if I'm being honest, has led to life-altering experiences.

Talon has left us for the drafts high above, and I can see Bane tolerates his time aboard a vessel, but Jilly and Lilit are living and loving each adventure at sea. Guin, though not having been crew on a vessel, ne'er the lesser has been aboard others and knows the terms shouted by a captain, and so she learns sail management quickly and is adept with the small boat's ways.

Each sun with my new found sister amazes me further still. At only fourteen year, she has climbed to prominence at the Wic'cha temple and has become its most accomplished acolyte. Well versed in not only the history of the isles, our mœther pushed her to study the history of all of Aeryth and particularly the Northern Reaches that the temple has many tomes discussing its history. This is something found in but a few parts and pieces in the Mid Realm or Southern Reaches. In verity, only rare histories are kept by a couple Druidae. But the Wic'cha temple knows and keeps all of these histories, and my sister has a voracious appetite and unfailing memory for these facts and tales likened to Sæm, I've found. Her knowledge and abilities with power runes shames Alænèa. But then again, she's been studying them for years more. And now, I can see her dexterity and strength serves her well aboard the skiff. I feel proud.

The fates grace us with a breeze sliding out of the hills we had recently descended in our flight. The open sea seems to be almost pulling us to her, and we take a moment about the tiller to discuss what had just happened.

"I've never known Rieka to act in such a manner, Arias. If ever she has an issue with anyone, she approaches them directly and sorts it face to face."

"There was purpose to what she did, sister. I could see it on her face. And I believe that mayhaps, even now, we have not realized the full of it."

Even as the words leave my mouth, Talon's echoing war cry pierces our ears from high above. We are fast approaching the exit to the small bay.

"Hold the rudder, Guin. I must visit Talon for a time. Keep a line due north till we are past the point a good ways then tac starboard if you can."

I then lean back against the gunwales and slip into my *Knowing* and a moment later feel as light as air, surveying all below as I'm lifted on a current of air eighty poles high. My intent though is on a large, meticulously built, three-mast schooner flying an Asgährdian flag. A pair of men in black garb stand at the bow with spyglass in hand. I know them immediately. 'Tis Mensæ and his assassin…Rieka's purpose. But why? How?

Their vessel is much more swift than ours, and our destination much too far to reach before they will overtake us. We need an escape plan. I fear a retreat to land will not be a good choice. We would be vulnerable and greatly outnumbered by Mensæ's assassins in the wide-open spaces. We have just experienced that with just one experienced warrior. I fear I cannot protect my sister in such a situation, and I've known the agony of Mensæ's assassin's arrow.

As we fly ever higher to assess our choices, I can see now what I've been told. Surrounding the entire isle is a dense fog bank that measures a half league in width and so thick any wise captain would avoid it at all costs. Clearly, this remains as much reason as any for the isle to stay hidden from the outside world. I can only imagine the strength of mægic involved in its creation. It being clear to me, it is not a natural phenomenon.

Due north of our small vessel's present location, less than another half league distant from the northern edge of the fog, lies the beaches of the Northern Reaches. Looming over the beach are sheer cliffs a hundred poles high. They look more impenetrable than on the maps I've read. The bare rock of the cliffs extend a league inland along the whole of the coast, its sheer surface broken only by the occasional crack, leading from beach to an endless jungle beyond.

Out from the beaches, the Northern Reaches look even more unreachable, as breakers made of pointed rock outcroppings seem to grow and recede again into the surface of the sea. White foam of cresting waves cause chaos and promise destruction to any captain foolish enough to approach too close with his vessel. I see a possibility in the fog. Dangerous, but mayhaps achievable with the help of Talon. I close my eyes and return to the skiff and my crew.

"See off to the west there. That is an Asgährdian ship, Arias. They will be able to assist us."

"Nay, Guin. They fly false colours. It is an enemy that seeks my capture or end. We must avoid them at all costs."

"Then what are we to do? I can see they are closing the distance between us even now."

"Aye. Aloft with Talon, I've surveyed our choices, and see but one to my opinion. It will be dangerous, but less so than letting them catch and board us. That vessel holds a dozen assassins sent by our grandsire, the king, and he does not favor me in the least bit, thinking me the bastard son of a traitorous Kingsman."

She's paused to take this new knowledge in. It is obvious, our mœther has not told her this tale. Resolving that I speak the truth, she asks,

"What is your scheme to avoid them, then?"

"We head for the fog bank. Any reasonable captain will not follow. Then we head east till we reach the Bay of Onæ and exit there, sailing to safety I hope. I see no other choice."

"How will we sail within the fog? I've crossed it once before in an Asgährdian ship, Arias. You cannot see your hands about your own eyes! It is why we came to the island the way we did."

"Talon will guide us from above, seeing the swirl of our masts and sails. Or at the least, that is my hope."

She looks skeptical. For good reason, as I feel it myself. But I do not sway from my plan. What I have not tell her yet, is that she would, needs be, man the rudder as I fly aloft with Talon. Looking behind us, I can see Mensæ steadily approaching. I turn the rudder towards the fog. And have Guin adjust our sail.

The assassin's ship lies no more than four dozen ship lengths aft of us as we enter the fog. It does not follow immediately, and this gives me some hope! And in addition, I feel a strong current pull is forward. As I adjust the tiller to take us just a little further into the concealing cloud, I sigh in relief that my scheme just might work. I lean toward Guin. When her face comes into view I am but a hand's breadth from her, and she clearly does not share my optimism.

"We will be safe within the fog, sister. Fear not."

"Nay, brœther, I do not feel your optimism. I cannot wait till the current brings us through the fog."

"Nay, Guin, I do not want to travel the full way through the fog bank, but let the winds carry us along inside just out of sight of their captain. I will need you to hold the rudder as I reach out again to watch with Talon's eyes."

I see her brow furrow instantly to my statement.

"Arias, with the feel of the current under us, I've just recalled my one other trip through the fog. The captain ordered the oars put out, as he explained the winds die to nothing within the cloud, and the current flows ever slightly away from the island. It will carry us through the fog to the far side."

I then realize the truth of her statement as I feel only the slight airflow on my face. Reaching forward, I inch ahead till I can feel the sail. It remains slack and empty.

I make my way cautiously back to Guin, and Bane lets loose a mournful howl. I can feel Lilit and Jilly scurry about my feet. All the creatures are sensing our growing anxiousness, and I can even sense Fæna pace to and fro.

"Guin, hold the tiller slight against the current while I go aloft with Talon." She nods.

My anxiety briefly leaves me as I again see through Talon's eyes. I can clearly see the ship in pursuit. It stays outside the fog and has lowered her sails. I also notice that the captain has called for the oars. He knows. But now I see a man with Mensæ at the bow and his arms are flailing as if in debate with the king's advisor. I do not believe he wants to follow us into the fog. I also believe his argument will fall on deaf ears.

My attention turns to the search for our skiff. There is no swirl of sails in the dense cloud, but I urge Talon to search with his remarkable sight. After a time I see it with him, the unmistakable flag on the high mast of our skiff, appearing for just moments a'times then disappearing again. It is headed not sure east as I'd hoped, but floats in the current towards the beaches of the northern mainland…and towards the chaos of the breakers, which at the direction the skiff is headed, will be just a half dozen skiff lengths from the edge of the cloud bank. My heart skips a beat as I can see that no matter how the tiller is turned against the current, the end result is inevitable.

I slip back into the skiff with Guin.

"Feel about for the water casks that are stacked near the mast, Guin. And drag any that are less full back here. *Hurry.*" I sense her beginning to feel her way forward, doing as I said. Meanwhile, I pull my pack from my back and pull out some leather straps and elven vine I keep with me at all times. There is a coil of strong sailor's rope at my feet at the tiller as well.

Guin returns with two casks, one after the other, each as tall as her knees.

"There are two small wine casks as well. Should I bring them?"

"Yea, quickly now."

I empty the casks and secure the corks back in place. Then I run the rope thrice around each and knot them in my best sailor's hitch. I've run it over a length of elven vine which then is also secured to the casks. Guin has returned with the smaller wine casks, and I do the same with them. Then a thought pops into my head.

"Guin, do you know how to swim?"

"Nice of you to ask, brœther dearest. You're expecting us to have a need then?" 'Tis expressed more as a statement than a query.

"Yea, and it isn't going to be pleasant. There are rocks the size of this skiff that we are headed into, and there is no avoiding them. I have little hope."

Even as I say this, the boat begins rocking. I quickly finish lashing up one of the smaller casks, and with two lengths of the elven vine, I make a makeshift leather harness for each of the furions and knot the to lines to both Lilit and Jilly.

The cords attached to the bigger casks I secured to Guin's wrist then mine. As soon as I finish strapping my bow and staff, I throw my pack back over my head and then we pass out of the fog bank. I can again see more than a hand's breadth in front of us. The surf instantly becomes deafening, and it is not an inviting sight.

"Bane and Fæna, Arias!"

I return her look. I am confident they will not want to be tied to a cask. I lift my barrel and show Guin how to hold the cask in front of herself, holding tight to the binding ropes. And that's all I have time for as the skiff lifts high and crashes upon a rock twice its size. I watch as Bane and Fæna leap from either side of the boat and Guin is thrown aft over the rear gunwales. The center mast breaks free and is headed right for me. I throw the cask with furions atop overboard and roll into the surf. The mast gives me a further push as it strikes my shoulder. The pain is excruciating.

I fall immediately into my *Knowing* and draw in a deep breath.

My eyes open, and I see Bane licking my face and a few paces afore me, the furions are furiously working at chewing through the elven vine to no avail as they scurry about the cask they are attached to. Guin is tending to an injured Fæna at the water's edge, and my head and shoulder ache to the point of nausea. Unbinding myself, I then go to Guin and her spirit cat. Her eyes are closed and she lies limp on the sand. Retreating into my *Knowing*, I reach for the cat's spirit self. It is very week, but it is there. Recognizing me, she opens to me and I immediately try to breathe life into her thoughts and being. She convulses before us and spews a great deal of seawater over and over again. She will live.

Turning to the furions now, I see that they are quite fine but sopping wet and looking like lizards of a sort. Coming back to them, I sit next to them and can not help but laugh. Fates be praised, I am happy to see them alive. After I cut them free, they savagely attack me about my ears and chin then sit back and laugh at me.

We are all alive.

I recall nothing of how I've made it to shore, but I celebrate that. We all do.

"I'm sorry. I did not know what to do, Arias. After I was thrown from the boat, I panicked as the mast fell and hit you. You disappeared from sight, and I needed to concentrate on just saving myself. The waves seemed to have swallowed Fæna, but I saw Bane's head bobbing. Your furions had vanished, and I found myself fighting to keep my head above the surface. Your cask idea most certainly saved my life, keeping me protected while crashing into rock after rock and taking the brunt of the collisions and even more for keeping me afloat.

"When I made it to shore, your furions were already in the shallows, sitting atop their little cask boat and doing fine. Bane seemed well and headed towards Lilit and Jilly and worked to pull their cask ashore. I finally pulled myself ashore as well, too exhausted to do more than sit up. Then you appeared. You looked lifeless, Arias. Bane saw you first and headed back into the surf, somehow pulling you onto the beach. Crawling over to you, I watched your chest rise and fall and sighed in relief. Bane started tending to you as I saw the waves wash Fæna onto the sands. I was devastated as her seeming lifeless body just lay there. That's when you arrived. Thank you for saving her!"

"Well, we've fallen from the spit into the fire and even as we've survived both, we are still not free from those with the knives."

Guin follows my gaze and now sees what I do. Further down and away from the breakers but now clear of the fog bank sits the Asgährdian ship. They will be able to tender ashore safely from where their ship waits, and we are in an even more vulnerable situation now. I recall what a dozen kingsmen did to Da.

"We must leave immediately. While aloft I spied deep cracks into the cliffs. Mayhaps therein lies a patch to further escape. Bane, can you scout ahead? Guin, let us quickly see if any of these casks that have washed ashore hold any fresh water. It may be hard to come by later on. But we must be off in either case, afore they leave their ship."

We have a bit of luck and find water in the first barrel we check. I pass my quiver and bow to my sister and after sorting my pack, discarding those few items ruined by the sea, I fill two water skins, and we head down the beach, away from our pursuers.

We have not been off too long when Talon's echoing war cry alerts us to the fact that Mensæ and his men are leaving the ship to continue their pursuit.

Bane returns to us shortly thereafter, excited that we should follow him. A bit of hope then, I think. I stride more swiftly in spite of my nausea and severely bruised shoulder. Mayhaps some eight hundreds of paces further down the beach and just around a jutting point of rock rubble and huge boulders, we come to a fissure cleaved into the cliff face. Taking time to retreat to my *Knowing,* I join with Talon and survey the way deep into the huge crevice.

There will be no deceiving Mensæ and his assassins as our trail in the sand remains quite clear. They will know when our tracks end that we turned inland. It will do us no good if there is no exit. Traveling above with Talon, it takes but a quarter turn to fly over the fissure in the rock face.

As I suspected, when whatever tremendous natural force cleaved the cliffs and formed the crevice, it left an avalanche of crushed stone and boulders flowing from the inland end to the beach. There looks to be sections that are no wider than what a single man could fit through. But after a long climb over sometimes loose surfaces, we should be able to make it to the top of the cliff. The trip would end at the start of what appears to be an endless, thick jungle from Talon's point of view. We'll deal with that circumstance when, or if, we make it there. I return to myself.

"Guin, you, Fæna, and Jilly and Lilit head up first. It will be a hard climb and rough going in parts, but there is an end. Trade me. I'll take my bow and quiver, and the staff will benefit you better."

My thoughts are that I might need my bow. The cat and furions set out with little trouble, but the gravel makes the early climb tougher on Guin and myself. Our feet want to slip from under us.

Even as we climb within the cleft, I continue listening into the dark behind us as the sun does not very well penetrate all the way to us. I know when they have started into the cliffside as my *Knowing* enhanced hearing recognizes the far off echo of voices and then the faint crunch of a dozen footsteps. They are less than a turn of a sand glass behind us. I urge our small troupe forward, trying to quicken our pace.

I have to help Guin scale some towering boulders which we encounter in our path. I know without doubt the trained men chasing us are gaining ground against our advance.

The sky above begins to darken. Pausing to let Guin catch her breath, I take back my Bo staff and set the mægical glow to its end. Then I placed her hand within mine and over my finger's bone encased in the center of the staff. When I release it into her hand, the light remains intact. We move forward. Dusk has arrived, and as the height of the cliff walls decrease ahead, mayhaps three poles in height, I know we are close. A myriad of stars light the clear night sky above us, and the worst of the climb up through the pass is behind us. But we have precious little time to escape the assassins too close on our tail.

27

Druid's Council

"Elsii, lass."

Enamored with her newfound ability to 'see' mægic in colours, my little ward has climbed to the roof of my tinker's wagon and has been 'reaching' into the tree branches as we pass under in what she calls "a chase of the elusive substance." We are close to the tinker's meet now, having been on the road most of three moons. It has been near to five moons since I've rescued her from a cruel and gruesome tragedy at the mountain lodge that she knew as home.

"Mæster Rõghæn, I can push the breeze in different directions now, blowing petals from the tree flowers in the branches above. Just small poofs, mind, but it is me doing it, sure certain!"

She's mastered a mægic it's taken me years to perfect in a single sun.

"Come, lass. We'll be out of the forest soon enough, then over a rise, and we'll see the gathering. More tinker's wagons than you can count!"

"Oh, can I do some trade and barter on my own?"

"Aye, lass. In just three moons, you may be the better of the two of us at it, ha!"

"And will you find your friends here and 'hold council?'"

"Aye, lass. That is my hope. I have not seen them in many years. They may have changed some in look if not manner."

"But they will come?"

"They will come. This Tinker's Bazaar will have been arranged by one of them, sure certain. And the maggie's will have found them all. It was I that taught the training of the birds after all's said. They will come."

"You trained the maggies to find your friends?"

"The original birds I did, decades gone. But I trained others in the art as well. There are bird tenders in all corners of Aeryth now. Which brings me to another thought. My friends will be calling me by another name most like. Röjjer, or just Röj."

"Why would they do that? Did you change your name?"

"Aye, I have from time a'times, from towne to towne, o'er the years. But you know me by my true name, Elsii."

Hitting a few deep ruts in the road, I take extra care maneuvering through and around them as Elsii desperately hangs to the seat's bench bar to keep from being thrown to the ground. Huni sticks her head out from under the bench and her cubs climb over her and then out to the edge of the wagon to look down at what is causing the bumpy ride.

"So why do your friends call you Röj?"

Memories lost in centuries long gone resurface for me. They are never completely gone, just stashed in my brain's library till I need them. This council will be four, mayhaps five, and there is an outside chance of even six of us, all told. Eschereon has emphasized some gravity to its need.

We meet once in a decade or two, mostly each living our own and varied lives though communicating by maggie ever so often betwixt council meets. We are chroniclers of Aeryth and her doings and history mostly. Also tutors to those wanting to learn from the past. A wise and noble track followed by ever fewer these suns. We have an older task given, though until now I've have not experienced the need. We were counseled by our mentors centuries past to be ever on the lookout for new mægic, should it appear. Especially if it takes strong form in a person. I've found it by chance, it seems, in Elsii.

The league of Druidæ, we were once called. We'd all been mentored for years together at one point, both in Aeryth histories and mægics. Our numbers have dwindled over the decades, through accident or even trouble and malice, and with a dearth of apprentice material about Aeryth, we are few in this age. Each of us have a mægic 'strength' and were taught to develop it and to look out for it in the general populace, for it is foretold that a time would come when mægic will be revived to greater extent in Aeryth once more. We've seen little evidence to date, and it's been centuries for some of us.

A maturing of mægic markers in the very blood of lines started centuries upon centuries ago, designed to coalesce and make itself known one day. As there are no living Source-Sayers, I've often wondered how this could be guided up through more than a millennium. But the ancient maegics, when harnessed and directed, are powerful tools.

Though residual mægic lingers in all things, of course, we rarely see it in people. Some animal 'whisperers,' healers, and 'seers' are out and about–their talent from latent mægic in their bloodlines–but true mægic the like of which we few control remains extremely rare. Until finding Elsii, what I've recorded is but a shimmer amongst the mundane.

I smile down on Elsii once the maneuvering through the trail ruts and my memories settle. She has become accustomed to lingering silence as I lapse into a memory of the past or contemplate an issue. "Your mind works mighty slow, a'times," she's apt to say.

"They called me Röj because it means spear or lance in an old tongue, and they thought my remarks biting at one time. I've mellowed quite a bit since." I chuckle as she shakes her head and shrugs at my much delayed response.

The harnesses clatters and the horses neigh and stomp a moment as I rein them in even as we come to the top of a rise in the travelway. And then, all quiets as we gaze down into a vale with a river running through it. Camped on either side of a wide stone bridge on the open plain with just a scattering of trees are a hundred and then some, of tinkers' wagons. Likened to my very own, they are brightly coloured of roof and wheel, with sides hinged atop so that they open as an awning to customers browsing wares. The interiors have just enough space to bed in, out of the rain on those eves when one cannot sleep out in the open or under it.

From this height, one can see groups of wagons parked about a single fire and looking like multicoloured spokes of a wheel. Or linked zig-zag in a line like loaves of bread sitting on a window sill. Then there are the outliers, tinkers that camp apart, alone even as they spend most of their lives. But they are the exception. It is a towne unto itself, and laughter reaches like gusts of wind, bursting from the valley below. I glance to Elsii, whose expression beams of awe and excitement.

Off in the far distance, east of the settlement, a city sits, filled with folk that bust with joy to barter and buy from this bazaar of tinkers. A valley of treasure for those seeking the wondrous variety on a tinker's wagon, now hundreds in one place!

"Ooh, I can see your friends from here, Mæster Rõghæn! … 'er Röj."

My look must be incredulous.

"How is it you think you see my friends, lass? Especially at such a distance!"

"They glow just the same as you! There, do you see? On the outskirts, near the great tree…do you see?"

I see the group she speaks of, but see no glow. But I have no doubt she will prove correct. There are four wagons, but they appear no different than others. The fact that she sees more unnerves me a bit. We have always thought we were invisible to the general public. Granted, Elsii has proven quite different than common folk.

"Let us proceed there then, Elsii. I am anxious to introduce them to you."

"And hold council, like the maggies said." She adds, and I give a quiet nod. For my part, I bring my news with me.

As we approach the bazaar from the south trailway, the hum of activity becomes enthralling and the cacophony of sounds lifts our spirits. Folk from Newcastle, the city off to the east, are plentiful. Many are merchants looking to stock their own shops back in the city. These men buy wares, tools, and trinkets and bring nothing to barter. But their coin makes the tinkers quite happy ne'er the lesser.

Elsii insists on walking aside my wagon and I oblige, happy to see her completely immersed in the atmosphere. She runs from wagon to wagon, inspecting merchandise and taking mental note, sure certain. I have no doubt she could find her way back to those wagons she wants to revisit.

We are nearing the group Elsii has pointed out to me when she stops dead still and looks my way with a look of terror on her face. Reining in the team, I throw the brake and near leap from my seat to the ground. Walking briskly to her, I stoop and look her in the eye, laying a consoling hand to her shoulder. She takes a breath finally.

"Mæster Rõghæn...behind me. The tall man in black with the pointy beard on his chin... He was there, with the king's advisor...and *her*. *He is evil*. Not just bad, but *evil*. He has the same *look* as *her*. And Rõghæn, he glows too. But his glow is a different colour than yours."

I lift her back up onto the wagon's bench and she immediately reaches for the comfort of Huni's fur. The wolf badger climbs into her lap. Before returning to the wagon myself, I query a nearby tinker as to the name of the tall dark stranger. We discuss it for a moment.

Kicking the trail mud from my feet on the wagon's wheel afore climbing back up, I observe the man a while longer. I note he employs body guards. Three I recognize as such immediately, never too far from his person. They look deadly. But he mingles among the tinkers, smiling most affably. He gabs as if old friends. A convincing act from what I gather in but a few moment's time.

We continue onto the outskirts of the settlement towards the great tree Elsii had pointed out, her mood somber and reflective now though as she looks o'er her shoulder now and again.

I smile as we all approach the circle camp by the tree. Elsii had been spot on. In the decade plus that I have not seen them, the men seated around a fire, sipping what I feel certain is ale, have changed very little. Elsii visibly relaxes and unwraps her arms from her shoulders. A good twenty paces away from them still, I lower her to the ground and Huni quickly follows and with her, the two growing cubs.

I sit back and watch at what she might do. She walks up confidently betwixt the two seated closest to her and extend her hands towards the fire. A small shiver clearly runs up her person, and the flames of the fire leap up and burn hotter for a moment. A perfect entrance for this group. Looking into each man's eyes in turn, she says,

"I am right, am I not? You are the friends of Mæster Rõghæn... I mean Röj..."

They are so focused on her now that they do not notice my arrival.

"We've sometimes called such a man friend. And who might you be then?" A big smile graces her face as she puts her earlier shock away for a time.

"I knew it! I knew as soon as I saw you from the ridge."

I cannot have asked for more stunned expressions on men that have lived so long that nothing could shock them. And then they notice me.

"Röj, who have you brought with you that seems so adept at recognizing *us*? And welcome to you!" greets Tymur Foxglove, his name borne out by his covered hands with gloves sans fingers. Well, he has fingers, his gloves do not. The outer edges of his red moustache rise away from his beard with his grin.

"Goodmen, meet Elsii, my new ward and apprentice!"

A chorus of greetings meet the smiling lass as she turns from the fire to look back to me, a quizzical look on her face.

"Rõghæn, why is it that your friends all wear long hair on their face? 'Tis not like all the other tinkers we've seen this sun. I would have known them for that alone and not the other."

Again, the others' eyebrows rise to a one in shocked expression.

"Well, friends. Mayhaps we stand out more than we thought, and a younger is the one to point it out." My hand rises to grasp around my lengthy beard and slide first around it then down it from chin to chest.

"Elsii–Röj's most observant ward–if you have carried a beard for countless years, it may be result of the memory of the drudgery of taking a razor to your chin each morn. We've become victims of an abused habit over too many years, I'm afraid!" But I can see a small concern about him ne'er the lesser.

"But, inquisitive lass, you mentioned in truth you knew us for another reason. Pray tell how is it we announced to you our connection to your Mæster Rõghæn and our Röjjer."

"Oh! It is your glow... Rõghæn says mægic can be felt by those with the right blood, and some might even see it. I guess I am one of ones whose blood lets me see mægic. It is all about really...in some plants and trees and things I mean. Some animals and the winds and clouds and water in some places...but when it is in people, it is brightest! I could see you from the ridge. Your colours were so loud!"

As I look around at my friends, I find them all gobsmacked. And to them, I am certain my eyes sparkle in delight. Finally, Trævor rises and curtsies with a flair to the lass.

"Well noticed, Elsii, young apprentice. Please come...sit with us a while and tell us more of the colour of mægic. For those in this group sometimes feel or know of it, but I dare say, none of us sees it as you do.

Please join us, won't you! Tymur, mayhaps you've a sparkling water for the lass? And a bite to eat?"

"Oh, that would be wonderful." And looking back to me, "I do like your friends, Rõghæn!"

"Well, sit then, Elsii, and chat with them for a bit. But, mayhaps Kobē, I might enlist your help in bringing my wagon around to camp?"

"O'course, Röj. Let us get you settled. We'll need leave room for Escher's wagon, though. We are still expecting him as well."

I can hear laughter from the campfire as Kobē and I back in my wagon and settle the horses. My ward seems to be continuing to make an impression on the others. Kobē motions to her as we work.

"Your ward is quite remarkable, Röj. How did you come to capture such an apprentice? I could not help but also notice her wolf badger and with two cubs and no less. I've never in all my years, and you know they are many, seen a sight. Wolf badgers are the wildest of forest creatures and to my knowledge, untameable. Yet this one she treats as she would a tabby!"

"They've an unbreakable bond, sure certain, Kobē. Her coming to me is a heart wrenching tale on its own, and I'll tell it. I think her mægic first started with the wolf badger there, but mayhaps it was the tragedy that befell her that brought out other mægics. She has three that I'm sure of and would not doubt another also. That she actually sees it in colours, I've just known a sun or two, and mayhaps it's only been with her for as long. I've much too discuss this council and most of it involves this lass."

"Three mægics and she's seeing it in colours as well. Mayhaps there is truth in the Source-Sayers' prophesy after all is said and done?"

"After countless decades of the mundane enveloping all of Aeryth, this development portends just that, I'll wager. But if it be so, there are other prophesies to be discussed then besides this one. Let us join my new ward and our friends, eh?"

'Tis good seeing my comrades once more, and as is our custom, fond memories and anecdotes abound early in our meets, and Elsii seems mesmerized by our tales. So much so that after evemeal her head begins to wobble precariously on her fists, attached to arms whose elbows are propped on swaying knees. She leans toward each and the other of us who might be speaking or telling a tale.

"Elsii, you might want to gather up Huni and the cubs. They are looking quite bushed after our long trail this sun. Time to set them in a corner of our wagon and you might settle there yourself under a blanket and away from this chill. There'll be plenty of stories on morrow's sun, and we're about to hold council in any manner."

"Aye, but hold the good ones till the morrow then. You've such funny friends, Rõghæn, and I do cherish their tales!"

"Aye, lass, that'll be an easy promise. Oh, and one last thing afore you go if you'll hear me. The man from earlier, did he have a colour about him?"

"Aye, Rõghæn, you did not notice? Twas a deep red that clung about him, like blood, I thought."

I nod.

"Well then, off to bed, you and the cubs, eh? They'll be needing their sleep!"

We all bid her pleasant dreams and settle to quietly smoke some pipeweed about the fire for a bit. The fire snaps and frogs 'n crickets sing about us. Gentle voices punctuated with laughter rise from nearby camps. I find this time most relaxing, with the waft of five different weed scents mingling together in the air and pleasing memories of these very men in adventures gone by.

I cannot help but notice the eyes of my friends coming back to me more than any other.

"Aye, I have a little to report on, goodmen, but I'd prefer to wait on

Escher so as just to be telling it one time and with all of us to discuss it together."

Nods all around, and we return to discussing the mishaps and hilarity we'd experienced together in times long past. The not so small barrel of ale Tymur had perched on his wagon gate is pronounced empty late into the night, when the moon has well passed its zenith, and we finally spread our bedrolls about the fire under a myriad of stars.

I wake from my bedroll next to the fire and to the sun cresting the eastern horizon two suns hence, the tinkling of metal on metal as I pull myself up to sitting. Eschereon kneels across the small, newly stoked campfire with a pot of java, by the smell, bubbling enough to rattle the lid. He sits back upon a stump as I reach into my pack to retrieve my cup in order to fill it with the hot brew. Perfect to clear the remaining cobwebs of morning's dream leavings.

"Escher, you've finally arrived, and you being the one to call us to this meet." The java clears my mind and wet my throat.

"Yea, I detoured to Esperance in the Southern Reaches to observe the king's son and his advisor for a bit. It was most revealing and further confirmed the need for this council."

"Aye, I'll not argue the need. I've news of import myself. But let us enjoy the scent and delicious effects of this hot brew afore we delve into such matters."

"Yea to that my brœther, and the others will need be here to discuss it all as well." I nod. It will be a most serious council, this meet. On a curious note, I notice his treasured beard had been cut to mostly a stubble and is more consistent with the other tinkers in the settlement.

"And I've, by chance or fate, have run into our young friend from the isles. Vicchi will not be joining us, but she has sent word to be on the lookout for him. But it is he who found me, a fortnight passed, on the roads here." At that moment, Illéron from the isles walks up behind Eschereon.

"His son will be an important topic for this council."

Elsii arrives behind me with the wolf badgers at her heels, mum and cubs. Escher's brows rise to the sight.

"Rõghæn, are these your friends as well? They've magnificent glows! There is wonderful mægic in them, I see. Should I get makings for a morn-meal, Mæster Rõghæn? Me and Huni are quite hungry." I smile as her tummy groans just then in agreement.

"Aeryth is becoming a wondrous land once more, sure certain. I see you have tales of your own to share, dear Rõj. A wondrous and dangerous place, I fear. After mornmeal then."

And my brows rise this time. It seems we both were experiencing co-incidental happenings in our lives. The java has indeed warmed me enough to tend to my ward's need. I get up and about just that.

28

𝔄nother 𝔚ending 𝔚ay

We have made it to the top of the cliffs just past dusk and a failing sun, and are astounded to find a clear path leading into the jungle. Even more so, there at the entrance stands a remarkably huge tree, or trees, with intertwining trunks and quite reminiscent of the one carved at the door of the Wic'cha temple. On the left trunk, Guin reads the rune as '*Care*' and at equal height carved in the trunk to the right, she reads the rune as '*Haste*' or '*Swift*'. She cannot decide which. After a bit of study, I notice a second trail to the left, somewhat hidden amongst the flora. Do the runes mean to be labels for the two paths?

Knowing our pursuers to be getting ever closer and after looking about in all directions, I follow my gut and make a decision. I cypher them to be well less than a turn of a sand glass behind us now.

"Guin, follow me and remain most silent. Stay clear of any sight line from the crevice."

I extinguish the mægic light that hangs above my staff and head out upon the flat, barren surface of the rock clifftop, heading away from the jungle and back towards the sea. The myriad of stars above light our way. The landscape I peer upon is barren of all life and flat so one can see a league in <u>any</u> direction but for a few huge boulders that look to have fallen from the sky and lie scattered widely about. It is one of these that I head for. Not the closest, but one a good ways from the manna tree and still within a line of sight to it. I bid all to settle quietly behind it. It is of a size to easily hide all of us.

The moon shines so brightly that it throws a shadow down and out from one side of our boulder. From the shadow and lying tight to the ground, I peer back at the tree.

When they finally rise out of the ground's fissure, a quarter turn shy of a full glass, I hope that Mensæ will be so anxious to continue the pursuit that he'll enter the forest immediately, and we would then take the hidden path. My hopes are dashed. Shadows move about the tree, some studying the runes, I imagine, while others venture about it for a short time. But then I see a campfire start, and I know they will not be continuing into the gnarled jungle of strange trees this night. I hope they do not think I've made the same choice but only decided for themselves that caution is a better approach. The morrow's morn they surely reckon will better show our tracks. To that end, we have traveled a short way down the right pathway before we retreat onto the rocky plateau of the cliffs.

I spend my night in my *Knowing*, watching and waiting and not sleeping. I wonder what Alænèa and Sæm are doing this night…and then, my mind wanders further still to Finnie and the youngers. I know I've done the right thing now in sending them back to Middenvale friends and safely away from my predicament.

Well after the assassins had made their camp, a pair of them start out back onto the barren clifftop on the other side of the crevice, clearly heading towards the huge boulders that are scattered about. My survival senses start to tingle. Will they send a second pair in our direction? My question is answered a very short time later. Yes they will. I feel I can handle two of Mensæ's assassins if they approach too near, but that would obviously alert the others and our odds of survival will drop precipitously.

The two on the other side of the chasm have already approached and surveyed four widely scattered boulders and the next lies a tremendous distance out. The pair on our side have only two more before they will discover us. Thinking and plotting furiously, I come upon a desperate scheme.

Reaching out to Talon, I express my need, then lie back and hope. Almost immediately, we hear Talon's war cry, and I know Mensæ recognizes it as well. Flying overhead and a distance inland from the tree and on the 'Haste' rune side of it, Talon gives three back to back war cries and makes it clear it is him.

Shortly after and before the assassins have approached our hideout, they are called back. Mensæ sure now he's scared us enough to enter the jungle and are now in trouble. I let out a breath I didn't know I have been holding. I have Talon continue the charade further into the night and further from the camp.

The morrow's morn brings a sunrise that paints the sky in reds and oranges with purple underbellies of clouds lingering above us. I'd watched as the assassins broke their camp and headed down the main trail in the direction of Talon's war cries throughout the night. He now sits hidden in the branches of the very tree they had camped beneath, watching them with me joined with him seeing what he sees. The lead assassin, the very same that had put an arrow into my shoulder just a few short moons passed, sends two of his men down the concealed path which they have found in the morning's light.

The others–there are ten plus Mensæ himself–depart into the wider path, more certain it would have been the way we had taken. I take time to examine them closely, these assassins. Each wears black leathers, with hood and cape in black as well. A small soldier's pack tucked under their capes. Half have quiver and bow and all have thin bladed longswords, long dirks, and throwing blades sheathed on shoulder, back, and waists. They work with extreme precision, breaking down their camp and extinguishing the signs they have even been. Professionals, every one.

I debate asking Bane to follow them but decide it will be better if he travels with us. When they have been gone a turn, I retreat to myself and beckon Guin and our troupe to follow me. We return to the tree with the runes, and I decide to make camp for a time there, wanting to discuss the runes with Guin.

We examine the runes now in the light of sun and find there to be more we had not noticed in the failing light of yester's eve. Two smaller runes are embossed under each. Guin cannot cypher the meaning of those on the right most trunk, but her words bring my attention to the others.

"'*Wending Way,*' the runes say here. The others I cannot read at all, and these hold no meaning to me."

I raise my chin to her proclamation and smile, as I think I know their meaning. Our trip to Sæm's home village springs to mind.

"Guin, I believe I know what these runes mean. There was a trail through a forest in the western part of these Northern Reaches that carried the same name. Sæm, at that time, explained why they called it the Wending Way."

I explain that if we take this route, we will be obliged to stay strictly on the trail as dire danger lurks for any that stray from the path. And any that do will become hopelessly lost with no sense of direction, to fall prey to unusually vicious predators.

"I'm not sure I fancy a trip that way then, Arias."

"We survived without incident, Guin, but Sæm insisted we did not dally or stop to sleep but continue through the entire way. That being said, and knowing Mensæ and ten assassins took the other trail, I judge this to be the safer route. But, I have not seen sleep in two nights over the last three suns, and if we take this path I must have some rest before. I propose we make camp here for at the least till the sun climbs full height. I'll ask my creature friends to stand guard. It would not do to be surprised by the two returning."

"On your say so, brœther. You are the experienced one in these matters, but afore we depart, I would share the history of this place as I know it, for I have studied this land at the temple."

"Sure certain, then. Any knowledge is crucial and forewarning if we are to survive."

Her eyes are hesitant with worry.

"I'll say but one thing before your rest. It is legend that only those who cross the breadth of this land and reach the Orakle Isle that lies just off shore beyond and to the north, ever return from these shores. And those that have, bring fantastical stories back with them. Our pæder is one such, and his tale sent shivers down my spine."

"We'll take time then to hear some of it, and if they are tales of our pæder, I'd fancy hearing all that you can recall."

With that, I collapse against the great manna tree just under her runes and search for deep rest in my *Knowing* for a time. Guin curls into my side, and it feels natural to accept her. *Family.*

Highsun brings me to the here and now. A shake to Guin's shoulder brings her out of a well-needed slumber as well.

"Roux," I say, and her eyebrows lift. "Is it acceptable that I call you by this, your other given name? It suits you, and it falls easier from my tongue."

"Yea, it feels right to me also, brœther. I've an urge to call you Ari. Would that be all right as well?"

"Yea, only one other has called me that, and she too is family." She pauses to look my way, her face a query, and a silent "oh" escapes her lips.

"I would like to hear more of this lass when you find time, dear brœther!" I feel the corners of my mouth curl up at this suggestion. I will love to tell her of Finnie. 'Tis nice to have a sister…a confidant.

With our camp essentials packed once again, we set off, and I become ever weary of the two assassins that have preceded us down this path.

"Remember, Roux, stay to the trail no matter the circumstances, as leaving it will not improve your fate." I take her mood, and we are off.

Immediately upon entering this jungle forest, all else falls away to it. The air itself feels closed and moist and different. Retreating into my *Knowing,* I perceive a glow along the pathway, encompassing us as we walk. Mayhaps my mægic senses are growing as I do not recall this sight whilst traveling with Sæm and his brœther, Tonk. But then, I had not used this sense back then. Now, I feel the strong mægic actually tickling my senses, and auras of many colours seep in from the surrounding forest in addition to the strong aura of the trail.

They seem almost palpable, the colours, as if I could push and pull them with my hands.

"Do you feel the mægic of this forest, Roux?"

"My skin is tingling if that is what you mean."

"Yea, I'll need to teach you to reach deeper into your *Knowing.* I believe you might see the colours of the mægic even as I do."

A turn into our travel, Bane returns to us. I know immediately what it means. We are on a collison course with the two assassins that are returning. I knew it was a distinct possibility.

"Roux, can you attach a voice to an object? Alænèa would sometimes do it as prank to Sæm and I. She would use runes to hold the mægic to the object."

"Yea, but what use could it possibly have here?" I take two of my precious arrows from my quiver. I will not be retrieving them.

First, I send the furions ahead to spy on the assassins.

I explain what I have to mind while we work on the arrow tips, etching the runes she requires to be placed on them. Then we speak at the runes. We finish none too soon, as I hear Mensæ's soldiers approaching at a distance. With careful aim, I loose both arrows, one following the other, twenty paces off the path and mayhaps fifty paces onward into the forest, each finding a tree and taking purchase.

Moments later we hear our own voices speaking loudly ahead of us and are confused as if searching for each other out in the forest.

The furions have eyes on the assassins not a hundred paces from us, around a few bends in the trail. They have heard the voices as well, and the furions watch each of them point into the trees. After a moment of discussion head to head, they disappear into the jungle, chasing our voices even as they appear again. My ruse worked, and we proceed forward with caution. In a few moments, other sounds visit us. Not thinking it the assassins, as they would be trained in stealth, I stretch my senses as far and towards the sounds as possible. It seems to me the sounds of predator and prey.

Bane and Fæna are on high alert, staring as I am towards the breaking of twigs and forest leavings underfoot. Then silence. Two things happen of a sudden. Our voices ring out again, and a surreal shriek pierces the air with a major disturbance happening in the underbrush. Sounds of a heated battle reach us for the best of a quarter turn to a sand glass.

Silence. Eerily so.

Of a sudden, an ear-ripping shriek and crash throws us to the ground as an animal or a tremendous bird, the likes of which I've never seen nor heard tell of, bursts through the jungle's thick, thorny underbrush that stands knarled to each side of the trail. It appears not two paces from us and immediately Bane's hackles rise as he leaps forward betwixt the beast and us. He bares his teeth in a vicious snarl, whilst Fæna also rises into an attack pose. Lilit and Jilly yelp and scurry behind us.

The creature stands as tall or taller than me, and its head swings huge on an equally thick neck. Its massive beak clenches something as it turns and stares at us.

But then it begins to shake…and huge, featureless wings spread all akilter above and out from it. Claws larger than Bane's head clench and reclench at the air as sparks and crackling fills the space about it. It throws its odd, oversized head up and wails pitifully before turning and diving across the pathway and into the thorned and thicketed brush on the opposite side of the trail. I swear I see wisps of smoke rising from its back and torso. Wails continue as it recedes from the trail and us.

Rising to my feet, I pull Roux to hers, and we dust ourselves, shaking with fear. All had happened in but a moment. Yea, fear. Looking down, I make out what the beast had been carrying in its mouth/beak. 'Tis the bloody arm of an assassin.

"The path's mægic drove the creature from it, inflicting a horrendous pain upon it, I have no doubt, by the beast's action. Did you see the sparks and glow of it, Roux?"

"Brœther, my heart was near to burst that I took little notice of such details. By the fates, what was it?"

"I've nary a clue. I've ne'er seen nor heard of such a creature but would prefer ne'er to run afoul with one ever."

Pushing my hands deep into Bane's furry neck scruff, I settle my heart and watch as my sister hugs Fæna. The furions reach about my legs wanting some reassurances as well.

"Two crises averted, and we know not to leave the trail till it ends then. Shall we be on our way?"

"Yea, brœther, but start a few paces ahead and leave Bane with me a moment. I've a need to relieve myself." I chuckle and shake off the last of my fright, leaving Roux behind for a short time. She runs to catch up in haste afterward.

With the distress mostly behind us now but for a weariness of the forest about us, Roux tells me her lessons regarding our current plight, here inland in the Northern Reaches. Some learn at the temple, others from tales our pæder told to her of his time here. She knows my/our pæder. She'd grown up with our mœther and pæder. I do not begrudge her it, and my life with Da had been full. But it is a strange feeling within me that such a thing could happen. We continue ahead as a chill breeze hits us face on and swirls the leaves at our feet. It softly chitters as it flows through the branches on either side of the travelway, the only sound about us now.

"Poppa was sent to seek out the Orakle years past. I was still a younger not six years yet. The Wic'cha knew it would be a dangerous quest and bestowed a special amulet unto him for protection. It is mægic that they do best. Like the one you wear even now about your neck and laying on your chest. It had been thirty years since the trek across the Northern Reaches had last been attempted."

"What is an Orakle, Roux, and to what purpose did the Wic'cha sent him to find it?"

"Nay, Ari. Not what, but who. The Orakle is an ages-old seer. But not just any seer, and one that sees forward and the far past as well, as it is said the present cannot be without both. She will advise if you can cypher her riddles, and it is said every word counts. The Wic'cha were in dire need and had exhausted all other means, but Poppa's tale did not include or reveal their need at the time."

"Why did they not just go to the Orakle first if the need had been so great?"

"But that is the lesson of the Northern Reaches, Ari, for it is told that she will speak to only those that reach her by traveling the breadth of the Reaches and no other way."

"And that is why our pæder was here and had the tale to tell." She nods.

"But what other way would there be to reach this Orakle?"

"By sea, of course. She resides on an isle in the Northern Sea just off the coast there and due north of Asgährd across the breadth of the Reaches. And there she is guarded by a warrior sect that is said to be ruthless and unyielding to those who approach without her leave."

"So, you are saying one must traverse the whole of the Reaches, only to be turned aside by her tenders?"

"Yea, but it is the only way out of this part of the Reaches also. Only there can a ship be found for passage away from the Reaches and back to Asgährd."

"Surely that cannot be so. There must be hundreds of leagues of coastline betwixt here and there!"

"Yea, Ari, and the coast is all the same as we found it upon our arrival. Rock cliffs a hundred poles high and most without as much beach as we landed upon. 'Tis why outlanders from Aeryth seldom bother with the Northern Reaches. At least on the eastern side."

"So you are saying we must cross the whole of this land and then find a vessel to return to Asgährd, and ships seldom even pass that way." Roux nods.

"But why not head west? I know there are villages and towns. I've visited one such that Da and Sæm hail from."

"Because of the Breach, Ari. You must know of the breach, surely?" My look betrays me.

"You spoke of your journey from the west to Esper keep and the druid, Eschereon. Did you travel the way direct, west to east?"

I understand her meaning now. We have to travel first south and around the uncrossable canyon that runs from the northern coast of the Mid Realm to the keep at Bladestone. It is half of what makes the Accadian Plains inaccessible from the rest of Aeryth.

"There is a canyon to the west?"

"Aye."

"Lore holds that Aeryth shook for a whole moon, and the Breach opened across Aeryth, splitting it near in two. The when of it is lost to time unwritten, but happened afore any mæge or Source-Sayers reached Aeryth." She continues as we walk the Wending Way.

"Time stood still on this side of the Breach mostwise. The land is trapped by sea and the Breach. Larger, more vicious beasts roam here still, and it's some of what Poppa told of. We witnessed it ourselves now from what you say."

"So, this land is inhabited by only wild creatures?"

"Nay. Poppa said there are folk that live here in villages like our own and on Aeryth proper. But even there, the people of the Breachlands are... different than folk as we know them. Of a more steely constitution and sly and not wholly trustworthy, Poppa said. He said there were other types of folk also. Some with powers left over from the mæges of old, and some just born different, like the Amæzonaens or the Titæns. Born in ages passed and not changed as the outlands had.

"Why have they not left then, if life is so tough and dangerous here?"

"Some have. Those that are weakest or hunted. There are but two ways to do such a thing in any manner, and one of those is thwarted by strong mægic. You see, Ari, the Breach ends afore it reaches the inland sea to the south. There is a land bridge there, mayhaps a mere fifty paces wide just at the cliff's edge. But mægic keeps those that would try to leave from doing so. Folk and creatures alike may cross from west to east but not back again. Twisters of mægic, high gusts of storm winds, and blinding hailstorms work in union to throw those who attempt over the cliffside."

"The other manner is by vessel. But few trading ships pass, and the few that do stop only on the isle of the Orakle and that is not a generally hospitable place for folk from this mainland. Most ship captains shy away from would be passengers from the Breachlands. Some have, no doubt, but their numbers are small. And so, the Breachlands have remained a world unto itself."

We have walked the better part of the sun, though we've seen it seldom and even with small respits, the strain of the last two suns have made my sister weary. Though she is of strong and healthy body, our travel and travails have been most unusual for her. I can see the strain in her.

"Roux, let us rest a bit here and trust the mægic of the trail to protect us. This toppled tree will offer up firewood, and we know not how long the Wending Way is. To preserve our strength would be wise as well. Mayhaps a few turns for rest as it is dusk even now."

"I'll not argue your point as my legs are truly heavy from this endless trail. I've seen what the mægic does to beasts that intrude on to the roadway, and it surely must be a deterrent to them."

I do not believe we are wholly safe, but I do not want to worry her. With Bane and myself watching, I think Roux in the least can gather some rest. I've been working with her some on reaching her *Calming* and feel this a good time to teach her to reach deeper into it. With a fire going against a growing chill, we pull some travel cakes from our packs and dine, giving a snack to the furions also. Bane and Fæna watch us eat but are not interested in the evemeal fare presented.

Finally, while leaning back against the fallen log, I coach Roux into a deep state of her *Calming*. I distinguish now for myself the *Calming* from the *Knowing*. The former for deep renewing meditation, the latter for special awareness. They are close but different, and I have not taught her the *Knowing* technique as yet. From what she described lies ahead of us, I will have time later for such lessons.

Bane lies vigilant in front of us, and Lilit and Jilly spread their lithe bodies over and into the deep fur of his back. Roux's spirit cat languishes but stays alert, lying but two paces from us atop the fallen log and occasionally digs her foreclaws into it. Even as I rest in an almost sleeping state, I remain acutely aware of all that moves about me. My senses beyond my sight, ever on high alert.

In what I judge to be the earliest morn, a turn of a sand glass or more afore sunrise, the quiet changes. All the creatures about me sense it and become immediately alert. No light to show it, but I sensed...hear, smell, *feel* the approach of several beasts. They travel to either side of the Wending Way but linger now as they sense us.

I shake Roux from her slumber and place a finger to her lips. She nods. I signal that we should leave and express that there is again danger outside the Wending Way trail. After quickly gathering our things, I pull my short sword from its sheath upon my back. Roux pulls a long dirk from her waist sheath. It is her favorite weapon for close battle encounters. I've tasted its sting in training sessions. She wields it expertly.

As we travel, though near to silent, the creatures hidden within the trees follow, though refuse to engage in the mægic of the pathway. Our advance and their vigil continues for two turns, a host of predators and their sensed prey. There seems to me to be indeed many, as the jungle begins to thin and only the lower brush and hedges move as they travel alongside to us.

The pathway lightens with the sunrise ahead, and we come to the end of the trees. I halt our small company, and I spy about us, But the beasts remain hidden, and yet I remain certain that there are many, and I sense their energy mounting.

Looking ahead along the path down a gentle slope, I notice a river lying ahead. It is wide, mayhaps forty long paces. And on the closest shore, a raft crafted of planks and barrels sits moored against the bank. Two iron rods, the height of my shoulders, stand with a fashioned eye hook atop each. A sturdy and heavy-looking rope passes through each eye, both to the bow and stern, and I can see that the rope spans across the river and appears anchored securely to a tree on either side of the water. The rope itself sags so that it nearly touches upon the water midstream. The rods holding the rope do not appear to be anchored too well into the raft. Its wood has an age to it and has seen better times.

Roux, of course, has cyphered the same thing. If we make it unscathed to the raft, our whole troupe would fit precariously on the less than stout and stable flatboat. But it at this time is the one and logical choice. By fate's grace, the shimmering aura of the path seems to extend the entire way to the shore. We continue as a tight group out and away from the treeline. Bane, Fæna, and myself face back in anticipation of the beasts following us. I am not disappointed.

Our adversaries make themselves known. They are no longer shy about it. But I know not what they are. I can see that there are many. A half dozen to my left and twice that many to my right. Never have I seen their like. They stand no more than knee-high, and still they look a worthy adversary. My gut tells me that the mægic of the path might not be enough. They act the part of a hunting pack, and I think mayhaps they have been in this situation times before.

They seem to be a cross betwixt a carrion bird and a lizard but larger than both. Leather skin of grey, with muddled orange stripes that circle their necks and travel down their spine and onto long tails the like of water lizards but more narrow and long. Their front limbs seem near useless and the size to match a raccoon's, mayhaps, and tucked tightly to their chests. They walk on two large, muscled hind legs likened to a hare that end in clawed, four-toed feet with the look of a rooster's and black talons nearly as long as my own fingers. Their heads and eyes give me great pause as well.

Their heads are overly large and heavy with long, sharp teeth exposed over lipless mouths and strong tight jaws. The orange on their neck and spine is matched in their eyes, which have two lids, one under the other and constantly opening and closing. All these observations I make in the space of a moment as I've retreated into my *Knowing*, slowing time for me. Around me, things do not wait, however.

They have done this before to my reckoning, and I somehow know we will not make the river's raft without consequence. It happens quick and vicious, like jackals in bloodlust. Four from the left come leaping from muscled hind legs and through the mægic veil of the path. One springs at me, and it lies in two smoldering parts upon the path. Another heads toward Bane and in defense, he springs back and away… and outside the veil to the right and into the path of the greater number of the beasts. I leap after him but look back to see what has happened to the other two. The first lies skewered on Roux's dirk but the fourth has succeeded in grabbing Lilit across her midsection in its massive jaw and continues with a second leap, outside the protecting mægic behind me. Jilly attacks the creature and is attached to its underside with her own claws in a death grip and with hind legs flailing at the beast's abdomen even as her teeth sink into its neck. A deafening, echoing war cry from above silences all but the cry of misery from poor Lilit. Her attacker lies dead. But Jilly meows hideously as she sniffs at her sister. I feel her spirit drop from my *Knowing*. I know the reason.

"Nooo!!" I scream.

Spinning, a rage like no other gripping me, I wish with all my heart that the Wending Way's burning mægic would strike all of these ugly beasts dead. I slam my Bo staff into the ground as I turn on them. The amulet on my chest burns. Then there comes a thundering roar from my Bo's drægon tooth end even as the golden veil from the path swirls about it and unleashes a second boom. The aura radiates like a wave in all directions outward from the end of the staff. The force blows Roux off her feet and backward and the Wending Way's ancient mægic strikes all the beasts where they stand. In a moment, they are but a dozen and a half smoldering cinders in heaps scattered about the ground.

Coming to my senses, I turn and sweep Lilit into my hand and urge Roux towards the raft. She regains her feet and stares at me. I throw my staff into the raft and lay Lilit's lifeless body aside to Jilly in the center of the barrel boat. I leap back to the bank to free the raft from the shore and urge Roux to start pulling on the guide rope. The raft sweeps out into the river as I jump aboard it.

"Keep pulling, Roux."

I drop to my knees and within my *Knowing,* I search and search for Lilit's spirit sense. Jilly stands on her hind legs, looking from me to her sister and back to me once more. I recognize the forlorn look and desperation in her eyes, and then she sinks to the deck nudging her nose under her sister's chin. She knows.

"Ari."

I look to Roux's tear-stained face and then follow her gaze back to shore. Three of the great beaked predator beasts, cousins to the one that had earlier leapt in front of us on the path with an assassin's arm in its mouth, stare back. They stand directly on the Wending Way path. I rise to my feet and take over for Roux. There is still a great distance to pull the barrel boat across to the other side, but for now, being beyond the reach of the gathering beasts on shore will do. We are half the distance to midstream, mayhaps twenty paces from shore. The beasts do not follow into the water but still stamped their feet and squawk at us, dipping their beaks into the river and clawing at the shoreline. I push down my urge to send an arrow their way. My rage turns now to a deep, deep grief.

After a moment of thought, I pull my pack from my back and fish within it to find what I am after. I explain to Roux my intent, and she says she'll do it for me. With my sewing kit and a piece of elkskin I had pulled from the pack, she sits cross-legged next to Lilit and fashions a swaddling burial pouch for the furion while I pull us toward the further shore. Jilly watches closely, never leaving her sister's side.

Leaving the pull rope for a time, I sit next to my small creature friends. Reaching over to Bane, I use my blade to cut a piece of fur from the scruff of his neck and place it next to Lilit in the burial cloth. Next, I do the same with a lock of my own hair. Roux sees what I am doing and offers a lock of her red hair also. Jilly watches intently. Fæna, a close companion to the furions for three fortnight now, ambles over and delicately sniffs about her friend. With a deep purring, she lowers her head into Roux's lap, allowing Roux to nick a bit of her neck's scruff. Jilly crawls into my lap and reaches up to lick the underside of my chin as if to give thanks and then turns to offer her tail as well. Placing our offerings tightly against our sweet friend, I cinch the swaddling skin tight around her and secure it with elven vine twine. We all gather at the edge of the flatboat as I lightly lay Lilit into the stream. We watch as her body drifts downstream on the gentle flow.

29

River Ride

An especially chill breeze and its accompanying scent from behind us out of the west brings me back to the barrel flatboat and our further predicament. I gaze now in that direction. Roiling grey-green clouds have materialized out of a previously warm and clear sun.

"Roux, we've a sudden storm brewing. I best pull to the far shore as quick as possible." She looks to the ever-growing storm clouds and nods.

"Let us both pull, Ari. You to the front and I back here. That storm does not look natural."

"Yea, to it then, shall we?" Reaching for the rope to hold my balance, I work my way forward. 'Tis not a simple task as light waves begin to rock the ill-crafted vessel.

Bane and Fæna pace our small space, glancing here and there over the edges as we two pull in an effort to beat the storm that begins thundering now. The creatures gather towards the center now as the current seems stronger and small white caps start appearing on the surface. At midstream, the pull of the current is strongest and the rope grows taut. Pulling the barrel boat becomes an onerous, grueling task even for the two of us working in unison.

The current only grows as the storm begins overtaking us and pelting rain makes it all the more difficult until it is no longer. The rope slackens in our hands, and the raft begins to float downstream ever faster. It has snapped loose of its anchor on the further shore. Attached still on the bank we'd left, the current pulls the clumsy vessel swiftly downstream and the rope whips through the eyelets. As it exits the iron rod on her end of the raft, the boat begins a spin and Roux grabs for the iron stanchion even as she falls over the side. It keeps her with us but overboard and fighting to stay with the boat. Diving across the deck onto my belly, I reach for her wrist as she still clings to the post, the river trying to wrench her from it. Taking hold, I pull with all my might and manage to swing her up onto the deck.

We crawl to the center of the raft and join our creature friends. I pull my pack back on and secure it, helping Roux do the same. We sit on our other possessions, hoping not to lose them. We are at the mercy now of the storm and the river.

I count the passing time as the heavy rain shows little sign of letting up. We are traveling within the storm, it seems. The trip is a bit rocky, but we are no longer in danger of capsizing. We are wet and chilly, and the rudderless raft slowly turns as we float with the current. But as the rain lightens a bit, I no longer fear for our lives.

As turns of a sand glass pass, and the storm has finally moved ahead of us. We sit up and take note of the landscape we are floating past. It is incredible. The sun, now halfway to the horizon behind us, brings out unimaginable animals. Some beasts so huge that they must weigh more and stand taller than three oxen each atop the other, and beyond that a neck so long that the beast grazes at the top of trees. A herd of elk-like creatures are drinking from the bank, each the size of Da's warhorse Bregœ, and I see a snake curled in a tree that I am sure I could not wrap my arms around.

As the sun continues towards the horizon, I see we are headed north and east which is a good thing. I start to seriously look for an opportunity to come ashore. We can swim it, of course, but only if necessary. Our weapons and other possessions will make that effort more difficult. The river being wider now, I notice it has shallows as well, a'times sand bars just below the surface. We've come more towards the further shore with the slacking off of the center current, and I see a possibility ahead. The storm has toppled a tall tree onto the river, its roots now reaching for the sky. Its trunk and upper branches extend near to fifteen paces into the river.

I use my staff to push closer to shore as we pass shallow sandbanks. Reckoning we will be able to catch ourselves into the tree …and we do. Ten paces or so from the bank, I can stand and touch bottom, enabling me to finally grapple, push, and pull the raft ashore. Our creature friends do not wait. Jilly uses the tree as her bridge to dry land and Fæna follows. Bane leaps into the water for the few paces left to the shore.

Finally upon solid ground again, Bane and Fæna venture out exploring the area, mayhaps to hunt their evemeal or just to regain their land legs. They have become unlikely but fast friends over these last two few fortnight.

With a majestic sharma tree nearby, it is an easy decision to make camp under its widespread canopy. I survey it first, however, to make sure no oversized serpents are hanging within its branches. Bow in hands, Roux, Jilly, and I set out in the waning sunlight in search for small game and other edibles. With a small copse of trees nearby, we hope the fates will smile upon us. They do, and a large hare will be evemeal this night. Jilly has found some 'shrooms and tubers. A waterfowl nest produces eggs that will serve for our mornmeal on the morrow.

Returning to camp, we spread our spare garb and other supplies from our packs out to dry. With the torrential rains of earlier, the most waterproof of packs could not have kept our essentials totally dry.

Having eaten our fill, Roux and I and Jilly settle about the fire.

"My suns have been eventful since my brœther has re-entered my life."

"Ha! I find myself apologizing frequently to my friends for just this same thing. I now must do likewise with family. It is not wise to travel with your brœther, mayhaps."

Jilly has settled into my lap, and I ardently stroke her to comfort us both. As Roux and I talk of our full and consequential past few suns, Bane and Fæna enter camp, and they, too, settle close. Bane greets Jilly first thing before curling at my feet.

"Ari, what happened back at the Wending Way? I know, I was there, but never in my life have I seen mæge's power and then such as that. I've read in the temple's histories of similar things, but even those did not speak to such a thing that I witnessed at my own brœther's hand."

I take a moment to compose an answer.

"Mæge's power, you say. I've denied for the longest time that it could be anything but fable and myth, and now I, of all people, can wield it. But the like of what had happened back there, it shocked not only you but me as well. I've had a few incidents, and Eschereon has tried to tutor me in these things, but they have only happened to me in times of great stress or emotion. I seem not to have control of it."

"It seemed very controlled to me, Ari. Those evil, vicious…I know not what to call them… You struck them down, nay, burned them to dust in one fell motion that appeared to come from your staff, or mayhaps the stone embedded within it."

"Eschereon says the stone and staff amplify or direct the mægic. When first we met, he held it high and made a sky bolt shoot from it. I've never been able to do the same, cause only a light to appear actually, and you've seen that."

"But Lilit." I need to take a moment. A rock and pain in my throat are preventing me from speaking.

"Seeing and hearing her cry of distress…an anger filled me so. I wished with all my heart that I could take all the mægic about the Wending Way and direct it at the beasts." Pausing, I reach for the amulet lying against my chest.

"This amulet, the one you say holds a very old and great mægic, when I have a specific desire, the mægic within it acts on it."

"Nay, Ari. Well, there is some truth in your statement, but it is not the amulet that holds the mægic, but it directs, even as your staff does, the wearer's mægic. *You* are the conduit of the mægic. You form the type of mægic you use or pull it from the ether, and then direct it with the aid of certain stones or rune mægic, or both." And *that* is a lesson directly from the Mœther Dominæ. She is a…Druidess? Would you call it? Likened to Eschereon in learning and mægic…a Mæster.

I think on this awhile.

"Eschereon has told me that mægic has been asleep in the peoples of Aeryth for hundreds of years, flowing in their blood and bloodlines. He says it has lived on in other things, both living and inanimate, like some creatures and trees and such, but that Source-Sayers of the ancient world had begun a grand experiment that he said had begun to awaken in our times.

"He says this awakening would be erratic and unrefined and that a greater purpose of the Druidæ would be to aid those with whom mægic awakened within.

"You are my sister of the same bloodline. Do you have mægic, Roux?"

"I don't know. I mean I can sense mægic in objects even as Mother Dom…Vicchi does. And because, afore having met you again, I've never seen it with mine own eyes, only read of it. I do not know. Vicchi has said it is strong in me and that is why I can spell runes so well, but I'd never consider that to be a true ancient mægic, the like that I witnessed from you at the Wending Way. And though I know she carries it, I do not even know what mægic Vicchi carries herself. She is most secretive in that regard. She is a master of deflection, that woman."

"I will not deny she is sly of purpose, your temple mœther. Tell me, could you see the shimmering veil about the Wending Way as we traveled within it?"

"Nay, not when we traveled, but when we exited the wood near to the river. Yea, I recall a shimmer in the air, but I did not relate it then to mægic."

"Then you can see it even as I do. Alænèa tutored me a little on recognizing the mægic of creatures, and she can see it about those that carry it, even as you 'feel' it about objects such as the amulet around my neck. I've spoken of my *Calming,* my *Knowing*…for it is when I am using it that I see mægic, even as Alænèa explained it to be. Mayhaps it will do the same for you."

"Yea, you've spoken that it is a way of rest and a rejuvenating of the spirit, and that you used it in healing Rieka. I would like to try it if you are willing to teach me."

It does not take long, as Roux is the most apt of any I've taught it to. She can take herself there…and to the *Knowing* in but one lesson. Because I've described it prior to her learning this first time, she can even sense the spirit energies about her and connects then to Fæna. I see it immediately. She is remarkable, learning in a first lesson what had taken me several.

"Oh, brœther, I see the auras that you spoke of connecting to Fæna. It… it's indescribable! Thank you for this."

We decide to stay awhile in our place on the bank and under the tree, fairly secure that Mensæ and his assassins will not be likely to find us after our experiences of the last few suns. And I think to better prepare Roux, as she is destined to travel with me through the Breachlands. I bring shelter making materials from the nearby wood and build a sturdy lean-to as a temporary home.

While I gather building materials, I also find a stout branch, long and strong enough to be fashioned into a fighting Bo staff. I've seen Roux train, both at the Wic'cha temple and also on the isle with the Amæz. She is lithe, strong, and quick, and I soon learn that she is a very quick study, even as Sæm had been.

We duel and train for seven and one suns afore anything changes. I tutor Roux in the *Knowing* and we connect, spirit sense to spirit sense, and it becomes an unbreakable bond…an underlying connection betwixt us at all times. Brœther to sister, sister to brœther. This makes our dueling especially straining but gratifying, as we can anticipate the other's moves instantly until we discover a more random and unpracticed method. And so our mutual efficiency grows, as do our lethal methods. I think Moor would have found our team an unbeatable foe, even though my sister has yet to reach her fourteen year-end. I will continue to feel very protective but confident in her abilities, ne'er the lesser for it.

But as I said, our pathway and purpose changes once more. While out hunting with bows on the surrounding plains which we enjoyed each after-highsun these past half a dozen suns, an astounding encounter meets us. Talon alerts us. Looking north, we watch as in the distance, a predator and prey chase ensues. We cannot make out the prey in the high grasses, but the beasts in pursuit are clearly large jackals or coyotes. Their howling very recognizable. They are headed south toward the river and across our path.

Still a few hundreds of paces out from us, I finally see their prey, but I am no less confused. The jackals are gaining, when of a sudden, what appears to be two small youngers rise into the air on glimmering green sails and shoot further ahead on the wind and land again into a full run. This sets us into motion. Bane has already left us. The youngers appear to be losing this race and growing tired, sure certain.

We can hear their voices now though not recognize their tongue. They speak animately with whoops, I imagine to spur each other on. They are close enough to us now and I stop, plant my feet, nock, and loose an arrow. Roux keeps running, knowing her arrow would have no chance. Mine hits home and fells the closer jackal to them, but the next closest even now pounces on the trailing younger. I wince.

I hear an anguished yell from the lad even as Bane arrives on the scene. The attacking jackal becomes the prey and immediately leaves off the lad to defend itself. It has no chance against Bane. Roux closes within twenty paces and has stopped to nock an arrow. Fæna arrives before she could loose it and somehow has attached herself to the underside of the next jackal, hugging around its chest and shoulders even as she bites into its neck and thrashes its abdomen with her hind legs. It howls in pain. The fourth beast looks to be waiting for an opening to attack the cat. Roux's arrow finds its neck, and it is done. Even as this happens, Talon's war cry echoes, and he comes out of sun in a swift dive to take the fifth jackal–the largest–by surprise as it seeks to sneak up on the youngers as they are the most vulnerable in hopes of salvaging the attack. Talon's tearing claws and piercing beak send it off missing an eye and most of an ear. Fæna's jackal follows, bleeding heavily. The three others lie dead.

As I approach the youngers, my expression must have betrayed me, as I most certainly show my surprise. These are not youngers at all, but full-grown…men? They have beards and lines about their eyes and if their height was not half the height of Roux, I'd have put them as men grown and seen thirty years or mayhaps even twice my years. But the one most certain lay injured, and in distress, though he has a strange way of showing it. As I had with Alænèa's people on the Accadian Plain after listening but a few moments, I understand their language perfectly, though at first it had been a foreign tangle of guttural sounds.

"Derri, you fool. Let's fly to the river you say! Nay, I'm the fool fer listenin', aren't I? That mongrel mutt's torn into me good, hasn't he?"

The one speaking looks away from me, staring at his friend who winces as he examines his friend's back over his shoulder.

"I'm not going to lie to you, mate. It looks a bit like ground meat, it does. Not appetizin' at all. We're safe for the moment though…" He takes a moment to measure their rescuers as he glances up to me and Roux when we approach. He gazes more nervously as Bane and Fæna wander over and lie watching them.

"They're here, aren't they, Derri? Is it out of the kettle, into the fire, mate?"

"Turn and look then, Mayo. 'Tis but a lad and lass then. They don't look the type, if you take my meaning, mate."

"What type would that be then?"

They both jump near to falling over and turn to face us. Roux looks askance at me as well.

"You speak Gnomon, lad?! How is that possible? He speaks Gnomon, Mayo!"

"I've still my ears, Derri. No thanks to you!"

"Mayo, is it? Mayhaps we ought to get you back to our camp. It's not far. I've my healer's kit in my pack there and can be of help, I believe. You've lost a lot of blood, and I fear you'll be getting a bit woozy soon."

"I'm there already, lad. I'd be obliged for some help. My mate here is more than useless this sun." He eyes Derri with a wavering contempt.

"Roux, help me remove his shirt and use it as bandage till we can get him to camp."

"Aye, a good idea that, lad! Do you hear, Mayo? He's a healer, he says. A bit o' luck, would ya say? Ha, a bit o' luck that!"

We wrap him up as quickly as possible, and I pull him onto my back, crossing his arms about my neck and holding them there. I cannot help but notice his feet, bare and as hairy as his back, reach around my body to grab hold of each and the other like two hands. I race with him back to camp as he passes unconscious.

30

Gnomon Vale Druid

His good mate, Derri, watches as I clean the deep wounds across Mayo's shoulder and back. Mayo has not regained consciousness during the whole of this process and that is fortunate as it would have been quite painful. I've brought my opæum out for that purpose, having restocked many moons prior from the poppies upon the Plains in Accadia.

Mayo's luck, and mine for that matter, does not hold, and the halfling, a term that Roux proclaims our father had used in describing an encounter with these same people, wakes to excruciating pain, as I start to stitch the deepest wounds on his shoulder back together. I have Roux feed him a bit of the opæum, but she may have been a bit heavy-handed in the attempt to help. Whilst pausing to let the opæum take effect, the two friends' conversation becomes a bit unusual.

"Mayo, the lad really is a healer! He's managed to pack yer bloody mess of back meat back into yer skin and sewed most of it tup till ya came to again."

"Derri, ppffft, why's yer skin so peek-ked and green… Oh, I'd not noticed yer ears are quite big and round, mate. Yer lips are movin' but it's just jibberish leakin' out, mate. Psnikkk, but not tellin' ya anything ya don' already know, am I?"

Derri seems taken aback.

"Well, yer nose noise is makin' more sense than you, Mayo! I'm tellin' ya, the lad is usin' a fish hook 'n elven thread, he says, to pull yer back together, dolt. Jenni would be mighty proud fer the look of it!"

My patient looks over his shoulder to me.

"Oooo, yer glowing in all sorts of colours, lad. Oh, you've yer fishin' gear, I see. Did Derri tell ya we was flyin' out to the river for the fishies? His real name's Derriwether, ya know… We call 'im Derri for the bird what knocks his head all sun long against the tree, ya know?"

"Ya do no such thing, ya rubbish babbler… Derri's jus' short fer Derriwether! Stop yer mouth fartin' then, mate!"

"Oops…words got out, shhhh… You've a pretty smile, lassie. Whatchya smilin' about. Kin I lick yer finger again?"

Roux covers her mouth to hide a further chuckle as Derri paces to and fro and I finish up my sewing.

"He's not usually like this, ya know. He's the logical and proper one of the two of us. Didn't want to fly over to the river. Never have before 'cause Jenni says it's not safe. Jenni's his wife, ya know, 'n she's the one always wantin' him to bein' sensible. But, I'm the trouble maker, n' I'm the one suggested we come, 'n he was steamed with Jenni cause of something or t'other. Which he never, he loves her so, but he was and I said let's fly to the river, knowin' it wasn't safe… This is all my fault. Jenni's gonna banish me fer sure of it." And the poor little guy slumps to his knees and begins to sob, large hands with tufts of hair atop them covering his face. His friend Mayo has passed out sitting up, not hearing a word of his friend's confession.

Later round the evemeal fire, Derri shares left-overs we'd scrounged up about camp with some roasted tubers Jilly has found for us.

"Ya gotta come back to the vale with us, the two of ya… Not sure about yer wolf 'n cat, though JabberJack wouldn't mind, I suspect."

"We were thinking of traveling further downriver. Our pæder told of townes along the river, and we thought to hire a guide to get us to the Orakle."

"The Orakle, you say. JabberJack'll know 'bout that. He's a druid, ya know!"

Our ears perk to that.

"A druid, you say?"

"Well, not sure, really. Cause everybody jus' calls 'im JabberJack the hermit, but my great, great, grandsire says so, 'n he's older than anybody else in the valley. Said JabberJack's the reason he's still livin' at two hunerd 'n thirty somethin'. Still flies some too!"

"So this JabberJack lives in the valley then?"

"Well, yea and nay, to that one, lad." I've introduced Roux and myself to Derri, but he persists in 'lad and lass' when addressing us.

"He lives in the valley but into the ruins, ya know."

"Ruins? Ruins of what?"

"They say a mæge of old's keep. But it's jus' moss-covered rocks 'n caves 'n stairs to nowheres now. But JabberJack likes it there. Sometimes folks won't see 'im for years a'times. My great, great, grandsire, we call him Froeds, says he's out adventurin'. I don' know what adventurin' ya kin do in holes in the ground. But there is a whole separate valley surrounded by cliffs, sheer like a cake tin. You'll see if ya come, so who's to know? And he's older than Froeds, by a hunerd years or more, Froeds says."

This makes up my mind for me. It holds more promise than a towne downstream, most ways.

"Well, Derri, we'll come see your valley, and mayhaps your hermit, if he's home, and we'll see Mayo back to Jenni."

He winces at her name but smiles at our accepting his offer.

"Will Mayo be okay to travel on morrow's morn then? Jenni's most like to be frantic and fit to be tied, even now, with Mayo not home yet."

With the ailing halfling under the opæum's influence, I am able to reach into Mayo's spirit self, enough to start some healing from within and can see evidence his body is healing extremely quick.

"Mayhaps by highsun on the morrow," I suggest. He nods. Later when we bed down for the night, Derri sleeps close to his friend.

On the morrow, I place more healing unguent upon Mayo's back when he wakes. He is extremely hungry, and my trip back out to the plains and an extended walk by Roux and Jilly along the river bank produces some good mornmeal fare. Eggs, onions, roast tubers, and hare. I swear the halfling ate two of my normal portions and is eyeing the campfire for more.

"Do you feel up for a trek back to your valley, Mayo?"

"Aye, we best be going, whether or not. Jenni'll be beside herself in worry, her knowin' Derri." I swear I see the corners of his mouth turn up at that. Derri's brow furrows.

We have little to pack since being washed up ashore and into the Northern Reaches, so we have little trouble leaving out at highsun, Mayo feels up to the task. The two halflings have naught but small, light packs on their backs. Mayo insists on carrying his own, in spite of his mauled back. But it is healing well, so I do not argue. Our trek over the plain proceeds uneventfully with Bane and Fæna ever alongside us at a distance and Jilly traveling in my pack. Missing Lilit gives me a chill and sure certain, Jilly also. We arrive to a rise over a most remarkable valley, not quite come dusk time.

Looking out upon it, we can see a wondrous sight. 'Tis a narrow vale with tiered hills rolling up each side, and it seems to go on forever into the distance, though bending first eastward then back west again. Pathways wide enough for two narrow pull carts meander along each side. Off in the distance, round wooden doorways and shuttered round windows appear as pockmarks against the hills. Some hillsides are tiered in crops, rising for and five levels high. Halflings move about, looking like ants at this vantage. And they also fly! Many sails dot the sky betwixt the hills on either side of the valley. Each, Derri says, carries a friend or cousin most like from one side to the other.

Mayo stares off into the distance to the left hillside and squints hard.

"Derri, she's gathered a posse, Jenni has. We best be off at once." Derri groans quite audibly.

"Arias, Roux, follow as you will. Do you see the door in bright yellow there? With the crowd around it on the path? That'll be my place. Just follow the path, and it'll be our turn to offer up evemeal!"

"Mayhaps I shouldn't come with ya, Mayo. We can talk on the morrow."

"Nay, ya will not, Derri knockhead. You'll face up, even as I'll do. Now off with ya! I want to see ya headed right."

The halflings then pull their own sails–they called them lifts–from their small, flat backpacks and pull the thinnest material I've ever seen from them. Pounded and sewed elven leaf, they explain, and I marvel again at the many uses of this very same plant. They deftly reach down and pass a loop of the sail over a thumb on the rear of each bare foot and take two others in the thumbs of each hand.

Derri walks to the edge and jumps into the air. Mayo immediately follows. At first, I think they'd fall like rocks and tumble down the hillside into the vale, but a draft lifts each of them up and into the air. They rise above us on a wind stream and then fly out above the valley, heading east with a pull from their left thumbs.

"Ari, have you ever seen such a thing?"

"Nay, but I've seen new and seeming impossible things since leaving my homestead, and the improbable has found a ready home now in my mind. Shall we be off then?"

"Aye…but for the danger in it, big brœther. I like this adventuring!"

I'm less sure. My thoughts wander to Finnie, and a safer home far away, thinking Da mayhaps had the right of it by settling outside of Middenvale. Learning of mægic and finding my family and new friends has its sway, but I'm finding this threatening by Mensæ does not sit well, and I know I'll be coming to terms with him in the future. There can be no doubt as he will not stop his chase for me, sure certain. Having to protect my sister from him weighs heavy as well.

But still, we goggle a bit in wonder of the valley afore us. True to his word, after descending some, upon the serpentine path through switchbacks and even a rock-hewn tunnel in the hillside, Roux and I come finally to the bright yellow door with a gargoyle knocker bolted in its center. As we arrive, Jenni, I assume, comes rushing out of the door and leaps up and hugs me about the waist, leaving her legs dangling for a moment.

"You wonderful lad, you! Saving my Mayo." Falling back to her feet, she looks up to me and frowns.

"You could 'ave left that Derri to the jackals, tho!" Her face redeems a bit now.

"Jenni, luv, I've told you it was just as much my fault as his!" Mayo talks of equal blame, and I think he makes a good mate to Derri.

"Well, I'll not speak of it anymore, and mayhaps not ever again to that scoundrel Derri, certain. But, come, come, you and the lass. I've made up a feast for the heroes! Come in, won't you?"

Mayo is a different person inside his home. He wears a vest, nice trousers, and a white under-tunic with ruffling about it at the collar and wrists. He has a smoking pipe to mouth and the smoke wafts about the cozy abode and smells of rich smokeweed. An aroma I've always enjoyed. We need to take care once inside, as the ceilings are just above our heads and any doorway lintel we need to duck low under. But once seated, their home proves warm and inviting.

They have a few guests for us to meet, and I think they are important to the community. Mayo explains that his healer spoke perfect Gnomon even though an outlander and that I travel with creatures that I speak to as people. He continues on about how the creatures have helped save his life, sure certain at my bidding. They ask what beasts I speak to, and Jilly makes an appearance. I explain that my creature friends include an echo eagle, a Linx cat, and a mountain dread-wolf.

"He means a dire-wolf," says Mayo. They all exclaim that a dire-wolf 'tis not possible. Dire-wolves do not abide any man as they are as wild a beast as there could be.

"But it is so. I looked into its eyes. There is no mistaking," Mayo insists.

"You've seen wolves such as Bane afore, Mayo?"

"Aye, once, but tales tell of the dire-wolves roaming about all the forests off to the north. They do not travel in packs, but they are sighted oft enough. They are, after all, the kings in all the forests. Even the borderland beasts do not tempt fate with them."

"The borderland beasts? They are different somehow? We've encountered two species I've never heard tell of." I query, more curious now.

"Aye, JabberJack would know more o'course, but everyone knows that ancient beasts still roam near the outer cliffs and are held there by ancient mægics."

We are treated to a feast by Jenni and her sister as it turns out, and the other special guests pepper us with queries of the outside world, though they hold no intent to visiting such places. They do not seem to notice our difference in physical stature, as if they deal with it in everysun occurrence. They take more note of our ability to speak their natural Gnomon tongue. Especially when we explain we have never heard it afore our encounter with Mayo and Derri. But Jenni does not abide hearing Derri's name and shuts down those discussions.

"There was a great war once, and our histories say we fought with the mæges and Wic'cha to turn back the old war-gods. We're not a warring people but fight to discourage the scoundrels and thieves from the lawless townes that come calling a'times."

The 'dinner party,' they call it, ends afore sundown, and the others go on their way as they all but Jenni's sister are traveling with 'lifts' and prefer not to fly at night. We are offered a room to stay in for the night. It serves as a large larder or storeroom, and Jenni and her sister, Jōddi, produce arm fulls of blankets and pillows for us to spread out.

Morrow's morn comes with dipped honey cakes, eggs, sausages, and taters with cheese. Then a second serving arrives with buttered flatcakes and heartberries. Finally, pipeweed for Mayo, and tea for us others. Jenni and Jōddi chat throughout, and we are beginning to understand that the halflings of Gnomon are both friendly hosts and most talkative. When we finally break away and step outside, we both find a long stretch in order. 'Tis good to have the room to manage it. Mayo follows us out.

"Mayo, your family is wonderful. Please thank Jenni again for us? Also, do you think you and Derri could show us the way to JabberJack?" He stands, shaking his head vehemently. His hands rub down both sides of his trousers, and he glances about furtively.

"Don't think Jenni seeing Derri 'n me together wou' be wise, ya know. An' Jōddi 'n he were getting sweet, too, if ya take my meaning. He's in it deep now, 'n Jōddi is siding with my wife. 'N ta top'n it all, Jenni isn't letting me out o'sight. Mayhaps Derri can take ya, tho?"

"I understand, Mayo. How do you think I can get a hold of Derri then?"

"I'll ask Jōddi. Jenni isn't watching her sister near so close as she's eyein' me. I kin send ya to a meet up, 'n then he kin take ya, eh?"

"That would be great."

True to his word, he sends us off and down a trail, telling we ought to meet the mayor. Jenni does not let Mayo take us himself, saying she has some urgent chores for him. She does have Jōddi escort us in his place, asking her to market while in Valetown if she gets the chance. That is how they refer to the center hub of the community.

The trek to the valley's floor spurs us to continual queries of Jōddi, who despite much shorter legs, ne'er the lesser keeps ahead of us, acting as tour guide. As we look to the sky, it becomes evident that all the tiny folk of Gnomon Vale employ the sails to travel from side to side, down and along the valley. They do not just float downward as one would expect, but they know drafts and lifts to climb into the air on and so can elevate and glide on the winds to most anyplace they desire. And the wind and competing breezes are constant here, in turmoil even it feels. Jōddi insists one could fly the length of the vale if need be which lies some thirty leagues distant. It seems mægic, but 'tis just inventiveness really and a marvel to our eyes surely.

We eventually make the valley floor, then find the market square. As it turns out, it is Mayo's set upon meeting place. Derri greets us enthusiastically, and folk near about do as well. Though not exactly museum material, we are a rarity within the town square, and with Jilly holding court upon my shoulder, we make quite the spectacle it seems.

"I'll just pick a few things up for Jenni whilst the three of you talk then," Jōddi says with a meaningful sideways glance to Derri.

"Jōddi says yer lookin' to visit old JabberJack," Derri offers.

"That's right, Derri. If you can't, mayhaps you could tell us who might."

"No worries there. I kin take ya. But if we're gonna be walkin' and startin' yet this sun, it'll be late time we get there. Best be usin' the market to stock up for travelin' supplies, eh?"

"Mayhaps you can help us with that, Derri?" A nod, a wink, and a huge smile plants on his face as my answer, and he turns toward the market.

We catch up with Jōddi and trade for some trail foods as she finishes her marketing for Jenni.

"I'll 'scort Jōddi back to Mayo's iffits all the same to you, Arias. If you twos follow the river road, I'll meet up with ya a bit outside of towne, eh?"

"Yea, Derri. That will be fine with us. Jōddi, thank you for your aid. Please give our best wishes to Jenni and Mayo. Your sister is most gracious. Please thank her for us."

With nods and fare-thee-wells, Roux and I are off. We can detect Bane and Fæna keeping a distance up in the hills while matching our pace.

"Ari, this valley is amazing. Watching the halflings sail overhead and visiting their homesteads… They are simply remarkable and seem such a pleasant, happy, and giving folk. 'Tis such a contrast to how we arrived into the Breachlands."

"Yea, Roux. It would seem there are good and honest peoples even in the toughest places in Aeryth. "I'm anxious to meet this druid they speak of. An unusual name he carries."

Keeping to the river path, Derri joins us well after the towne is left behind two bends and two turns of a sandglass. The sun is already hidden behind the steep hillside to our left. Their sunlight wanes early in the deepest parts of the valley, and we can see why the halflings prefer to live higher on the valley's hillsides. We watch Derri deftly maneuver in the winds and comes to rest directly in front of us, having arrived from behind and over our shoulders. We are seeing fewer and fewer of the halflings' unique homesteads. Having swiftly packed his elven leaf sail, Derri fills the quiet of the aftersun with his amiable banter.

"'Tis the Darling River, 'n it flows the length of the vale. The Calgua Falls feed it jus' where we turn to the Ruin's Canyon 'n that's where we'll find him, iffin he's home. JabberJack, I'm meanin'.

"They say 'twas the very canyon the Breachlands own 'Sorserors' of more built his mægic keep in."

"Do you mean Source-Sayer?" Roux queries with furrowed brow.

"Aye, the Sorseror. Tha's what I said, dinnit I? The one in the tales of drægoons 'n such to scare the wee ones, eh."

"And who are 'they,' Derri?"

"You know, the ones 'at sing the tales 'n pass 'em on!" I nod.

"And when did your people come to the valley, Derri?" asks Roux.

"Oh, we've been here forever 'n always, even afore the Sorserors. Least ways tha's what me great grandsire says. He says the JabberJack even has books about it. Says he seen 'em his very self, he has. It's why I know the way. He's taken me and Mayo both to the canyon. Was a long time ago, mind, but I 'member the ways. Can't git there in the air. Ya gotta know the way from here in the vale. 'Tis no secret, mind, but nobody bothers as few know the paths nowsuns."

"So you've met this JabberJack?" Derri seems to mull his answer to me.

"Well, not 'xactly, see. But, we've been to the ruins, Mayo 'n me. And great grandda insists he's still there. Says he's huners' a years old. Most wise immortal, great grandda says. That means he lives on forever, ya know."

My hopes of finding this hermit Derri called a druid once diminishes a bit on hearing this. But we walk on, and Derri continues telling the history of the Gnomon Valley. From how they learned to fly to great battles against outlanders and others that would have driven them from their ancestral home. His high voice and the occasional gurgle of the river as it rushes over rocks are all that we hear for three more turns and into the darkening eve.

Finally, Derri pauses and stare at a monolith of a bolder to the side of our path. Pulling some branches aside near its bottom, he smiles and turns west and unto no path that we can see. First through brambles and then down a steep hillock, we make our way to ha's, and woohoo's, and whispered giggles from the halfling. A new path is found though less clear as such. Derri starts up his tale again, sure in his desired direction now, though we feel less sure. It appears we are heading directly into a cliff face.

But likened to the entrance to our frost cellar back home, there is a fold in the rock cliff face, and there, an entrance into a cavern of sorts. I produce my mægic light atop my staff, and Derri's eyes widen in it's light.

"Well then, we are near to getting there, Arias and lassie Roux," as Jilly pokes her head from my pack. "Just through this cavern way, it is."

The way is not long and exits back to an almost failed sun, but there is a host of glimmering stars.

"We should mayhaps camp here for the night, Arias. The way from here is a bit tricky, here amongst the ruins."

We are on a rise and can see in the starlight and the rising moon, a great expanse of valley completely encased within sheer cliffs in every direction. Sure enough, as we look out upon it, we see the ruins of what had once been a great keep and village long ago.

We set up camp at Derri's suggestion and settle in for the night. But the hairs on the back of my neck rise as I feel eyes upon us. Any apprehension dissolves though as Bane and Fæna wander into camp to join us. They seem at ease, so I settle and give little further thought to it. It is a benign feeling in any case, and I feel no threat.

31

Temple Counsel

Alænèa, Therrien, and I follow a young acolyte through winding halls in the temple proper. The only sound the clack of hard soles and heels of the young lass' shoes against the marble floors and echoing off the tall stone walls. A random thought crosses my mind that her pæder might be a cobbler. The acolyte's just gathered us from the library, a wondrous array of chambers, some wide and tall and well-lit through rose windows as high as two stories, others small and cozy and lantern-lit, with but a few chairs and small tables scattered about.

Our trek ends in front of two high, arched, and heavy doors, a smaller twin set to those at the main entrance to the temple itself. Whispers of wonder pass betwixt us three. We had not come across this chamber in our explorations of the temple. A relief sets upon the doors and holds the same twisting trunks of a majestic tree, each bearing an ancient rune. Though the door is massive, it swings in with only a light push from Romilly, our young guide. She smiles and stands aside, beckoning us to enter. When we do she pulls the great door closed as she leaves us. We are not alone in the chamber.

Astounded, I look upon an amazing group. Vicchi, the matron of the temple who I expected, but the other guests are quite remarkable. Vicchi is standing to the right aside a large stone fireplace, her head level with its mantel and holding a cup of tea I imagine, as it seems her favorite drink. On the other side of the firebox stands what I can only describe as a warrior queen. She stands so regally. She is garbed in the finest armor I've ever seen, the king's guard's livery I've seen in Kings Court not excluded. The mantel stands only waist high to her majestic stature. I come from a village of tall folk, but anyone among them would be dwarfed in comparison.

To this warrior's right, a compatriot, though in slightly less armor, is sitting upon a great chair, one of four designed, it appears, just for them. This warrior woman sits with head stooped in shame, her head in her hands. To Vicchi's left, a determined-looking woman paces to and fro across the room, stopping as we arrive and pulling herself away from the window she had spent a moment staring out of. Týr, whom we also know, stands behind another chair to the right, hands gripping its back. But most curious of all, Talon sits perched on the back of another chair. He spreads his great wings in recognition of us and settles again.

"Good after-highsun, Sæm, Alænèa, and Therrien. Please come forward and mayhaps take a seat. I'd like to introduce you to a few people."

"Of course. Though, by her hair and eyes, I suspect I might know one of your guests." My eyes roam to the woman at the window, and she returns my gaze with a half-hearted smile playing across her face, in direct contrast to her lined brow.

"My son has spoken of the three of you, I believe, but most oft about you. I am sure you must be Sæm?"

"Aye. We've traveled together for many moons now, and my father's brœther you surely know as Ètœn Braveheart."

"Yea, and I owe a debt to him I cannot repay. Your uncle was very dear to me."

"Please come, sit, the three of you. It is concerning Arias and his sister that we need to speak." Vicchi offers again, and Alænèa speaks my thoughts.

"His sister? Arias has a sister? How wonderful! And then as Sæm has said, this lady is surely his mœther. He must be beside himself with the joy of it!"

Vicchi nods, then continues.

"You are already acquainted, though neither of you knew it at the time. Guineƒere Roux Côeurdrægon is his sister, and she is the acolyte that first brought you all to me. You know her as Guin." My face, I'm sure, shows my surprise. "Come, sit. We have some disturbing news."

She then informs us of news the two warrior women had brought to her. The one shamed, Rieka, had returned to the warrior queen and explained how she drove Arias and Guin onto a skiff and out to sea, noticing then that an Asgährdian vessel gave chase to them.

"I raced to the point and stared out to sea as the chasing vessel passed by. Standing at the bow stood a group of soldiers, I am most sure, all garbed in black."

"Mensæ!" Therrien notes.

"Mensæ? My father's court advisor? Surely not."

"Aye, 'twas my immediate thought as well. He has been chasing us, with a dozen assassins in tow since Arias escaped the Bowels at Kings Court. Eschereon thinks him a mind mæge, whatever that may be, and it left him quite disturbed after Arias shared his encounter with the man. Eschereon sent us away and left to other parts immediately as well."

"The tinkers bazaar," Vicchi speaks aloud. "'Tis why Eschereon called the meet, no doubt, and I should be there. But I sent Illéron in my stead."

All of us look to her, confused.

"If indeed this Mensæ is a mind mæge, it is serious trouble we are up against. Brewing for two millennia or more. It is the very reason the Source-Sayers of old established this very chamber, and they were the highest mæges in all of Aeryth history."

Her statement does not clarify any of our concerns, I see on everybody's face. I see something else though.

"You chased Arias and Guin out to sea and near into his enemies' arms, warrior woman. Why would you do such a thing?"

"I've wracked my brain for the why of it and can find no explanation. I hold only highest respect for him and his pæder and his mœther as well. I can only say that I felt compelled to do it."

Silence reigns for a bit, and then Vicchi speaks again.

"This is further evidence of my fear. I believe it was indeed a compulsion, and this Mensæ did extort Rieka to do as she did. And at no fault to her, as I understand the power of a mind mæge. Most like, as the Amæz are of strong mind, he could not enthrall her to kill the two of them, so he did the next best thing. He compelled her to deliver them to him. And even the part that she played was unknown to her at the time, or she would have refused it also."

"How could you know such a thing Vicchi?" I ask.

"I know the ways of a mind mæge, because I myself, am one."

We all know, by this time, the lore of the mæges that escaped the oppression of a different land, coming to Aeryth and bringing mægic with them. But Vicchi has just admitted she practices the very mægic that they were escaping from. Confusion reigns among us all.

"Though little known, it was not an inherently evil mægic the Source-Sayers were fleeing, but rather those that wielded it. Particularly three very powerful Source-Sayers in their own right. They named themselves the Three Eye Council and had strengthened their abilities tenfold when they joined in spirit form. Though still individuals, they could act as one a'times to become omnipotent. This is what the Source-Sayers of old fled from. And there were a few mind mæges amount them."

"But if this is the case, are you saying it is not my pæder, the king, that hunts for Arias but Mensæ, his advisor?"

"Yea, Aeglèsia, if this Mensæ is who I suspect him to be, the king himself has most surely been under his sway for as long as they have known each and the other. Further, I believe that it's not merely your son, Arias, he seeks, but the Druidae themselves and further the Elders as they know them. They are who we know as the Source-Sayers of Aeryth legend. I am sure he believes Arias will lead him to them. Alas, if he is here and has been, as you indicated for near to four decades, I fear he is not alone. The great invasion your pæder vanquished may not have destroyed the greater enemy. This is dire news. I am sure Eschereon has deduced the same and has called a council to address this threat."

"So, Vicchi, you yourself are a druid? And what of Arias and Guin? You speak as if you know Mensæ has not caught him yet."

Talon lets out a small echoing cry. All eyes go to him.

"We must take to the sea immediately and try to intercept them somehow!" Alænèa bursts out and rises.

"Settle, Alænèa. You will not catch them at sea. That time has passed."

"What then?" Therrien joins.

Vicchi speaks again.

"Our ship has returned to port without her captain. Mensæ and his assassins, as they've been indeed named such, have gone ashore into the Northern Reaches, following Arias and Guin who narrowly escaped death in the rocks and waves offshore. The assassins have murdered Captain Fein."

"So we follow them," I say.

"Nay, it would be near fruitless, Sæm, in a land as vast as the Breachlands. At any rate, they have traveled well inland, and the assassins are far from Arias and Guin. But you and your vessel will be needed."

"How do you know all of this?" Therrien queries.

Vicchi looks to Talon.

"But how?" Alænèa voices all of our concern.

"Likened to how Arias can connect to animals, as he had explained to you, I too can do the same. In fact, it is this very mægic that Arias uses to accomplish it. You see, Arias I believe is a mind mæge. Indeed, with his claim he could read all of the runes upon the temple doors marks him as having all six of the ancient mægics. I believe he is the culmination of the Source-Sayers grand experiment. He is Mægic's Heir. The first and mayhaps only person on Aeryth to carry all the mægics in his being."

"You, yourself carry three Maegics, Sæm, and Alænèa, though each carries different mægics."

This comes as a shock to me, as I do not recognize any Maegics the like of Arias. I say as much.

"They are there. I see the auras of them, and recognizing the power of the runes confirms it. You just have not been trained as yet in their use. It might take three different mæsters to draw them out. One is mind mægic by the way."

"This is for another time, Vicchi. What must we do to help Arias and Guin?"

"Ah, to the heart of it then. We can mayhaps track their process across the Breachlands, with the help of Arias' raptor friend, but they must get there on their own. It is only once they reach the Orakle's isle that you will most like be able to aid them."

"This is what we will do then. How far is it to this Orakle Isle?"

"From Arias' eagle friend's mind and thoughts, I believe he calls him Talon? Arias and Roux have but a third of their journey completed. Roux will have told him where they must go. We are in luck also, as they have somehow found the Gnomon Valley, and there they most likely will find aid. Even still, they are at best a moon to three fortnight from the northern coast of the Breachlands to where the Orakles Isle lies off the coast."

"What is this 'Orakle's Isle,' and why will it be their choice of destination?" Týr speaks up.

"'Tis where the foolish go to have their fate revealed to them, and not somewhere I'd want to visit on purpose! But it's the only place in all the Breachlands where the cliffs fall and access to the beach is possible."

His statement answers my query but queues up another. I look to Vicchi.

"The Orakle's Isle is home to one of Aeryth's strongest seers though she prefers to give her sight to those who visit most oft in mystery and riddle. But Týr's other statement is the most pertinent and why it is there that you must sail to… It is what Roux knows and will advise Arias."

"Then we shall leave on morrow's morn." Alænèa and Rien nod in approval.

"We must address those that are following them, Sæm. From what you have told me and more what I suspect, these assassins may be waiting for them even as they approach the beach."

The huge warrior woman speaks up at this point.

"I am responsible. I ask leave to accompany you… Sæm, I can be of aid. I need to be of aid."

Her sincerity and determination is written into her expression. Týr speaks next.

"I as well, Sæm. I have sworn an oath to protect Illéron's daughter with my life and fear I might fail the man I owe my life to."

"The help is appreciated as we are to be outnumbered and must fight against trained assassins and a mind mæge now, it seems. But what if this mæge takes control of your mind once again, warrior woman?"

"Rieka, man-child. Sæm." The corners of her mouth turn up at her moniker for me. "Vicchi promises she can guard against it happening again."

"Yea, Sæm. I can help with this by doing our part here at the temple."

She reaches up and lifts an ornate æntwood box from the mantel behind her. She places it on the table before us and opens it to reveal a half dozen amulets, similar in design to Arias' amulet he'd received from the tinker.

"They mayhaps are not as powerful as the one Arias wears but will turn aside this mind mæge's early attempts to enter your minds. You must not give him many chances though. I fear he is of great talent and power with his mægic. As you see my supply is limited, as the stronger mægic used to craft these has passed from Aeryth more than a millennium ago."

The filigree is similar to the one Arias wears and I see as I examine one that the runes woven into the intricate filigree about the center stone is in likeness to his as well. Each is similar, but a few carry different gemstones.

"I've but these half dozen, and one should be for Roux when you meet up with them. Your fellowship is set then, you five alone. The morrow's morn may be too soon though, Sæm. I'd prefer you spend some time with one of our best captains, so he can teach you how to avoid the dangers you will encounter within the straits you must sail through. Fear not, there will be time to reach the Orakle's isle ahead of their arrival."

"Ne'er the lesser, I would meet your captain on the morrow's morn then, as I am anxious to leave out as soon as is possible." Vicchi nods to my request.

"Let it be so, then. Rieka, this shall be your amulet. Blue amethyst is the center stone. It's a gem compatible with strong wills and pairs best with women."

As Rieka places it about her neck, she takes in a deep breath as the stone blazes brilliantly and then settles upon her breast. Her eyes glaze for a moment, then she turns to Vicchi.

"I have memories I did not have a moment ago. Memories of being attacked from behind and overwhelmed by a dozen men garbed in black. And then another approached, and I lost all ability to strike back against them as I struggled to even clear my mind."

"Yea, Rieka, the amulet offers a certain amount of clarity of mind as well as protection. A mind mæge will find it difficult to penetrate the shield, and as you see, you now know the scars he has left behind. Be not ashamed of what he has done, for he is a powerful mæge."

Each of us accepts an amulet in turn. Ryen seems most affected as he feels for the first time real mægic about and within himself. Vicchi speaks a final time to our new fellowship.

"Fates be with you, each and every one. Take care and be utterly ruthless with this mæge. Do not give him further chance to reach within your mind."

32

Myrmidon Guide

This towne is the closest to Destinæa as anyplace I've come across in the whole of Aeryth. These people are not like the typical folk in any towne in the Mid Realm. I'd encountered 'rough' cities in the Southern Reaches along the coast but this place is different, and the very undertone of every whispered comment I hear is as near to sinister as any I've experienced in my homeland. There is no trust here. I can see it in every eye. My smirk is evident to all, I'm afraid.

Charan is accompanying me into the ale hall. He has two of his men take a seat at a table close to the door, but where they can easily spy us in case of any trouble. He is down two of his company, leaving us at ten soldiers plus myself. The two that have been sent down the second trail back at the cliffs have not returned as yet. He expects them any time now.

Six others he sends in three groups of two, to visit the inns and other ale houses to query after the lad and the lass. They will stick out in a towne such as this, and I hope they will be found without much trouble. One final man he has posted outside the front door. Charan is thorough.

The patrons may be of a different mindset, but the atmosphere in an alehouse does not change much. My nostrils flare with the scent of the house draught, and the back-slapping camaraderie underscores the cacophony of friendship, real or perceived in the crowded hall. Charan leads the way to a table where we can place our backs against an outside wall and have a view over most of the hall. His earlier nod to a house lass has two stouts in front of us even as we are taking our seats.

"This lad is resourceful, Charan. He escapes the Bowels with battered and broken body, into the sewers below the dungeons. Then somehow returns across the barrier mountains to the cliffs above the inland sea. Even as we are close, he again eludes us to vanish into the sea in a ship of ancient design."

"It seems clear he has help from capable allies."

"Aye, Charan. Though those with him at present are not those capable allies. This is our chance to corner and take him. We must not let him slip away again. There is much I can learn from him. He is key."

"He and the young lass he is with will stand out in a towne such as this. They will need supplies for their further travels. I do not believe they will remain here long."

"They are traveling with their wild creatures, yet tamed to them. A towne would not suit them, but as you say they will seek out supplies. Where they will be headed is a mystery though. It would be good to know at least this."

We are not speaking loudly, but it appears we have become noticed by a local. He has arrived only recently and has taken a seat alone in a corner. I sense his interest in us. He looks at ease in this environment. I set aside my thoughts of him for the moment.

"Let us give your men time to do the search and queries then and have a bite to eat. I see they serve a nice charred slab of beef here."

We are just finishing our meal when the local, who has been eyeing us from his corner, steps up to our table. Charan's men start to rise and intercept him, but I wave them off with a nod.

He arrives with a whispered belch and a hand to his belly. I can tell you what he's eaten. He nods a greeting but holds his distance at a pace and waits while I finish my drink. He packs a smokeweed pipe with deft hands from a pouch on his belt, watching me all the while as I chew a few last bites. He is not a soft man.

"Can I offer you both another ale?" He does not wait for an answer and with a quick gesture, has a bar wench hustling to do just that.

"They serve a fair steak here, but their ale is what I come for. Might I join you for a moment? Mayhaps I can aid you in your search. Your men will have little luck with it." He has yestersun's growth on his chin still, and a scar runs from his forehead through his left eye and trails to his lower cheek parting his whiskers.

"What do you know of our search?" My curiosity piqued, I push a chair out from the table with my foot. He sits, even as he lights his pipe. It is good smokeweed. I enjoy the scent as he exhales and leans back into the chair. Charan is taking his measure.

"You've six men in teams of two, canvassing the inns and alehouses of Myrmidon. They will learn nothing. No man nor woman will weasel to a stranger, not for coin and not under threat. Any in the Breachlands would already know this, so you are clearly outlanders. I, however, will have the information by morrow's morn. But the information will cost."

I like this man. Our ales have arrived and he tips a toast to us. His eyes are unique. Coppery with the pupils of a predator beast. I've never seen their like on a man.

"And why would you help... 'outlanders?'"

A wink and a half-smile forms around his pipe.

"Because it is my business to deal in Myrmidon affairs. He runs the fingers of his free hand through his long, grey hair. I am her premier guide and expeditor. Name's Faolán." He doesn't bother offering his wrist in greeting.

"We would be obliged for your aid in finding our friends." He scoffs at that thought.

"Surely they will be joyful to be reunited with their friends." It is my turn to offer a disingenuous smirk.

"So, Faolán, what can we do to help you find our friends?"

"Let us meet here again mid-morn on the morrow, you with your coin purse, eh?" I justify a nod. He leaves, finishing his flagon of ale as he rises.

"Till the morrow then." A moment later, I watch as he repacks his pipe just outside the alehouse window before moving on.

"I'll have him followed."

"No, I believe he may be of use. I'll wager that the bar wench can give us all we need to know of the man."

Something about this stranger has given me pause. There is both a familiarity about his actions and a confidence that belies his true self. My light probe of his mind as we spoke told me more than a little of who he is…or rather, who he knows.

***

(Faolán)

It has been years since I've last spoken to him in person. But Shæ-Kahn knows where to find him. I lightly run my finger from her beak to the crown of her head. Fore and back, fore and back as he had taught me to do when I want her to carry a message to him. Though we have not spoken face a'face, we do communicate with help from this magnificent bird…raptor really, for she is a deft predator in her own right. A hawk with talons that even now pierces deeply into her perch. I tie my missive to her leg and she lets me, peering down at the tightly rolled parchment I've slid into the leather cylinder pouch made especially for this purpose. There are no cages or raven keepers here on this rooftop, only a single wooden perch embedded into the stone wall that shields this part of the roof from the near-constant western breeze…and the view of prying eyes.

Because of this magnificent specimen of hawk and the notes we send to each and the other most every moon, I know he is still out there, listening and watching and growing his special breed of army. What he had fore-told to me has come to pass this very eve. An outlander in search of him or someone else, mayhaps, with special powers, even as he has. His only instructions those many years back–to aid him, query him, and send a note immediately that we have met.

I know already this man and his assassin lackey are those that my master had spoken of. He has even touched the outer boundaries of my mind in a way that no other than Vulkar has. He is the one that the master was expecting to come. And this man is in pursuit of another. Another outlander that he intimated would mayhaps act unusual to other men. Mayhaps display unique *abilities*. I know he spoke of the ancient mægics.

Vulkar has taught me of them. He'd plucked me out of the alleys as a younger not yet reached my ninth year-ender. An orphaned, street waif wise to the ways on the streets. I'd already had this scar across my face by then, a gift of a merchant who'd near caught me with a sack of his precious goods. Master Vulkar told me I had a special gift deep in my mind, a remnant of one of those very mægics. I know it must be true, not only because I have the ability to sway men and women alike to my way of thinking, but because I've felt him in my very brain. He can talk directly to my mind when we're close a'times. Those days are long past, but he's taught me well.

I am now my own master, and master of a network of like-minded compatriots throughout Myrmidon. Vulkar tutored me that it matters not whether a man or woman is strong or weak, evil or good, honest or deceitful. They matter only to what ends they can be used. I have assembled just such a cadre of individuals, and they their own groups, but each remains beholden to me.

I already know that the two this Mensæ seeks are not in Myrmidon, nor have they ever been. But a river merchant has spied the abandoned pull raft from the border cross just east of the breach mountains and I can surmise what has transpired. The merchant also said the Wending Way has been disturbed in some manner as border beasts pay no heed to it near the river anymore. Those that this outlander seeks are unique as well, it is sure certain to my mind. This all makes me quite curious, and I want to associate with this man, this mæge, for a time more. There is surely risk, but I wager there will be measurable gain also.

I will not be able to deliver their prey to them on the morrow, but I am certain I can lead them to a place that they will be able to meet up with them.

33

JabberJack

erri stoops over the makings of a campfire, working his flint, blade, and shavings with his back to us. He rambles on about this or that, but we are distracted. Roux and I stand atop a boulder aside the campsite and gaze out over the vale afore us. I've never seen anything in its likeness. When we arrived the previous eve, the sun had already passed over the western wall and the sky had darkened to the point that we could not see the wonder that spreads afore us now.

We stand at the highest point just outside of the cavern tunnel we have arrived through. A path leads from our campsite and down into a jungle forest of every manner of tree, vine, and plant. Tremendous trees reach the height of the surrounding cliffs and are as big around as fifteen men with outstretched arms standing side to side, I'd wager. They line one end of…a bowl of sorts made of sheer cliffs of rock thirty poles high at the lesser end. The vale, cliff-side to cliffside, surely measures a few leagues across at its narrowest point.

A river winds through it but seems to disappear into the ground in front of the cliff walls to the north and come into the valley as a high falls on the south end. Mayhaps fed by the larger river we traveled down a ha'fortnight past. Brilliant birds of the brightest yellows, oranges, and greens fly about singing songs I've never heard. Some have beaks as long as my hand and streaked in multi-colours. They join us in the trees about our campsite and dance in the air above us.

"I've gotten this fire agoin' now. And I've a pan and eggs and taters in my sack…a sweet onion if ya like. Jōddi made me pack it all, and I'm grateful she did, just now." Derri shows nearly all of his teeth in pride as he turns to us.

"Mind, I told ya we might not even meet up with JabberJack. It's been years since me and Mayo's been here, and like I said, we never met him, but granddad says he'd tell him tales and those is what we've been told. That's why he's called a recluse. Lore and legend to most really. We was jus' lads no more than twenty-year back then. I ain't promisin' we'll find 'im."

"Jilly, can you find that bag of tea leaves you've been napping aside in my pack? A warm cuppa will be nice in this morn chill." Derri watches in amazement as she does just that.

"I imagine if he wants to be found we will indeed find him. But I'm sure certain that if he resides in a wonder of a place as this surely is, he will know he has visitors." As I discuss this with Derri, I nonchalantly gaze up to the trees over his shoulder.

Roux speaks to Derri as she helps steep the tea leaves Jilly brought over in a small kettle he had pulled from his sack. Derri's mornmeal is sizzling against his pan on the fire. As we eat, I query Derri.

"What is this place, Derri? The ruins themselves are magnificent. Stone staircases I see in the trees below, winding to nowhere, and tower and spire off in the distance sits unused and overrun with elven vine and bloom. I see arches and pillars broken in half and who knows what else."

Derri takes a moment to peer out over the valley of jungle and ruins. "'Tis the City of Mæges, me grandda called it. Its true name lost centuries past, I imagine. 'Tis so old the songs don't even know it anymore."

"But why have your townfolk not rebuilt it? It is magnificent here." Roux asks.

"Ha, nay, maämel Roux. Not one in a hundred would even know how to find it even living so close, and not one in a hundred of *those* will dare come here. 'Tis the food of night terrors, this place. But me grandda is one who would, and he brought Mayo 'n me time a'times, and I never have forgotten the way."

"But why, Derri?" Roux insists.

"Beggin' pardon, but it's the mægic o'course. Folk here know it exists, but are mostly afeared of it. Grandda says it twernt always so, but this place is the reason most like. They say the ghosts of the mæges still live and breathe here."

"Oh…"

"Are your friends afraid of us, Derri?"

"Well, Mayo 'n I've not told any'un of any mægic you've done, though I've seen it in what Arias has done with the healing of Mayo, sure certain, and he does carry a mæge staff, but I don't think they are afeared of you. Just nervous of the mægic a bit, ya know, in the back of the minds mostly. And that's why none but a few would bother to look for JabberJack."

"I remember Grandda's stories though, 'n Grandda wasn't afeared so I didn't mind bringing ya here."

"Well, if that's the case, Derri, I suppose I could join the three of you for some of that tea. The scent is brilliant. Is it Asgährdian?" A gruff, but friendly voice seems to spring from the trees just a few paces away and a movement belies a man standing just afore them. He steps forward.

Derri near jumps out of his trousers as he turns and stares at the man speaking to him. I've been waiting for him to appear. I've known we were being watched but had not informed Derri or Roux, waiting to see what our secretive guest would do. I know him to be no danger, as Bane has not bothered with him and this is quite strange unto itself.

Derri bows low to the compact and elderly man twice…and continues to show deference while remaining quiet before him. It is something we have not experienced from Derri afore.

"Mæster JabberJack...welcome, ser!" whispers Derri, finally getting some words out.

"Yea, welcome, ser," I second. "Please do join us, and yes it is from the isle...the tea, I mean."

JabberJack turns out to be a diminutive man but not quite so short as the gnomen...and stockier. He wears a mousy grey beard down to the center of his chest and tied at it's end with a woven leather strapping to keep it from becoming too unruly. His eyes carry a mischievous sparkle under the thickest eyebrows I've ever seen. The twinkle of his eyes seems to pull at the corners of his mouth. He wears a tunic in multiple shades of green with brown leather straps and belts crossing every which way across his torso, strategically hiding pockets that I know are there by their slight bulging beneath the belts. He has about his shoulders a hooded cloak in the same mismatched tones of greens and browns. If he were to stand still betwixt two trees, you would not know he was there. And he carries a polished wooden staff with split and twisted branches atop that swirl about a large ruby red stone gem that appears to be floating within. His hair falls about his shoulders, and when I look down, his trousers and boots look two sizes too large as they hang so loosely. He wears an amulet about his neck and rings on his fingers. In that respect, he reminds me of Eschereon.

He lays his staff aside as he sits upon a stump near to Derri's campfire, his legs spread. He stares at Roux's kettle, anticipating a warm liquid treat in the tea. Derri and I join him around the fire, Derri staring at him in awe and speechless still. I believe he was not actually expecting to find him. I study the man as Roux passes tin trail cups around then wraps a rag about her fingers, lifting the kettle and pouring us all a bit of her brewed tea, steam rising from its spout.

"Ahhh, I believe the plant these leaves are picked from grows nowhere in Aeryth but the isles with temple mægic from eons past giving it it's flavor! And I would know, being a connoisseur of such things and having traveled the whole of Aeryth many times over."

Derri's eyebrows rise at this.

"What, Derri? You didn't think I spent all of my time in these old ruins, did ya? Where'd you think all those tales I told your grandda originated from, eh?" JabberJack treats Derri to a wink.

"If you've traveled about, Mæster, have you mayhaps met my mentor? He goes by Eschereon, and my da named him a druid, even as Derri has called you."

"Ha! Eschereon, Sage, and Mithur and a few others as well. Yea, we are well acquainted. He's called a council to be held even as we sit here. Outside of Newcastle it is to be, in the Mid Realm. I meant to leave out a fortnight past, but the fates kept me here, and I'm seeing the why of it now... This tea is capital. It soothes and sparkles in the throat as it goes down. I've missed it so."

"I've plenty to pick back home. I'll certainly leave my remaining supply with you." Roux offers and JabberJack's eyes sparkle all the more.

"Thank you, dear lass. From your offer, I take it you are one of Vicchi's acolytes?"

"Yea, my mœther and pæder brought me to the isles twelve years passed. I've studied at the temple these past five years. I am Roux, and as the usually talkative Derri has neglected to introduce us, this is my brœther, Arias."

"Hmmm, the fates, and by that I mean Source-Sayers of old, have indeed wended the future to their purpose."

"If I may be so bold, druid JabberJack," JabberJack quirks his head and turns steely eyes of intense lavender, laced in gold, to me, "you speak in more circles than my mentor, Eschereon!"

"Ha, and I see Mithur has taught you to turn a curious ear."

"I know druids take an oath to speak only truth, but I've known two, nay, mayhaps three in my life already, and their truths seem to surely contradict each and the other," I add.

"Do they now? Mayhaps, it is but the point of perspective, eh?"

Derri and Jilly both are sitting up straight, swinging their heads to and fro betwixt the two of us, one in complete confusion, the other because it is her wont. Roux listens closely. JabberJack takes another sip of tea, his long, pointy nose rising with the scent of it. His hands close around his cup, holding in its warmth. The sun has just now risen enough to start burning off the morn's chill.

"And I might say, I've studied the Source-Sayers a bit. As matter of fact, 'tis why I've spent as many as forty decades and a few more making my home in this very place."

Derri looks down to his fingers and starts counting, his eyes going wide.

"Ha, Derriwether Smelters, I've told my tales to your great, great, great, great, grandda when he was just a younger himself. You favor him sure enough, by the by!"

I smile as Derri becomes himself again, though his never-ending chatter remains under his breath as a muttering only he can cypher. His eyes dart back then forth betwixt the corners of his lids.

"I've met a blind seer many moons past, and now see he may well have been a druid in his own right. You speak of mæges controlling the future and specific souls within it, yet his only imperative to me was that I must remember that I have a free will and I alone may determine my fate and future."

"Ha, they are astounding beyond compare, the Source-Sayers of old! I wonder if that could be their doing as well, or some free-wheeling mægic they are made to deal with. I must take time to ponder it." At this, JabberJack seems to be speaking to himself. He looks up to me again.

"A comment and a query, Arias, if I may." His eyes twinkle in anticipation, it seems to me. "If I haven't missed my guess, I'll ask you to recall–and I believe you can–the exact words of Tìrsius, my blind but all-seeing friend. Search your memory and see if he said specifically that you *alone can* or *alone do* determine your fate and future."

"And my query… When you gazed upon the temple doors at the Mæge Tree, how many of its runes could you read?"

"I saw six. And I fail to see the distinction in your query."

"Ha! So then, you are a part of why Eschereon has called a special council. But I fear there is more. How is it that you and your sister have come to be here in the Breachlands of the Northern Reaches?"

For what Derri has called a hermit and recluse, JabberJack seems quite attuned to what is happening in the whole of Aeryth. Certainly, he is quick to a point. Derri sits still, but his face contorts continually from wonder to confusion to wonder once more to all that he is hearing.

For my part, I explain how Roux and I came to be here, taking the tale all the way back to my capture and escape from the Bowels beneath Kings Court Keep and that my friends remain on Asgährd Isle.

"So, this Mensæ is the other part of Eschereon's tale for the council."

Bane strolls back into camp, having left us earlier. He does not come directly to me, however, but rather eyes JabberJack first before ambling over to him and sniffing about him in a manner I've never seen him do with anyone else. The druid just smiles. To me, he observes,

"Hmm, your spirit beast does catch her scent, I see." JabberJack turns directly to Bane, and he smiles. "I told you it was the fates that have kept me here when I had meant to be traveling to Mithur's council… I've been nursing a young dread wolf back to health after she had a run in with a grizzly. The grizzly will not make the same mistake again, I'll wager, ha!"

Derri and Mayo had said the forests north of the Gnomon Valley hold dread-wolves.

"Your friends include spirit beasts, both you and Roux, I cannot help but notice." Fæna had returned to camp with Bane. "Spirit creatures have not been around for tens of hundreds of years here in Aeryth, you know. Oh, how Eschereon's heart must have pounded on seeing you for that first time upon your return to him. This indeed has turned into a remarkable age, sure certain."

JabberJack turns his attention to Roux now, his curiosity piqued to greater heights it seems.

"And you, lovely lass, how many runes on the Mæge Tree cast auras for you?"

"Five."

"Hmm, the alchemy of blood seems to be fickle. But that can certainly be seen in the lines and progeny of kings, can it not? Even still, you must be a prized acolyte of Vicchi." I wonder, does he also know our blood connection to the king?

"I've reached the tenth level of the twelve."

"And you're what? Only a lass of fourteen, mayhaps?" Roux nods.

"Has she taught you more than runes yet?"

"More than runes?" Roux's curiosity also measuring high at his suggestion.

"I expect that Arias here has already been taught to reach for his mægics, but lass, you are very special as well. I would be delighted if the two of you would spend some time with me. There is much I can show you here." He looks out from our camp, and in a grand sweeping gesture of his arms, he indicates the valley. "And I might be able to show you a few tricks that Vicchi cannot."

JabberJack flicks his wrist and my Bo staff which I had leaned against a tree some paces away, flies through the air and to him. He deftly catches it in both his hands. I rise to regain it on instinct alone. I have no control over my reaction.

"Steady, young Arias. I mean only to show my specific sort of mægic. But I see why you are so fond of this staff! Who crafted it for you?"

"My da."

"Illéron? I would never have thought he had such talent."

"Nay, I mean my guardian while I lived in the west… You know my pæder is Illéron?"

"I know the pæder of Vicchi's favored ward and student. And from what this lass has just told me, I deduce that she is one and the same. I do know Illéron, the favored son of Asgährd. And then, you must mean Ètœn Bearheart, Arias. Eschereon has spoken of him. He has a fates guided hand in this craft indeed." The druid studies my staff a bit longer then hands it back to me.

"Do you know why he chose those specific runes he placed to each end of your staff?"

"They were some that were on a box he held for me from my mœther, three of the four of them. The fourth rune, to my shame, I learned upon his death and I know its origin as he told me when I was but a younger. But I never saw the box afore his death, so I could not query him further. When I once asked him, he at the time said only that he'd seen them somewhere and fancied them, that he did not know their meaning though he was sure they held significance."

"Hmm. And did Eschereon not explain their meaning?"

"He did, those he knew, but one he did not. He knew its origin, as I had explained it to him so as to help assuage my shame. He promised he would search its meaning for me, but life turned us all from such menial tasks."

"Most curious. And what did he say their meanings were?"

I point to the drægon's tooth ends of my staff as I hold it in front of me.

"This first represents mægics, and he explained there were six parts to the rune. He tutored me on the strokes to form it, saying even the way it was crafted held importance." The druid smiles and nods.

"This second he explained meant 'a bond' or 'binding' and he called it a strengthening or protecting rune." Again a nod, and I feel somehow proud, as a student would afore his mentor.

Roux joins our discussion.

"I know the one on the furthest end, nearer the red stone. It is the rune for bloodlines and legacy." Roux bursts with pride at her knowledge.

"Da named it drægon's firestone," I say as I run a finger across the gem. JabberJack adds,

"Even those particular stones are rare. I'd love to know their tale."

"I can oblige you, as I found them myself." His bushy brows rise once again in interest. As a druid, he seems a polar opposite to Eschereon, his expressions and manner so animated. Back to Roux, he speaks,

"Excellent, lass. You've named it true. The other is the one that brings you shame, lad? Why would that be?"

My thumb goes to the underside of a ring I wear on the middle finger of my right hand even as I touch the rune upon my staff. I see that the druid notices the movement.

"Might I see your ring, Arias?"

Though Eschereon had counseled me that I had no need to feel any shame, there still lies a lingering doubt in my mind. I step across the fire and bend to a knee to show him the ring. I will not remove it.

"It was a gift from his grandmere to him. To Da, I mean, before he left his village and went out into the world. It is shame that racks me when I removed it afore burying him, but I wanted something personal to him so as to keep him close. It is shameful. I feel I was robbing him."

The druid gazes deep into my eyes.

"And yet, you hesitate to remove it from your finger even to show it to me. I see it is precious to you, in spite of any shame you feel. Rest assured, Arias, this ring is not meant to be buried with any soul. Ètœn Bearheart and his grandmere would be proud that you wear it, and others as well."

"Others?"

JabberJack ignores me.

I take a moment to look around me. Roux sits leaning towards me, trying to espy the ring. I still cannot call it mine. Derri and Jilly are a pair, each staring up betwixt JabberJack and myself with wide-eyed intent. Derri, in quiet awe of this conversation of Maegics and runes and levitating staffs. Jilly, I believe is looking for a little handout…a leftover from somebody's plate. The druid has emptied the kettle of tea and now sips it from his cup with glee. Bane has found a place within our circle and is keeping a close eye on JabberJack. The druid nods towards Bane.

"Your dread wolf recognizes the scent of another of his kind on me." Turning the conversation elsewise again, I give him a puzzled look.

"'Tis why I have not left to travel to Eschereon's meet. As I said, the fates have kept me here, and I count myself quite fortunate for it. You see, I happened upon a female dread, near the size of your spirit beast, near death after vanquishing a grizzly thrice her size. I've spent the better part of a moon nursing her back to health. She is ready, even now, to return to the forest."

"We found Bane in a trap as only a pup. After nursing him back to health, we traveled four suns up into the mountains to return him to the wild. He returned to me the day following Da's death."

The druid looks to Bane. "He most likely had made his bond with you when you first set eyes upon him."

"Others. You were speaking of the ring." I turn him back to our previous conversation. This druid is scatter minded or shrewd beyond even Eschereon.

"Hmm, yes. Did you wonder that a ring that belonged to Ètœn's grandmere could fit his finger and then yours? He was a large man, was he not?"

I recall that the ring had slipped easily off of Da's hand, and though it was much too large for any of my fingers, when I placed it upon my finger it adjusted to the size of mine, fitting snug around it. It had astonished me at the time. But Moor had just arrived and my mind left it.

"The rune. I am familiar with it. Have you noticed that though the ring itself appears to be a simple pewter setting with an unremarkable jade stone fashioned into a rune, it does not turn your finger black as you might expect a basic metal to do?"

"You know the rune's true meaning!"

"Few would, I do. It is here that I first saw that very rune. It was used seldomly. You see, it is the rune of the last council of six, Source-Sayers all. They named it Æerythesperi which translated means 'Aeryth's Hope'... and aptly so."

"I must say, Arias Côeurdrægon, I feel I've just held in my hands an artifact that will one day be numbered amongst the greatest tools, or weapons, in the history of Aeryth."

The meaning of his words are not lost on me. Their weight is a towering burden on me for a moment. But then I look to Derri's face, gripped in awe and worry, and I laugh aloud. I most like will be found stuffed under the bushes for ant-feast by Mensæ's assassins. It is a nervous laugh. These times must be a legend meant for somebody other than me.

"Your words are too deep for my ears, Mæster JabberJack. But speaking for myself, I am eager to take respite in your canyon and mayhaps learn some of your mægic, if I am able." In my side vision, I see Roux enthusiastically nodding her agreement. Derri, however, rises and bows low again to JabberJack and then to Roux and myself.

"I've seen yer to the canyon, Mæster Arias, as agreed, but I feel an urge to be gettin' back, yer know. Jōddi will be 'spectin me." It is clear to all of us that this talk of Maegics has disturbed him a great deal.

"Oh, will you be leaving immediately then, Derri? Let us help you gather your sack and cooking pans. We are much obliged for your help and hospitables. If we must say our fare-the-wells, please give our thanks to Jōddi as well."

"Peace go with you, Derriwether. And when you are looking for a greater adventure out in the greater world, come find me again!" Though he is the one to convince Mayo to fly to the river, I feel his wanderlust mayhaps is stunted as his head shakes in the negative towards JabberJack.

He takes his leave back through the tunnel in the cliff's wall within a turn of a sand glass. In the meanwhile, we have broken the campsite down and doused the campfire. After Derri has disappeared from sight, Mæster JabberJack leads Roux and me down the path and into the jungle forest.

34

Tinkers and Assassins

(Assassins & Mind Mæge)

"I have news, Mensæ."

This Faolán, he intrigues me. Charan's assassins have little luck in finding any news within this towne of the king's grandson and his companion. I feel certain that there is knowledge of them to be had here, but in the fortnight since we had arrived, little…nay, nothing has been learned. The folk of the towne are indeed tight-lipped. First, inquiries throughout the inns and alehouses produced naught but hearsay and whispers. Then, more serious coin was offered to little avail, but throats needed to be slit for failures and unsuccessful dupes. I have circled back to our first encounter. The scar-faced man of confidence we'd met our first day here.

I had been tempted to dig direct into his mind when he'd proposed he could find all the information I needed for a purse of gold, that next morn when we met again. But I sensed there was more about him that a mind search might spoil. He's proved himself correct in his assessment of our coming failure. Yesters-eve I had instructed Charan to pay the purse of gold but to follow him till we met up again today. He disappeared from their sight within a half turn of a sand glass, and I expected I'd not see him again. But this morn, he's sent word for a meet on a rooftop. We do not have to wait long once we arrived. Charan set guards about the building, inside and out, and we two followed a winding stair three flights up and onto the roof.

The eve is warm and the sky clear. The noise of the city has all but disappeared by the time we reach the rooftop. We find a table set with a quarter round of cheese, bread, and a jug of wine. A single lantern lights the table area. Charan's final two guards that had followed us up search about the rooftop. Having found nothing, he sets them to guard the stair, just down from the rooftop door.

We stand at the front parapet, looking out over the city.

"It is a wondrous sight, this city, at night, is it not?"

"Faolán...you have news?" I refuse to show any surprise when he appears of a sudden behind us. A lite growl surfaces from Charan's throat. He is not pleased.

"Assure, Master. Though it was a bit more difficult with the disfavor your cohorts have sown throughout the city...and it was for naught, as your *friends* have never arrived here to the city."

"How can that be? We did not overtake them, and the road leads only here."

"Which would have a reasoning man believe they have taken a different path," he reminds me. *Of course.*

My mind immediately goes to Charan's two men not returning. The lad is clever. I'll need to be warier still in the future.

"And where does the other path lead?"

"Oh, many places for certain. But your quarry traveled to one place in particular."

"You mean my friends."

"Ha, Mensæ. If we are to work together–and you *will* need me–we should dispense with such subterfuge and future lies. If we are honest with one and the other, we can be much more efficient. A fortnight is quite a bit of time wasted, do you not think?"

He has a self-confidence and thinking mind, I will give this man that due.

"So tell me, Faolán, where is my *quarry*?"

"They traveled the path into the Wending Way. They are smart, these two that you seek. And resourceful. The Wending Way is safe until you reach the banks of the river where the mægic is weakest. The creatures then will gather and force travelers off the path and out of the safety of the mægic. There, you must be swift or resourceful."

"The lad is resourceful, if nothing more. Yea, he is remarkable in that, and he carries a mægic as well."

"Hmm, that would explain a further detail to my tale, but that is for later."

"Go on then. How is it you know this?"

"Information from sources, of course, but a level of deduction on my part as well from even the little I know of you. You see, you've come to our city from the travelway that originates at the cliffs overlooking the breakers and it being the only beach in the south that an outlander can arrive to the Breachlands from. From there, there are but two choices. You took the one, so they must have taken the other."

"You said you know where they are now."

"Yea, there have been some strange happenings upriver, starting at the intersection of the Wending Way and the river. There is, rather there was, a raft and pull line to get travelers from one side of the river to the other. A merchant of my acquaintance has recently arrived from a towne west of that point. He reports that the mægic of the Wending Way has been fouled and disrupted there, and the raft turned loose from its tethering.

The merchant found the raft a good way downriver, hung up on a fallen tree extending out into the river. He pulled ashore there and observed a campsite, well used, as if somebody had stayed there for a few suns at least.

He is a curious fellow, mind, and he found some evidence of gnomes about the camp also."

"Gnomes? What are gnomes?"

"'Tis but the local name for them, as they live in the Gnomon Valley. They are also called halflings. They are a queer folk and mayhaps have lived in the Breachlands longer than any other human, tall or small."

"So, you believe they were in this camp, met some halflings, and have traveled to this Gnomon Valley? How would you deduce such a thing? And if they are there, we shall go to this Gnomon Valley."

"Aye and nay. That would not be advisable."

"And why would that be, Faolán?"

"First, it is not just the campsite that suggests their whereabouts, but further news. You see, some of the more adventurous halflings have a taste for our towne, and our alehouses…and mayhaps even our oversized women. And one thing is certain, the halflings talk a lot. Endless chatter, the lot of them. A couple of those that barter betwixt us and them were visiting recently and had a tale. It seems a lad and lass what saved two of their own from a pack of marauding sher-jackals have arrived to their valley near to a fortnight passed. Five carcasses of that very same creature were found by my merchant friend with arrow wounds and torn out throats, not too far from the campsite.

I will assume your quarry travel with some sort of beasts and that is their mægic. I've seen it in others, the control of beasts."

"They travel with beasts, yea." It is not the type of mægic I thought the lad possessed, and it gets me thinking about the lass accompanying him.

"So Faolán, why would we not follow them there?"

"Because while we mind little that halflings visit and trade with us, they do not abide uninvited guests into their valley. And though they are small, they are many thousands throughout the valley, and legend has it they are very clever and very dangerous. I am quite certain they would refuse the sort of men you travel with."

I ponder this for more than a moment. Though I can easily control a halfling's mind, I cannot of a sudden control the minds of many. He is right in his assessment, even not knowing my abilities.

"So, you suggest that we wait until they leave this valley of halflings and travel here, mayhaps?"

"Aye and nay." Again a contradiction. This man is not simple. "They will undoubtedly leave the valley if they wish to return to the isles, but I am quite certain they will not come this way if their intent is to return to the isles sooner rather than later. The path through this towne would greatly slow them down. No, they will leave through the northern end of the valley, sure certain."

"We must leave soon then if we cannot follow them into the valley, and our way is the longer path."

"Nay, I think not." And I feel my brow rise. This man is touching a nerve against my urgency. "Yea, we should leave before the next full moon, but from my conversation with this specific halfling, we have some time and should travel prepared."

"We, Faolán? Why is it we will be traveling together? And how is it we must prepare?"

"Ha! All good questions, Mæster. Let me explain. The loose-lipped halflings just so happen to be cousins of the two that were aided by and brought as guests, two outlanders, into the valley. Their cousin claimed that a cat and a dread wolf helped in their escape from the sher-jackals, and they used mægic to heal the deep wounds that the jackals tore into his, their cousin's, back.

"Their cousin further bragged he had guided and accompanied the out-landers to the canyon ruins to meet the JabberJack. And he insists they truly did."

"JabberJack? What, by the fates, is a JabberJack, and what are the can-yon ruins?"

"Ha, you see, Mæster, your purse, in but a single day, has wielded information your men could not find in a fortnight."

I notice Charan's gaze turn a bit darker toward Faolán. A small smile creeps onto my face.

"The ruins are but rubble from times of lore and legend, said to be hidden within the valley. I have not seen them, few have. But the JabberJack is a hermit and sage, and some say a man of mægic himself. There are two hundred years old rumors of the man, but there are those here in the city that insist they have met him still. They swear he carries a staff that has a gem suspended in air above it, and he is mighty clever."

"A mæge. The lad travels in unusual company, Charan, and finds aid in the most peculiar places. I would most like to meet this 'JabberJack.'"

"It is most likely that you indeed will, Mæster Mensæ, as I believe he will be the one to guide them out of the valley and to the Orakle Isle. The halfling's cousin told of a wondrous visit with the JabberJack and that your...quarry's intent is to visit with him for a fortnight or more."

Another mystery pops up in our conversation with this Jack-a-many-trades, Faolán. I find myself settling into my chair, feeling the warm breeze, and helping myself to his food and drink. Taking more time to study him.

"I assume you will offer your services as a further guide, Faolán." He smiles. "And what, pray tell, is the Orakle's Isle?"

He pours himself a cup, reaches for a date, and leans back into his chair.

***

(Rõghæn)

"Mæster Rõghæn, did your council go as you planned? Did you enjoy visiting with your old friends? I found them quite fun to be around, especially... Eshereon, is it? You know, the one the others called Mithur? I don't understand why you all have so many names, it's quite confusing. He is stuffy and formal around the campfire with the others, but when we walk about the bazaar, he is quite funny and ever so nice to be with…more like you, I guess."

Ha. Mithur–or Eschereon, as he has gone by for many decades now–is indeed less aloof than he oft appears when sitting amongst us. I know him mayhaps better than any of the council. He was my Mæster and I his apprentice and ward a hundred or more years past. And this past fortnight as we've counciled, I've noticed a keener edge to his demeanor. Aye, the news we'd brought to the council is decidedly grim on its face, but it has awakened in our group a greater purpose once more.

We will do more than be chroniclers of the goings-on throughout Aeryth now. A long-prophesied threat has materialized upon the shores of the Realms, and it apparently has been here for near to forty years, unchecked.

The long-ago mechanizations of the Source-Sayers of old has begun to materialize before our very eyes. Young Elsii being one such, and Mithur also has brought tales of a new apprentice with at least five ancient Maegics within him. Not to mention the two others that arrived with him, carrying mayhaps three Maegics each. A northerner, no less, and a lass from the Accadian Plains. It has become an exciting and dangerous age all and in one. Nobles being advised and controlled, without doubt, by mind mæges from a land across the great Southern Sea. The king himself, it would seem. And Illéron, Vicchi's surrogate to the council, and a ranger known to a few of us, is the sire to the lad Mithur has informed us about. He himself is unaware of the lad's latent talents. It would seem the Source-Sayers of old, when combining their talents, could indeed influence the future…and our present.

"Aye, little one, it was a welcome gathering of olde friends. But now we must be about serious business for the foreseeable future. Your identifying one of our foes at this very gathering…the master merchant with the dark aura, will be a subject of our attention. And your parchment picked up off the floor at the lodge is powerful aid to us as well."

And it is, sure certain. We have deduced–now knowing some of the lodge participants at the 'summit' as Elsii named it–that the list is an assassin's assignment. Important lords or other notable figures that would need to be removed to advance the mind mæge's purposes. Interesting that it was a charge dispensed at night and not by the council governor. Mayhaps, there are cross purposes within the council itself. Some thought would be needed on this alone.

Our compatriot, Ferryn, and his news of soldiers being trained in the southwest, seems to play a part in the story as well. He will persue that aspect further.

The clap-clop of the horses and the latersun's warming breeze bringing the scent of recently turned soil and sown grains settles my mind. I look over to the small but intelligent lass I've taken as my ward, as she has the face of somebody cyphering some thing or other of import in her mind. This olde tinker's wagon we ride upon now will be put to use as a tool in our search and espying of the mind mæges and their many acolytes.

We each have taken our own assignments in counter-purpose and in search of more answers to the threat. Elsii has exposed three of the mind mæges, and four by association, of the council that had convened at her parents' lodge. We must discover who the others are and find a way to eliminate or at the least mitigate the risk they surely represent.

Forty years is a long time for a council of mind mæges to go unchecked.

"I will help as I can, Rõghæn. I know the look of evil now. I will not be fooled again by nice words and false gestures. Help me know the uses of the maegics I see all about me, and I'll use it for good too."

I knew she would. She's seen what evil can do and has a strong desire to avenge her losses, sure certain. So young still, but I fear she will need to grow fast in the coming years, mayhaps bypassing some of the pleasures of other youngers her age. But she is bound to be a powerful mæge one sun if I do my part right. I've the mægic of the elements likened unto my mentor,

Mithur, if not as powerful. But betwixt the two of us, we see the beginnings of four maegics, mayhaps, in little Elsii, and they are strong within her, we feel, even as she recognizes the maegics about her in hues and colours.

'Tis our tasked assignment to infiltrate the court of the king's son in Esperance and stop any of the assassinations as might be possible. Two, it seems, are to happen in our watch there. And in the meanwhile, I have a ward and apprentice needing my guidance. I will take up this charge enthusiastically, for she is a lass deserving and destined for greater things, sure certain.

35

Source-Sayers

ane and Fæna bound off together into the jungle that is too tangled and overgrown to be named just a forest. The myriad of different trees and knotted thickets are no great obstacle to the creatures, this being close to their natural habitat. Jilly, standing on hind legs, watches them go and decides her place is to accompany Roux and me as we follow JabberJack down a clear path into the wild and noisy growth.

It seems a totally different manner of forest as I enter into the tree line. I look to Roux to see if she notices. It reminds me of the Wending Way in that the trail is protected on sides and above with a shimmering mægic clearly evident to me, and as I glance to Roux, I know she sees it as well.

"Are there many dangerous creatures here in the canyon, JabberJack?"

"Most definitely. And many creatures of mægic also."

"Creatures of mægic? Like Bane and Fæna, who wear an aura to distinguish them?"

"There are certainly beasts of their type about the canyon, but nay. I'm referring to beasts made with mægical intent. The Source-Sayers that inhabited this canyon put many years into doing just that."

"They produced...er, crafted beasts? From mægic alone?"

"Nay, not from pure mægic. That is not possible, at least to my knowledge, and I'm quite familiar, but with mægical beasts of different types, merged into another creature altogether."

"That sounds gruesome." Roux chimes into the discussion.

JabberJack does not answer, and we walk in silence for a while. I'm very good at reading expressions, but I cannot read his. Where Eschereon can manage a face most stoic to be almost unreadable, JabberJack's face contorts dozens of different ways, seeming to express as many thoughts that are running through his brain. His bushy brows, expressive eyes, long nose, and wide mouth do a myriad of striking combinations.

While he continues to ponder Roux's comment, we take in our surroundings, which are spectacular in and of themselves. The sounds alone are extraordinary. I've studied the noises of the wilderness, growing up with Da and Moor and even Grayce. We'd oft make a game of matching beasts to their distinctive voices, even the insects. I was proclaimed a master at it by my fifteenth year-end. But as I listen here, there are many I cannot name, and when I reach out with my *Knowing* I sense a number of creatures that are unfamiliar to me.

The very air here in the canyon seems different even, and somehow I feel…welcomed by it. I pose the question to Roux, and she mirrors my thoughts on this. It seems a place we are meant to be.

Looking forward again to JabberJack, I study him some more as well. I notice his stride being '*off.*' Mayhaps an old injury? His gait seems stiff, or in the least, a bit awkward to other men. Granted, his stature itself is not like others. Taller than Derri and the halflings in the valley, but shorter and more…diminutive than most men. Though his upper body and torso seem natural to any man, as I had noted when first we met, his trousers and soft leather boots hang crumpled about his legs…oversized to them. And yet, he ne'er the lesser moves with a grace.

The piercing cry of Talon comes to me at this very moment. JabberJack hesitates a moment to listen and notes it is a voice he has not heard in quite a while. I look to him and explain it is Talon and who Talon is. The druid's eyes sparkle at my words, his bushy brow raises, and a wide smile spreads across his face. All the while, his head shakes in knowing wonder.

"Source-Sayers, Source-Sayers," he whispers.

He turns and continues to lead us deeper into the jungle. A'times the thick trees part, and ruins and rubble can be seen about it. Sometimes we pass great arches and ascending stone stairs leading to nothing more than more open spaces, but there is clear indication that something...some great edifice once stood there. Further on, there are towers broken in two with clinging vines and throwing marvelous scents, unfamiliar to me, but com- forting ne'er the lesser.

Everything, I note...the sights, the sounds, the scents, the very feeling of leaves upon the branches as I run my fingers across them...all gives me a sensory perception of a place far from the ordinary, yet familiar and welcoming, indeed. Almost comforting in my awareness of them. There is so much mægic here. I sense it in most everything. I mention this to JabberJack, Roux's head nodding aside me. Even Jilly lies about my pack and shoulders, taking in the sensations produced by this place.

"Hmph," the druid's only response.

We have traveled near to two turns when I hear the gurgle of running water. It turns out to be a swift river, fifteen paces across and swirling about large rocks as it flows across our path. It does not appear we will be cross- ing here.

But JabberJack continues towards it, up a rise, a stone ramp I notice upon looking closely. Another, its like on the other side of the river. He stops and plants his staff aground, bending his head in concentration.

As we watch the river below, stones, in-line with each and the other and a few paces apart, rise from the river's surface as the water momentarily crashes against the rising obstacle. But quickly it becomes clear that it is a stone bridge as the water drains off from it to either side. As it reaches the height of the incline we are standing at, we see it connect seamlessly to the paths on either side of the river. The weight of it must be measured in tons. An impossible happening, but I see it with mine own eyes. JabberJack merely starts his walk across it. We follow, stunned and looking back as it retreats back down into the river.

As we descend the bridgeway on this side of the river, we are immediately presented with another obstacle. A wall of hedges, appearing near impenetrable, stands four long paces tall…twice my height and extending past my sightline in both directions. The druid barely pauses as he passes his staff, right to left and back again, the hedges bowing away from each other and offering us a pathway through. Two steps in, and we are through the hedges as they spring back into place and we are left in a long corridor of living plants. Filtered light finds us through the leaves above, and our pathway is lined in blossoming vines of flowers in a myriad of colours about its walls. We are now walking on a flagstone path. I cannot see the end of this tunneled hallway of living plants.

Ne'er the lesser, we do find its end, and it empties into a courtyard garden open to sunshine once more. This garden is not overgrown but manicured and fine. There are marble and other stone sculptures and water features and fountains in a space fifty paces wide and as many long. Benches line paths about the gardens, beds of different varieties of scented flowers and plantings making a masterpiece of the garden.

"You have made all of this, JabberJack?" Roux queries the druid. He smiles, pride evident on his face.

"The fountains are the originals, dating back countless years, but most of the statues I've transported from other parts of the estates to occupy the gardens while I travel. The flowering plants I gather, arrange, and grow, year to year.

"It is wondrous and brilliant," adds Roux. "I could spend an entire sun just ambling about in the beauty of it." The druid is pleased with her appreciation, I can see.

Tiny birds of bright coloured feathers fly about us, seemingly dancing in the air over our heads. They chirp and whistle tiny melodies.

"Mayhaps another time," he says. "We've other things to see yet, and I've a tale to recite if we are to become true friends."

We take our time still and take in the garden's beauty. The scents presented are almost dizzying in their variety and intensity. The colours are bright enough to shine in the black of night, I'd wager, and they complement the scents wafting about us. The fountains seem to frame the gardens, classic and beautiful with trickling streams and bobbing spouts performing a visual theatre.

The sculpted statues are more uncommon though and reflect the druid's comments about the Source-Sayers' unusual doings here in the canyon. It is quite a contrast, to my mind. There is one of a large wildcat with wings and talons of an eagle on its forepaws, caught as though ready to take to the air. Beautiful, but fierce. Another is a large jackal, but its tail is the segmented curved tail of a desert whiptail about to strike, sized to match the scale of the jackal. Feral and lethal. As I look about, all the statues are of this same type, two beasts merged as one. Though as I look closer, there is another type also.

More disconcerting, or in a vein more personal mayhaps, some are of men and women with head and torso of humans but legs of beasts. There is a forlorn look about them, even though many mime a cheerful attitude. But not all. In one case, the entire and huge body of a man, carrying the head of a bull ox, it appears. The statue holds a brutish pose at the entrance to what appears to be a labyrinth of high hedges. Queries form in my head to ask JabberJack later. These statues give off an all too lifelike mean and manner.

Having passed through the gardens, we come upon a wide flight of steps made of granite, yet worn in their center from what must surely have been ages of being tread upon. They rise to a chiseled wall with the same trunk-entwined tree that lies upon the temple doors in Asgährd. No runes mark them here, but coloured auras differentiate the entwined trunks of the single tree. The building itself is covered in climbing vines, elven vine, sure certain, but with a host of different coloured blossoms. Even the familiar carries a different air here.

At the top of the stairs, the druid speaks as if directly to the tree in what I recognize as ancient mægish, as Sæm, Alænèa, and I had named it when being taught by Eschereon. I watch in a silent wonder as a single trunk of the tree retreats back into the wall, offering an entrance to the great edifice. We enter, following JabberJack into a large vestibule bathed in soft light that seems to emanate from the walls themselves. A calming comes over me and Roux also, I can see, and this in turn pulls me into my *Knowing* and reveals a different world about me. It feels I have been transported to a different time altogether as I look around in awe and wonder.

Where a moment before drab walls and dull stone floors met me in the soft light when we entered the hall, now bright frescoes of gardens and sunlight and brilliantly blue skies cover the walls and shine as if wet slate floors in hues of blue and greys lie about me. Intricately carved tables of finely polished walnut stand against the walls, and huge colourful vases holding bouquets of blooming, long-stemmed flowers give the vast room a vibrant life of its own.

Ahead of us, great doors open into a finer chamber still, with a long, heavy stone table at its center and a huge fireplace of beautifully chiseled stone with a blazing fire within on the farther wall. There are a few majestic beasts and a half dozen finely garbed men and women standing about. They all turn to me as I look in on them.

"Welcome to Aeryth House."

The druid's words break what surely is a spell, and of a sudden the doors are closed and the frescoes and flowers have disappeared. I jump at the sudden change.

JabberJack gazes at me and his bushy brows wriggle like furry caterpillars.

"You are staring most intently at the council doors, Arias."

"They were open a moment ago with a grand stone table and finely dressed goodmen and ladies about and discussing things among themselves before they turned toward us."

"Hmmm."

"You doubt me?"

"Nay, I marvel at you, lad. Those doors have been closed and locked and beyond my power to open for all of my years here…which have been many, I assure. In my life, I've never seen their other side. The chamber is named the Sanctum Prise and was the exclusive council room to the Hexad…the council of six, Source-Sayers all."

"It was so real, and the walls about us were painted in brilliant frescoes and the floors polished to a shine with tremendous vases filled with a myriad of flowers. All gone now."

"'Tis the sight…a mægic of yours, I see. A strong one within you too, if you see into the past. Most seers mægic allows only glimpses of prophetic scenes of the future."

"I saw it too, Ari. All the painted walls and flowers, but the doors were not open to me. And, yea, it seemed real to the touch."

JabberJack stamps his foot and smiles wide. He's pleased.

"Come, you two. I've made my living quarters near the kitchens not far from here. We can have some cakes for mid-sun meal and talk a bit more, eh?"

The doors pull back at me as we follow the druid. I know I will need to return and try to open the doors. It feels as if I am meant to be here, at this very time in my life.

JabberJack clearly feels at home here as if the huge echoing halls and vast spaces, some shored up with makeshift lumber, are but a cozy cottage.

As we turn a corner and traveled down a long hallway, he raises his staff and the shuttered windows are mægically thrown open, and fresh air swirls through them, a number of birds alighting upon the sills. His gait changes, and a joyful bounce replaces the awkward strides he had used previously, but still, it is unusual to me.

We pass through a great hall with statues that are clearly sculptures in process, representing other beasts similar to those in the garden. After passing next through a long, domed room encased in yellowing glass, some of it patchwork repaired with newer, clearer panes. Every sort of flower we'd seen in the garden has a twin here.

Finally, we reach the kitchens. What had obviously once been a much larger kitchen has been scaled down. There is a smaller table with three miss-matched chairs aside it, and a second firebox, once used in the greater kitchen, is now decorated with an added mantel holding two candles and a few knick-knacks. Three softer, cushioned chairs sit facing this fireplace. The total area has a cozy cottage feel.

JabberJack lights a fire in a small iron stove and places a kettle upon a hotplate to bring it to a boil. Then he turns to a small countertop with three lidded pots to the back of it.

"Please, have a seat, the two of you. The tea will be ready in a moment, and I'll just put together some cakes and throw them in the ovens."

"Oh, how wonderful. Might I help? I do love helping in the kitchens back at temple."

"Ha, yea, lass. Come help. It's been a few years since I've had hands working with me in my kitchen. I've missed it."

I watch as the two of them quickly bond. They run about the kitchen with bowls and eggs and other ingredients, happily putting together cakes for the ovens whilst gayly conversing about times past doing just that same thing. My younger sister looks at home with the task and quite pleased to be allowed the chance. It is a different side to her I've not seen as yet. JabberJack himself clearly enjoys the company. I find myself in charge of keeping the tea mugs filled and dodging dough balls tossed in fun.

We spend the next two turns of a sand glass in a most comfortable manner, simply drinking tea and eventually savoring hot cinnamon cakes straight from the oven and drizzled in a most phenomenal honey cream topping. Roux speaks of her life and then I, mine. The first part of my tale is a story of my life with Da and Moor and Grayce and Effie, the second the details of my search for the Druid Eschereon and all that it involved. Then my life with Eschereon and mægics learned afterwards. Finally, my capture and experiences with Mensæ in Kings Court, my escape and all that it entailed, bringing us to the here and now. It springs from my lips as easily as it did in the temple for Vicchi.

"Remarkable tales you both tell, it being such a wee bit of time for it all to have happened. But I find it ever so. Long languishing years of ne'er any hint of the fates pulling us forward, and then when least expected, an explosion of remarkable events, changing the very course of history once more."

"Ha! I'm sure our lives are not so remarkable as the great tales of lore and legend, Mæster druid, even if they've touched upon the lives of the great people of this age. I've been described as but the bastard younger of a king's daughter, to fit at most, as a footnote to a footnote in a lost tome someday."

"And I am a simple acolyte in a temple on an isle that is most wise unreachable. My life is simple. This kitchen, the furthest I've been in my life from that very isle."

"Nay, dear lad and lass. You are both entangled in the very happenings constructed over an eon past, by my own pæder and the Hexad Council of Source-Sayers that called this canyon home for a while. It is a purpose of my life, I am certain, to teach you more before sending you on your way. I hope that you will do me that honor."

"Your pæder? You mean that you trace your bloodline direct to the Source-Sayers beyond the legends? How could you know such a thing?"

"Nay, Arias."

JabberJack rises and paces fore and back in front of us for a moment.

"These are momentous times, Arias and Roux Côeurdrægon, sure certain. So much so that I am now going to reveal a secret of my own that no other that lives today in Aeryth knows." His caterpillar eyebrows, nose, and beard-covered chin contort in too many ways to count before he turns directly to us and drops his trousers.

We are stunned. Before us stands a man above the waist but with the legs and hindquarters of a large mountain goat. He kicks off his ill-fitting trousers and boots and offers his true self to us.

"My name given at birth was Gilænos, last son to Atelæs, Source-Sayer and of the Hexad. Later I became known as *Jahab Bœra Jakká* here in the valley and canyon. 'Sage Man-goat' if translated literally from the oldest mægish."

A twisted smile crosses his face.

"I was pinned under a massive tree trunk as a younger about your age, Arias. An ambitious attempt of my mægical abilities I'd not yet mastered. The damage was so great that I could not be saved in any typical fashion by even the strongest Healer-Source-Sayer of the Hexad herself. I begged my pæder and the others to find a way. I am their first attempt at mægic merging a beast and a human. Used only as a last resort to save my life."

"Jahab-Bæra-Jakká...*JabberJack*...I see. So, your true name is Gilænos. Oh...I called it gruesome, the Source-Sayers playing at making new species of beasts. I'm so sorry for that comment...*Gilænos*. Please forgive me." Roux bows her head in sincere apologies.

"Ha, no offense taken, young lass. But it did drive me to this decision to reveal myself to you both. Secrets will be our greatest enemy in this new age, I fear.

"Wait. You name yourself son to an original founding Source-Sayer of Aeryth. That would put your age at…"

"I no longer keep track of mine age, but to chronicle the happenings of Aeryth as the other Druidæ, they are too many to count, Arias. It is a result of the mægic used in my merge healing, made possible in part by all the members of the Hexad. I am near immune to the aging process of other men, even the Source-Sayers themselves. I age but a few moments to another man's year. I self-heal after an accident or wound, given enough time. And I recognize the mægic within a man, as they all reside in mine own body, though I can call upon my original mægic only."

JabberJack appears to be bewildered that we are not more astonished to see his true self. Roux does have a further few queries regarding his just presented new identity.

"Gilænos. It has an appealing sound to it, Mæster druid. Might I ask what your peers called you back then?"

"Ha, it is strange to think of them all these years…centuries later." He retakes his seat and lifts his mug of tea to his lips again. "But some still reside strong in my memories even now. Your query pleases me more than you can know, young Roux. My closest friends called me Gilli. If you would like, you may also."

"Yes, I think I would. Somehow, it would be as if I'm connected to that age and time. A time when great mægic was practiced here…and elsewhere in Aeryth. A marvelous thought. I would be honored. Another question, *Gilli*." Their smiles, equally bright. The centuries-old man with the whiskers and hindquarters of a goat, and the spunky auburn-haired lass, one of the few in Aeryth who could understand his birth language.

"They are your sculptures in the garden, are they not? Do they represent real creatures?"

"Some. And others but spring from my mind of imagining. I am the only half man and half beast ever crafted by the Hexad, so the oxhead of a man you saw there is but the imagining of one of those dear friends gone many centuries past. He was as represented though, quite bull-headed."

"It was indeed an incredible time in history. I am the breathing proof of it. But this too is the beginning of an amazing age, as the two of you are the culmination of the Hexad's greatest goal. If their writings on the effort are correct, you are not the only ones in Aeryth either. Your friends, Sæm and Alænèa, did you say? They too would be evidence of the Source-Sayers' success.

But, Arias, your tale also points to the Source-Sayers' greatest fear as well. If these mind mæges that they fled from are even now here in Aeryth, times are dire." The druid quiets even as his long fingers begin to lightly drum on his tin tea mug.

"You said you can help us further with our abilities. Gilli. Is it true?"

"Yea, lad. The Hexad's Source-Sayers that crafted this lovely body recognized that they had, indeed, left a piece of each of their mægics with me in the fashioning of my new self, and they were determined that I might use those powers. After their handiwork with me, I could recognize the mægic in a younger before they themselves knew it.

So, they theorized, I should be able to harness each of their mægics as well. Alas, though I could 'see' mægics about me and within others, my birth mægic is all that I can control. They did express that my situation had turned their thoughts to other ways of crafting mæges just likened to yourselves. So you see, I am the early inspiration to mæges such as you. And my earlier lessons with them make me uniquely suited to help you control yours."

***

We all agree, over tea and cakes, that JabberJack...nay, Gilli, will tutor us both in our mægics.

For a moon, we travel the canyon visiting ruins, meeting unique creatures, and bringing forth our mægics. Eschereon, during our time with him, had tried, from his learning through tomes, to aid us in this, but Gilli is familiar with the tricks and techniques he's learned from the Source-Sayers themselves, and this makes all the difference.

Soon, we are both lifting and moving objects with our minds, 'conversing' with beasts, and bringing forth healing techniques I was not aware of. He teaches us triggers to make the 'sight' come more readily to one, and it turns out that going into a deep '*Knowing*' trance is the biggest aid to this.

He teaches me to speak into his mind directly and to 'pick up' his thoughts, though he cannot put his in mine. And he describes how I might 'hide' my thoughts from others. In the past, I could 'read' the feelings and deduce their thoughts. Now if concentrating, I can do even more. Gilli cautions me though. It is forbidden to honorable mind mæges to go where they are not invited, as this will lead to the dark mægic that our very enemies use. These mind mægics Roux cannot, no matter how hard she tries, summon to her.

This morning over eggs and green sprouts covered with a special sauce of his, Gilli, quite pleased with the results of his tutoring, proclaims that practice is the only thing we lack now. Warming his hands about a mug of tea from the isles, he smiles at us both as we sit at a table in the back gardens.

It is in this garden, a moon past, that he introduced us to his recovering dread wolf charge. Bane is with us, and the two wolves seem smitten with each and the other. After a few suns, they leave out of the garden together, never to return. I do see them from time a'times, running together in and about the ruins of the canyon when Gilli has us out and about.

"Gilli, can you help me with the lifting of the bridge?" my sister queries. "Ari has mastered it now, and I have not."

"Certainly. The size of a person does not matter, in the mægic of it. It is the determination and strength of mind that count for more."

This brings to mind Moor's lessons on my old homestead regarding this same thing. Da had named it 'toughness' of mind, an apt description from a soldier. This, in turn, brings to mind my opening of my mœther's gifted box just before my quest to find Eschereon, the druid of Esper. And this brings another thought to mind. After Gilli and Roux leave the table, I decide to head in another direction.

My destination is the entrance hall where my *sight* mægic has reached back to show me an age when the Source-Sayers still lived. It is just me and my staff, which JabberJack has taught me can magnify and concentrate my mægic if I channel it through the stones within it. That is my intent. The box from my mœther with its gems and runes does the same thing, I cypher.

After arriving, I sit in the center of the entrance hall, falling deep into my *Knowing* and running my hands over it, one to each end of the staff. I let all other thoughts go except my memory of the frescoes on the walls and the flowers populating vases upon tables all around. My fingers lightly trace the runes below the drægons tooth gem and the drægons firestone, just as I do upon my mœther's box. I've not closed my eyes. It's not necessary.

A chill breeze flows from behind me, and I catch the scents of the flowers as they pass by me. The light breath of scented air is enough to push open the doors. They swing in now on silent hinges. As they did a moon ago, all the Source-Sayers eyes turn to me, welcoming me. All but one. The one with brightest blue eyes speckled in gold sits off to himself in a corner, staring beyond us all. I marvel at the likeness he holds to the blind elder I met in Sæm's village those many moons ago. He is the Seer of the Hexad, and somehow I know *his* vision is me entering this very chamber.

"How is it that I can see and communicate with you, when you inhabit an age long past and I live in a time more than a millennium beyond yours?"

"Because you are real, even as we are. Our combined mægic has put into motion the circumstances that will and have culminated with your existence. Your sight has merged with that of Tírēsias here, and you both hold strong mægic within yourselves."

I realize that I am not speaking aloud but they are. They are speaking in old mægish, but I am projecting my thoughts into their minds. Ne'er the lesser, I understand them. An elegant lady smiles at me.

"*I am Athæna*," she says without moving her lips, even as I hear her words in my mind. The Source-Sayer of mind mægics. The others have long ago fled others of her kind, yet I know her to be of pure heart and intent. The mægic cannot lie.

As I enter the grand hall, I take in my surroundings, and the Source-Sayers standing about the great polished stone table in the center of the room patiently watch. A high domed ceiling of leaded glass sends beams of sunlight down into the room. Floating flecks of golden dust within them make the scene that much more real. Seven large chairs sit around the table.

At the far end of the hall is a broad and quite tall man in a striking white robe with matching hair flowing about his shoulders and falling in waves from his chin and cheeks. He is leaning against the mantel. In his tremendous hands, he juggles and spins two ball-shaped bits of sky bolt. It is he who has been addressing me.

"I am Ōdæn. Behind you is Meilæki with Wölfe and Pantær." He is meaning a statuesque woman wide across the shoulders dressed in leather tunic and trousers, ready for a hunt. Having left her side now is a great cat, black as coal and a twin to those I met in the tall grasses of the Accadian Plains. The cat sidles up alongside of me, and I *feel* the cat's body against mine. The wolf, an orange hue of thick fur quite near in colour to Bane's, sniffs about me. She is the same size as Bane. My thoughts cannot help but wonder if they are of the same bloodline. Their eyes sparkle in copper and gold even as Meilæki's do. She takes a seat to my left and the beasts curl up at her feet.

A third woman, again a lady of stature and clear inner strength, looks across the table at me.

"I am Hermítæ."

"You are the Mæster of Healing."

"Yea, it is a part of my mægic."

I look to my remaining host as he nods, and the chair that I am nearest moves out from the table as if beckoning me to sit. I do. The others follow my lead.

"You must be Atelæs then." His brow raises as do the others. They stare with looks of shock. "And how is it you would know my name?"

"Your youngest son, Gilænos, still walks Aeryth and is Mæster of all of this in my time. He has told my sister and me his story, and what the six of you have done for him. He has been tutoring me on the use of my mægics."

A low chuckle as if in satisfaction rises around the room.

"He made oath he'd honor our service to him, and he has Atelæs!" It is Hermítæ that speaks.

"And what may we call you, lad?" Atelæs queries.

"I am called Ariastone Côeurdrægon. But you may call me Arias, if it pleases."

Ōdæn then queries, "And what station do you hold?"

"Station? I carry no title other than my name. I've a grandsire that sits on the throne in Kings Court, but I've been labeled 'bastard' by him, so 'bastard' is my title, I presume."

"This is a miscalculation then," Ōdæn says. "We had planned that you might have sway over great numbers in case the Three Eyes were to find us."

"I know nothing of this 'Three Eyes' of which you speak, but if he is in consort with the mind mæges that have come from across the great Southern Sea, you have miscalculated by more than twice my age. And we have only just become aware that they are here in Aeryth."

They all rise and gazed back and forth amongst themselves for a moment. The one called Athæna speaks.

"Our efforts to dissuade them to look north did not hold as long as we'd hoped. It is clearly a complicated construct." A query directly from her mind to mine then… *"How old are you, Arias? I have eighteen year…"* Aloud, "A few decades miss over 120 could be expected."

"Still, we will need to consult with Tírēsias after this council." This from Ōdæn.

"All that have been told of this have called the news dire," I say. "And I have met one of these mind mæges myself to no good outcome, escaping barely with my life. But I know there are seven others of his like here in Aeryth as I have seen them in his mind. He hunts me because of it, with a dozen assassins even now. What are we to do?"

Athæna speaks to me in our mind link.

"You must kill him, Arias. If you have linked minds with him, he will always know where to find you. You must keep moving until you have an opportunity to destroy him. The more direct the manner, the better."

I detect more than a hint of fear for me. Mægic does not lie about such things. Her thought is that the danger is great to me.

"Do they know that you know them to be here in Aeryth, Arias?" Ōdæn, again.

"From the time we met mind to mind, he–his name is Mensæ–he has been chasing me. I know not how he and his acolytes communicate, but the chase has lasted near to four moons now. His chase has been continual. I do not believe he has returned even once to Kings Court."

"That's twice you've mentioned this Kings Court. There is no such place in our time."

"It is the seat of the king over all of Aeryth, and Mensæ is the king's chief advisor."

"And who knows of this Mensæ and his acolytes?"

"The Druid Eschereon and Gilænos, your son, Atelæs. Though

Eschereon has called a council of the Druidæ, but he has told us that they number less than ten in this age."

Again, a gaze passes amongst the Hexad council.

"How must we battle these mæges and this Three Eye council you mention…"

"*You must…*"

They dissolve afore my eyes. I am left standing in a room with cracked stone floors, thick vines crawling up the walls to an iron grid mostly rusted through with the open sky above. Three large ravens look down upon me from above.

Looking back over my shoulder, I see Roux and the druid Gilli are standing in the open doorway.

"Gilli, I've just met your pæder." He nods to me, a bit of longing in his eyes.

36

Ragnu

"What did you learn, Ari?"

"The vision dissolved before they could advise me, though they were very aware that these mind mæges would someday appear in Aeryth. It is fact, even as you have said, Gilænos, that one of their own is a Source-Sayer of mind mægic. Her name was Athæna. They indicated that it is not the mægic that is evil but rather the Source-Sayers themselves that turn the mægic to evil device. They mentioned a Three Eye Council. I must ponder what they have told me further."

Later when I have time alone with the druid, I discuss the matter more. He says,

"There is a tome I found and read one hundred, two hundred years past mayhaps. It mentions them…the Three. I remember little of what I read at the time, but I recall I took the book to the isle's temple. Vicchi will be able to find it, I would think. It may be relevant now."

"One other thing that Athæna said to me directly. She said that because Mensæ and I had linked…in our minds, that he would always be able to detect me. This is how he has continually been able to track and find me. For that reason, I endanger the lives of any that are with and around me. Many of the valley could be in extreme danger even now. And especially Roux and even you, Gilænos."

"Do not worry on my account, Arias."

"Nay, mayhaps not. But I must return Roux to the isles and then leave, so that I can deal with this mind mæge without putting others in peril. I've decided we must leave immediately. If we are traveling, he will have a harder time in finding me and therefore less risk for my sister. I feel it must be me that chooses the time and manner of our final meet."

"If you insist, then I will accompany you to the Orakle's Isle. I can get you there with more haste, and from there help arrange transport back to Asgährd. Mayhaps I can aide you in your further designs against this Mensæ. I feel a duty to that purpose also."

"It is settled then. How soon can we leave, JabberJack?" He looks to me, bushy eyebrows raised. "Ha, I'm sorry, Mæster druid, but I find it hard to think of you other than JabberJack now even though I know your proper name."

"Do not apologize, lad. I take no offense. Truth be told, a person's real name has power that can be used against him so JabberJack is fine with me."

JabberJack is a man of simple means, it turns out, and the three of us are ready early on the morrow's morn. I have always been easy to pack and ready myself for a trip, Da and Moor have trained me such. Roux wonders at our strong desire for such haste as she has enjoyed our adventure in the canyon of ruins. JabberJack has spent near to two fortnight tutoring us in all our mægics. Realizing she holds more abilities than Vicchi had ever taught her, she is more reluctant to go. But JabberJack promises her the way is long and that we will have plenty of time for more lessons while we travel and promises even to accompany us to the isles so she is content and even excited at the prospect.

JabberJack leads us not the way we came but rather in what he explains is a much more direct route. At his direction, we make our way to a dock aside the river and climb into a long canoe, easily large enough for the three of us and Jilly. Bane, Fæna, and the recovered dread wolf that has been in the druid's care and with whom Bane has befriended, travel along the banks, weaving in and out of the jungle, at home there, and with each and the other.

Jilly finds the canoe more to her liking, weaving in and out amongst our legs, packs, bows, and staffs, watching her friends appear and disappear along the shoreline. When they aren't in sight, the furion amuses herself with the fish surfacing alongside the canoe. Her grief in losing her sibling seems to be lessening a bit, becoming a little more her old self.

As I have learned over this past moon, my estimate of the size of the canyon from our perch high aside the cliff face we had first arrived from, is lacking to a far extent. The river, from end to end as it passes through the canyon, measures not a few but rather forty leagues in length. It turns out also that what we had originally thought was the river that JabberJack had raised the bridge over, had been a moat around the Hexad's keep only, and the larger and wider river flows behind it.

Our trip down the river takes us the better part of two suns, with further lessons in all six mægics with JabberJack along the way. He insists with me that I speak to him by mind link only. Though he cannot project his thoughts to me, I find that I can *read* the thoughts he wants me to if I keep a mind link active with him. He does not feel I am intruding into his thoughts. It seems that living hundreds of years has taught him that secrets and lies are the greater danger. I certainly have grown to trust him implicitly through this experience.

Roux continues to prefer to call the druid Gilli, while his JabberJack name here in the canyon and Gnomon Valley, I thought suited him. He seems equally fine with either, each appealing to a different side of him.

Whatever we call him, he keeps us busy with our mægics, and with the mind link we are able to work then in perfect concert, one to the other. Roux has worked through her early astonishment that she can move objects with her mind or *push* a breeze and grows stronger and more precise the more she practices.

"JabberJack, what drove people from this canyon? It seems a pleasant enough place to make a home."

"It did stay inhabited for near to fifteen generations after the passing or the leaving of the last of the Hexad council. But they sent teams and lesser councils out into all parts of Aeryth to further their *great experiment* and thus reducing the canyons populace. Then, more and more, the youngers wanted to experience the greater world outside these walls with less and less to keep them here, as with the Hexad dissolved that purpose had gone. With each passing generation and a lessening of the population, heredity of this staring, suffered with many of the issues of not introducing new bloodlines. The last generation moved out in a great mass, leaving only stragglers who eventually passed into history's abyss."

"The creature population thrived though, eventually finding a balance, prey and predator."

We have witnessed this in our moon with him here in the canyon, even occasionally seeing a few of the 'mixed breeds' the ancient Source-Sayers had introduced into the canyon. His statues are not all of species imagined. Some really do exist. When we stop and camp the first night out from the Hexad's keep, I ask JabberJack more about just that. Earlier in the sun, we had seen what appeared to be a half dozen ponies with unusual colouring running along the farther bank.

As we approached, gliding along with the river flow, we caught up to them as they stopped to drink at the bank. It is then that I realized that they were not ponies at all. Not *only* ponies in any case. With head and body of ponies, their ears, eyes, and teeth were those of wildcats and their markings and body fur also. Looking close, I could see they did not have hooves either, but instead had tremendously large paws and claws likened to a cat. They are a striking mix of the two animals, JabberJack explains.

"The Hexad had picked this very valley, this canyon enclosed on all sides, for just this reason. It was their great experiment. It helped that the mægic is especially strong here. They had a name for their work...their grand experiment. They called it the *Öffælos*...or the *Benefit*."

"The *Benefit*. But who was it to benefit? To what ends, to what purpose would it serve, to combine different beasts, JabberJack?"

JabberJack's smile is broad to my queries.

"To the *benefit* of all of Aeryth, Arias. And to what ends? You, Arias... and *you*, young Roux...and indeed your friends. You all are the ends to their means. Mæges with the abilities of many mægics, and furthest, the culmination of their efforts was to conspire to produce a few persons in Aeryth that could use any and all the mægics as strongly as any Source-Sayer could."

"How does the interfering in the natural order of things, the mixing of beast attributes, cause mægics to be born into people?"

"As I said, lad, it was a grand experiment. These were just the beginnings of their studies. The *Öffælos* was conducted over more than two centuries. First, with insects, then birds, then beasts, learning more in each cycle. They learned to break down even our very blood to its basic parts and the very fluids that form together to produce a beast's or human's features. They studied how sons and daughters inherited their mœther's and pæder's characteristics and eventually how to mix and direct them. But in their studies, they realized the changes would need to take fifty generations or more of guided pairings betwixt heirs to different mægics."

"But how could they control such things, well beyond their lifetimes?"

"With the aid of their combined maegics and the Source mægic of the seer amongst them. My pæder once confided that Tíresias, the seer, would indeed be the crucial element to their scheme. There were groups developed and trained to live on, generation to generation, with specific goals to the Hexad's ends, well past their own lifetimes. The temple on Asgährd is one such. The Accadian Plains people are another."

His words, of course, give us plenty to cypher and ponder.

At the end of our second sun on the river, we come to its end. Not its true end. JabberJack explains that it split in two directions after entering the canyon wall. Neither of which we can follow. He tells of a great falls, dropping fifty poles into further caverns and tunnels not too far inside the cliff wall. From there, the river is said to go either to the great sea to the east or into the Breachlands chasm which divides it from the rest of the Northern Reaches. Our way is to be a tunnel that could only be traveled by foot into the dark recesses of the mountain and through it.

"The way is risky and perilous but will shave more than a few suns off what a very long and tedious trail through the Gnomon Valley would otherwise be. It will also make our journey out of the valley a secret. The way is a labyrinth of tunnels and dead ends, but I know the way. Beware, there are creatures ne'er seen in the light of day that call these caverns home. Light is a strong weapon to guard against them, and should we get separated, stay put. I will come and find you."

"Well, JabberJack, you put a light and adventurous spin to our future travels! Please, lead the way." My tone clearly sarcastic but friendly as Bane and his new she-wolf companion sniff about the wide entrance for a while before the druid enters and looks less than thrilled to be entering the cave. Fæna shows less concern, and JabberJack ventures in ne'er the lesser, with lantern floating above his head to light our way. As I enter, I also bring a light of maegic to aid us. Bane and the creatures relent and enter after us, quiet and watchful.

"How long will our trip be within the mountain, Gilli?" Roux asks.

"It has taken me as few as three suns and as many as ten times ten, when curiosity has gotten the better of me. I've studied ruins of an even older civilization than even I can imagine. Driven into the mountain depths to avoid some cataclysm in the outside world, I presume. We will make camp tonight next to an underground lake and you will see them. It is quite fascinating."

We start our journey on sandy ground with a far off echoing of falling water deeper within the mountain. JabberJack notes it is the falls we hear and that he has described earlier. There are a few tunnels leading to the west and towards those same falls, but the druid leads us more north and easterly for the time being, following the greater pathway.

It is not long before the entrance light fades behind us and we turn in a direction more northerly to my internal reckoning, deeper into the mountain and now headed down into the bargain. Every so often, we pass another byway, but so far JabberJack does not hesitate in the pathway he chooses to take. Fæna will on occasion detour and explore the way but is quick to return to us, preferring our lighted way over the pitch black of the other. We have traveled three turns of a sand glass when we approach a juncture that JabberJack decides to hold us up at.

"We are approaching our first peril. Arias, if you can shine your light brighter or lower to your feet, it would be wise here. We are about to cross a deep chasm on a stone bridge that has no side rail. It is narrow enough that we must pass in single file only. Please take care." With those words of caution, he leads us into the left tunnel at the junction afore us.

His words do not do the experience justice. After fifty paces, Roux suddenly stops and a gasp escapes her as I see a shiver run from her neck and down her spine. Ahead of her, JabberJack calls out.

"I find best to look forward and not down as you cross. The bridge is quite sturdy and safe."

Looking over Roux's shoulder now, I see her hesitation. Sending my light forward, I pull more mægic to it and will it brighter still. We are not at the edge of a *small* chasm as I was sure JabberJack had described, but rather a canyon that my light could not reach across, nor even the ceiling nor the canyon floor. All that is visible to us is a stone shelf leading out past the druid who now stands fifteen paces from us gazing back over his shoulder with mostly a dark abyss surrounding him.

I can see the distress in my sister's eyes as she bites her lower lip. Jilly sees it too. The furion climbs from my shoulder to Roux's and then down into her arms. Roux immediately begins to rub about Jilly's ears and chin. Roux takes in a deep breath and sighs it out again, settled now. They start across.

For my part, I slip into my *Knowing,* stretching my senses as far as I can. This alarms me to an extent as I realize that there are other living creatures in the mountain about us. I sense there is indeed a ceiling above us and it is populated with hundreds of small heartbeats. Bats or their kin, I suspect. What is surprising to me though is that I can actually sense the walls and, just barely, the chasm's floor far below. My sense of them grows and fades with my inhale and exhale. As an experiment, I let out a low whistle and find that my sense of the physical cavern walls grow more distinct. Roux looks sharply over her shoulder at me in clear rebuke of my antics.

The bridge widens at about eighty paces out, and we reach the other end in twice that. The path on the other side leads us steadily downward. Nervous chatter has come now to Roux, as she peppers JabberJack with queries of this and that. I remember now that she is but fourteen and seeing a greater more wondrous world than she had ever expected. In reflecting on this, I myself wonder what JabberJack at his age has experienced. Our lifetimes to him were the equivalent of but a few suns to date. How young we must seem.

The time does not drag so much now as we travel on. Stopping for a break and a small meal a little after crossing the chasm, we have become a little more comfortable in the deep underground. I teach Roux the art of gathering mægic to form a light ball, and like all things mægic, she learns it quickly and we each now have our own source of light.

After a trek of mayhaps four turns we have been quiet for some time, each with our own thoughts. I see light ahead and it confuses me. The wolves and Fæna squeeze by me and head towards the light which is but fifty paces afore us. We arrive a few moments later to find Fæna stopped and drinking at the edge of a small lake in a tremendous cavern. Bane and his new friend are playing in the shallows together. And there is light.

The whole of the cavern is lit by a natural luminescence coming from… well, everywhere. It is clear to see what is producing it. Large veins of soft white line the walls and ceiling and even the bottom of the lake. They appear as huge cracks and spider out everywhere. The ceiling of the cavern is easily thirty poles high, and across the lake from us is another wonder.

Built into the walls are clearly man-made abodes. The face of them are intricately carved stone. A mix of quarried and stacked stone with chiseled-in-place reliefs, producing a cliffside city in stone. It is Roux that breaks our silent stare of wonder.

"It is brilliant, Gilli. Who could have built such a city in stone and so far into the mountains?"

"I've studied it in great detail, trying to cypher its origin, and it was not hard as the people that built it left written evidence on great tablets of stone that I have spent years cyphering and studying. The people that once inhabited this city in fact predate the Breach that separates the Northern Reaches, and it is that very cataclysm that forced them to abandon it. What you see before you is but the smallest bit of what is truly a vast lost and abandoned city. The higher born inhabited this side, overlooking the lake, but in caverns larger than this a much larger city of stone lies hidden behind. They were great miners and craftsmen of metals and gems once, many centuries past. They had left even before the Source-Sayers found the canyon above."

"They spent their whole lives underground?"

"Nay, they would hunt and forage and even farmed small amounts of crops in the lands outside, but in the times they lived, greater beasts roamed the hills above, and so they lived in the safety of the mountain and cherished it. I believe I have met their brethren in the mountains of the desert in the Southern Reaches, for they live in smaller keeps in the mountains there and resemble the stone carvings here. They were a small but stout people, and strong if judged by the heft of the axes and hammers they left behind here. They wore thick leathers with heavy iron clasps and belts."

"This is amazing, JabberJack. Do we travel around the lake to camp within the stone city?"

"Nay, lad. The quickest way through the mountain keeps us on this side of the lake. But return someday and we can tour them, for they are magnificent to behold."

We make camp upon the shore of the lake. A deep, fine sand mixed with the luminescent crystals found in the walls make for an interesting bed. I sleep soundly, with dreams of the stone city teeming with life.

Upon rising to the soft glow of the sand and cavern city, we eat another small meal from our packs and head out to another sun without natural light as we travel through countless dizzying turns on our trek through the mountain. I have cyphered JabberJack's method of finding his way through the labyrinth of tunnels, however, as I see high on the walls a cleverly hidden but distinct rune directing him to the correct pathway. He smiles at my discovery and explains the marks were left by the dwærvs, the people of the cavern city.

The turns of sand glass wear heavier this sun, the dark and endless tunnels become oppressive after the excitement and wonder we beheld on yestersun. Occasionally, we enter stretches that are veined with the glow, but even Jilly has retreated to my pack to escape the monotony of the trek. JabberJack halts us finally, and we settle for another soundness, light deprived night.

"We've made good time, we have," JabberJack informs us on the morrow's morn. "We will most like make our exit from the mountain later this sun."

"It will be a welcome relief, Gilli. I already long for the sounds of the world outside. And the sun, I crave it!" Roux is quick to reply.

"Have a care though. We will pass through larger caverns with narrow ledges and will need cross flowing streams. As we get closer to the outer world there may be beasts and creatures that make den in the caves. Be wary."

"Ha, I believe I will welcome the signs of life, JabberJack, as half our trip has felt like we walked through catacombs." With that, we set out.

His description does not do justice on this last leg. The narrow ledges he referenced are aside chasms that my *Knowing* and a falling stone cannot find a floor to. The few streams we cross are either swift and hazardous or freezing cold, which brings back memories of our homestead frost cellar.

We pass under a falls and stand to marvel at it from the backside until Bane's growl alerts us to a cave filled with piles of bones near to knee-high behind us. When we shine our lights back to them, I notice a honeycomb of large holes in every direction on the cave walls...a distinct smell wafts from them. We continue on our way with a gathered haste.

"It is not far now..." JabberJack turns to us as he rounds the next corner. We catch up to him in the next moment and stop in surprise. He is doing his best to extract himself from what is clearly a spider's web that extends across a large chamber we've just entered. His lantern is suspended above him, held tight in the web also.

I've noticed less stone in the makeup of the tunnels we have been passing through and more soil. It is the same in this cavern chamber. The spider's silk is thick and glimmers in our light. And as I look about the room while JabberJack continues to extract himself from the sticky strands, I can't help but notice a number of holes bored into the caves soil walls and similar to those we encountered in the room behind the falls.

Falling instantly into my *Knowing* even as Fæna begins pacing and deep growls come to the wolves' throats, I peer about me and extend my spirit sense. Roux comes to full alert as well.

Staring into the holes, I see, as well as sense many creatures …spiders, peering back at us in anticipation. There is one much larger just inside a goodly sized stone tunnel at ground level. While the others express only an aggressive posture, this larger one I get a distinct sense of an intelligent being. Her…I *know* instantly that she is the matriarch here. Her many eyes gaze directly to me as I press my spirit sense forward, then hold, letting her mind accept mine if she will.

Her mind's guard dissolves, and I know I am speaking directly to her. But not just her. There is a further link to all that are her *family*, and there are many. A dozen here in the cavern with us but many more throughout the mountain.

"No humankin has spoken to me in a time uncountable. Most who wander about in my home are witless and poor food. You travel with beasts that will taste better though."

"I travel with my 'family' and would be obliged if you looked elsewhere for a meal."

"The pocpoc are hungry, man-child. Why is it I would deny them?"

"Do you recognize that I tell you the truth when I say that many of your family will die in an attempt to secure us? We are, the three of us, mæges of some considerable power, and though you might eventually prevail, as I sense a great number of 'pocpoc', all of these here with you, and mayhaps yourself, are in imminent peril."

I show her my memory of what I had done at the river's edge at the end of the Wending Way. While doing so, I put a glow to both ends of my staff. She jerks back in her cave a pace.

"It is the way of the world…the stronger survive. And I see you hold a tremendous power. I give you leave to pass, but though I am the matriarch, there are some that do not always obey me."

I nod my understanding. She gives us leave, but we might still be attacked by a rogue that does not acknowledge her wisdom.

I speak to my group by touching their minds, explaining that we can pass but to be wary still. There comes a hissing from one hole in particular. JabberJack moves forward, retrieving his lantern and striking through the webbing with his blade. I let him know that I will watch over them as they cross the large cavern. Roux and Fæna follow him.

The wolves stay back with me, and we watch two great spiders with bodies half the size of Bane and eight eyes each a glowing crimson. Long hairy legs end in pincer claws, and I can clearly see in my staff's light, keen pointed fangs with a venomous liquid glistening at their tips. Their bulbous back bodies pound up and down in a fierce and threatening manner. The two pay little attention to JabberJack and Roux as they finish their walk across the cave. They turn then to watch us as we slowly proceed towards them.

For each step I cautiously take, the colossal arachnids advance also, one along the strings of silk of the tremendous web, the other having fallen to the ground and now pumping its torso up and down as if about to pounce. It seems they think one victim will be recompense for the two that have escaped their death chamber. I think otherwise. There are three of us, myself, Bane, and the she-wolf, and they are two…until two other of their brethren advance, half out of their holes in anticipation of meat and blood.

My *Knowing* sense recognizes the moment they twitch in anticipation of their pounce. The two emerging spiders act first, as a diversion mayhaps, and leap for the wolves. But these are not any wolves, and each is ready.

Only a fraction of a moment passes before the first two spring at me. Roux has not been idle. Whilst the first is still in the air on its death strike towards me, Roux's arrow is as quick. In my *Knowing* state, with time slowed because of it, I see her arrow slice through the spider's head, two of its eight eyes exploding. Even as it falls away in front of me, not an arm's length from my face, the second and more fearsome one arrives, climbing in mid-air over its dead sibling's falling body, trying to reach me all the sooner.

That split moment of delay means its end, as my staff crushes into its head between its two largest blood-red eyes and then across its open fangs.

As I stand back and assess, three immense bodies look less so, as their furry legs hug prone, contracted torsos on the ground. The she-dread wolf is just releasing the fourth, its body spasming in its last throes in this life. A quick glance and feel about with my *Knowing* sense assures me there will be no further attacks. As I pull Roux's arrow from its victim with my foot on its head, I reach out to Ragnu, the matriarch. There are two brief responses, and I know them for what they are. A nod and a small grim smile. Her charges will not go hungry now. As we head away from the cavern, I sense the scurry of many other great spiders, weaving sacks about the fallen. Sustenance for a time more, and a threat to her rule removed. Life to the fittest...or more intelligent.

"I've not encountered their like afore, though I've heard the scurrying in the walls," JabberJack whispers as we move on.

"We are almost there," he assures us a little further on.

37

Unexpected Encounter

A half turn later, we break out into the fresh air and stiff breeze swirling in a sky dimmed by billowing clouds with grey underbellies, promising a chill rain. The landscape is a vale with tossed about boulders the size of small cottages and smoke sheds, buried in tall grasses. As I look south, I see we've come out just past what looks to be the end of the Gnomon Valley. Ahead of us to the north, a thick wood to our right with a travelway emptying from it and then heading further north. Before we make the travelway, we stop for a rest. A few smaller boulders make for a suitable place to sit and discuss the next leg of our journey. Our beast friends are less anxious to rest, fidgeting even, wanting to stray into the woods ahead mayhaps, but I am anxious to discuss the way with JabberJack. Jilly even wriggles free of my pack and onto the ground, standing upright and sniffing the air.

I am a fool for not reading these signs.

Of a sudden, Fæna jumps and knocks Roux over and to the ground as an arrow twangs past her and buries itself into the ground beside the two of us. We all react immediately and fall behind a large boulder. Bane, the she-wolf, and Fæna leave out from us, heading in different directions, becoming hunters instead of the hunted. A few more arrows fly by but miss them. The bowman distracted with their scattering in differing directions saving them, no doubt. Instinct of natural-born hunters.

In my *Knowing* instantaneously, I reach out with my mind. I'm sure of what I'll find, but I do it anyway. *He is there. Mensæ.* The others as well. I reach out and count…Mensæ, his right arm assassin, and ten others like him…and then another. I sense mægic in this last one, not practiced or strong, but there ne'er the lesser, in his spirit sense. Mensæ's right arm man is very dangerous, and a bead of sweat comes unbidden as I recall he is the one who put an arrow into my shoulder and sent me over a cliff.

"We must react, JabberJack, or they will have us pinned and easy picking. They are thirteen in all, and trained assassins. They're with Mensæ, the mind mæge."

To his credit, the druid accepts my assessment. I reach out to Talon, hoping beyond hope that he is not far away. I almost laugh when I immediately hear his echoing war cry in the distance. After warning Roux, my spirit self leaps to join the raptor.

He/we are not close. Mayhaps it is my heightened hearing combined with his extraordinary cry, but even with his phenomenal sight, I cannot make out where we wait behind the boulders. Talon is flying swiftly with the stiff breeze aiding. He knows exactly where we are.

***

(Charan/assassin)

Eljin has just come running into camp. The others know what it means and don their blade belts and other weapons, rising before he has even reached me. Our scout knows too and is smiling.

"Marcus has them pinned behind a boulder, sir. They arrived with three beasts, two great wolves and a large linx cat. The beasts have left out from them. They are three. The lad, a lass, and another, and he is a strange one. He is the size of a younger but wears a beard and carries a walking stick."

I signal the men to spread out and track towards our foe. He's been crafty. He's been lucky. Mensæ insists the lad has mægic, I've not seen any yet. He travels with well-trained beasts, but I've seen that afore. I know that mægic exists–seers–I will not deny. And I'd seen Mensæ torture a man's mind without speaking or touching the man and force him to do his bidding. I've even seen parlor tricks where a man lifted a fork off the table with his mind. I saw nor felt no string as I watched it happen. But I had taken this lad once, and I would again. My men are the best at what they do. They will not escape.

Mensæ knows what is happening as well. He comes over, and we leave out together, following the men. I whisper Eljin's assessment to him as we go. It does not take us long to reach Marcus' perch upon a high boulder overlooking the valley's northern entrance where Faolán insisted we would meet them. He was right as well that there would be no hurry. We had made camp and have waited half a fortnight for this sun. I do not trust the man, but he is earning his gold.

Marcus points out the place he has them pinned down. They cannot leave without exposing themselves. Mensæ insists the lad is a resourceful warrior with phenomenal ability. We will be patient and see, for the time being. Starting cautious and alert.

A wolf howls in the distance and then another. The screech of a wildcat reaches us also. Trickery only, I suspect, but I pass word to the men to stay aware. I watch as Faolán rubs his whiskers but readies a short sword that looks well used. The winds pick up and I look to the sky, and even as I do, a deafening, almost unnerving echoing cry erupts from high above. It is the same raptor's cry that had us following the first path away from the cliffs when we first arrived to these Northern Reaches. Trickery. I respect the lad for that, in the least. And one cannot pinpoint where the hawk is calling from.

***

We are here, and Talon screams out another war cry. Bane returns with a howl, followed by another.

I see through Talon's eyes our enemy. The wolves and cat are keeping a distance and continually move in a great arc behind Mensæ's assassins. I see the man himself, perched on a high boulder with an archer and another. I assume it is the assassin captain. There is another bowman fifty paces to their left, standing on a similar boulder. His men are low in the tall grass, and though I will not be able to see them when I return unto myself, I take note of their location.

I leave Talon and return to JabberJack and Roux. I see Roux is anxious, but I know that she is capable of holding her own, even at only fourteen year. I had seen it in the caves with the spiders. As I come out of my *Knowing* I fill in the two of them on our dire circumstances.

"JabberJack, where is it that we can best reach safety?"

"Do you spy the three monoliths standing side a'side, north of here and west? If we can make it there, we can find sanctuary."

"Yea, JabberJack, I see them. They are a good two hundred paces away. What safety do they bring?"

"They mark the start of the Mæge Fields. Though arrows still fly true there, if we can get a safe distance into the fields, we will be safe from all but other mæges."

"How is that so?"

"I'll explain more when we get there, but suffice to say there are strong mægics placed there that will attack any that do not carry mægic themselves. We all will be quite safe there unless the assassins chasing you are mæges also."

"I think not, other than Mensæ and one other that travels with them now."

"It is the way I planned to take you, as it is the way I use when venturing out into Aeryth on my forays. For it is this way that offers routes the mæges had crafted in ages past to cross the Breachland chasm. Seldom used since the age of the mæges as only they could access them."

"Some sun, JabberJack, if we survive this one, I will love to hear tales of the age of mæges."

"Let us make it so then! Now tell me, what must we do to foil your nemesis' plan for us?"

I explain further who and where they are, and we make ready to act. Each of us have a specific part to play until, as in all battles, our plans go awry. The bowmen are our first concern, and the druid will use his mægic in hopes of disarming them, allowing us opportunity to run and shelter, if need be, further on. We will have little time before the assassins swing the arc around to block our retreat. I let Bane and Talon know our need for their help. We make our move.

As we leave out from behind our boulder, the two archers rise simultaneously and pull their strings. The closest, and the one with Mensæ, gives a look of astonishment as his bow is mægically ripped from his grasp and tossed high into the air. The second is set upon by Talon as the great echo eagle attacks his head with his mighty claws, blinding him.

We move quickly now as all the assassins have risen from the grasses and head directly towards us. Roux and I have both loosed arrows, each to lethal effect. But I see that the captain and Mensæ have joined the battle. The captain has retrieved the archer's bow and has it raised and nocked with an arrow. My chest burns and the tinker's amulet there glows crimson for a moment. I *feel* Mensæ's attack on my mind, but I've repelled it.

I've been distracted just long enough as the captain's arrow is released. Roux has already recognized the captain's threat, and I see that it is the two of them that are exchanging arrows. From the corner of my eye, I watch as Fæna leaps from the grass.

JabberJack lifts a dozen rocks the size of my fist with his mægic and sends them flying with a great force towards three approaching assassins with blades drawn. I see a large ruby ring on his finger glow even as he lets them fly. *He looks to Mensæ.* In my *Knowing*, I am taking all of these things in and processing them. I am spirit linked to Talon, Bane, JabberJack, and Roux. Talon is causing chaos from above as Bane and his she-wolf companion are attacking the closest assassins to them.

But an arrow strikes down another as I drop it and take up my staff. Three more are near upon us. And then as I pass my awareness across all that my mind is touching, JabberJack's thought hits me like a ton of bricks.

Arias...the mind mæge...now!! I sense he is in real pain, and when I look to see, my sister is stabbing him with her dirk from behind, and I cannot *sense* her anymore. I instantly know the reason and an anger within me boils over in the very moment.

Sensing all the assassins, I wrap my spirit sense about each of them, feeling for Mensæ especially. I gather all the mægic that I feel about myself, and I know it to be a tremendous amount. In my mind I see myself physically lifting them all off the ground and bring my anger forth. I will myself to throw them back and away from us. *It happens even as I've seen it in my mind.* They are gone. Thrown back from us. Unmoving, any of them, from what I can see. I feel drained.

I look back to Roux and see that she has collapsed onto the ground. Aside her, the druid is on one knee holding his side and barely able to do that. Blood is seeping in too many places for him to grasp. I'm dizzy but make my way to him.

"Lay down, JabberJack, and let me in." He takes my meaning and nods as he lies back.

I join with him, and I let myself find his wounds from within. I gather what mægic I find left within myself, and also that which surrounds him now, and use it as I wish upon him a *healing*. Even as I feel it working, a darkness envelops me. As my conscious world recedes from me, I sense Jilly and Bane licking at my face and hands.

Thoughts gather in my head, but I have no sense of my body. Eschereon comes to mind, and his lesson to the three of us, Alænèa, Sæm, and myself. Using mægic exacts a cost on the mæge. It is temporary, but it is real. And then, my sister comes to mind and JabberJack. I will my eyelids to open. It is a struggle and I feel I am failing in it, but I persist. I feel them flutter, and the smallest bit of light seeps in. There comes a shivering cold and wet. A deeper darkness now.

Thoughts again. Riding in a coffin in the back of a buckboard wagon, feeling every bump in the travelway. Have they captured me yet again? *A memory*? A memory, I judge, as I feel rain hitting my face and I can't feel rain in a coffin. I try to open my eyes, and it works this time. JabberJack is staring down at me.

"You've given me a scare," he says in a pained whisper.

"JabberJack…are you okay?" I'm able to lift myself onto my elbows. Yea, it is truly raining. "Roux?" He sees my desperation.

"She lives but is unconscious still."

"Still? How long have I been out? Mensæ?" The fatigue is lifting a bit now, and I can sit up. JabberJack is quite pale.

"Mayhaps a half turn, lad. Be still a moment more. *Listen.* Mensæ has used your sister in desperation, and that is not good. He'll have done harm to her mind. You've saved my life, though I'll need to heal much more as I've lost a significant amount of blood. The lass' spirit beast, Fæna, lives no more. She took an arrow to save her. The she-wolf is down as well and in dire shape once again, but she tore the throat from an assassin. There is no sign yet that the mind mæge has recovered nor any of the others, but they may, and you must get Roux back to Vicchi. She will know what to do. I fear her recovery is not in your power to heal."

I need no accounting of Jilly and Bane. They are with us. With my strength near returned, I help the druid to sit up against a boulder. He has told all to me, even as he can barely rest on his elbows. I can see now Fæna dead, a pace away, and the she-wolf laboring to breathe. Bane is at her side.

I stand cautiously and look around for Mensæ and his cutthroat soldiers. I cannot see them, but the heavy clouds above continue to block the sun and pelt us unmercifully. A moan escapes Roux, and I quickly go to her.

"If she is able, you must get on your way with her, Arias. If not, when you are able, you must carry her away to the safety of the Mæge Fields."

"What about you?"

"I will not be able to go with you now but listen close and I'll tell you the way you must take." And he spends a few moments doing just that.

"I will be fine. When Mensæ and his assassins arrive, they will see a dead, halfling druid, and after they are gone, I will nurse the she-wolf back to health again. But you must go now while you can."

I hesitate, but then think that he has made it through a very long lifetime of trials and knows better his own abilities. And Roux needs my help. She is sitting up now, but her eyes are glazed and I cannot touch her mind with mine.

Gathering my bow but leaving hers, I put it in its place upon my back across my pack. Roux understands and acts on simple directions, and I set her to walking aside Bane. I explain where we are headed to the great dread wolf. He looks back to his she-wolf companion then to JabberJack. He then heads out. Jilly climbs up Bane's back and sniffs at Roux, wondering at her state. I lift my staff and lead them out, falling back into my *Knowing* to guard against any surprise from Mensæ's men.

***

(Faolán)

I open my eyes, and excruciating pain radiates from my head to my toes. Too dizzy to rise yet, I take stock. The last thing I can recall is being lifted into the air and losing all control. The air being forcibly pushed out of my lungs, and then all went dark. A thick rain pelts me as I lie in the long, thick grass. Rising to my elbows, I notice a pace away to my left, one of the mind mæge's assassins lies broken against a boulder. He will not rise, and I count myself fortunate I landed in the grass.

Six paces from me, Mensæ and his captain lie side a'side. I see that their chests rise and fall. They live. I wonder what has happened to their 'quarry.' A lad, a young lass, and the halfling hermit that before today was but a figure of lore and legend to me. The lad is a mæge of incredible power, and but without it he would have been dead or captured now. And I should take more care with this Mensæ, I know now. I see that he has forced the lass to turn a dirk on the hermit and stab him thrice. Then the hermit…he himself is, or was, a mæge. He stole the bows from the archer's very hands and raised rocks from the field with his mind and sent them to flight as weapons. All of this, and they commanded wolves, wildcats, and eagles as well. I shake my head in awe of it.

Able to get my legs under me now, I crawl to the boulder painted red with the broken assassin's blood and use it to aid in my climb to my feet. A moment more and the world stops spinning about me. Making my way to my employer, I lightly slap his cheek in hopes of rousing him. He responds, and I reluctantly move to Charan, his captain, and do the same.

"The lad, Faolán, is he still about?" He has his wits about him much sooner than it took me. I climb the nearest boulder and gaze to the east, where we had encountered the three of them. I stand high enough that I can see our battlefield. The hermit, the halflings call JabberJack, lies dead from his wounds from the lass. One wolf and the wildcat lies unmoving next to him. Turning to the north, I see the mæge lad walking aside the other wolf and the lass.

"He is leaving. I see him, the lass, and a wolf. The halfling hermit mæge is dead."

"Charan," the mind mæge speaks. "He must not escape."

"You will not reach him here and now." I inform them.

Charan's remaining men gather about him when I look back and down to them.

"My men can catch them."

"Your best bowman's arrow might just reach them, but if it does not, you will not reach them now. They have reached the Mæge Trail and are untouchable now to mortal men."

"Enough of this man's idiocy, Mensæ. After them, Eljin. Twenty gold to the first man to him."

And with that, Mensæ's captain leaps more than climbs up to me with his bow. He nocks an arrow, takes aim, and looses it. His men pause to watch the arrow's flight. Mensæ also.

It is a high flying, perfectly executed shot. I can almost hear the collective intake of breaths as we watch the arrow's flight, every one of us. I cannot hear the thud as Charan's arrow hits the ground short of his target, but the mæge lad has. He turns and pulls his bow from his back. Walking back, the lad pulls the arrow from the ground. In what appears to be three swift motions and no more, he strings his bow, nocks the arrow, and looses it.

The arrow leaves his bow with not enough lift to make it half the way back to us. But I am wrong in my assessment. I lose sight of its flight for a moment then jump to the side and off the boulder and Charan does likewise in the other direction. We've moved not a moment too soon. I hear its swoosh as it flies past where we have just been, and it carries another twenty paces more before slamming into the ground. I join the mæge, and Charan, aside from his men. Mensæ turns to me.

"What do you mean, Faolán, 'they have reached the Mæge Trail?'"

I pause a moment, gazing to Charan as if to say, 'the lad is better than you.'

"It is much like the Wending Way that I spoke of earlier, Mæster, but with a much deadlier twist. Mæges of old have cursed the very ground and skies above against any that enter and do not carry mægic. None that have entered escape and live to tell if it."

"Again with the idiocy, Mensæ. This man is but a grifter, out to pocket as much of your gold as he can."

"Have I as yet told you anything but truth and guided you directly to your target? Have I not earned my pay?"

"Not yet, you haven't. Our 'quarry,' as you put it, is still loose."

I want to say that it has nothing to do with a failure on my part but hold my tongue.

"We still know his destination and with a damaged lass that you have left him with… Yes, I saw what you have done to her, Mensæ. I know not the how of it, but to know that you could travel the Mæge Trail unharmed, but she looked to be a burden to him now, walking as if in a trance."

He studies me.

"Send a man, Charan, just to the rise to spy and report if they are heading north still."

"Let us send the grifter, Mensæ."

"But you do not trust him, Charan. So, send him *and* one of your own." I feel a bead of sweat and a chill at the same time form on the back of my neck.

"Send your man, and if he returns alive, I'll hand you back your gold and leave you to your own designs from here." I propose in a last effort to sway them from his mad idea.

"You will both go…Mikhail," Charan calls over one of his men. "You and Faolán here to the rise and spy their travel direction."

At some unseen sign, all of his men place hands to sword pommels and look directly at me. This will not go well either way, I fear. We head out, I and Mikhail.

Passing the monoliths I know to be the entrance to the Mæge Trail, I reflexively put my hand to mine own sword. All of the assassins do likewise again. This is happening. My throat constricts.

The rise is only eighty paces away. Mayhaps it will not be far enough to trigger the mæge curse, I tell myself. Or if it does, I need only outrun this fellow, but he looks fit…and lithe and swift. *Damn my luck.*

We reach the halfway point and nothing has happened. Then, in but a few moments more, we are at the rise. Looking down, I spot the three of them. They have left the field we'd been crossing and are now on a defined travelway and headed north. Mikhail nods to me as my advice had been accurate. He confirms that they are headed north as I had informed them.

As we turn to go back I hear a hum and then more of a buzz in my ears. With furrowed brow, I look to the skies above us and see a moving yellow cloud, almost looking like a golden dust in the air but all abuzz and moving in some pattern only they can discern. I begin to run. I know what they are, and they are not simply bees. Drægonflies. One sting can be painful, two deadly.

Mikhail, I don't think, knows the species, but he clearly sees my fear, I am sure, and starts to run himself. He is faster than me, but they are faster still and for some reason are chasing only him. I hold up as they are in front of me now, betwixt me and the safety of the monoliths.

The drægonflies are like a cloud about the man now, and he is screaming in torment and pain. In a moment, he goes stiff and falls to the ground. I see his wide-open eyes and his contorted face as he does. But then, the murderous insects leave him…and me. Not a single one even flies in my direction. I stumble in a daze the remaining twenty paces to the others. Mensæ and Charan both stare at me.

"There is a travelway, and they are headed north. If you don't believe, go see for yourselves."

Looking back over our recent battleground while the others argue about retrieving their compatriot's body, it dawns on me that something is missing. I no longer see the body of the hermit…or the wolf. I do not say anything, and instead head off towards the camp to gather my horse. They have till then to decide if I am still their scout and guide.

38

Mæge Trail

A blood-curdling cry reaches my ears as we travel up the trail and further into what JabberJack refers to as the Mæge Plain. Looking back, his words come back to me. Only those with mægic within them can travel past the three monoliths and into the Mæge Plain, no others will survive. Mayhaps, we will be safe for a time.

I have tied a tether, like a horse's rein, about Bane's neck and direct Roux to hold it at all times. She can handle no more instruction than that. After passing the three monoliths, I find another large boulder to shelter behind, and delving into my *Knowing,* I venture into my sister's mind. We have merged before while in the canyon and are comfortable with doing it, one with the other. My hope is to heal, or help her to heal, whatever damage Mensæ has done. However, I find naught but a vast void within her mind. Searching as far as I dare in a faraway corner, I sense more. But it is impenetrable and even repels me with a fierce jolt. I retreat, dismayed.

It is imperative for me now to get my sister to the Orakle's Isle and then back to the temple where JabberJack insists Vicchi can help. Guilt racks me. And so we rise to continue on our way. But it is not an easy trip. It is a moon's journey from the Hexad's canyon to the upper coast of the Northern Reaches. The three of us are caretakers to Roux–Bane, Jilly, and myself.

I have plenty of time to ponder my past and future and my present plight. Until my encounter with the Source-Sayers of the Hexad, I have ignored the danger that the mind mæge presents. Not only to me, but any that travel with me, and if Eschereon and even more so the Source-Sayers insist, all of Aeryth as well. It is time to take the threat more seriously. At this point, it is Roux that needs me most, but I turn my mind to the elimination of the greater evil and what I must do.

I have two fortnight to craft a scheme to both send Roux to the aid of the temple and draw Mensæ away to a showdown betwixt only the two of us. Sæm would be a good sounding board for ideas, but in the same vein, he would insist on staying with me to battle the mæge. I must do this on my own.

I ponder how I can best protect my sister, and my face grows red with anger at myself when I realize I have the tool to so on my very person. I reach for the tinker's amulet around my neck and squeeze it. It is the amulet that saved me from Mensæ's attack on my mind in the Bowels under Kings Court. Of course. I ponder the necklace and its jewel and the filigree setting of mæge runes surrounding it. I now believe the Hexad, though long dead, played a part in its finding a way to me.

This means I must accept that they have the mægic, or rather the mægics, between the six of them to ordain the future over a thousand years. But the blind Elder, the Seer in Sæm's village, had made a point that I could control my own destiny. I must then take charge of my own fate. Knowing the intent of the Source-Sayers, mayhaps the best method will be to not fight against their purpose but to navigate my own way through it. I become determined now to make my own choices.

The first is to use the tools they've given me, and the learning I've acquired along my journeys. The tinker's amulet plays a large part in that. It is time to see what it can really do for me, for it won't be long in my possession. I know when we reach the coast, I must pass it to my sister. Come midsun I decide to make camp for the day and give caretaker duty entirely over to Jilly and Bane. I must slip into my *Knowing* and learn the further secrets of the tinker's amulet.

Making camp, I quickly roast up a rabbit I'd caught on yester's eve. Having seen to my sister's needs, I watch a half turn as Bane and Jilly take over watching and entertaining her. She interacts with them on a basic level when they nuzzle, tug, and play about her, but most of the time she sits and stares about her, her face showing intent even though I know her mental ability near non-existent at the moment. Ne'er the lesser, she waves her hands and arms before her with some sort of purpose, pushing, pulling, and gathering the empty space before and around her. I wish to myself that I can see what she is seeing.

At this thought, the amulet warms, and for a moment I witness a myriad of colours all about. I shake my head, and the warming of the amulet brings me back to my purpose. I sit with my back against a great alpaca tree and delve into my *Knowing*. I'd been told by JabberJack–and the notion reinforced by the runes on the doors at the temple and on their twins in the Hexad ruins–that I carry all six mægics within me. If I am to defeat Mensæ, I will need to properly know how to use them. Eschereon had started my lessons but we had not been entirely successful, due in part to my malaise from being apart from Finnie and that he himself practiced only one of the six.

My time in the Bowels, after nearly being killed by Mensæ's assassin and the loss of my memory at the time, produced a thirst to learn more in order to protect myself from the mind mæge, after inadvertently delving into his mind and memories and learning his and his compatriots intent here in Aeryth. But I've been on the run and hunted by him since, with a little respite only. First on Asgährd with Vicchi and my sister learning rune mægic, and then recently with JabberJack. JabberJack is an ancient druid and has been exposed to all mægics in the Source-Sayers of the Hexad's attempt to produce a mæge such as myself. And though he can only work one mægic, he knows how to bring them all to the fore within me and Roux.

It is my intent, with the help of the amulet, to build and practice my mægics, so that when the time comes, I will be ready to stand against the mind mæge. I have only the time of our travels to the Orakle's Isle to better and ready myself.

I believe the amulet is the key. It has hinted to me that it is such. Besides protecting me from the mind mæge's advances against my mind, it has shown me that it can use my maegics at the behest of my subconscious by manipulating my maegics to bring wishes to fruition and gather maegics about me in concert with my subconscious thoughts to expel great forces through my staff. And so, as I once unlocked the box my mœther had bequeathed me, I will try now to learn the knowledge weaved and held within the amulet. I believe now it is an artifact forged by the Hexad themselves, evidenced by its finding its way to me specifically.

Delving now into my *Knowing* as I sit with my back against the alpaca tree, my fingers trace the filigree of the amulet's setting, letting my energy flow to it and letting its energy flow to me.

The world about me dissolves. Once again, I am back in the Hexad's council chamber. Tírēsias sits in his corner, brilliant blue eyes staring, but otherwise immobile. The others' eyes all turn to me. Athæna speaks first this time.

"The mind mæge? This Mensæ, you've mentioned?"

"He hunts me still. We've just had an encounter with him and his assassins two suns passed. He has damaged my sister's mind severely and nearly killed Gilænos in the effort. I have escaped into the Mæge Fields with my sister, spirit wolf, and furion. I've cyphered your intent in crafting the amulet I wear and am using it now. I will use it to further my learning in each of my maegics, as you have perceived my need. We are headed to the Orakles Isle to find passage for my sister back to Äsgarhd and the temple there, so that the temple mœther might heal my sister's mind."

The five glance to each and the other, and Athæna turns back to me. I feel her mind touch mine.

"The mind mæge still hunts you after more than a decade?"

"Nay, it has been but a moon since our last visit."

"A moon to you and ten years for us. Most curious."

"I am hoping to develop my mægics before I meet him again, as I am sure he will be awaiting me when we reach the end of the Mæge Fields at the coast nearest the Orakle's Isle. To be honest, I did not expect that I'd be drawn back to you when I activated the runes of the tinker's amulet. It is a most incredible thing that you have crafted."

"Yea, is. And we will endeavor to aid you. The Mæge Fields, why did the mind mæge not follow you there?"

"I reckoned it is because he travels with his assassins that cannot enter into the Fields, as they carry no mægic. JabberJack...er, Gilænos has explained the properties of the Fields and the ultimate danger to those who wield no mægic."

Athæna continues aloud now, and I wonder at it.

"Arias, we must ponder and discuss what you have told us. Of course, we will aid you in any way we are able. Contact us again in two suns time, and we will be better prepared to do as you ask."

I gaze about the council chamber, and they all nod in agreement to Athæna's statement, and then the room dissolves into a mist again. They are gone.

***

(Mensæ)

I know now that Faolán carries a mægic. I believe he is as surprised as I am. He walks out from the area he named the Mæge Fields, leaving one of Charan's men in what surely looks to be an excruciating death. The drægon wasps did not touch our scout and guide. Which means, if his tale of the Mæge Fields is true, that he himself carries a mægic.

I feel now I must know which of the five he possesses. While Charan and his remaining men decide what to do with the corpse, I follow Faolán back to camp. I approach as he saddles his horse.

"You possess a mægic, Faolán."

"Oh, so now you trust my words, Mensæ. If so, it is the first time since we've met that you have."

"You mentioned earlier that we could work more efficiently if we would drop any charade and be truthful, one to the other. I am a mind mæge, Faolán. From the first I have known you were keeping something from me. I actually respected that in you. I could have as easily probed your mind for the answer but that respect has kept me from doing it."

I study him as he thinks through my meaning.

"I have no mægic that I am aware of. I do not understand what happened in the Mæge Fields. I expected to die."

"What would you say is your strongest attribute?"

"Men and women both say I have a convincing way about me."

"Hmm. And do you get on well with beasts?"

"I'm no animal whisperer, but I've been known to settle a guard dog or two in younger days. I carry no beast mægic. I cannot command creatures to my will."

"How much do you know of mægic, Faolán?"

"Just what's in the fables and tales. If it is real, it is not found in these parts. The halflings feel there is some truth in it and fear it." I watch him carefully, and again I have the sense he is holding something back.

"I have studied mægic for many years, Faolán, and I can assure you it is very real, as I am sure you believe after our encounter with Arias Côeurdrægon, the lad who is escaping into the Mæge Fields as you have named them."

"There have been tales all my life about the Fields. I had no desire to test them. And I have met another not unlike yourself. In matter and fact, he told me that I might expect to meet you, or another like you, one day."

I feel my brow raise of its own accord. So this is what he has been holding back. I let it ride for a moment.

"There are two sides to the mægic that is attributed to beast mægic. They once called such mæges empaths. They can read intent and thought in the face and slightest body movements of any man or beast. They can detect an untruth and lie in anyone. You would do well not to gamble at cards with such a person." Faolán's pupils dilate for a moment. I have learned some of these tells myself, though the mægic is not native to me.

"I do well in any card game. I just thought some were shortsighted or deaf to such signs. Surely not all are so ignorant."

"Not ignorant, just not attuned nor practiced at such things…and but few possess such mægic. What did the other tell you to expect of me?"

"That you would be hunting him, or hunting somebody. But in either case, I should send notice to him."

"So, he is still alive. I never doubted it. Not like the others. And how is it that you contact him?"

He's given me a raven. One that will take my messages directly to him, and his missives back to me if he so desires." I nod.

"When you next send word, please let him know that I wish to meet with him. Until then, if you'll agree, I would like to continue our relationship on a more equal footing. I promise to respect your advice more. Where must we travel next, to intercept this thorn in my side?"

Faolán does not pause.

"The coast, across from the Orakles Isle. We will need keep an eye out for highwaymen. The Breachlands are, after all, a lawless territory. Mayhaps, we can renegotiate my fee?"

"Ha. As you say, Faolán. I find value in your services and knowledge."

I had left out of Kings Court with Charan and a dozen elite, well-trained assassins to hunt a broken lad, garbed in rags and barely able to stand. Left unfed and his wounds untreated for near to a moon's time. He somehow managed to escape the unescapable dungeons beneath a soldier's training ground. We are here in the middle of the Northern Reaches, near to three moons later and he has managed to dwindle our ranks by more than half and has revealed extraordinary mægic.

A mere lad threatens our plans and advances in Aeryth. Just as I am discovering the greater maegics hidden here, though not the original Elders of mægic the Three Eye Council seek, our schemes could be foiled if the lad lives to contact the Elder mæges to alert them. He must clearly know them or how to reach them. I am torn betwixt allowing him to live so that I can extract his knowledge or just destroying him and all those he meets so as to silence the threat.

Later a thought strikes me. Pulling away from Charan and bringing my horse aside our guide, I query him.

"Faolán, are highwaymen for sale?"

"Aye, you could offer them coin, but odds are you'd be throwing half away. If it is mercenaries you are after, we will be passing through two townes on our way. I can gather mayhaps ten who will be more trustworthy and able."

"Ten will be adequate, I think. Get it done then, Faolán."

In a fortnight's time, we travel with a contingent that includes nine additional men. Though not regular trained soldiers of a lord's regiment by the scars they wear, all are clearly battle-tested and confident, bearing bows to longswords and a number of varied weapons besides. In camp at night, they spend time honing their blades and tending their horses like men who know their craft well. Murder and mayhem. Faolán has done his job well.

In another few sun's time, we have made our destination. Peering out from the cliff's overlooking the Northern Sea, Faolán points the direction to the Orakle's Isle and then to the edge of the Breach which we are also in sight of. It's a chasm a hundred paces wide at this place and falling easily fifty more to the beach below. The cliffs on the other side are shear and unscalable as they are the whole length inland, Faolán explains.

There is an unexpected sight as well, and when I notice it, I pull us back from the cliff's edge so as to remain unseen. There, anchored offshore, are the mæge ship that Arias Côeurdrægon and his compatriots had escaped in, back below the druid's village on the far side of the inner sea. His friends await him here then.

This settles my earlier debate with myself. The lad and the lass with him must die afore he can reach them. We will make our scheme accordingly. I pull Charan and Faolán to me in war council.

***

A fortnight into our trip, Roux remains unchanged. I've tried unsuccessfully to reach the depths of her psyche that I am sure hold her memories and conscious self, but they lie steadfastly locked away within that corner of her mind.

We've reached the Breachland's chasm, as we have been traveling north and west on JabberJack's last instructions to me. Again, I hope he has managed to reach safety away from Mensæ's band of cutthroats. I know he is as capable as any. I've been practicing the new skills he's had a hand in teaching me during our stay in the canyon. With the aid of the amulet, I've become quite successful in some of the mægics. I can command some elements. Water to some extent and especially winds as they and their controlling mægic are everywhere. I have become more nuanced in the control of lifting and moving objects with my thoughts alone. And recently, I've had a dream or two that I feel might be more than just dreams. Wishing into the amulet to guide me with lessons JabberJack has outlined to me, I am finding success. I hope it is enough and in time.

I spend as much time as possible in trying to train my mind mægic. I find I can do this even as we walk. My thoughts are to hone the defensive powers that the amulet has shown me are possible. It has been this very ability that the amulet has best served me. It has protected me from the more trained mind mægic of Mensæ. I must be able to withstand his attacks against my mind, even without the amulet's aid, if I am to survive an assault such as Roux has experienced. This is important, as I must give up the tinker's amulet to my sister when the time comes. She *must* make it back to the temple. It is the sole objective in my world now. I cannot look past this first and foremost, whatever the cost to me.

Deciding to camp here for the day so I can do some hunting, I ponder the Breachland's chasm that we have made our way to and what JabberJack has told me about it. Where others must travel to the Orakle's isle and wait for ship's transport to escape the Breachlands, JabberJack has told me the secret of another way. Many ways, actually. The first of which he described as being at this very place. Just as he portrayed it, another two monoliths mark a bridge over the chasm where it is narrower here.

I queried JabberJack on whether it would not be faster back to the isles using this way, but he nixed the thought, explaining there were still the cliffs to maneuver down and severe terrain afore them. These crossings lead to the greater Northern Reaches and are meant as such. But he explained also that some mægic is required to read the bridge entrance runes in the ancient mægic speech to access them. It is my backup scheme, should the skiff JabberJack says the isle inhabitants leave on the beach does not await us.

When I approach the chasm after passing by the two monoliths, I see a third as he'd detailed in their likeness at the edge of the cliff. It is triangular and stands half again as high as me. A stiff breeze meets me and I shy back from the cliff's lip. Three runes lie on one side of the large stone pointing skyward. I ponder their meaning and practice their sounds.

"*Eth-Brăkar-Wäaff.*" I am certain I have them right.

"*Eth-Brăkar-Wäaff.*" I speak again and understand their meaning better. "Skies Breath Surrender." And that is what happen. The winds die to a stillness.

Walking now to the edge, I spy what I did not before. Almost invisible to the eye, a stone bridge, attached to a dozen descending stone steps, arches across the canyon. Its design such that it blends seamlessly against the backdrop of the face of the opposing canyon wall. I can only keep its shape before me by continually moving my head side to side. It is only a pace wide and the winds, if they had continued, would surely blow whoever ventures out upon it off and to their death. It will take a nerve to cross this bridge even without the stiff breezes. I will not test it, this sun.

Our path north keeps us always within sight of the canyon, and we pass two more mæge bridges, each with a different mægic protecting and disguising it. One requires descending into a cavern with hidden traps held from triggering by the mægic runes. They are never needed as only mæges have passed through the Mæge Fields, I assume. Or if others do, they never make it this far.

A second fortnight passes, and it finds us in a forest that I see ends up ahead. Just past the tree line, I can make out three tall pointed monoliths, the end of the Mæge Fields protection. Cautiously, I approach the forest trail's end, and thinking the worst that Mensæ awaits, I move off the travelway to peer out from the tree line in search of any sign. None.

But I remain less than assured. Retreating back behind the forest's edge, I lean back against a tree to think a moment. I can hear, smell, and feel that we are close to the northern shore as a very stiff breeze pulls the sounds and smell of the salty surf. A sea birds call gives me my answer. I call upon my friend in the skies, never too far from me in all these moons since we've met.

Slipping into my *Knowing* I search for Talon's spirit sense, hoping he is not too far away. I find him perched on a stiff branch of a tree extending above its neighbors, allowing him a point to survey all about him. We gaze upon a rippling sea of leaves topping the trees below. I catch my breath as I feel a freedom only a bird can feel at such a sight. As I join with him, I immediately sense our physical distance apart as his mind is capable to judge it somehow. He lifts into the air on a tremendous wingspan, aided by the sea breeze from the north. He rises high into the dusky sky, some hundreds of paces, and flies north towards the coast.

I feel we must survey both near and far out to sea to discover our destination, the Orakle's Isle. I sense as the great raptor passes over our hiding place twenty paces inside the treeline. We are looking out to sea now and the isle's hilly and green coast is immediately evident, less than half a league due north.

Before the sun's light fails us, I suggest that we turn east and back to shore. In doing that, a sight unexpected greets me. The mæge ship. Sæm, Alænèa, and Therrien are here!

My spirits rise and then fall immediately again. As Talon and I approach the beach again, I spy two disturbing things. First, there is a skiff against an old pier. It lies mostly submerged with its mast clearly askew and broken. This leads my eyes, Talon's incredibly far-sighted eyes, further east and down the beach to a jetty of rock from cliff to water and just past it to an encampment of a count of ten fighting men as if in wait of an ambush. They amble about, hidden behind the boulders, a few sitting about a small fire. Two are high upon a boulder lying flat, surveilling the beach to the west.

As we cross back to land, I notice now another scout atop the cliff at its edge, standing close to a small solitary tree rooted in the rock. He carries a longbow. And among a copse of trees nearby, a half dozen more men, two aside and appearing to be in conversation. Mensæ and the assassin. They have hired mercenaries and know exactly where we will approach from. What our destination has been all along. Near to a dozen and a half-trained soldiers.

I think to pass over the chasm, searching for the monoliths marking a mæge bridge that JabberJack had assured me was there. Three passes and we finally find it. But the monoliths are just rubble on the ground, as is the single marker at what should be the location of the bridge. Knowing what to search for, Talon's superior sight recognizes the bridge, and it is like the others I have found earlier on our path, but the first three paces are no more. It is evidence a battle has once played out here. Not knowing the how of it, I realize I must get Roux to the mæge ship and my friends.

Withdrawing from Talon, I settle back into my own body and mind to contemplate how I can save my sister and get her back to the temple. Contacting Sæm and Alænèa will not be a problem. Getting passed a dozen and six assassins, mercenaries, and a mind mæge will be a near impossible challenge. My newfound mægic skills will be needed.

Sitting back against a tree as I have become inclined to do while removing myself to the solace of my *Knowing*, I stroke Jilly's tummy absently and gaze over to my sister who sits cross-legged with Bane's great head in her lap. She stares blankly while fingering the deep fur about his ears. Pondering a good bit on my task at hand, I finally formulate a scheme and go over it countless times in my mind to tackle each of its flaws before becoming satisfied it is a solid plan. My first step is to contact my friends. They will be crucial and I must put them in grave danger, which I am loath to do but feel trapped by the circumstances.

Searching my pack, from deep within I retrieve a small cylindrical leather tube that was once sent to me around the neck of Bane. Pulling from it a scrap of parchment, I search and find my quill and sealed ink bottle. Unfurled, I read again its contents and my thoughts immediately fall to Finnie, for it is the very same note that was sent to me discussing her arrival to my Middenvale friends. It is over a year since we parted, and my heart hurts to think on it. Reaching out to Talon, I await his arrival, knowing he will come.

I write my scheme on the back of the note and send it off with Talon to the 'Odyssey.' Preparing a cold meal for Roux and myself, I await Talon's return. It is dark but I cannot rest. The trees rustle about me and my senses are on hyper-alert. Every sound seems the sound of my enemy approaching. The chill penetrates to the bone. When finally Talon returns, I lie back in fitful sleep for but a few turns of a sand glass.

Before dawn I rise and begin my preparation. I will be attempting a greater mægic than I have ever attempted before. My plan is to *not* confront Mensæ or his assassins at all. Stealth is my objective.

I prep Bane and Jilly for their parts. Bane is to be Roux's guide and protector at all costs. Jilly her calming spirit beast. Roux is to follow Bane, no matter what is happening. She has been doing just that for the past moon and is comfortable with it. I tie a tether betwixt the two of them, two paces are as far apart as they can get. I place a clothe sling about Roux's shoulder and head to be Jilly's home under her chin and against her breast, there to soothe and encourage. With staff and amulet alive to my thoughts, I begin to gather and trigger the needed mægic.

With moisture from stream and sea, I gather the mægic, and will a dense fog to form above the sea and creep in and over the sandy beach. From the stream aside me I do the same, the fog growing thicker and drifting towards the cliff. Sæm should already be on his way to shore. I will the shrouding mist and fog to grow ever high against the ground. Beads of sweat tickle my forehead from the effort in spite of the chill air.

Before setting out, I remove the tinker's amulet from my neck and place it about Roux's. Taking my bow in hand, I set off slowly towards the pathway that descends from the cliff's edge to the beach. Bane follows with my sister's hand tight about the rein around his neck. The veiling fog hides all but the tops of our heads, I hope. I cannot be with Talon at the same time, so I've impressed upon him my need for him to watch for me.

After a nerve grinding quarter turn, we make the distance from treeline to clifftop across the thick grasses of the open terrain from there to here. Before descending the path, I look to the sea and can make out a mast, like a cattail stalk cleaving the sea fog towards shore on calm waters. Sæm. I breathe in a sigh. Ushering Bane and Roux onto the pathway before me, this will be the time we are most exposed. Glancing up the beach eastward, I'm hoping Mensæ's contingent of mercenaries there are lax, knowing the scouts above them will see their approaching foe first and alert them.

My hopes are dashed as Roux's foot sends an errant rock over the path's edge and tumbling down the cliffside. The sound is deafening to my ears, though I hope beyond hope that it is not heard further down the beach. Moments later I hear the call of the mercenaries, and then Talon's echoing screech above. All are alerted and I hurry Bane on. A third of the way down the cliffside, I pause at a switchback and gaze up. An assassin with bow appears at the cliff's edge thirty paces away, staring directly to us. As he yells and nocks his bow, I've already done the same and loosed my arrow, urging it straight and swift with a push of mægic. He falls over the edge, my arrow lodged deep in his chest. But I find myself winded in the effort. Gathering the mægic has brought me near to exhaustion, I am realizing.

Looking back to sea, I notice my shroud is failing as Sæm's skiff is pulling up to the dock. The sun has breached the horizon. I urge Bane and Roux on down the path. They are halfway to the beach now, directing Bane to the skiff at the dock. I stay put. Roux must make it, and I'll protect them from here for now. It is a good vantage to both beach and clifftop.

It is good that I do, as an assassin starts down the pathway and there are two more behind him ready to follow. Another bowman appears at the cliff's edge above me, and even as I loose an arrow at the descending man, that bowman does the same at me. In my *Knowing*, I am able to move enough to avoid a heart strike but take his arrow in a more than glancing blow to my side. Ignoring the strike, I pull an arrow, nock, and release. My arrow finds the man's chest, near his shoulder and he falls back. The first man falls into me and in the process knocks my staff that I had left leaning against the cliff wall. It slides over the edge of the pathway. His body, however, takes a blade thrown by a compatriot above.

I toss aside the assassin's dead weight and pull the blade from his back. My attackers have pulled back for a moment and I look and see Therrien running to help Roux, while Alænèa is loosing arrows into the quick advance of ten mercenaries. One falls to her arrow. Sæm has nearly reached the first attackers to fend them off as Therrien gets Roux to the boat. What astounds me most is the sight of the warrior Rieka, the very same that drove Roux and I from the island and almost into Mensæ's grasp. She passes Sæm and crashes into the onslaught of mercenaries and with long knife in one hand and short sword in the other, she is a flurry of lethal motion. Three quickly dead at her feet. But a fourth's sword has found purchase in her side.

I see Sæm look up to me, just before he engages... Our eyes meet and there is an intensity to our connection. He knows my will, I am sure of it. In my side vision now, as I turn to address my attackers, Ōdæn's sword in Sæm's hand is glowing and with one swipe, there are two foes less.

I must move, and I do, but up not down. I will my staff to me even as JabberJack did when we first met, and it responds. I've pulled the arrow from my side and replaced my bow upon my back.

39

Orakle and Vision

The mist is thick. I lean forward over the bow and wonder how Sæm can steer the boat through it. He's put a mægic breeze behind its small sail, as the sea is unnaturally calm in these wee turns of early morn. I gaze east at the sun cresting the sea's horizon. My head jerks to the cliff face as I hear a rock clatter down the wall, each crack of rock against rock echoing across the beach. Though the fog lies thick on the beach and above the cliff, the wall itself leaves Arias, Bane, and Roux in stark relief against it in the rising sun as they make their way down the narrow switchbacks of the steep trail downward. I know it well as we have scaled it thrice in the three fortnight we've been here to hunt for food during our wait for Arias to arrive. We held no doubt he would make it, even with Mensæ in pursuit. We were excited to see Talon swoop onto the mæge ship yester's eve but distressed to read his message.

Our skiff makes contact with the pier. With the echoing rock falling, I hear an almost simultaneous shout from further down the sands. A sentry stands upon a high boulder of a rock jetty a hundred paces eastward down the coastline. Another call echoes from the cliffs above. My heart begins to pound. Men begin to appear, climbing over the boulders. A lot of men and heavily armed. The mist is dissipating.

Leaping from the boat, I nock my first arrow. Aiming to take down a living human being. It will be another first. But they are heading towards dear friends with murder as their intent. Arias' sister seems to be walking in a daze, only moving because Bane is guiding her. Keeping her safe against the wall side of the pathway as they descend. Two of the soldiers of fortune are swifter than the rest and are already forty paces nearer to the pathway's exit onto the beach. An archer appears on the cliff's edge above, and I see Arias stop and nock an arrow.

Aiming with intent, I loose an arrow even as I see the archer above fall from the bluff above. A second arrow leaves Arias' bow and the two advance assassins go down even as Sæm and Rieka leap past me and onto the shore. A moment later, Therrien has tied off the skiff and is racing towards the pathway and Roux.

The huge Amæzonian is carrying a spear in one hand and a short sword in her other. Sæm has unsheathed Ōdæn's blade. Rieka pauses and looses her spear then runs again, quickly passing Sæm. Her long, muscular legs beat hard against the sand. Her throw is true where my next arrow misses, and moments later she is charging through the mercenaries, stopping most of them in their advance. Sæm arrives on her heels.

Therrien has reached Roux and is helping guide her back to the boat, but I spy two men that have slipped past Sæm and Rieka. One is headed towards Roux and Therrien while the other bounds up the pathway towards Arias. Dropping my bow and drawing my blade I start running as fast as I can towards them, yelling.

"Therrien, cut the tether!"

To his credit, he acts without thinking why, even as he turns to see why I am staring past him. But Bane knows and is already moving. The approaching killer hasn't a chance now.

"Alænèa, thank the fates for your quick thought. Help me! The lass, it is as if she is in a trance of a sort."

As best we can, we hurry Roux towards the boat. I look back over my shoulder, and the scene is chaos. Arias is not coming down the pathway but climbing instead. His staff's ends are glowing. Talon is sweeping the air about the upper cliffs, diving then retreating, only to screech an echoing war cry and dive from on high again. The raptor is clearly what has kept the assassins from attacking Arias from above. But the last of those from the beach is in a chase to catch him from below.

My gaze drifts to Sæm, fearing for his life. I need not have. I see Sæm dispatching the mercenary who has struck the blow to Rieka, even as she strikes down the last attacker from the beach.

"Therrien, go help Sæm with the Amæzonaen. She is wounded. I can handle Roux."

He nods and is off. I settle Roux in the bow of the boat below the gunwales and facing away from the beach. Jilly is tending to the underside of her chin as she absentmindedly rubs the furions ears and head. Surveying the top of the bluff once more, my eyes are drawn to movement at the chasm. I watch astounded as I see Arias high above running as if on thin air! Even as he reaches the other side, the thundering sound of a land-slide–rubble splashing the river and pounding the ground in the canyon floor–reaches us all. Sæm, Rieka, and Therrien turn to see what could have caused it.

As Sæm unties the skiff from the dock while his eyes are still on the scene above, we drift away from it. The only sound is that of the water lapping against the shore. Arias looks to have collapsed on the far edge of the canyon bluff, and three figures stand on the near side. He is safe for the moment.

The three turn their gaze to us for a time and then back across the chasm to Arias. One points away from us and downward, and I know what he is doing. Like the pathway down to the beach on this side of the canyon's mouth, there is another switchback trail leading up to the clifftop there on the far side and deeper into the canyon. It will take some time, but they will be able to reach Arias, and he appears unconscious.

A collective exhale leaves us all as we see Arias make his way to his feet. Almost immediately, I see Arias raise his hand to his head and stumble but then point his staff back across the chasm. One of the three falls a pace back and yells so that his echoing curse even reaches us. The three storm off. Arias clearly turns to us and Bane bellows out a blood-curdling howl. Arias raises his staff and then turns and walks off.

Sæm makes his way to the stern and gives Therrien a few orders regarding the skiff's sail while he takes the tiller to hand. Bane curls up at Roux's feet as she simply looks past us all. I look to Rieka and sit across from her. As I reach over to pull open her tunic, she slaps my hands away. I slap back at hers and she stares at me.

"I am fine."

"You are not fine. You were struck with a sword to the ribs. I have mæge healing and I'll see to it." She stares at me for a moment, then nods.

Sæm addresses us all now.

"Arias has asked us to get Roux back to the temple as soon as possible but the Orakle's Isle is right here, and they have a temple too. We will sail there first and see if anything can be done for Roux there, and Rieka also. My thanks, Rieka. You had my back there on the beach."

"And you, mine. Though I would rather have taken the head of the thug who did this to me myself." Sæm nods and smiles. I finish tending to her wound and see that though it is deep, no vital organs have been damaged. It will heal well.

I make my way up to the bow and sit down next to Arias' young sister. I know not what to do, so I wrap my arm about her shoulder and pull her to me. The soft sound of the sea against the bow is somehow comforting as my own body calms down from the stresses of the past turn. My psyche has buried that I have just killed a man. But my mind is also processing the greater threat that the mind mæges present to my friends, and mayhaps the whole of Aeryth into the future. My carefree days on the Plains have disappeared, and I am realizing the outside world is more than just an adventure and indeed is a very dangerous place.

***

Leaping to the top of the bluff, I swing my staff in a wide arch pushing outward and away from myself all the mægic I've gathered as I race back up the path. The exploding force of energy throws Mensæ and two other assassins to the ground and knocks the breath from them, incapacitating them for a bit, I hope. But it takes me to my knees also. I am light-headed and feeling weak. Of a sudden, a large mercenary, with a scar the length of his face from forehead to chin and traveling through his eye, bursts from the pathway I'd just leapt from and a blood rush clears my mind. I've no time to battle him so I sweep his legs from under him and take off at a run towards the chasm.

I look over my shoulder and see that Talon is keeping the thug fighting for his very life as I make my escape. The fog I'd conjured is now just wisps against the ground and swirls about my ankles. I am running to where I know the shattered monoliths lie where they will indicate to me where I'll find the bridge over the canyon. I fall back into my *Knowing* and focus on that one thing. Not slowing and looking very much like I am planning to jump from the cliff's edge, I bound down a half dozen stone steps and leap into the air in full stride. I've judged correctly and I find myself landing directly in the center of the pace wide bridge of stone crafted mayhaps a millennium ago by a mæge of great power.

I do not stop to consider his genius though but keep running across the bridge. I must quirk my head to and fro to keep its shape afore my eyes as it blends with the far cliff wall. It is a good choice I've made to not have stopped. I hear the stone cracking beneath me even as I take each step forward. Sixty unhesitating strides and I know I've made it across, but as

I turn to see what is happening behind me, a wave of vertigo overtakes me and my vision fades to…black. I do not feel the ground as it hits me hard on the back of my head. My last thought is that I've expended too much mægic…and the sky is a beautiful cerulean blue.

When I awaken, a wave of lightheadedness engine me once again as I strain to rise onto my elbows. Talon is circling above me and it takes me a moment to realize where I am. Rolling over to my hands and knees, the wooziness dissipates a little as I squeeze my eyes shut for a bit. Falling into my *Knowing* as I rise, I stiffen and look back across the canyon. I sense a pressure against my psyche and know immediately its cause. My mind locks down in defense. Mensæ and two others are staring back at me, and a fourth is struggling to his feet. Scarface will carry a few more, courtesy of Talon.

I strike back immediately. Channeling my mind maegic through the drægon bloodstone of my staff, I push back on the mind mæge's assault with all my will. I find I've entered his mind almost instantaneously, but just as quickly, his mind shuts out my push into it. Not before giving him the shock of his life, I suspect. I glare at him across the ravine as he of a sudden steps back, the blow to him like a physical strike. He screams out his fury, and it echoes into the chasm.

Turning to the sea, I raise my staff to my friends on the skiff as they head back to the mæge ship, my sister safe with them. Turning my back on Mensæ, I walk deliberately away, doing my best to walk steady and assuredly even as my vision is tunneled and my legs are shaky.

Somehow, I make it to the treeline and the forest trail leading away from the chasm cliffs. I do not head further down it, however, and choose a game trail I spy that leads in my chosen direction. My *Knowing* ever aware, a large tree's canopy catches my eye. It is there that I am headed, hoping for some respite and protection. My mind clears a little more even as I reach the far branches of the great tree. It is as I suspected. I call them mæge trees now, and I've encountered a handful in my travels. The same tree is depicted in the doors of the Azgärhd Isle temple and the Hexad's Council Chamber. This one with four distinct trunks, always one of an Æntwood tree.

The other trees, on the Accadian Plains and in the Deep Wood to its north, are the same. I feel a little rejuvenated as I approach the base of the tree, though I'm still exhausted beyond measure. Looking up into its branches, I have a thought. Removing my bow from my back, I wedge it and my staff tight in betwixt two trunks on the backside and away from the direction I arrived from. With a smile, I take a cue from a prank Alænèa once played on me. I pull my blade from my belt and carve a small rune into the tree trunk. Covering the rune with my right hand, I place my left upon my bow and staff and say the name of the rune. The bow and staff disappear, camouflaged perfectly within the tree. With a sigh of determination, I start climbing the tree. Six paces up, I find what I am searching for. The trunks spread apart here, and where they do, a small nook opens betwixt them. I settle within it, feeling safe and secure. Even as I do, Talon alights on the extended branch. He is perching on one leg and I can see the other is injured. I beckon him to me, and he hops into my lap and nuzzles into my chest. Reaching under his body, I gently grasp his injured leg, and as I delve into his body to give some healing, darkness envelops me.

***

(Sæm)

The bay we arrive into at the Orakle's Isle is small with one long and a dozen shorter docks lining a wide wooden pier. The village about the bay is home to a few hundreds at most. The buildings are stuccoed clay, painted in bright colours with red and orange and grey roof tiles. Behind the village on a hillside green with thick foliage of palms and fruit trees that I am finding are typical to small isles, clearly stands our destination. A temple that is the smaller sister to the one on Azgärhd.

I still marvel at this ship as it glides silently towards the pier. I see a number of townsfolk making their way to the docks as we arrive. We will have a welcoming party to greet us. I drop the sails as I judge we have enough momentum to reach the pier. Therrien and Rieka toss the tether ropes to a few dockhands. I go below to gather and escort Roux. When I come back topside, the outside gunwales have been opened and the gang-plank set to the dock. The others are already speaking to our greeting party.

It is midsun, and the skies are clear. The sounds of a typical fishing village greet me. I can see the fishermen have by now sold their catches in an open market on the pier at the end of the docks. The sights and sounds, however, do not make it any easier to forget that we have just left a battle for our very lives, only to have once again lost contact with Arias.

"We've explained what has happened back on the beach in the Breachlands, Sæm. Szil and Labena here have offered to accompany us to the temple." Alænèa nods towards the two. They are garbed alike, two young acolytes akin to those on Azgärhd with rune patches sewn to their tunics.

"We are much obliged for your aid. Vicchi of the Azgärhd temple speaks highly of your temple healer, and we are in need." The two offer a short head bow. The others of our greeting party seem more interested in our vessel.

Alænèa places Jilly's sling back around Roux's neck and shoulder, and the furion takes her place tight to Roux's breast. Our two acolyte guides lead us down the pier into the heart of the village and directly to the road that clearly heads to the temple. The village buildings and townsfolk are no different from the dozen or so that I have now seen in my travels, save one exception. As I look about I cannot help but notice the dozens upon doz-ens of maggies perched everywhere—on fences and roof ridges and even in window sills. The birds I have become familiar with in Esper, trained and housed by Giorgi, are present here in greater numbers by tenfold. What is more, they seem very curious in us as we pass by.

Shaking the feeling of being spied upon by the birds, we continue up the roadway out of the town and into the hills, our destination clearly in sight now. My hope is the healer there can help Roux. If so I plan to carry on with my travels along the coast of the Northern Reaches, following the direction that Arias is headed in.

As we reach the doors of the temple, my feeling in that regard is strengthened; upon the doors stands embossed the same mæge tree that is found on the Azgärhd temple. As a pair of maggies look on from perches on either side of the massive doors, our acolyte guides stand before them and utter in ancient mægic speech, the words necessary to unlock the doors. Once done, the great doors, three pole high and half a pace thick, open with the slightest push from the smallest lass guiding us.

We are greeted by the wizened Mœther Superior of the temple's order. She is clearly expecting us. Her eyes sparkle, and I want to hug her more than pay deference to her.

"Come, come, guests. I am Diantha. Libena, please escort this young lass to my surgery. Roux, is it? Oh, and her little ferret and the dread wolf also, I see. Do not worry for her. She is in good hands now." Looking back to us, she seems not at all bothered that a dread wolf whose height reaches near to her shoulders has followed us into the temple. My heart leaps for Roux even as I wonder how the Mœther Superior knows her name and ailment.

"So you can heal her, Mœther Diantha?"

"Fates, no. I can calm her psyche for a time and her body as well, for your trip back to Azgärhd, but her deeper upset can only be cured by mind mægic such as Vicchi can gather. And please, Diantha will suffice for my part. Formalities are not necessary." My heart falls once more...for Roux and Arias.

423

"Szil, please take our guests to the refectory garden. Let me see, you are clearly Eshæm Bearheart, and I've exchanged messages with Therrien here though he knows me as Heræ, I believe." At this, Therrien's eyes widen.

"You are Eschereon's great aunt? I've sent his missives by Giorgi's maggies from time a'times! Oh, the maggies, they are everywhere here on the isle." Diantha chuckles aloud.

"Great aunt? Is that what he calls me? Bless his soul. I was there for the birth of his great aunt, so I'll take it as a compliment, ha!

"Well, now, the other two of you are easy to place. Alænèa from the Plains and of the bloodline there, so my sister tells me, and Rieka, warrior guard to Hippolæta, queen to the Amæz. My sister, Delphæa, is ecstatic to meet you all. She can speak of nothing else! But first, you must relax and have a bite and a sip in our gardens. It will do your souls good. Szil will see to it. I will meet you there when I get Roux here settled."

I wonder at the woman's age and that she treats us as my grandmere would. We follow Szil on a twisting labyrinth of halls until we come to a large courtyard garden somewhere in the center of the temple. The garden is open to the sky above and there are several women and young lasses milling about, either in conversation or eating at a number of small stone tables with stone benches adjacent. We are led to one of these, and Szil excuses herself. We get a number of glances and nods from everybody close by. Others further away make a point of passing by us for a casual inspection.

We sit about the table. Rieka eschewing the benches, sits cross-legged on the ground next to us. The table, even still, is not at a comfortable height for her. It seems only a moment and the table is filled with a variety of fare, from fishes to fruits and steaming root vegetables. Three large flasks of water and wine accompany the feast.

"Eschereon, it seems, has friends in every part of Aeryth. And if few others have ever visited the Northern Reaches, he knows them well, sure certain. Vicchi also. And the age of his friends is astounding. And how is it that Diantha's sister is excited to meet us? Vagabonds all, save Rieka here."

"Mayhaps it is our mægic, and tales Eschereon has sent her," says Alænèa.

Therrien pipes in now.

"He has not, and I would know. I write and deliver his messages to Giorgi to be sent by his maggies."

"Then I wager this Delphæa is a Seer, like the elder in my village back home. If so, I am anxious to meet her as well. Mayhaps she can tell us how we might aid Arias."

The scents of lavender and other plants in the garden seem to engulf me as we take our meal, and I am heavy-handed with my own cup and the wine. I soon find myself fully relaxed, the stress of the earlier sun now drained from me. Diantha had the right of it. Arias' plight somehow escapes me for a time.

She joins us after a turn.

"Well then, have you had your fill?" she queries, even as she sits down across from me and next to Alænèa and grabs an apple from the fruit basket.

"We have, thank you. How is Roux?"

"Roux is doing fine and presently asleep."

"But you cannot help her further? We were hoping... Arias will be needing us."

"Nay, young Eshæm. I can see you are a great friend to those about you and most certain, Arias. Let us be off to see my sister. She is insistent on meeting you, all of you, and she mayhaps will have news of Arias too. She has the *Sight*. I believe you might have guessed by now."

"I thought as much. Your comments remind me of the elder in my home village."

"Ah yes, the handsome young man with the deep blue eyes. Does he still favor his tea from the isles?"

"Arias said he offered him tea when they met."

"Hmmm. He would be especially anxious to meet your friend…Well, then," Diantha slaps the palms of her hands on the table. "I see that you've settled a bit. Let us be off to visit my sister, eh? She has sent a lass to me, insisting that we all meet." The plump lady winks at us and rises from the table, reaching back for a few grapes. We follow her out of the garden.

Winding our way through a number of more halls, we come upon another set of great doors. A light music–I cannot tell what instruments–lightly surrounds us and follows us through the doors.

Here we are greeted by an all-encompassing calm, one that I know well from my own personal *Calming.* The music is still about, and water trickles down a far rock wall. From there, it streams lightly into a shallow basin in the stone floor, which at its center becomes a faster swirling whirlpool before disappearing altogether. It is not a chamber at all, but rather an enclave out of doors. The sun's light beams down from above here and there, and warming the entire space but leaves shade and shadow for a respite from it as well. Sitting cross-legged at the basin's edge is a woman with a timeless look about her. She smiles and looks right through us.

"Ha! You carry it with you, Eshæm. Ōdæn's blade. And Alænèa, even still in your pockets you carry two manna seeds from the Mœther on the Plains. You have chosen well. And Therrien, you carry quill and ink and parchment in your bag. Ever the scribe. Finally, Roux's guardian, you also have chosen a rightful path, as she will need you more than the queen of the isle."

I look to Rieka in a new light just then, and I see that it is true. She is bowing her head and sighing at the words. Therrien claps his hand to his bag and Alænèa reaches into her pocket. All things seen by the lady at the basin, even as I can see that she herself is blind in all but her S*ight.*

"Come sit with me, friends. I have waited countless years to meet you in the flesh… These are exceptional times indeed. But please, hold hands if you will, and with me close the circle. I would look on how things have changed from the Source-Sayers' first scheme and mayhaps give a little guidance."

"The Source-Sayers? Of ancient lore in the libraries in Esper and the temple at Azgärhd? What have they to do with us?"

"Roux can explain further once she is able, Eshæm. But suffice it here to say that you are all their children; heirs to their mægic. It is a grand experiment in the making, and it is the hope they have given to all of Aeryth." Her voice is soft and soothing, barely more than a whisper, but each word spoken rings crystal clear to my ears.

With brief glances to then fro, we each find a place and sit around the shallow pond. Even as we do, it turns an inky black.

"Please, clasp your hands and close our circle with me and each and the other of you."

When we have seated, it feels natural to me to fall into my *Calming* even as Arias has taught me. If her words were the slightest bit soft a moment ago, when we are all joined they ring as clear now as if she is whispering directly into my ear alone.

A soft exhale escapes her lips and I sense she is settling deep into her mægic S*ight.* For long moments, nothing happens, and then a calming warmth envelops me. I glance lazily about our circle and see that all the others are relaxed and serene and gazing down into the inky indigo waters of the basin. My eyes follow and I am captivated. The swirling waters are coalescing into a scene, and I am being sucked into it, as if falling from the sky. The scene expands and becomes more lifelike as I speed in descent towards it. Is this how a Seer feels when experiencing a S*ight?*

Swoosh. I alight near to the ground like a bird to a branch except I am not outdoors. I am in a great hall with soldiers lining three deep along the walls to each side. Court dignitaries are bunched about the lower steps of a dais. I am on one knee and garbed in a soldier's leathers and iron. Ōdæn's blade is sheathed upon my back. I am larger and taller than my present being, and still, the sword is too large to carry on my waist. Somehow, I recognize that I am in Kings Court. In front of the king as he descends the steps of the dais and looks down upon me. He touches my shoulder and leans further to whisper into my ear. *The scene dissolves and becomes another.*

I am on the deck of the mæge ship and looking back into the seas about me. Fifty large vessels are following, each waving the king's flag. I look solemn and in deep thought. *Darkness envelops me.*

A sunbeam awakens me. My friends lie about me in similar stages of wakefulness. The shallow pond is still there between us all, now crystal clear again. Delphæa is no longer with us.

"A sleepy bunch, the lot of you are. Dozing the whole of this after-highsun. If you can rouse yourselves, I've some sustenance in the refectory garden, and mayhaps a little conversation afore you take leave of us. I've a parting gift for each of you if you will have them." Diantha exclaims, playing the part of great sent to all of us.

At evemeal, we discuss what we had seen in the Seer's pool, each a different tale. I sense now that my fate must diverge from that of Arias'. It seems all of ours do. Each of our individual fates await us now. I wish good tidings to my friend as he makes his way towards his destiny, and I hope we will meet again.

***

I spring awake and find myself soaring high above the treetops. My attention is far below. Three riders are exiting the trees on a travelway heading towards the setting sun and a good-sized town in the distance.

Instinctively I know who they are. Mensæ, his assassin chief, and

Scarface, his mercenary captain and guide. We leave them and fly north. Within sight of the cliffs and the sea below, another town appears. I determine it is my next destination. Leaving Talon, I awaken from my *Knowing*, once again in my mæge tree niche. I sit up and take stock.

40

Black Market and Slave King

(Rõghæn)

I open my eyes to a throbbing pain in my head and close them immediately. Confused and not knowing where I am, I venture another try,
more slowly this time. I hear a throaty groan and then realize it is coming
from me. As I try to raise my head…or what is left of it–as it must surely
be in a screw vice in some dungeon's torture chamber–spins the world too
fast and I'm taken by nausea, which makes it only as far as my throat to add
a burn to my misery. I taste blood. I hear sobbing. *Elsii*!?

"Elsii?" It comes out as a thick whisper.

"Oh, Rõghæn! I thought you might be dead. But then not, cause they
tied you to the chair. You were bleeding so…and I couldn't reach you to
stop it. They've tethered me to the leg of this table, and you are just out of
reach."

I realize I am indeed tied to a chair. My arms are useless. I manage
to finally open my eyes and lift my head. It feels no better but not worse.
Two small square windows, high on a wall to my left, stream two identical
beams of late sunlight, laden with heavy dust particles. I see Elsii at the
end of one. Her leg is shackled and tethered to a table holding a few small
crates, canvas sacks, and what looks to be a ledger book lying open. A slow
survey of the room in front of me–I don't dare turn my head too far left nor
right–holds more of the same. Crates, barrels, and sacks. A closed door sits

below the windows and which I assume, is locked. Another table, a desk, is directly in front of me.

"What has happened, Elsii? I cannot recall any of it."

"We were attacked on the trail out from the bazaar, Master Rōghæn. They waited in a tree with low branches hanging over the road. One swung down and hit you with a club straight on, and you fell right over the side and to the ground. Another climbed up my side of the wagon and grabbed me. Huni leapt out at him though. Started clawing and biting at his face so's he let go. Ooh, but Rōghæn, another still! He climbed up on your side to grab the reins, and when he saw Huni, he stabbed her! Now...she is dead too." I watch as the poor lass bows her head into her lap and sobs so as to near break my heart.

When she finally raises her head again, I am thinking clearly once more, trying to deduce the intent of highwaymen who would bring us to a place such as this.

The Mind Mæge who we came across in the bazaar.

Elsii whispers more now.

"Her cubs stayed hidden though. We got to get back to them." She wipes her eyes on her sleeve and looks to me. I nod back, a small bit of assurance I'm in no position to give.

"It's the man with the dark eyes, isn't it? The one we saw at the bazaar and that was at the summit at our lodge?"

I nod, sure certain it is.

We are startled as the lock of the door rattles and opens. Two men walk in and our suspicions are confirmed. The first a brute with muscled arms and then the mæge. The thug moves to stand behind me, and the mæge pulls out a chair and sits at the table across from me.

There is silence as he studies me.

"I'm called Marlowe, druid. It is my great fortune to meet you." He holds a long dirk which he pointedly stabs ever so lightly into the tabletop

431

and spins with his thumb and index finger before laying it aside and turning for a moment to look at Elsii, his brow furrowing. I need turn his attention to me.

"Druid? You mistake me for a character from a book of fables and lore? I'm but a tinker who's been waylaid by your thugs. My wagon's goods stolen, I assume?" This elicits a tight smile as he turns back to me and away from Elsii.

"You wish to play games?" His smile is malicious. "Two of your brethren have suffered the ultimate penalty to such things. The others will soon follow in their footsteps, or yours, mayhaps. It matters not. I only need one of you to bring before the council. One mind peeled open will do just fine."

"And who is this council that would decide the fate of a tinker that has done nothing wrong?"

"Hmph. Very well, I'll play your game. The council are the whispers in the ears of Aeryth's great rulers and noble families. They are nobles themselves, gathering armies for the battles to come. Battles to wrench the whole of Aeryth from the likes of you, druid, and then they, *we*, will find and return the traitorous Elders to Destineæ to face the wrath of the Three Eye Council."

The thought of the likes of this man capturing even one Source-Sayer of old and transporting him across the sea makes me snicker. In small part they will be sorely disappointed to find that Source-Sayers no longer exist. But, the mind mæges' threat to Aeryth is quite real. And if what he claims about the others is true, he alone is a very dangerous man. *Mæge*. I do not forget for long.

He turns quiet again, but not inactive. I feel his mind touching mine. It has been a long time since I've experienced this. The Wic'cha temple mœther was the last to do it to me. The last mind mæge in all of Aeryth, we thought, and one of the Druidæ. She was preparing us should we ever find ourselves in this very situation. She had given us each a ring that we should

432

always wear as protection. Fortunately, I have heeded her advice, as her lesson was brutal. The ring warms about my finger.

"If I was not convinced before meeting you, I am now, druid. You might be able to repel my attempts but not Mensæ's. There are sometimes more direct methods that work, in any case." His eyes glance up to the thug behind me, and he in turn lays a very sharp blade against my throat.

Elsii immediately rises at the sight of this, and I *will*, with my mind and with all my might, that she sits down again and not draw attention to herself. *To no avail.* But she is no longer a sobbing younger. To my astonishment, she starts to wave her arms as if pulling and pushing the air around her, waving and grabbing at apparently nothing. Her face is a study in extreme concentration and the eyes of both men are drawn to her.

I recognize it, as I've seen it previously when she sat atop the wagon, summoning and pushing the colours of mægic she sees and moving leaves and branches about with it. She whispers in a tight voice now.

"What is your lass doing, druid?" Both their attentions are drawn to Elsii now. I do not have time to explain that she is gathering colours… mægics, from the air about her.

"You were there…at the Summit. You spoke the most with Lady Maya, deep into the night." I'm not looking at the mind mæge but drawing his attention all the more.

Marlowe's eyebrows raise in a manner that cannot belie the fact it takes him totally unawares. While this transpires, I watch as his blade rises ever so slightly above the tabletop and Elsii continues to wave, push, and pull her hands and arms, appearing a crazy, unhinged younger to our two hosts, no doubt.

"Who *are* you lass?"

"Your friend Lady Maya and Mensæ killed Mummy and Poppa, and you think you will kill Mæster Rõghæn and me now. *YOU WILL NOT!*" Her eyes suddenly turn to Marlowe.

A push forward with both her hands leaves me astounded as the mind mæge's own dirk instantly lifts off the tabletop before him and a fraction of a moment later finds itself embedded to its hilt in the right eye of Marlowe. His lips are still moving as the thug behind me steps back in the shock of seeing it happen. Elsii immediately turns towards Marlowe's man, and I cannot see but hear a gurgle and then he falls to the side of me. His blade, moments ago tight against my neck, now deep into the soft underside of his chin and up into his brain.

Elsii looks to me, and I see concern in her face but no remorse as she collapses to the floor herself.

Moments later, the door bursts inward and off its hinges as Illéron, Asgährd's Ranger, and Eschereon rush through, looking to face off against the mind mæge.

"Mithur! Your timing is almost impeccable." The two of them assess the scene, and Eschereon queries me.

"You've managed just fine without our aid, I see Rőjj…even bound to a chair!" He seems quite impressed and a little puzzled, but I see relief in his eyes also.

"I cannot claim credit… It was Elsii. And could you take a moment and unbind the two of us?" Eschereon comes to me and tends to my knots as Illéron releases Elsii's tether.

"Is she okay?" he asks, and I nod.

"She's just performed a trying bit of mægic on her own, and it has taken a good bit of her energy reserves, I would suppose. She will be fine physically. It is the mental part I am most worried about."

"Mithur, you have not, by chance, come across my wagon?"

"Yea, Rőjj. It is parked in the mæge's courtyard out back. We saw it as we crossed from his gaols to this warehouse and show blocks."

I have an idea of what he means as I fear Marlowe mayhaps dealt in more than physical goods. A black market slaver as well, I judge. But that tale can wait.

"Illéron, could you carry the lass out of here for me? It would not do to have her wake and see this scene again. Please lead me to my wagon, Mithur, if you would be so kind."

On the way, I tell them of the manner and loss of Elsii's spirit beast, and that it had probably been the inciting incident to push her use of her mægic the way she had.

Arriving to the courtyard, I bid Illéron to set Elsii down against some sacks piled against the warehouse wall. Walking over to my wagon, I pull a piece of jerky from my robe and split it in two. Approaching the buckboard seat, I wave the jerky to the underside of it and patiently wait. Huni's two cubs make an appearance and take the proffered treat and let me lift them out of their hidey-hole and carry them over to Elsii. I place them on her lap.

The two still tiny cubs, after finishing their jerky, climb the front of Elsii's tunic and settle, one to each shoulder. Reaching into her chin and neck, they begin to nuzzle and lick the lass. When she wakes to find Huni's cubs about her, she pulls them in and cradles them like a mœther would her babes. She looks up to me, and her warm smile melts this old man's heart.

I pull Mithur aside and query him.

"The mæge knew of us…has been spying on us at the bazaar, Mithur. He bragged that he has killed two of us and has assassins following the others."

"There is a sorry bit of truth to it, I'm afraid. We've lost one brœther, Ferryn, but no other. We discovered the mæge's plot with the one death and then his sloppy assassins followed Illéron and myself. We, in turn, were able to foil two other attempts…and almost made it in time to rescue you."

"Well, I'll forgive your tardiness as you seemed to be quite busy, and in any case, I'm fortunate to travel with a very capable apprentice and ward."

"Aye, she is that, sure certain. We'll need to adjust our plans a bit now, Rőjj. But you've solved the issue with Marlowe and that is to our advantage. Our foe, however, will learn of it soon enough and we must plan for that."

Mithur and Illéron have freed a dozen youngers hidden in the bowels of Marlowe's warehouse here on the outskirts of the city where they were being made ready for the blocks…being readied for sale to a select clientele. That will not happen now.

Taking a seat next to Elsii in her place against the warehouse wall before we leave, I ask how she is doing.

"I've found more perfect names for Huni's cubs, Rõghæn. Bark and bite will no longer do. This here is Puffy, 'cause of the way she puffs up her cheeks when she reaches in good kisses. And this is Lumps, 'cause he's the clumsy one. But together, they are the softest, most huggable team ever… PuffyLumps!"

If she ever wants to talk about what had happened inside, I'll be there for her.

Illéron makes arrangements for the bodies of Marlowe and his henchmen to 'disappear.' Who will follow in his footsteps we do not know, but they will be watched. The Ranger assures Eschereon and I that he will make those arrangements.

Elsii and I set out again. I will be more aware of my surroundings this time. Assignments have changed amongst our group with the loss of one of our own and one of mind mæges. We are headed to the south and west, to Coffs Harbour.

41

Reckoning

Understanding I must not pause for long, I ne'er the lesser settle into a chair at a corner table across the dining hall from the tavern's entrance. It has been three moons since I last ate a meal in such a place, surrounded by common folk and not mæges nor enemies outside my campsite. There are laughter and scents of food and pipeweed wafting in the warm air as it spreads from a large fireplace set in the very center of the hall. It conveniently blocks the sightlines from the door and that suits me as an extra protection. I order a large portion of roast pork, and it arrives charred and sauced nicely with a heaping pile of garlic mashed taters and glazed carrots aside. I tuck in, feeling normal again if only for the night. There is music and a bard, and the ale is good.

I wash in the inn's bathhouse and later sink into a soft bed in one of the guest rooms. I open the window to let the cool breeze penetrate the room, and to my surprise, Talon swoops and settles upon the window's sill. I will sleep feeling safe this eve.

On the morrow's morn, I search out the town's stables to find a horse. I've decided where I'm headed as my night in the mæge tree left me with a *vision*. In it, the sun sets into the sea with the mountains to my back. The vision portends that I would travel to the west coast of Aeryth, as that is the only place I could witness such a thing and that felt like a good decision to me. Da had recited tales of visiting the shores of the western sea, and if I am to die at the hands of Mensæ and his assassins, I decide I would like to visit such a place before that fate befalls me. Also, as a trip to the Western Sea would take a few fortnights at a pace to stay ahead of my foes, it would give me time to better hone my mægic abilities and better prepare to face them.

I travel now perpetually in my *Knowing,* and it is becoming a phenomenal learning experience with mægic. When in the past the colours of different mægic auras visited upon me oft times only in a peripheral sense unless in my *Knowing* and focusing on them, now I am seeing the colours of mægic everywhere. Being able to see them, I find that I can gather specific mægic at will, with only my thought to guide them. I realize that the amulet I wore about my neck before surrendering it to my sister, had been doing this for me.

I also find that I can 'store' gathered mægic within the stones of my staff and thus build upon the gathered energy. This will save me from the draining effect upon my body when I expel the mægic, as there is no effect on myself as I release the energy from the staff.

I have been traveling for two fortnight now, with no sight of my enemy. Jabberjack explained to me that Mensæ, having connected to me mind to mind, will always be able to find me given enough time. Traveling constantly makes this harder, but inevitably we will meet again. My intent is to be ready when the time comes. Meanwhile, I gather and store two different mægics within my two staff stones, drægon-tooth and drægon-fire, as Da had named them. One mægic is of the elements and I've gathered it during storms I've ridden through. The other is a mind mægic that I have named chaos and hold in the drægon firestone. It is the same mægic that turned away a slave trader in the middle of the road as he headed directly for me with evil intent in his mind. It was carried in my amulet at that time.

Life becomes an easy routine, stopping for the night from time a'time in a village or towne I pass through, to bathe and eat properly and join in fellowship and an ale with the everyday folk that I meet. These are the times that thoughts of Roux visit me. I feel sure that Sæm and Alænèa have safely rescued her. But the damage to her mind weighs heavy on me. I should have thought to give her my tinker's amulet. Will Vicchi be able to reverse the damage I've allowed to happen to my sister? I've refused to call myself prey, yet those about me suffer for even being in my presence. I admit am surely hunted still. A reckoning will come; sure certain. If Mensæ wins, will my family and friends be safe even then? I think not, and it makes my predicament that more dire. The rest of Aeryth be dammed, it is they who are most important. This weight is becoming unbearable, and I know not if I am up to the task.

In an all too short a time, the faraway Western Mountains are no longer so, and I've reached the last towne afore them. The mountain scene now is one of jagged peaks of gray, which the locals call the Dragons Teeth. In the sunset, the name seems appropriate. I settle into a loud and bustling inn the stableman has suggested, and I am thankful for the recommendation. The owners remind me of Johan and Susii of Seas End where I plotted the demise of Lord Tullamoor. The food is brilliant and the master innkeep sits and regales folk of tales in proper bard fashion. The ale is good.

Sitting across from the innkeep my second night there, I query him, late into the eve.

"Hrókr, I have traveled to the west, to the outskirts of towne, and see no trail to the west. Is there no way to the sea from here?"

"Why would you want to go to the sea? There is nothing there. It is just the end of Aeryth and no more. Sand and sea monsters as what the lore is. They say the sand and mountains run on forever…all rock and little sustenance. The depths creep up to the shoreline and so fishing is near to impossible without a boat, and the winds and waves are harsh. There is a lake so large that is hard to see across, a few leagues south of here, if water is what you are after."

"Nay, I long to see the sun setting into the sea."

"You are a strange one, lad, but I have a friend, a man who can show you the way if you insist on going. Promise me you'll come back with the tale of a sea monster if you spot one, eh?" We both laugh. And I tell him a few tales of the beasts in the Breachlands, and he listens intently.

His friend, who knows a way, draws for me a map but tells me a horse cannot make it through the mountains. "Mountain goats, wildcats, and men with no sense" are his thoughts about it.

With my horse traded and new quiver and arrows acquired, I set off on a very chilly morn, two suns hence. The way is easy for a sun, but I soon learn why a horse is not an animal equipped for such a trip. The way wends and winds through increasingly more treacherous ground aside the mountainside I have climbed. Ne'er the lesser I always head west. I've purchased trail supplies but hope there will be small game available. My thoughts are on looking out onto the open sea as in my dream, though deep down, I sense the vision portends a greater event.

Three suns' travel across narrow, mountainside trails through long, jutting and jagged boulders pushing through the ground at different angles, brings me to an eve in which I can hear the sea in the distance, spy gulls overhead, and smell that familiar scent that is all-telling. I camp knowing that on the morrow, I will have truly crossed the breadth of Aeryth. I'm hit with a few searing thoughts and feelings. My life and days with Da, not my true pæder, but truly my pæder; my friends are closer to me now than more than a year's in passing, just down this coastline and inland a bit; and Finnie. My heart aches in this last regard. I must settle accounts with Mensæ if I am ever to see her again.

The morn's meal is sparse and I am anxious at any rate, so I am off early, sensing I am close to my vision's reveal. I do not understand its true meaning, but I recognize that it is significant. Visions always are.

At midsun I round a bend and I am hit in the face with a stiff breeze as the sea is revealed in all of its vast glory. The sounds of it are, of a sudden, all-enveloping. Waves lap against a sandy shore and rock jetties, backdropped against fast-rising mountains, both barring the sea and offering it bits and pieces of itself. An age-old battle. The sound rhythmic and relentless. The gulls are dancing in the air and feasting at the water's edge, singing a chaotic chorus of caws and shrieks. I stretch and take it in. Like its sister to the far east, there is little to see afore the far off horizon, where in the east the sun is born and here I'll see it fall away and disappear again. I wonder what could be beyond that horizon.

Making my way down to the sands, I cross to a pier of rock extending fifty paces out into the pounding surf. The sea lapping against the rocks is dark and full of mystery here as I make my way to its furthest point. Near the shore, the waters seem almost angry, but here at the jetty's end, there is a calm. Sitting on a flat boulder, at the farthest point west that I can spy, I pull my pack from my back and lie down, using it as a pillow. Delving into my *Knowing* I experience a deeper calm than I've felt in many moons. I linger with its influence, the sun upon my face, and a soft breeze inspiring me to breathe deeper still.

I awaken with a pressing urge to travel south along the shoreline, and so I do. The sun has already crept halfway down towards the watery horizon. I have the will and press of a man nearing a fate he knows awaits. I am both at peace and carrying the weight of my destiny with each and every step, my *Knowing* keeping my mind sharp and taking in everything around me in singing detail. But all remains silent save the lap of the waves upon the shore.

The sky grows lavender nearer to shore even as burning shades of yellow and orange and reds hang farther on the horizon as the sun has grown in size before my eyes. I sit on the sands and watch a scene I'd witnessed a few fortnight previous while dreaming, 'tis identical. I expect the sun to set the sea sizzling and steaming as it makes contact legions of leagues out to sea. The sight is stunning but my imagination has outstripped the reality of it. Even as the sun rises out of the Eastern Sea with growing brightness with no reaction from those waters, the setting sun is accepted into the Western Sea with an incredible calm.

It leaves me in a similar calm. My psyche was expecting more, I realize, but it is simply the end of another sun. I quickly gather wood that is plentiful at the toe of the mountainside and build a fire. Shedding my pack, I dig within it to retrieve the last of trail bread and jerky I've left of my stock and settle about my small fire for its warmth. No great clash with destiny this night.

A shiver pulls my eye open. My fire's embers wane in the pre-dawn. But that is not why I am aroused. Fifty paces down the beach in the direction I'd arrived from, three shadowy figures stand on the further side of a great driftwood log. The moonlight reflects off some metal on the tunic collar of one and then off the tip of a nocked arrow in his bow. I squeeze my staff as it lies aside me. On instinct alone, I raise it above the sand and send my will through it.

A sky bolt explodes…from my staff's drægon tooth end. Rolling right, I feel and hear an arrow thud into the sand where a moment earlier I lay. But in that same moment, I watch as my mægic crafted sky bolt bursts apart the chest of the assassin who had fired the arrow. The light of it reveals the two other figures at his side…Scarface and Mensæ.

The two of them disappear behind the log they were standing behind. I do not wait for them to reappear. Grabbing my pack, I spring up and in four strides I am ascending the rocky mountainside. I run away from my pursuers and climb into the slope, throwing my pack over my head one-handed, somehow finding a way to cinch it tight even on the run. Stopping a moment to glance back as I reach a ledge I can stand upright upon, I see Mensæ following me aways back. I have no sight of Scarface. I look forward and see a hundred paces ahead a cleft in the mountainside, mayhaps a cave, and a position to defend from. I make for it. Mensæ is climbing now.

The mægic I have gathered in the other end of my staff is meant for Mensæ. A quarter turn passes as I make my way to the cliffside cave. As I reach its mouth, I turn and back in, looking to spy the progress of Mensæ and to catch a glimpse of the other mayhaps. Mensæ is still following, and there is still no sign of the other. Turning back to assess the cleft I have entered, I see it is a much deeper cave than I was expecting and I reason it favors me in my defense. Even as these thoughts materialize, however, a heavy thump sounds behind me. Scarface appears, falling from the outside top of the cave entrance. As he rises from the cave's entrance floor, his longsword is already in his hands and he is approaching me with it swinging to and fro in a ferocity I've never experienced.

Instinct takes over. I find myself with short sword in one hand and throwing blade in another. Neither is a match for his weapon in offense, but defense is my only thought at the moment. He has me backing further into the cave, avoiding as best I am able his flurry of deadly swipes. And then he pauses…fully stops actually, and I do not think on it but flip my throwing blade in my hand and throw it, taking advantage. In my peripheral vision, it has lodged deep into his eye and he is crumbling even as I reach for my staff, aware that Mensæ is only moments away from reaching the cave's entrance.

Retrieving my staff and rising with the cave wall at my back, I turn to take stock of my surroundings once more. I stiffen and look back into the cavern's darkness. A reptilian eye stares back. It is a third my height and has two lids, top and bottom close over it, one then the other, then open again, and even as they do I am struck in my total consciousness with a swirling kaleidoscope of colours and sounds. The colours flash in blinding bursts and make my head throb in excruciating pain. I fall back against the cavern wall and slide, nearly paralyzed, down the wall.

I hear a deafening yell and somehow recognize it as my own. And then another joins it. This one an unholy screech, scraping painful cuts in my very soul. My *Knowing* is doing its best to wall off the attacks against my psyche. Every nerve is screaming now against what I perceive as attacks on my mind. A random thought reminds me of my staff in hand and I send my will into it. I know not where I am aiming it, just away and out, I hope, at whatever is causing this pain.

The yell I hear has stopped and as has the piercing screech. That alone is a little comfort. And darkness envelopes me. Also, the conscious pain, the sounds, and the kaleidoscope of bursting colours slips away… Why did I not come here sooner? Memories flood me in the darkness, and yet they are not familiar. *How can memories not be familiar?* But all is calm in these memories so I let them begin to flow, so as to examine them in my leisure. *Leisure?*

The scenes are no longer swirling so fast I cannot visit upon them. My mind seems to be sorting the images for me.

The darkness ruptures and I am, of a sudden, in the air and flying. Talon has somehow rescued me, my thought. But no, I am much higher than Talon has ever taken me. I glance left and right with no will of my own, and I see long leathered wings to either side. My gaze is directed downward now and I am flying above clouds. A'times they part and below them are alternating scenes of open sea or forested mountains. I feel no sense of time. The scenes below…just are. Sometimes there are clouds, other times only the blue sky.

I alight to the ground and all about me are beasts, huge beyond measure, of a nature I've never seen nor heard of in my life. No fables or tales describe the likes of these. Some have heads the size of the boulders I used to climb as a younger and teeth the length of my arms. Others the size of a team of six and a wagon behind, and then with a tail its equal in length and studded in horns. All of these are about me as I drink from a pond. As the water settles, I see and recognize the face staring back. It is the same that my last vision in the cave beheld. Green, gray, and blue scales surround a reptilian eye with two lids. *I am living the memories of a drægon.*

Now I am flying with a score of drægons of every colour and size. They swoop and dive about me. They turn belly up and fall away, then climb again in swirling grace. And now I spy a village below…and now a wending river through a valley. I am alone again. Turn upon turn of a sand glass I fly alone. And now in this memory, I am chasing the sun as it begins to set into the sea, but it does not as I continuously fly towards it in a never-ending quest to reach it. Stopping only briefly to feed and drink I fly ever on, over sea then mountains and plains and sea again…until I decide it will not be caught, and it finally settles again beyond a different horizon altogether. Another memory has me staring into another pond, but I am a different drægon now, slate blue leather of skin and with scales only upon my shoulders and back.

Contrary to my self memories though, all of these drægon memories hold sounds and exquisite colour. I am living the very long life of this drægon. I feel I know him, as more than even brœthers would. There are very personal memories of mating and nuzzling a small drægon kin in deep caverns below a mountain's surface. And with all of this, I now wonder if the drægon is experiencing my memories too.

Your memories are short though intriguing, Human-beast. Is that what you call yourself?

The voice is booming in my head and my eyes pop open. The reptilian eye has a great scaled head attached to it now as it studies me.

"I am called Ariastone."

You squeak when you speak…Ariastone. It is a small name you call yourself, like your life experience.

I look around me, wondering about Mensæ.

You seek the other human beasts that followed you into my den. I've cleaned up both our messes. The one you slew and the one that would not stop the incessant and loathsome shriek. I put an end to him.

Did he eat them? What messes did this great beast, that speaks directly into my head, clean up…and how did he?

445

I did not eat them. The time the shrieking one spent in my mouth proved him to be distasteful in more than one manner.

Walking over to the bluff's edge outside to the cave, I look down and see two bodies lying broken on the hillside below. Looking back into the cave at the drægon, I feel no fear. And am even a little grateful to him for having settled the score with Mensæ for me. No trepidation at all. It is as though when it was established that we can communicate with each other, we became equals.

"There are stories of drægons in our lore and legend. You are the first I've met and know of no other man who has met one, even the druid Eschereon and he has lived a long life."

You continue to squeak when you speak. Why is that, little one?

I realize now what he means. I am speaking aloud even as we are communicating, mind to mind.

"It is how we speak to each and the other. Mankind, I mean. Person to person."

Hmmm. I feel his shrug, as he moves on. *You say my kind is lore and legend. I do not understand these thoughts.*

I stop speaking aloud. He is right, it is less efficient.

I mean that drægons have not been seen for ages. Are there many like you? In your memories I witnessed others. Where have they gone?

You name us drægons. We are some, we are here, we fly to all lands. I do not understand your term… 'ages.' I see you, you are seeing me. I see human beasts as I fly above.

By 'ages' I mean the far past.

I do not understand this concept…far past. Explain.

Can it be that this drægon does not understand the concept of time?

What is this time?

I have forgotten he is reading my thoughts. This can be awkward. I watch as he quirks his massive head. *"Awkward?"* It somehow hits me just then that I am conversing with an exceedingly intelligent creature, asking about concepts like time.

Drægon, how old are you? How many moons and suns have you seen in your life?

You ask silly questions…Ariastone Human-beast. The sun is. The moon is. Even as you are and I am. The moon hides and the sun seeks. They meet and play their game again.

I try to explain. *I am in the beginning times of my life. I will change as I grow old…I will change as more and more suns pass across the sky. My hair will gray and I will become infirm and will some sun die.*

You will? I am as I have always been.

Nay. Your memories tell otherwise. Do you not revisit them? In one, I watched as you gazed into a drinking pond. You were much younger. You had not then scales over all of your body. You were much smaller than you are now. Time passes and we change, others change.

I observe his bewildering actions to this. His thoughts are awhirl and I cannot cypher them as he tosses them about to himself. I have more to learn of this mind mægic. He seems to be attempting to establish points of reference so that he can grasp the concept of time. I realize at this moment that he must be very old indeed. And then he does something wholly unexpected. He laughs!

It can be nothing else. There is mirth in his movements. A great huff issues forth from his snout. His head waggles to then fro and shakes up and down.

I must study this thing you call time. You say ALL beasts are young once and then grow old, only to die? I believed all lived until others killed. This is a remarkable thought. You must tell me more.

Yes, all creatures know time. Save drægons, mayhaps. The male and female mate, and this produces offspring…babes at first, then growing larger and wizened with further age throughout their life. Learning and living

and then all beasts die, their lifeforce gone. Their soul leaves their bodies
to go on.

This excites him more. Apparently, he has never stopped to note the life
of other beasts.

I must fly and think on this. I think best when I am in the air. You must
come with me, Ariastone Land-beast, and tell me more of...time! This is
amazing.

I do not fly, Drægon. I cannot come with you.

I can see that you have no wings and you are a land-beast, Ariastone
Staff-wielder. But many a tired winged creature has alighted upon my back
and flown with me over the waters. You can do the same.

To ride a drægon. Is this possible? I've ridden with Talon, though not
physically. The feeling is always exhilarating. I find myself smiling at the
thought of it.

Come to the beach, human. And you may climb to my back. We shall see
if a human land-beast and a sky-drægon can fly together.

I begin a climb down to the beach as the drægon exits the cave. He
opens his tremendous leathery wings as he does, pinning me to the hillside
for a moment. His mighty tail trails across the ledge that I'd entered from
as he crawls like a giant tree lizard toward the bluff's edge and then starts
down the escarpment to the beach. His massive body seems light, as the air
under his wings lifts it when he leaps away from the mountainside. I am in
awe at what I am seeing. He is lithe but fearsome as iron-hard scales across
the whole of his body seem to expand and contract like a serpent's skin in
motion. He raises his head and twists around to face me again in a fluid
motion. He is magnificent to behold as he settles to the beach, immense
and weighty again.

As I make my way down, I pass the two bodies of the scar-faced mercenary and Mensæ. I pry my throwing blade from the former and observe the
devastation to the corpse of the mind mæge. His body is pierced through

in a score of places along his length from the lethal bite of the drægon. He must have had the mæge wholly within his mouth to cause such damage. I waste no more time with them.

Drægon, I wish to retrieve my bow and quiver further down the beach before we attempt our flight.

As you wish.

Arriving back to my campfire's leavings, I look over to the assassin I had turned my staff to before the sun had risen. There is naught but ash that I can see. *Mægic sky bolt is a devastating weapon.*

Did it come forth from your staff? In my den, you brought forth a flash of brilliant fire that confused me for a moment and made the other's screech that much more annoying.

I had stored an enormous amount of mind mægic into the drægon fire-stone, and it had hardly phased him.

Shall we try to fly now, Ariastone Land-beast?

I smile at his settled name for me.

I have another name, Drægon. My full name is Ariastone Côuerdrægon. I'm told it means 'heart of the drægon.'

He huffs in mirth.

It will need to grow many times over to be the size of even one of a true drægon's hearts. But I will remember this name, however small. Shall we fly? I wish to contemplate 'time.'

He lays his head and shoulders flat to the sands, and I climb first to his foreleg and then his shoulder. I settle finally at the base of his neck and above his shoulders, clambering across his upper wing to gain a position. He does not seem to mind. I find that I can lift the larger scales there and slide my legs along his neck and under them. I do the same to those directly in front of me and tuck my pack and bow and staff within. He clearly can control each individual scale if he desires, as he clamps right over my legs and pack.

With no warning, he rises up on his tail and hindquarters, shoving himself upward, wings immediately unfurling and pulling us into the air. I feel his body rippling from head to tail as we rise and head out to sea. He gains speed quickly, and I *feel* now what I can only sense when I fly with Talon. At this thought, an echoing war cry rings out overhead. Moments later, Talon is flying side a'side with us.

A friend, I think to Drægon.

Hmmm. Another concept I do not wholly understand. You are a wonder, Ariastone Côuerdrægon.

We are flying over the waves and the wind in my face is stealing my breath away and I fall into my *Knowing.* The solution comes to me, and I gather surrounding mægic to form a shield against the windy onslaught, sending it around me but not directly into me, allowing me to keep a breath. And then I survey everything about me. The sea is becoming a deeper blue as we travel further from shore, and the very lands behind us are shrinking away. I feel an unbridled passion released in the great beast below me, and he climbs now and circles and flips and sends my head spinning until I gain the feel of it. I am flying.

We turn back towards land, and I suggest we head south along the coast. Drægon has no objection, and he begins his queries regarding time. Not knowing how to start, I communicate to him the story of my life, recounting my years growing up with Da on our homestead. Our life as I grew on the farm and in the forest and mountains hunting. I tell the tales of my year-end giftings and training with Moor, all the time showing the progression to my life. He falls silent, unquestioning for a while as we fly, and then more queries come. We fly inland now but much higher. So high that we leave Talon below and behind.

I see the mountains and landscape rolling by at an unimaginable speed. A distance it would take me fortnights to travel pass in a few turns. And then something below strikes me as familiar in the mountains and I ask

Drægon to head in that direction to assuage my curiosity. I've been grab-bing bites of trail jerky all the sun long from my pack afore me, and aside my curiosity, other bodily functions call. I lose sight of the mountain lake that has caught my attention as we are flying nearer the ground now.

As we descend, my heart starts pumping a beat faster than its norm when the lake appears again. I recognize where we are. It is Moon Lake, sure certain. I beg Drægon to the ground. As we fly betwixt the moun-tains, he flies just over the surface of the waters, his wingtips dipping into the flat, plate glass surface of the water. It is dusk as we settle on a shore I remember well. Climbing down on stiff legs and creaking body, I wander over to the bushes along the treeline, and as I water the broad leaves, I recall a sun from long ago when I did the same thing as a seven year. *Time.*

Recounting the tale to Drægon, I sit on the beach eating berries I've picked, growing anxious with the deep familiarity of where I am. A full moon is rising on the far horizon.

You have a mate nearby?

Yes.

Then I shall take you there and leave you. I must contemplate the things you have told me. And visit the places in your tales, mayhaps.

Climbing the drægon's back once more, it feels almost a natural thing to be doing. We climb above the lake again in the moonlight and head east over the trees.

The stars are bright in the cloudless sky as the moon illuminates the fork rock boulder that Da had once wedged an Æntwood log from Moon Lake on its peak, waiting for a sky bolt to strike. Smoke is rising from the cottage chimney and lantern light is shining from its windows.

Talon gives off echoing war cries over and over again, and I look to the rear door of the cottage. A figure steps through the door even as we settle to the ground, Drægon's wings fanning the ground for a moment. Even as he is dipping his head, I am already throwing my pack and weapons to the ground and sliding from his back.

I reach out to her spirit sense but there is no need. She knows it is me even as I am sure it is her. *Finnie.*

"Ari," she calls in a voice both believing and unbelieving.

I am running towards her as I feel Drægon lift into the sky again behind me. She is running towards me. The embrace is immediate, the kiss fierce and full of yearning until she pulls away from me.

"Ari, was that a drægon?"

"Yes, a friend." My need is great and I embrace her once more. We stand out under the stars and can feel each other's heartbeats pounding heavy in our chests. After several moments. She speaks with a wide smile.

"Ari. You smell like drægon. Meet me at the well, and I'll bring soap. Shed those clothes or I will refuse to touch you further."

I am totally naked and thoroughly doused, wet from head to toe when Finnie returns with soap and an old nightshirt. She helps bathe me under the stars to laughs and wet hugs. We walk hand in hand to my homestead... our homestead cottage. Stepping up to the porch, Finnie pushes open the door for me as she stands in the doorway and forces me to squeeze by her. I do not mind and stand there with her.

The warm fire is too alluring though, and I draw her inside with me. We have barely spoken a word. Turning, I take in the sight and scent of the cottage I grew up in. *Home.* But it's different than I remember. There is a woman's touch that Da and I could never give it. A smell that was never there before.

Finnie pulls me to our small table and bids me sit with a finger to her lips.

"Quiet, Ari. The youngers are asleep."

I nod, gazing to the loft and sit, content to watch her as she swings the kettle out of the fire and pours two cups of tea for us. From the cupboard, she pulls bread and cheese and fruit preserves. Doing the little things I have forgotten.

We whisper and hold hands and kiss lightly, enjoying the closeness, the touching. It's a turn of a sand glass in a blink. *Time.* Finnie clears the table and comes to me, taking both my hands. I follow her as she leads me back to the bed-chamber, lantern in hand.

As I enter, this room is new to me as well. It no longer has the scent of Da. There is lavender, I think. I gaze around and notice with surprise, a small wooden cradle in the far corner under the window. Too small for little Evie.

"Finnie," I whisper, as I approach. "Have you adopted yet another younger?"

"Nay, Ari. Come meet your son."

Epilogue

Ètœn comes swinging into the barn, the large door pulling on its hinges as he rides it in.

"We've company coming, Da!"

Looking up from my work bench, I take in my son's smile beaming back at me. He's nearing his ten year-ender and not hit his growth spurt as yet, so the hinges don't groan much. His hair is streaked with fly-away shocks of sandy blond in an otherwise mop of mousey brown. His ears peek out with small points on their tops leading the way. He is his da's son, sure certain.

"They've all auras too, Da." This catches my attention. Ètœn has just come to recognize the mægic auras about me and creatures that hold them, such as Bane. There are few to see in Middenvale asides the creatures, himself, me, and his mum.

"I was over to Auntie Grayce's helping her with the goats, and they came riding up like they were knowing exactly where they were heading. Grayce didn't see them, I don't think, as she was busy in the barn milking ol' Coddles. Anyway, they kept on riding past. I ran the short way, fast as I could."

I stand and step out of the barn. Even as I make my way into the sun, I glance to the trailway heading back to Grayce's and as I do, three riders are exiting the treeline, eighty paces out. Walking further out into the yard, I hear the cottage's front door squeak as it opens and Finnie appears on the porch. She is ever attuned to my thoughts when we are close, even when we are not in sight of one to the other.

I catch my breath as I instantly recognize two of the three, and as they approach, a furion leaps down from the horse of the first rider and bounds towards Finnie like a long lost friend…Jilly. She springs up the steps of the porch and flies into Finnie's arms, twirling around her head and shoulders, kissing her cheeks and chin to raucous laughter from my wife. They've always had a special connection.

The three have stopped afore me now, two smiling brightly, the third surveying me with a deep curiosity. Ètœn is at my side to my left and Finnie joins us, sliding her left arm around mine, whilst cuddling a much settled furion in her right arm. She is, as is usually the case, first to speak.

"Welcome, ladies. If I am not mistaken, I am meeting my husband's sister for the first time. It is lovely to meet you, Roux!" My sister, ten years older than when I last saw her, looks to Finnie, dumbstruck that she could know such a thing.

"And you must be Alænèa. Your pranks are legend in the tales Ari tells to the youngers while sitting about the fire in the eves. It is such a pleasure to be meeting you." I watch as Alænèa's eyes sparkle to hear such a thing. Ètœn touches his ears as he sees another—the first aside myself—with the same distinct feature as us.

"I confess, I do not recognize your traveling companion though. Please forgive me!" The third rider speaks up now.

"Nay, you would not, as I am fairly new to this troupe. But I certainly concede to knowing at first glance the mæge of the tales my new companions tell. And not just them, but more than a few bards and minstrels over the past years. His aura glows stronger than any other I've ever seen. It is a pleasure to finally meet you, Arias Cōeurdrægon…and, of course, your lovely wife. Call me Elsii, if you will."

"Call me Finnie, the three of you, and please, accept my welcome for myself and my tongue-tied husband. Please come sit with us under the tree and out of this sun. I'll go fetch some drinks."

"Let me help," offers Alænèa as the three dismount. Roux and I are in a clenching hug as I hear Elsii say to Ètœn, "Lad, will you help me with the horses? Mayhaps we can pull their saddles and set them out to pasture for a bit."

Letting go of my sister for a moment, I watch as Ètœn and Elsii lead the horses off. I cannot help but notice a full-grown wolf badger following them and another sniffing at my leg.

"Roux, I can't tell you how good it is to see you."

"And you for I, big brœther. I'd hoped you'd come back to the isles, but I can see why you have not. Finnie is lovely, and your homestead is a wonder," looking after Elsii and Ètœn now… "and your son is the spitting image of his pæder." We head over towards the great oak and take seats in the half dozen chairs I've crafted as a gathering spot for friends and family.

"I've longed to do just that, Roux, but being near you has nearly cost you your life, and it has been the same with all my friends. I am a true danger to all. Mensæ is gone, but others of his ilk still exist, and I've thought to keep you from harm's way by staying hidden these many years. I'm so sorry for all that has happened to you because of me." I can't help but now note my sister is wearing the tinker's amulet I gave her when we last parted ways. It rests against a chest covered in a thickened leather cuirass likened to those of the Amæzonians our mœther has been living with.

Taking in the look of Roux, I see her garb has changed much over the past years. She looks no more like the temple acolyte I sent back to the care of the Wic'cha Mœther, with her mind in need of healing from the attack of the mind mæge, Mensæ. Her style now includes elkskin trousers and high riding boots, adorned with sheaths carrying throwing blades…four that I can see. Roux has removed a well-crafted pack afore she takes a seat, and a full quiver also. The pack has a sheathed short sword, even as mine does. Her cuirass has upon it not a sigil but a mæge rune branded deep upon it, and I know its meaning—truth.

Alænèa and Finnie are returning now with trays of sweetened lime waters, a favorite of mine, and honeycakes that Finnie made last eve with Evie, Ètœn's older sister. Effie, a dear friend and the town's healer, had picked Evie up earlier this morn to continue her apprenticeship in the art. My oldest son, Tristan, at sixteen year, is gone as apprentice to Argo, another true friend and the town smithy. Argo is a genius with metals and had a hand in fashioning all of my weapons, along with the brand used to sear the drægon sigil onto the breast piece of my own cuirass-pack. A drægon. I glance back to admire Roux's very similar design and placement over her heart. It dawns on me in that very moment, the mæge rune for 'truth' holds the look of a wingless drægon!

A breeze from the west whispers through the leaves above us and lifts the scent of the cinnamon honeycakes into the air and the wolf badger at Roux's feet sniffs at it. Reaching down, my sister lifts the one intended for her off the tray and feeds it to her animal friend.

"Ari, your friends and family from all your tales have come to life! Alænèa is just as I have imagined her, and Roux is as lovely as you've described. I am so glad to finally be meeting them!"

"And Arias, I see now why you pined so for this charming lady. That you have hidden her from us these many years is a shame."

Elsii is returning with Ètœn now, and though the lad might typically grab a cake and run off to other affairs, he does not disappoint in fetching a honeycake, but placing it firmly betwixt his teeth, he proceeds to climb up into the tree and stays close by. He appears smitten by Elsii.

"The horses are watered and pastured. Ètœn was a great help, Arias," Elsii says and glances up into the tree. Taking a seat and joining us, she immediately tears off a piece of honeycake for her wolf badger friend. She glances to my sister as Finnie fills her cup, and then down to the badgers again as they join up and go wandering off together.

"Fear not, Finnie. They will not bother your farm creatures," Roux says.

"I did not expect they would. I but wondered that you and Elsii have the same spirit creature."

"That would take us to how we had met, Elsii and I. 'Twas under fascinating circumstance but can be for another sun, mayhaps. I would rather become more acquainted with my brother again, and his lovely wife and family!"

"And I, the circumstances and manner that have sent you out to find me," I added. "How is it you have found me, by the by?"

Roux reaches to her breast and fingers about the tinker's amulet, and I know before she tells of the tale.

"You gave me your amulet to guard against the mind mæge, that day on the beach across from Orakles Isle, forsaking it as your own protection. If you had known the Vicchi had sent Sæm and Alænèa with another for me, as well as giving them their own, you would not have needed to part with yours. It seems that the stones within the amulets hold an affinity to their true master. When I put it back on, I merely wished I could find you, and it brought us to you, over sea and mountain and vale." She lifts the necklace from about her neck and hands it back to me. It warms, and the gem within glows as I take it from her.

"We are glad that you have searched Ari out at last Roux…may I call you that? Ari has told me your true name is Guinefere? I will call you that if you wish, it is a beautiful name. For all the tales he has told me of you, Alænèa, and Sæm, I feel I know you." I cannot help but notice the glances that pass betwixt the three friends. There is more to their being here, and they feel Finnie will not like it.